"Heart-wrenching and powerful. *The Warsaw Sisters* left me reeling but in a good and necessary way. Amanda Barratt shines an uncompromising light on the devastation and cruelty of life in occupied Poland—a light that needs to be shined, because through Antonina and Helena, we see. We understand. We *feel*. Elegant prose, thorough research, and intriguing characters thread throughout this outstanding novel. Truly an exceptional work."

Sarah Sundin, bestselling and Christy Award–winning author of
The Sound of Light and *Until Leaves Fall in Paris*

"With her signature attention to detail and commitment to historical integrity, Amanda Barratt gives us a story not to be forgotten. When two sisters choose their own paths of resistance under German occupation, both are irrevocably changed. *The Warsaw Sisters* is a wide-eyed, unflinching look at the heartbreaking plight of a people grasping courage even when they can't find hope. For fans of Martha Hall Kelly and Amy Harmon."

Jocelyn Green, Christy Award–winning author of
The Metropolitan Affair

"In *The Warsaw Sisters*, Amanda Barratt has created a suspenseful and deeply emotional journey through the perils of the Polish resistance during WWII. Readers will be kept up turning pages as these sisters fight for their cause and try valiantly to protect the ones they love. But it is the relationship between Helena and Antonina that readers will remember long after the last page. I highly recommend this evocative novel of thrilling escapes, desperate heroism, and the courage it takes to choose hope in a time of turmoil."

Amy Lynn Green, author of *The Blackout Book Club*

"Amanda Barratt honors the victims of horrific brutality during Poland's Holocaust by sharing a glimpse of their stories. Twin sisters battle against the evil that permeates their beautiful city in *The Warsaw Sisters*, a tragic and poignant reminder of the cruelty of

war, the courage of the Polish Resistance, and the immeasurable cost of freedom."

the

WARSAW
SISTERS

the WARSAW SISTERS

a novel of **WWII POLAND**

AMANDA BARRATT

R
Revell

a division of Baker Publishing Group
Grand Rapids, Michigan

© 2023 by Amanda Barratt

Published by Revell
a division of Baker Publishing Group
Grand Rapids, Michigan
RevellBooks.com

Printed in the United States of America

Library of Congress Cataloging-in-Publication Data
Names: Barratt, Amanda, 1996– author.
Title: The Warsaw Sisters : a novel of WWII Poland / Amanda Barratt.
Description: Grand Rapids, Michigan : Revell, a division of Baker Publishing Group, [2023]
Identifiers: LCCN 2023012640 | ISBN 9780800741716 (paperback) | ISBN 9780800745011 (casebound) | ISBN 9781493443420 (ebook)
Subjects: LCSH: World War, 1939–1945—Poland—Fiction. | Sisters—Fiction. | LCGFT: Historical fiction. | Novels.
Classification: LCC PS3602.A777463 W37 2023 | DDC 813/.6—dc23/eng/20230324
LC record available at https://lccn.loc.gov/2023012640

Scripture used in this book, whether quoted or paraphrased by the characters, is taken from the King James Version of the Bible.

This is a work of historical reconstruction; the appearances of certain historical figures are therefore inevitable. All other characters, however, are products of the author's imagination, and any resemblance to actual persons, living or dead, is coincidental.

Published in association with Books & Such Literary Management, www.booksandsuch.com.

Baker Publishing Group publications use paper produced from sustainable forestry practices and post-consumer waste whenever possible.

23 24 25 26 27 28 29   7 6 5 4 3 2 1

For the sparks of light in the night of war,
the ordinary who quietly resisted.
For the ones who fought and fell in Warsaw,
a city of two risings.
For the six million Jewish men, women,
and children who perished in the Holocaust.
For sisterhood, the most resilient of bonds.
For Your glory, Lord. Always.

ANTONINA
AUGUST 31, 1939
WARSAW, POLAND

Antonina-and-Helena.

That was how I remembered our names. Spoken in a single breath, always blended together.

Antonina and Helena. Helena and Antonina. Two lives braided into a single strand. A tie as certain as the ground beneath our feet and the air flowing through our lungs.

A bond that would remain immutable even as we watched our father go off to war.

For war would come to Poland. Few remained in doubt of it. Only the delusional, or the desperate, clung to the unraveling hope of peace.

I wasn't delusional. But weren't we, all of us, a little desperate? Maybe desperation bred delusion as we sought assurance that the ordinary would remain unbroken. That nothing would happen in the end. That the rumblings would die away, after all. We told ourselves and each other and kept telling ourselves because who, in spite of the flush of patriotism and bravado, could reckon with the alternative?

I stilled in the doorway of the bedroom. Beside the bed, Tata stood, his back to me as he fastened his rucksack. I stayed where

I was, taking him in, gathering the moment close. The constancy I always found in his presence without him even speaking a word. His hands, steady and methodical, as they secured the rucksack. The way morning light touched his profile, outlined his uniformed shoulders.

He turned, caught sight of me. "Tosia."

I gave a little smile, abashed to be found hovering in the doorway like a child, and crossed the room. "I wanted to see if there was anything you needed." My fingers brushed the rucksack on the bed, the lumpy canvas out of place against the cream-hued counterpane.

"I think I have everything just about sorted."

"Good." I paused, trying to look only at his face and not at the uniform that transformed him from an attorney in a pressed suit to an officer in the army. He'd served during the last war—not the Great War, he hadn't been old enough then—but the one that followed, between Poland and the Bolsheviks. Helena and I hadn't been born yet; our parents hadn't even been married. Tata returned in 1920, the Bolsheviks defeated, the independence of the infant Republic of Poland established. I'd glimpsed his old uniform hanging in the back of the armoire and seen the earnest young man in the photograph taken before he left, but neither had prepared me for the reality of him in uniform, as if time had unrolled backward twenty years, to another war and a younger man.

Silence lay between Tata and me. I didn't know how to fill it, what to speak, what not to speak. The women of the previous generation were no strangers to sending their men off to war.

I'd had no practice. Not yet.

He paused, drew something from his pocket, held it in his palm a moment. "Your mama gave me this the day I left. The first present I ever had from her. When she found out I would be leaving, she came straight away, didn't even stop to put on a coat. I can still see her, so young and lovely, her cheeks bright, shivering as she insisted she wasn't cold. Stubborn as ever. Quite like someone else I know." He gave me a pointed look and chuckled.

I tried to laugh, but it tangled in my chest.

"We stood in front of my parents' house, and she unfastened

the chain from around her neck, placed it in my hand, and told me to keep it safe." His mustached mouth softened, his gaze far away. "I suppose that must have been the moment I realized she cared as much as I did."

He'd told us the story when we'd been young, but never quite like this. Then it had seemed a scene out of a novel, the heroine bidding farewell to her sweetheart before he marched into the glory of battle. How romantic I had thought it. For it had been only a story, a glossy reminiscence.

It had not been real then.

He pressed what he held into my hand, the small oval still warm from his touch. The medallion he always carried, the tarnished silver engraved with the image of Christ. "I want you to keep it now, while I'm away." He swallowed, and it twisted something inside me, such a look on my father's face.

I inhaled a breath. "We'll be fine. I will look after Helena. And Aunt Basia will be here." She'd come last night to say goodbye, for they couldn't spare her at the hospital today. Throughout our growing up years, our aunt—Tata's only sibling and a respected physician—had reared her twin nieces as if we were her own, filling the place of the mother who died when my sister and I were scarcely a year old.

"Yes." He nodded. "Basia will be here. I am glad of that." He gave a brief smile. The same one he'd worn last night when we packed his belongings and he said he wouldn't need much because he would be back soon. Then, as now, I read in his eyes what he did not speak.

Tata—so strong and steady—was afraid.

I did not let him know I knew this. Or that I was too. Our fear remained unvoiced, its presence thickening the air between us. It wouldn't do to speak of such a thing, not at a time like this.

He'd spent the years sheltering my sister and me, making our lives safe and good and beautiful. Now I wished I could protect him as he had shielded us.

I wished . . . but I could not.

So I would give him what I could in these last moments together.

The memory of his daughter, steadfast and smiling.

And he would know he did not need to fear for us and that we would be here.

Waiting, until he returned.

HELENA
AUGUST 31, 1939

There were no memories before him. He was my first and part of all the ones that followed. Drifting asleep to the sound of his voice spinning tales of mountains of glass and princesses in distant towers. My hand tucked in his as we walked to school, the September morning crisp, my heart beating fast beneath my coat. His rumbling laughter blending with crackly records as he taught Antonina and me to dance. His arms solid and comforting as I sobbed because the boy I'd secretly been fond of had begun a flirtation with one of my prettier schoolmates. My father's voice gentle as he told me that I did not need to change to be loved, that the right man would prove himself worthy of my heart, not the other way around, and that I would always be his kwiatuszek—his little flower. The days working side by side at his firm, him meeting with clients in his office while I managed his appointments and typed his correspondence.

For as long as I could remember, he had been a constant in my—our—world.

Now a different world lay before us.

Sunlight warmed my face as we stepped onto Marszałkowska Street, the broad thoroughfare lined with edifices of stuccoed brick, shops and cafés with brightly lettered signs and elegant awnings, squat domed advertising pillars and slender iron lampposts, manicured trees planted at intervals. Red trams glided along the rails embedded in the cobblestones, automobiles and taxicabs sped up and down the street, carts and droshkies clattered and clip-clopped, bicyclists rode past, and pedestrians thronged the sidewalks.

In recent days, Warsaw sizzled, an electric current pulsing faster, faster. Passersby no longer walked, much less strolled. They hurried, rushed, strode, as though driven by wind at their backs, every step one of purpose, nearly all carrying the now-ubiquitous gas masks. Women hastened along the sidewalk, laden with shopping bags and baskets, expressions agitated, almost hunted. People sought to lay hold of what provisions they could, fearing shortages. Last month, at Tata's advising, we laid in a supply of tinned goods, dried peas, kasza, sugar, and coffee. We bought no flour, for it might grow musty if stored too long. Four days ago, we'd gone to the shops and found them alarmingly sparse, no flour to be sold.

How could it be that only a few weeks ago all had been ordinary, the storm clouds gathering, but yet in the distance? Over the years we'd read the papers and talked of foreign politics, of Germany and Adolf Hitler, hailed as Führer by his adoring people as he regenerated a country crippled after the Great War and the Treaty of Versailles. Somehow it all seemed far off, removed from our lives in Poland. Troubles happening "somewhere else."

But as Germany annexed Austria and then occupied Czechoslovakia, the storm swept closer. Closer still as Hitler issued demands to which our government staunchly refused to cede, among them the return of Danzig—a major port on the Baltic coast and a free city under the Treaty of Versailles. Only a few days ago, we had listened, stunned, to the announcement over the radio that Germany and the Soviet Union had signed a nonaggression pact, the two countries, once bitter foes and agelong enemies of Poland, agreeing not to make war against the other.

In that moment, a memory had surfaced. I had come into the sitting room one evening, just as Tata rose and turned off the wireless, Hitler's fiery oration reverberating in the silence. He had turned to my aunt, sitting on the sofa, and said with a look I had never forgotten, "When a man is a fanatic, he is capable of anything, and that man Hitler is one of the greatest fanatics I have ever heard."

The years had tested my father's words, but only time would prove their measure.

Tata hailed a taxicab and asked the driver to take us to the Main Station.

War had not even begun, but already it had left its mark upon the city. Almost every window of the buildings we passed bore a pattern of thin white strips of paper, ours no exception. The newspaper said it would protect the panes from shattering due to the vibration of nearby explosions and thus safeguard against injury from flying glass. I wondered if it had ever been put to the test.

Posters on walls and advertising pillars announced a general mobilization of our army. Amid the mobilization sheets hung a different poster. This one depicted a swastika from which an enormous hand seemed to sprout, bony fingers reaching, almost encircling a map of Poland. A Polish soldier stood in a warrior's stance, bayonet fixed, poised to plunge the blade through the grasping hand.

Why had the artist rendered such a large hand compared with the height of the soldier?

Though the sun shone bright, I shivered.

We reached the Main Station, and the taxicab stopped. As we made our way into the station, I kept glancing at Tata, distinguished and somehow strange in his crisp tunic and peaked cap with its Polish eagle badge. He had been a soldier once, and with the mere act of the uniform mantling his shoulders, he returned to that part of himself again, as if a soldier was something one donned instead of became. But I could not admire him in military dress, no matter the chorus ringing out as men marched past, voices lusty.

"War, oh war, what a grand lady you must be, that you are being followed, that you are being followed by such dashing fellows."

There was nothing dashing about a man leaving his home, his family, without knowing when or if he would return. Though, of course, he must go. Of course he must fight, if necessary. Perhaps I should have been filled with pride as my father left to defend our country, but my chest tightened so I could not tell if I was proud, only afraid.

The station swelled with men, youths who barely looked of age shoulder to shoulder with the more mature. Some boisterous, mingling with comrades like schoolboys setting off on an excursion to the zoo, others somber and silent, staring down at their feet or into the distance. A couple embraced, holding each other for a long and quiet moment. A woman waved a handkerchief in a gloved hand, calling out, "Goodbye, see you soon," though to whom it was impossible to tell. Loudspeakers echoed, announcing boarding calls. The air was thick with heat and cigarette smoke and the unknown.

As we wended through the swarming multitude, I suddenly wished I could cling to Tata's hand as I'd done when I was a child, his broad palm enfolding my fingers, an anchor when the world felt so very great and I so very small. But I was eighteen, a grown woman, and so I must make my way on my own.

When we reached the platform, he set down his rucksack. Antonina stood beside me, an emerald hat slanted over her reddish-gold curls, her features serene. But the rigid set of her shoulders and the way she clutched her handbag betrayed her inward struggle. I bit my lip hard.

Since the moment I glimpsed Tata's mobilization orders—who could imagine one could hate and fear a simple white rectangle so much—I'd steeled myself for this parting. Told myself I would not break, nor even crack.

For long seconds, he stood, gazing at the two of us. "Take care of one another for me. Hold the other close."

"We will." I looked back at him steadily, gathering his face into the folds of my memory, wanting to remember for this and every moment until he returned.

"That's how I can leave you this way. Knowing you'll be together, no matter what comes."

"You're not to worry about us." Did Antonina hear how her voice caught at the end? Did Tata?

"I'll be home soon."

Of course. Of course he would be.

He opened his arms and pulled us close, my sister and me. Crushing us against him, his breath tickling my ear, my own snatched from my lungs with the strength of his embrace.

"My beloved girls," he whispered. "My Tosia and Hela."

He drew away.

"I love you." I smiled, forcing out the words through the swelling ache in my throat.

How fragile they sounded. They weren't enough. How could they be?

He shouldered his rucksack, met our eyes, the tenderness in his unraveling me piece by piece.

Then he turned away, faded into the crowd, one in a mass of uniforms. I blinked hard. Though tears burned, they did not fall. I should have been proud of myself for staying strong. But I wasn't. Not really.

Time lengthened as we stood side by side, our shoulders brushing. The whistle gave a piercing blast, and the wheels of the train began to turn, slowly at first, then gaining speed. The faces of the men filling the windows passed as shadows, blurred by the rise of steam. I wanted to push forward, try to catch one more glimpse of Tata, but the crowd pressed too tight and the train passed too quickly until all that remained was the echo of the whistle and the people left behind.

HELENA
SEPTEMBER 1, 1939

The cool stillness of early morning greeted me as I stepped into the kitchen. I crossed to the tall oak dresser, eyes gritty as I stared at the dishes neatly arranged on its shelves.

I had woken at half past six, though indeed, I barely slept, the hours stretching as I lay on my flattened pillow staring into blackness. I told myself it was the coffee I'd drunk last evening that kept me awake, but in truth, the fault lay with my mind. My thoughts wouldn't silence, no matter how I sought to quiet them. They traveled a path of fears, speculations, and uncertainties that ran in loops and circles and never reached a destination.

But with dawn came clarity. Or at least renewed determination. I would prepare breakfast. Go to Tata's office and attend to any business left unfinished. Put emotions aside.

Crash.

I jumped. Heart thumping, I rushed into the sitting room.

Antonina sat in a chair drawn close to the wireless. Brown liquid dripped down the front of her peach satin dressing gown. Bits of china scattered the floorboards.

"What happened?" I gasped, my jittery nerves on edge.

"Shh." She didn't look at me, her gaze on the set.

It was only then I registered the crackle of the wireless, the measured tone of the announcer.

"Early this morning, German forces invaded Polish territory . . ."

It's come. The words repeated in my mind, a rising clamor, inescapably real. *It's come.*

My stomach tightened. *Where are you, Tata?*

Antonina turned. Our eyes met.

She pressed her lips together, face chalky.

Static garbled the announcer's voice.

Antonina smacked the top of the set with the flat of her hand. It only made the static worse. She turned it off with a soft huff—the same sigh she gave when she smudged her lipstick or the tram was late.

Silence echoed in the room that suddenly seemed so very empty. Antonina ran a fingertip across her splotched dressing gown, as if only just realizing she'd spilled coffee on herself. I chafed my arms, my summer frock no match for the ice slicking my skin.

Tick-tick went the clock on the wall. The delicate black hands read 7:05.

Antonina rose. "I should dress." She gave a glance at the splattered floor and shards of china. "Then I'll see to this." She started to leave the sitting room.

I looked down. Bloody footprints tracked the floorboards.

"You've cut yourself," I called after her. The first words I'd spoken since the broadcast. Surprisingly, my voice sounded the same as always.

Antonina came back into the sitting room, feet bare beneath the hem of her nightdress. She lifted her right foot and held it up with both hands, wobbling on one leg. A tiny slice marred her heel. Though the cut continued to bleed, it didn't look deep, but I wouldn't be able to tell until it had been cleaned.

"I should see if there's any glass in that."

She lowered her foot. "I don't know how it happened. I couldn't sleep, so I made some coffee. I thought there might be news." She drew a shaky breath, my usually poised sister anything but in her stained dressing gown, her hair tied up in a scarf. "When I heard the announcement, I—I just dropped it."

"It's all right," I said in a soft voice.

How easily my reassurance came, though I wasn't certain what it really meant. Wasn't certain if anything could be "all right" anymore.

Antonina gave a little smile, but her features were strained.

She was afraid too. Somehow, I was glad not to be alone.

ANTONINA
SEPTEMBER 25, 1939

Death was coming for us, there in the cellar.

I did not want to meet it. Not in the stagnant darkness among strangers as terrified and certain of their end as I was. Once the cellars of Warsaw stored coal, potatoes, firewood. Now humanity cowered in their depths, hiding from death.

I have barely begun to live. I have barely—

The drone of the planes. That terrible, grinding whine.

Then silently I counted in cadence with my shallow breaths.

One. Two. Three.

I had been doing this since daybreak. Measuring the seconds between the first shrill of a falling bomb and when it struck its target, instinctively gauging the distance. That and wondering when we would die.

Four. Five. Siiiix. Sevvven.

The whining amplified, a kettle shrieking untended, pressure building, building—

Impact. Crushing. Quaking the walls, resonating in my bones.

Not us this time.

In the early days, when there was still a reprieve between air raids, *not us this time* meant something, even if only a few moments of relief.

But days had become weeks and now there was no relief. Only the roar of the planes and the shuddering crump of explosions as wave after wave of bombers darkened the skies, mechanized birds of prey swooping low to disgorge deadly loads, pounding the city to rubble.

"Speaking to you now, I see her through the windows in all her

greatness and glory, shrouded in smoke, red in flames. Glorious, invincible, fighting Warsaw!"

Mayor Starzyński's deep, steady voice returned to me. He had addressed the population every evening, his broadcasts a lifeline of courage. So long as Starzyński still spoke, people said as they queued for a loaf of bread or waited out an air raid, surely we had reason to hope.

Two days ago, the radio fell silent. Bombs struck the power station and we heard the voice of our beloved mayor no more. We had no gas or electricity. Our taps had gone dry—the waterworks had been bombed. Now Varsovians had nothing but sand and their own strength to battle the inferno. Food had become all but unobtainable. Bread could scarcely be found, and women stood for hours outside the butcher's in the hope of a little horsemeat. I would have been more worried about starving, but I had begun to doubt whether we'd last long enough for that.

Since the first day of September, I'd wanted to fight—fight with everything in me. For Warsaw, glorious, fighting Warsaw. For Poland, the country of my birth and of my heart. But in the airless cellar, bodies pressing around me, Stuka bombers screaming overhead, muffled explosions juddering the walls, I wondered, *Are we fighting or are we only dying?*

There had been hope at first. On the third of September, we cheered when Great Britain and France declared war on Germany, embracing friends and strangers in the streets and chorusing "God Save the King" and "La Marseillaise" and then the rousing words of our own anthem, "Mazurek Dąbrowskiego."

"Poland has not yet perished . . ."

But only two days later, rumors spread that the government had evacuated Warsaw. What a tidy word, *evacuated*. In truth, they had fled, abandoning the capital and its more than a million inhabitants. Mayor Starzyński, however, remained. The following evening, the army issued an order for all men able to bear arms to leave the city and make their way east where they would form a new line of defense. This news suggested the capital would be surrendered without a fight, and thousands streamed out of Warsaw, not only men but women and children too, a panicked flight as the German army continued to advance.

Contrary to the order issued on behalf of the army, Mayor Starzyński called upon Varsovians not to evacuate but to stay and aid in the defense of the city. Those who had left, he urged to return. Each must do their part. If we held fast, we would be victorious. Morale rose; our purpose had been renewed. Warsaw was ours, and we would not abandon her.

Yet as the curtain fell on the first full week of war, the city lay under siege. By the twelfth day, they no longer sounded the air raid alarm, for hundreds of enemy aircraft overtook the skies each day. We ventured out only when necessary and, then, at a dash. Bombs descended like molten rain, artillery whistled and slammed, tearing craters in the street, in the very place my feet had touched barely a moment ago.

But for as long as I could, I had refused to cower belowground. In an instant, a bomb could fall on our building and I could be buried under the ruins as easily as I could be machine-gunned by a low-flying plane or struck by an artillery shell while crossing the street. Though I could not be a soldier, I certainly intended to do my bit. In response to the call for civilians to dig trenches to fortify the city against the advance of tanks, Helena and I reported, digging as bombs exploded, far enough away for us to continue the work but still uncomfortably close. I flinched at each detonation, but I did not leap into the trench and cover my head as others did. Instead, I gritted my teeth and stabbed my spade into the ground, impaling the baked earth as if it were Hitler's chest and my spade a bayonet.

Scarcely had the war entered its third week when the news reached us. The Soviet Union had invaded Eastern Poland. Germany from the west, north, and south, now the Soviets from the east, squeezing Poland in a vise, crushing her slowly but surely, even as she fought with every particle of her crippled strength.

Hadn't we believed that if war came, it would quickly bring about the defeat of Germany and the restoration of peace? Hadn't people said the German military was poorly equipped, their tanks flimsy, their aircraft running on synthetic fuel not fit for a cigarette lighter? Instead our troops had been forced repeatedly to retreat. Some had returned to the city in bedraggled columns, their filthy uniforms and glassy stares speaking without words of the situation at the front. Tata had not been among them, and we'd had no word since his departure.

The city was surrounded, cut off, gasping for air, suffocating in the smoke and the flames. Burning alive, and with it, its citizens. Two days ago, German planes had flown overhead, dropping not bombs but leaflets. *"This is our final warning"* declared the message. If Warsaw did not surrender immediately, the city would be utterly destroyed. Not one inhabitant would be left alive.

Warsaw fought on, and our enemy was not one for empty promises.

The quivering flame of a candle stub threw shadows onto the faces of our companions—fellow tenants, refugees, and passersby off the street who had sought shelter in the cellar of our building. There were at least thirty of us. We'd been thrust together, not as neighbors or comrades or even as strangers but as human beings united by the sole desire that the next bomb find its target anywhere but the roof above our heads. Though perhaps some did wish for it, anything to end the awful waiting.

Helena sat beside me, her shoulder pressed against mine. I drew an unsteady breath, the atmosphere rank with unwashed bodies, stale cigarette smoke, and a baby's soiled nappy.

The wail of diving bombers swelled.

One. Two. Three.

The building tremored with another blast.

The old woman opposite us recited the rosary, her gnarled fingers entwined with the beads. "Our Father which art in heaven, Hallowed be Thy name . . ."

The throb of planes over the roof all but drowned her papery voice.

I found myself murmuring the prayer along with her, my throat dry from lack of water.

"And lead us not into temptation, but deliver us from evil."

Deliver us.

It wasn't only for us that I meant the prayer but for Tata. For

Marek, too, somewhere in the vast unknown of war. He had tried to enlist the day of the invasion, but the army wouldn't take him. Perhaps the fact that he was Jewish had something to do with it. Though even if he hadn't been, he still might not have had much success in joining the army upon the outbreak of war, for other acquaintances of ours had not been called up and presented themselves to the military authorities with similar results. The manner in which the mobilization had been handled had been a grievance I'd often heard repeated during past weeks.

In the end, Marek left the city on the seventh of September in response to the call for all able-bodied men to head east. He shouldn't be out there. He was born for a world of concertos and sonatas, not bombs and terror. When Marek Eisenberg took up his violin, he didn't merely draw his bow across the strings but gave himself to the notes, each one an invitation not to listen but to experience.

And I loved him. That was why he shouldn't be out there.

In the guttering candlelight, Helena's face was pale, and though she didn't speak, I could feel her slight frame trembling. I wanted to say "it will soon be over" or "we'll be all right," something to comfort her, to steady both of us, but there wasn't anything to say. Nothing that would be true, at least, so I slipped my arm around her and she rested her head on my shoulder. We sat, holding each other, our backs against the clammy wall, as explosions crashed, so many I no longer counted the seconds between the piercing whine of the planes as they dove and the impact of the detonation. One of the neighbors clung to her husband, whimpering as she'd done for hours.

"Why won't it end? Oh, why won't it end?"

The building convulsed. Fragments from the ceiling dislodged in a rain of debris. Women screamed.

"It's a hit," someone shouted.

I coughed, choking on the dust that filled my throat.

A man burst into the cellar. "Fire's spreading to the back of the building." His words came in gasps. "The house next door took the worst of it."

In the murky light, Helena's eyes shone with panic.

"Children and the old, stay here. Everyone who's able, follow me."

In an instant, I was on my feet, Helena beside me. Others rose, moving toward the cellar steps in a herd, our leader's electric torch a bobbing light ahead of us as we ascended the narrow stairs.

It can't burn. I can't let it burn.

"I'll need strong men on the roof. The rest of you, fetch buckets of sand," the man yelled. "Form a line."

I darted into the courtyard after the others.

I stilled. The crackle of burning, the *vrrrrr* of the planes, the deafening boom of explosions, my own ragged breaths . . .

The scrape of metal yanked me from my daze. Women and old men dug with spades, filled buckets with dirt. They'd buried some people here last week, so the cobblestones had already been pulled up in a portion of the courtyard.

One of the women thrust a full pail at me. I ran into the entrance hall, pushed the bucket into waiting hands, and rushed out again. Helena had joined the digging, her hair straggling around her cheeks. Our eyes met, a fleeting glance, then someone shoved another pail into my hands.

Running inside, taking the empty pail handed to me, dashing into the courtyard again. I stopped thinking about the planes swarming overhead or anything at all. I only ran.

Flames writhed in the shattered windows on the fourth floor of our building. The fire was spreading.

I snatched a full pail and raced inside. Footsteps clattered as people flooded down the staircase. A stout woman trotted past, arms overflowing with a fur coat, a jewel box, and a silver platter. Pani Puchalska from the second floor.

"What's happening?"

Pani Puchalska turned, shook her head. "Can't be done. Not without water. Best save what we can."

Before I could answer, she'd moved on.

I pounded into the courtyard, the abandoned expanse cast in a strange, dancing light. Only a lone old man continued to dig, shoulders stooped as he filled buckets left behind.

Helena.

Panic tasted of metal. My heavy pail clattered to the ground. I ran inside, started up the stairs. One flight, two. My lungs burned, my eyes stung. I coughed, gasping for breath.

Smoke filled the third-floor landing. I reached our door, jerked the knob. It turned. The smoke wasn't as heavy inside. Yet.

"Hela!" The shout scraped my raw throat. "Hela!"

Through the sitting room, into the dining room, I ran, shouting my sister's name, the darkened rooms eerily alight.

Into our bedroom. Empty.

I pushed into Tata's room. "Hela!"

My heart stilled.

On the floor beside the bed lay my sister's crumpled body.

No. Please, no.

I rushed to her, dropped to my knees. She lay curled on her side on the glass-strewn floor, her face turned away from me. Blood trickled from a gash on her temple. But her chest rose and fell.

"Hela." I bent over her, touching her shoulder. "Hela."

Somewhere above came shuddering, cracking. I raised my gaze to the ceiling.

"Hela, wake up. You need to wake up." I slapped her cheeks gently, trying to rouse her.

Her lids flickered, her eyes unfocused. "Tosia." Her voice was raspy. "What—what happened?"

"You must get up. We have to go." I put my arm around her, helping her to her feet. "That's it. Come." I led her from the room.

"No. Wait."

I glanced at her.

"Mama's picture." Her words spilled out. "I came to fetch it."

Blood trailed down her cheek, but her eyes sparked. She wasn't leaving without that picture.

"I'll get it." I ran back into the bedroom. The oval frame wasn't in its usual place on the bedside table. Panic swelled. There wasn't time for this. My gaze swept the room.

There. On the floor. It must have fallen. I snatched up the frame, a crack now webbing the glass, and rushed out again.

A sickening crumbling. The building shook.

Not a bomb blast. The roof. The roof was collapsing.

Bits of plaster fell from the ceiling as we ran, bent into ourselves, choking on the suffocating fumes.

Down three flights, through swirling smoke, clinging to one another.

We sprinted across the entrance hall, staggered outside. Helena coughed. I gulped in air.

A bloody glow illuminated the sky. Marszałkowska Street was burning. Flickering silhouettes rose stark against the night, masses of black smoke roiling above the buildings. Brilliant flashes burst on the horizon, the ground shuddering with detonations. Somewhere close by, a woman screamed.

A man said something about a shelter nearby, called out for everyone to follow him. Wind whipped a dry, crackling heat as we darted down the street. The air was alive with burning cinders, whirling and dancing in the glow of the flames. If they landed on us, I didn't notice. Planes roared overhead, their pulse filling my brain as I ran, my feet pounding the cobblestones, my sister's hand clutched in mine.

A whistle. Searing brightness. A building erupted. Flying brick and glass and enveloping smoke.

Nearly to the other side of the street, I flung a glance over my shoulder.

There it stood, illuminated in a nightmarish radiance. Crackling flames leapt in the gaps where windows used to be, consuming the four-story structure. The place I would always remember as home.

Then I ran. And I did not look back again.

I barely remembered reaching the courtyard where the shelter was. Along with the others, Helena and I stumbled down the short wooden steps into the musty dimness.

Only after I sank to the floor did I realize how badly I was shaking.

As a child, I'd feared sleep and the terrors it held. For months, the sound of my own screams lurched me awake. Tata would rush into my room, his warm arms and strong chest a shelter for my trembling body. Though the panic of those moments had been real, I viewed them now with a kind of wistfulness.

Huddled in an overcrowded cellar, as fire fell from the skies above Warsaw, I said goodbye to the girl who had only dreams to fear.

HELENA
SEPTEMBER 27, 1939

I blinked as we emerged from the shelter. How bright it was. But it was the sun, daring to shine in a hazy blue sky, that dazzled my eyes, not the flash of a detonation. After indefinite hours crouching in subterranean darkness with several dozen strangers, praying death would not find us, the sun seemed strange, a confirmation of life I did not quite believe.

We'd already bid farewell to our companions. There wasn't much to say, really. Everyone's thoughts were absorbed with the fate of relatives, friends, dwellings, perhaps even the city itself. No one knew what awaited us aboveground.

Now we made our way toward Marszałkowska Street, Antonina and I. The skies were silent now. No swooping planes, no plummeting bombs, no whistling blasts of artillery. It brought no peace, this stillness, for it was a lifeless silence, like a funeral. Perhaps it was, in a way.

I couldn't take more than a few steps without scanning the blue expanse above for the familiar shadow of bombers. At any moment they would return, darkening the sky, filling our ears with their whining drone, and we would need to run for cover. I braced for it, even now.

The shakiness of my limbs, the lightheadedness that left me unsteady and somehow detached from my surroundings, did it come from hunger and thirst? The wound on my temple that Antonina had bandaged with a strip torn from her skirt? From shock at the landscape that greeted us? Or disbelief at the simple fact that somehow we were still alive?

Warsaw had become a wilderness of rubble. It strewed the streets and lay in heaps. Bricks, stone, shattered glass, and debris mingled with leaflets scattered by German planes. The enemy's confetti, remnants of their macabre revelry. Barricades erected of uprooted paving stones, overturned trams, and household furnishings stood at nearly every street corner, as if such would stop the Germans who struck mercilessly from the skies again and again. We navigated around them along with everyone else.

Fire gnawed at the bones of buildings. Smoke and dust hung in the air and turned it into a world of grit and gray. Though some structures remained untouched, others had the appearance of corpses with their entrails spilling out—a twisted mass of bricks, boards, plaster, and the contents of whatever the building formerly held. What had once been the windows of stately residences had become empty eye sockets, gazing down on Warsaw as if to say, "You too shall become like us."

A group had collected around the body of a horse killed in its traces, cutting off chunks of its flesh. Though we'd eaten horsemeat in the past weeks—forced it down out of hunger—the sight of the crowd setting upon its carrion like vultures, the steaming, bloody scent as they split the carcass open with penknives, made bile rise in my throat.

How easily our human needs betray our higher sensibilities. How soon we turn feral.

The dry wind carried the caustic stench of burning, the putrid sweetness of decay. I told myself it came from those poor horses, only animals. But I knew more than animals rotted on the streets and under collapsed buildings.

Two nurses bore a wounded man on a stretcher, people wandered the streets searching for relatives or friends, grim-faced men shoveled rubble from the site of a building in another kind of desperate search.

I stumbled. Antonina grabbed my arm, jerked me back. "Look out."

I glanced down, found myself teetering at the edge of a gaping wound in the pavement. A bomb crater. It still smoldered.

"Sorry," I murmured, my throat raw from the smoke.

Antonina didn't reply. She hadn't said where we were going, and I didn't ask. Perhaps I already knew, deep down. I stayed close at her side, careful where I stepped.

Bodies sprawled in pools of blood, startling crimson amid the gray. Three corpses lay in front of a boarded-up shop, awaiting burial. A man crouched on one knee, drawing back the sheets that covered them, studying their faces. Farther down the street, under an iron lamppost, was a woman—or what remained of one. She lay curled up on her side, her arm outstretched. Her head had been blown off.

One might imagine that in the scope of devastation, human loss would be the most difficult. That the sight of death would move something in me. It did, but the emotion held the same remoteness with which I viewed everything else, a blend of pity and relief. Yes, relief it wasn't me laid out on the sidewalk as strangers filed past. Pity where there should have been grief over the ending of a human life. I was the child who wept heartbroken tears after a sparrow in flight struck our window, then together with Tata, carefully placed its crumpled little body in an old tin lined with a scrap of cloth and buried it under the tree in our courtyard. I'd seen films at the cinema—pathetic melodramas—that moved me more than the reality now confronting me.

Perhaps my frozen mind could not fully take it in, the horror, the loss. Or perhaps the weeks of war had withered me into a husk of the living, feeling woman I had once been.

We walked on until it was before us, its ravages laid bare by daylight. Where our building once stood, a gutted edifice now smoldered, outlined by a sky tinged yellow-gray with smoke. Of the adjacent structure, only a skeleton remained.

For long and silent minutes we stood on the sidewalk, two women gazing at the remains of the life we had once known. Smoke stung my eyes.

Home. I want to go home.

I should cry. In the face of sorrow, I'd always found tears. "My tenderhearted girl," Tata called me. I'd always been sensitive. Antonina cried less and flashed with anger more.

But now I could not cry. And I did not understand why.

Still, I ached. A pain not sharp but swallowing. My chest consumed by nothingness.

How it would break your heart to see this, Tata. Oh, Tata, where are you?

Antonina did not cry either. She grew pale, her jaw set, a deep burning in her eyes.

"Tosia. Hela."

I turned. Aunt Basia came toward us. Blond tendrils strayed from her chignon, her blouse and skirt stained with grime and dried blood. During the days and nights Warsaw had been under the heaviest bombardment of the siege, I'd feared constantly for her. But she was here. She was all right.

"Aunt Basia, I was so worried."

"Ah, my Hela." She wrapped me in her arms, her embrace motherly and warm. Like all of us, she smelled of filth and sweat, but a whisper of jasmine and rose—her favorite perfume—still clung to her skin. For a moment, she clasped me close, and I leaned into her strength. She embraced Antonina, then drew away, taking in the devastation before us. The past weeks had left shadows under her eyes, haggard creases in her skin. Marks made by weariness and war. She stared at the charred ruins, her lips pressed tight.

Then she turned to us. "Come. You'll stay with me. Until your father returns, at least." She paused. "We can only hope it will not be long now that . . ."

Antonina frowned. "What? Now that what?"

She drew a long breath. "I met an officer at the hospital. It's over, it would seem. Or soon will be."

"You mean . . . ?" Antonina's voice faded.

Aunt Basia nodded, resignation bleak in her eyes. "I'm afraid so. It won't be long before the official announcement."

I looked at my sister. In the cellar we'd heard rumors that the

British had landed troops in Danzig and the forces of our own General Bortnowski had broken through at Radom and even now were marching toward Warsaw. I had not known if they could be believed. I had not known what to believe, save the reality around us.

But now?

Surrender.

"For nothing," Antonina whispered. "All for nothing."

Wind blew strands of hair into my dry eyes as I stared at the smoke drifting from the remains of our home.

Then this was how it ended. It had happened so suddenly. First invasion, then the blurred days of siege.

Now, defeat.

What had been the purpose of continuing the struggle as long as we had if such an end had been inevitable? What pride could there be in fighting after all hope of victory was lost? How many lives would have been saved, buildings preserved, if the city had surrendered a week, even three days ago?

What a waste. A cruel, senseless waste.

Warsaw had been stripped, but she still stood. The Germans had not fully destroyed her, as they had vowed. Perhaps there was hope in that. Capitulation would bring peace, at least. No more planes raining fire and sowing death.

And Tata would come home. We would face whatever lay ahead together and we would be all right.

"Come." Aunt Basia put an arm around my shoulders. "Let's go home."

We turned and started down the street, three women picking our way among the ruins.

ANTONINA
OCTOBER 1, 1939

For nearly a month, Poland had fought. Bitterly. Bravely. And we had fought. With her and for her.

No. That wasn't quite true. The soldiers had fought, but we hadn't.

We'd dug useless anti-tank trenches, rolled bandages, and cowered in cellars.

Now Warsaw, the gallant city, who had vowed to stand defiant until her last drop of blood was spilled, had fallen.

Notices had been posted on shell-scarred walls, the official announcement of surrender. They asked the citizens to accept the entry of the Germans peaceably. According to the statement, the destruction of the water supply had been the reason for capitulation. Without water, the city could no longer defend itself.

Aunt Basia rarely left the hospital, tireless in her efforts to tend the injured and dying. Thousands of civilians had been wounded during the siege. The city had no electricity. Nor had the water-works been repaired. The only means by which we could obtain water was to join a queue at one of the few wells or fetch it from the river.

For over an hour, we stood in line before our turn at the pump. Now Helena and I left the weary column and started toward Aunt Basia's flat. The heavy pail banged against my leg, and sweat collected under my arms, despite the cool morning.

What I wouldn't give to run a steaming bath and soak for an hour, scrub the filth from my skin with lavender-scented soap. With water scarce and toting it through the streets an arduous chore, we allotted only a glass a day with which to wash ourselves. Not that it did much good. Wind churned up clouds of yellowish-brown dust from the ruins, ashes embedding into our very pores. Women had taken to covering their hair with kerchiefs, knotting turbans over their unwashed curls.

We spoke little as we trudged toward Hoża Street. There didn't seem to be much to say these days. Or perhaps it was easier not to speak of what inhabited our thoughts, as though voicing our fears would somehow give them life. Existence in a city left ravaged and bleeding allowed little space for anything beyond the daily grappling of survival.

When we did talk, it was of mundane matters—where we might obtain food, what tasks needed to be undertaken. Sometimes we speculated about the war, our allies, and the situation in the rest of the country. Rumors were all that remained to us, for Polish Radio no longer broadcasted and newspapers had ceased to be printed, save for bulletins posted on the walls, which provided scant information. Warsaw had been cut off from the outside, and we remained trapped, dangling in the gap. The space between the end of the siege and whatever awaited us upon the arrival of the conquerors.

The aftermath but not the beginning.

"We must find something to board up the windows." I shifted my grip on the pail as we passed men scavenging through wreckage, a building with its roof caved in standing behind them. "It's only growing colder at night."

Though Aunt Basia's flat had suffered little damage, the floor had been littered with particles of glass, dust, and ash, and a fresh layer of debris settled every time the wind blew. Hardly a windowpane remained intact in the city. As Varsovians scrambled to find ways of fortifying the gaping spaces in their homes, glass and even boards became sought-after commodities.

With what naivety we'd sealed our windows with paper strips in the days leading up to the invasion. In the end, it had proven as futile as so many of our preparations.

"We'll be fortunate to find heavy cardboard. It would keep out a bit of the wind, at least. I'll see about some candles. We're down to our last . . ." Helena froze, her voice trailing away.

It came faintly at first, a distant tread tugging at the edges of my consciousness. Then closer. Clearer. The rhythmic slam of boots.

Men in gray-green uniforms marched down the center of the street, rifles at their shoulders, their ranks stepping in unison. The handle of the water pail bit into my fingers as I stood motionless on the sidewalk. Something surged in my chest, hard and raw.

Out of the corner of my eye, I glanced at Helena. But she did not meet my gaze, hers riveted on the soldiers. I, too, could not look away.

The soldiers strode past, youthful faces impassive beneath steel helmets. Our first glimpse of the enemy who had done this to us, to Warsaw. How proud and strong they looked, sturdy, well-fed. A conquering army in their fine uniforms and obsidian boots, parading past bombed-out buildings and mounded rubble, haggard civilians who looked on warily or defiantly.

I couldn't move. I could barely breathe. I could do nothing but watch as the boots of Hitler's soldiers struck the cobblestones of my beloved Warsaw, every step gouging a wound deep into her heart, and with hers, mine.

4

ANTONINA
DECEMBER 21, 1939

Warsaw found itself locked in the grip of an unyielding winter. December in Poland had always been cold, but this . . . this was a different kind, hard and angry. It drove burning needles into our cheeks, its icy breath penetrated our homes. It sank into our bones and leached our strength. The numbing dampness stiffened my joints so even if I had a piano, my cracked fingertips would doubtless stumble over the keys. Since my cherished instrument had gone the way of the rest of our possessions—burned and destroyed, left behind in the remains of our flat—my theory had gone untested.

It did not help that there was a shortage of coal. The little available could be obtained only at exorbitant prices. Aunt Basia, Helena, and I wore our coats indoors on the bitterest days and slept three to a bed.

The cold or the occupiers. I could not decide which was more bent upon increasing our misery.

Wind cut through my coat as keenly as ever, but I minded it less that morning. I kept my head down as I hastened along the sidewalk, one among a crowd of men and women with drab clothes and drawn faces. Snow limned the gray ruins of blasted-out buildings. The structures that had suffered only mild damage or escaped unscathed had boards instead of glass in the windows. Shops and businesses had reopened, and streets and squares teemed with vendors and stalls.

In the weeks after the entry of the Germans, the citizens of Warsaw had resumed the grim task of living.

It had taken over a week before the damage to the water supply had been repaired. By mid-October, electricity had been partially restored, but it wasn't until November that electric lights once again shone in Aunt Basia's flat. Now that the streets had been mostly cleared and masons and carpenters had begun repairs, the extent of the damage wasn't as great as we'd believed in the immediate aftermath of the siege, yet we couldn't walk about without confronting evidence of devastation—the Royal Castle, the Grand Theatre, and the Philharmonic Hall, proud government edifices and majestic churches disfigured, decimated.

Somehow we grew used to the sight of the city's wounds. Or perhaps numb to them.

The clatter of carts and droshkies and the clopping of hooves mingled with the calls of a boy hawking the *Nowy Kurier Warszawski*. In place of the variety of newspapers once available and now permanently suspended, we had the daily *Nowy Kurier Warszawski* in Polish and the *Warschauer Zeitung* in German. The former existed for the purpose of transmitting the edicts and proclamations issued by the occupation authorities, along with filtering political and military news as they saw fit, which largely consisted of lauding Germany and its victories and vilifying Great Britain. Though loath to spend even twenty groszy—the price of each edition—we had little choice but to read the awful rag to keep up with the latest decrees lest we be in inadvertent violation of one and find ourselves dispatched to prison or worse.

In the autumn, the authorities had issued the order for Varsovians to turn in their radios. For the first time, I'd been glad our beautiful mahogany set had been destroyed—better it be burned than handed over to the occupiers—but Aunt Basia and I had hauled hers down to the commissariat of the police district and stood in line with everyone else. All weapons also had to be surrendered. The penalty for withholding either had been made clear. Execution.

Downtrodden and shivering, grappling for daily sustenance in a conquered city, was it any wonder the coming holidays found us without any of the joyous, expectant bustle of former years?

Breathless and windswept, I hurried along the snowy avenues of Saski Gardens. In summer, in peacetime, the broad lanes and English-style gardens were thronged with women pushing perambulators, couples strolling arm in arm, children playing. But on this bitterly cold morning, the park was nearly deserted.

He waited for me in front of the fountain. It stood silent, no cascades of water sparkling from its tier in graceful arcs. There was a barrenness to the landscape, the white expanse of the avenue, the magnificent Saski Palace in the background, the pale stone fountain, the lone, dark-coated figure etched against the snow.

My steps crunched as I approached. He turned. The moment our eyes met, a soft, spreading glow, like a candle's flame, rose within me.

"Hello, Marek."

"It's good to see you, Antonina." He clasped my hands, his lean violinist's fingers enveloping mine. He frowned. "Your hands, they're nearly frozen."

"I forgot my gloves." In my room on Marszałkowska, to be precise, but no sense going on about that now. I tightened my fingers around his, smiling. "They're all right now."

"Here"—he tugged off his own leather gloves—"take mine."

"I'm fine—"

"I insist. Anyone whose fingers hold such talent should take more care." He took my hands in his—first one, then the other—and slid the gloves over my fingers. The fur-lined leather that still carried his warmth enfolded my numbed hands. "That's better." He smiled that crooked half-moon of a grin that had taken hold of my heart from the moment I held it in my gaze. I'd fallen in love with him for his music first, his smile second, and then for a thousand other reasons, great and small.

"Thank you." I stood before him, our hands still entwined. It had been weeks since we'd last met. His doing, not mine. I took him in—gulped him in, really. His dark hair and irregular features, his lean cheeks and firm jawline.

Then I noticed it. A white band emblazoned with a blue Star of David, outlined against the right sleeve of his overcoat.

Ever since the decree that came into effect at the beginning of December—*"All Jews in the Warsaw district over twelve years of age must wear an identifying badge in the form of an armband whenever they are outside their place of residence"*—people had appeared in the streets wearing the armbands, white slashes against dark outer garments.

Still I had not been prepared for this . . . for Marek.

I must have done something. Started maybe or stared too long, because almost imperceptibly, his features tightened and he released my hands.

"You look thinner," I said, because I did not know what else to say.

"There's no need to pretend, Antonina."

I swallowed, glanced away.

"I don't mind." He gave a short chuckle. "Well, I mind a lot, actually, but compared with the rest, going out with a strip of cloth around my sleeve is almost immaterial."

"I'm sorry," I said, voice quiet. Because of my response or because the occupiers had enforced the branding of the Jewish people? An identifying badge. Identified for what purpose?

"For what should you be sorry?" His tone softened.

"This is why you wouldn't meet at a café, isn't it?" I drew a breath. "I should have known." I looked up at him. "How are you? Tell me."

His lips angled. "You wouldn't prefer to speak of Chopin? The nocturnes, perhaps?"

I didn't laugh. "I want to know, Marek." I searched his face. "Please."

Without a word, he motioned me to precede him, and we started along the avenue. Once he would have offered me his arm, but he didn't now. I didn't want to consider the reason, so I slipped my hand through the crook of his elbow, determined to span the distance between us. He glanced at me, but neither moved closer nor drew away, though there were few passersby about to notice us. I kept my hand there, tucked against the wool of his overcoat, the white fabric of the armband just above.

For a moment, the muted crackle of our footsteps against the snow-carpeted gravel remained the only sound. "We get by. Father and I have begun giving private music lessons. It's not my salary from Polish Radio, but it helps. Many have no work at all."

"And your parents?"

He exhaled, the smoke of his breath falling on the frosty air. "They manage."

"There's a couple in the building where my aunt lives. The Germans have come to their flat three times. Sometimes there's someone with them. A Pole, I think. Once I asked the officer what business they had there. He told me they'd come to search for hidden weapons. But each time, they take more. Carry it all out and load it into the back of a lorry. Furniture, valuables, I don't know. Has your family . . . ?" My words came in a rush, then faltered.

A slight hardening of his jaw, his eyes straight ahead. "We've had our share of visitors."

My stomach tightened. "What did they take?"

"A couple of paintings, the silver, Mama's fur coat, the sitting room furniture. They'd have taken the piano, I think, if they could have moved it. You should have heard the officer banging on the keys. Like trying to play in allegro with sausages." He gave a dry laugh.

I couldn't smile. "Your violin?" If they'd stolen his violin, his beloved Guadagnini . . .

He shook his head. "After I told them who I was, they didn't touch it."

"I could keep some things for you, if you like. They would be safe."

He glanced at me. "It's good of you to offer, but we've put some of our valuables in a safe place. They won't find them. They're not intelligent enough."

"But if they discovered you'd concealed something." The shiver that passed through me had nothing to do with the wind. In November, a Jewish man—a thief newly released from prison, it was said—shot and killed a Polish policeman and wounded another. In reprisal, the Gestapo raided the building where the man lived and rounded up fifty-three others, all Jews. They'd been shot, every last one, mere days later. Executed for the "crime of rebellion." It had been nothing less than murder.

In the proclamation issued not long after the Germans arrived in Warsaw, the Jewish people had been assured of their rights and the inviolability of their property. How soon those promises had proven cheap. The population of the Warsaw district of the Generalgouvernement—Polish territory under German occupation, but not annexed to the Reich—had been laden with restrictions and decrees, but the Jews had been singled out, dealt with as a separate, inferior body.

"Don't worry about that. Now, tell me about you. Has there been any news of your father?"

"We think he's in a camp for officers, but we don't know where. If we could just hear he's well and—and . . ." I pressed my lips together.

Untold numbers of Polish men had been taken prisoner during the fighting and its aftermath. We should have expected it perhaps, but still, we'd told ourselves Tata would come home after the capitulation. But he had fought in defense of his country, and according to the conquerors, must be punished for its defeat.

Though captivity wasn't the only possible fate. One other remained.

Marek stopped. "If he were dead, you would have had word." His voice was steady, certain. "I'm sure he'll write as soon as he can."

"That's what I keep telling myself."

"And your studies? Will you attend the conservatory once it reopens?"

Education had not been spared the consequences of German rule. For a time, all schools had been closed, then primary schools had been permitted to resume classes—with alterations to the curriculum. Polish history and geography were now forbidden. Universities and secondary schools remained closed, vocational schools the only higher education sanctioned by the occupiers. All Jewish schools had been terminated. But official consent to reopen the conservatory had been granted, and courses would begin in the new year. What form they would take under occupation had yet to be determined.

"How could I manage it now?" Snow drifted around us as we stood in the middle of the avenue. "We've had to close my father's office. The Gestapo arrested his partner in the firm. Helena and I must find work. We can't expect our aunt to bear the burden of providing for us."

Marek's brow furrowed. "But your music—to give it up?"

"We're under occupation now. Or haven't you heard?" I gave a shaky laugh. "Other things are more important."

"What gives life meaning must always be preserved, Antonina." The intensity of his voice stilled me. "Or else what is the point of going on at all? You have a remarkable gift. It's breath to you, as it is to me. I knew it the first time I heard you play."

"'Étude in E Major,'" I said softly. "Our Chopin."

"Yes." His gaze held mine. "Our Chopin."

There had always been music between us. It settled in our silences, for those who spoke its language needed no words to be understood. We didn't even need to touch our instruments for it to join us; we could meet at a café or in the park and share it still. From the first, our hearts had met in melody. Through it, we had found one another, and in it, we had been bound together.

But the days when the union of piano and violin could set the world to rights had become a memory.

"Come," he said, a sudden spark in his eyes. "Let's go to my flat. We'll play. You on the piano, me on the violin, just as before."

"Wouldn't your mother mind? I don't think she approves of me." I glanced away. "Of our seeing one another." In the months I had known Marek, I'd only met Pani Eisenberg twice. She'd been unfailingly polite but aloof. Her disapproval of her son's association with a young Gentile woman a false note I couldn't help but detect.

"Even Mama wouldn't deny you an hour or two with the piano. Please come. It's been far too long since I've had any accompanist but Father."

I found myself smiling. How like the old Marek he looked in that moment. Though the past months had left me little time to long for what I lacked, I still yearned for the press of cool ivory beneath my fingertips, the abandon of losing myself in a piece. Music had always been my constant. So long as I could turn to it, the rest would come right in the end.

"Very well. For an hour, perhaps."

"Excellent." He grinned, almost boyish in his anticipation.

We left the park. Snow flurried as we hastened along the sidewalk. Together, on our way to do what we both loved, war and occupation receded. He could have been walking me home after I'd dropped by the broadcasting centre, his overcoat-clad shoulder brushing mine, our glances speaking in the silence.

The rasp of tires and the low rumble of an engine sounded behind me. I glanced back. A lorry trundled down the street. The even clip of our footsteps didn't slow.

The lorry drew alongside us, stopped at the curb.

"Walk away from me," Marek said, low-voiced. "Don't turn around."

Boots struck the ground and a door slammed as a soldier in a greatcoat emerged.

"Halt. You, Jew," he called in poor Polish. "Come here."

Marek stopped. From inside the vehicle, another soldier looked on. Pedestrians cast furtive glances at the lorry before quickening their stride. They had learned to walk with their heads down, had grown used to distancing themselves from danger lest they become its target. I, too, had learned to do this, but now I remained motionless.

Marek turned and calmly approached the soldier. Wind bit my cheeks as I stood a few paces away, gripping my handbag.

"Get in the lorry." The soldier jerked his thumb toward the vehicle.

"If this is about a work detail, I have my documents here." Marek reached into his overcoat.

"Did I ask for your papers, Jew? Into the lorry."

Marek hesitated.

A fist cracked. I gasped. The soldier struck again. Marek sprawled on the cobblestones.

I rushed forward. "Stop!"

The soldier's booted foot slammed into Marek's body.

"Let him alone."

The soldier's gaze flickered to me. "Get away from here. This Jew is no concern of yours."

"Go home, Antonina." Marek's words came almost too quiet to catch.

Interest kindled on the soldier's blunt features. "Ah, so the Jew and the pretty Polish girl are acquainted, are they? What's a girl like you doing with a Jewish swine?"

I burned inside. "Do you know who this man is?" My voice rose. "This is Marek Eisenberg, the famous violinist."

The soldier glanced at Marek. "You're a violinist?"

Blood trickled from Marek's nose. He picked up his hat and stood, attempted to brush snow and mud from his coat. "That is correct."

"Regrettably, I have never been musical." A pause. "Get into the lorry, Jew."

Marek didn't so much as glance at me as he walked toward the lorry. A clank as the soldier let down the hinged panel, the back of the tarpaulin-clad vehicle already crowded with men. They looked on in silence, though one reached down and offered Marek a hand as he climbed aboard.

I drew myself up. "Where are you taking him?" If my voice shook, it was from anger, not panic. At least that was what I told myself.

"Work detail. Now, get out of here." The soldier's eyes slid over me. "Unless you'd prefer to come along."

For an instant, I expected him to grab me by the collar and haul me into the lorry.

For an instant, I almost wished he would.

I looked at Marek, who now sat among the group huddled in the lorry.

With every scrap of my being, I wanted to go to him. To pull him away. To protect him. But I could do nothing.

"Marek."

He didn't meet my eyes.

"I'll go to your family." Wind carried my words. "Tell them what's happened."

He said nothing. Only dipped his head slightly, an offering of unspoken thanks. For the space of a breath, I held his gaze, then turned away.

"Stay away from Jews, pretty Polish girl," the soldier called after me. "They spread disease, or didn't anyone tell you?"

I didn't look back. Bits of snow stung my face, my shoes tapped the sidewalk. Tires ground against cobbles as the lorry passed, its gray-green outline fading into the swirling snow.

HELENA
DECEMBER 24, 1939

Snow whispered from the vast darkness. I chafed my arms, my breath emerging as frost from my parted lips. I was a grown woman, past the traditions of childhood, yet still I searched the sky for the first star on Christmas Eve. When Antonina and I were small, Tata would carry us out to the balcony to wait for it to appear, for only then could the festivities begin. Cold would nip at my nose, but I'd never minded, not in Tata's strong, warm arms.

How unquestioningly five-year-old girls believe this wide and frightening world cannot harm them because their father will always be there to hold them close.

I drew a shuddering breath, shivering in the wind.

I'm watching for the star, Tata. Perhaps you're watching for it too, wherever you are. Next Christmas, we'll watch for it together.

At the sound of footsteps, I turned. Antonina came toward where I stood on the sidewalk, her coat thrown over her shoulders.

Wind tugged her hair away from her cheeks as she gazed into the sky. "Remember how we used to go out onto the balcony to watch for it? Bouncing up and down, ready to burst with waiting?"

I nodded, smiling. "You always saw it first."

"Did I?" She gave a laugh.

"Then you would run in to tell Aunt Basia, and Tata and I would stand on the balcony until I saw it too."

"It's easy to forget such things, isn't it? Then when you wish most to remember"—her voice caught—"it isn't there anymore."

How quickly the once-tangible slipped away, became part of the memories from before, the blurred remnants of a life that had ceased to exist.

Our gazes held. "We'll help each other remember." My words came quiet, fervent.

We stood together as snow drifted softly around us.

"Look." Antonina pointed, voice scarcely a whisper. "There."

Against the deepening darkness, a single star glimmered bright.

"He's thinking of us," Antonina said fiercely, her voice a little choked. "I know he is."

I stared into the night, the brush of falling snow against my cheeks. "He's always thinking of us."

We returned to the flat where Aunt Basia bustled about, laying the table. There would be no feast of twelve meatless dishes as was the custom for Wigilia—the vigil for the Christ child. No barszcz—beet soup with tiny mushroom dumplings—ruby-hued and glistening in the tureen, no carp and herring, no cabbage stuffed with mushrooms and rice, no plump pierogi. No kompot—a beverage made with dried fruits. No poppy seed cake layered with sweet cream and studded with raisins, no array of nuts and candies.

Still we'd done our best to gather the ingredients for a supper finer than any we'd tasted since before the war. Dried mushroom broth, smelt, and a small gingerbread prepared with carrots instead of honey.

Antonina had trekked across Warsaw in search of a tree. The stall owners had apparently feared putting out their stock too early lest the Germans requisition the trees for their own use and leave the Poles with nothing. Late this afternoon, she'd returned, rosy-cheeked and triumphant, hauling a tree with her. It scarcely came up to my waist, and had already lost a great many of its needles. When she brought it in, I'd stupidly wanted to cry. Compared with the trees that had sat each year in our sitting room at home, majestic and gloriously full, trees we'd decorated with Tata, bedecking the branches with our favorite ornaments, it had seemed as forlorn as everything else this Christmas.

"The star is out," Antonina announced. In the past thirteen years, my sister had really not changed all that much.

Aunt Basia placed a small plate on the table. "And not a moment too soon. Everything is ready." She moved to light the pair of candles in the center, for it was the tradition for the Wigilia meal to be eaten by candlelight.

We gathered around the table, laid with Aunt Basia's best cloth. The snowy linen had little bulges from the bits of hay spread beneath, symbolizing the hay that filled the manger in which the Babe lay the night of His birth.

"In the name of the Father, and of the Son, and of the Holy Spirit." We crossed ourselves and Aunt Basia continued. "O Lord, we thank Thee for the bounty which Thou has bestowed upon us. Grant us Thy presence on this holy night and grant it also"—her voice cracked—"to the dear ones absent from this table."

I raised my gaze to the empty chair across from mine. This Christmas Eve, as always, we kept the tradition of leaving one seat empty, so if a wanderer knocked on the door, we would be ready to offer them a place at our table and the welcome of our home.

Now I wondered if there were enough tables in the whole of Poland to hold all who were lost.

After our amens, Aunt Basia picked up the small plate with the opłatek. The delicate wafers embossed with images from the Nativity could not be found in the shops this year, so we made do with bread.

"Let us break this opłatek. May next Christmas find us all together in a free Poland, and may the coming year bring those who are not with us safely home once more." Though a smile softened her lips, quiet desperation lay beneath the surface of her gaze, a wondering that clutched at the tiniest pieces of hope and drew them tight. We were all reaching for our own tiny pieces of hope. Reaching out only for our hands to be met with empty air, which we pretended was something more.

Something worth holding onto.

She stood and carried the plate to Antonina. They each broke off a small piece. "Health and happiness to you, my dear."

"And to you."

They ate the opłatek and embraced, then Aunt Basia came to me. Her eyes were gentle with understanding as they met mine. In response to her well-wishes, I could only nod as I broke off a corner of the bread, my throat too tight for words.

Next, Antonina and I exchanged good wishes, breaking and eating pieces of the bread. The opłatek finished, I left the table to fetch the soup. We savored each spoonful of the flavorful broth as Antonina regaled Aunt Basia with the story of haggling with the stall owner for the tree.

In moments like this, it was easy to remember peace. When belief in "good tidings of great joy" still held the wonder of innocence.

When we trusted the future instead of feared it.

How many families shared opłatek this night, knowing a beloved face would no longer be found around their Christmas table, a place ever remaining empty?

Later, as we sat together, our humble tree aglow with a few candles, our voices rising with the words of age-old carols, I wondered where, for all our well-wishes, next Christmas would find us. The ones with me now and the one who passed this night so very far away.

I prayed he was warm and well. I prayed he would know he was in our hearts, with us this Christmas as he had always been, and that the memory of us would give him strength.

And I prayed for peace.

5

ANTONINA
OCTOBER 12, 1940

"Attention, Attention!"

The whine and spit of static broke over the street, the now-familiar rousing of the beast that transmitted the edicts and propaganda of the German authorities. Occupation humor dubbed the loudspeakers "barkers" on account of their droning racket.

I kept walking, a net shopping bag over one arm, the heels of my worn oxfords clicking on the sidewalk.

"On the basis of the decree on restricting residence in the Generalgouvernement of 13 September 1940, a Jewish district is to be created in the city of Warsaw, in which are to live Jews residing in Warsaw or moving to Warsaw."

My steps halted. Around me, others had stopped, silence descending upon the street, save for the toneless voice resounding over the loudspeaker.

"Poles residing in the Jewish district must move to other areas of the city by 31 October 1940. Jews residing outside the Jewish district must move to the Jewish district by 31 October 1940. They are allowed to take with them only refugee luggage and bedclothes. Allocation of flats will be made by elders of the Judenrat. Signed, head of the Warsaw district, Dr. Fischer."

I stood motionless, clutching my handbag. How to understand? To grasp what this meant?

Rumors of the establishment of a Jewish district in Warsaw had ebbed and flowed since the early months of occupation, and truth be told, I heard them only in passing. Near the end of 1939 and in the early months of 1940, there had been an outbreak of typhus in the part of Warsaw densely populated by Jewish families. Many dwelt in poverty, only increased by the privations of occupation and the decrees that stripped them of their livelihoods. Barbed wire fences had soon been erected on streets bordering the area traditionally inhabited by a large number of Jews. "Area Threatened by Epidemic" read the signs posted around the perimeter.

This past spring, a sight as startling as it was unexpected appeared. First came the uprooting of cobblestones and the digging of long trenches, the hauling of bricks and the mixing of mortar. And slowly, steadily, it began.

The building of a wall.

"The Jewish quarter must be separated from the rest of the city for sanitary reasons," reported the *Warschauer Zeitung*.

Since the beginning of the occupation, Jews had been routinely evicted from their residences, but in spite of everything, many remained outside the walled Jewish quarter—Marek's family, who lived in the district of Mokotów, among them.

Now, this order. Not an ordinary decree of occupation, like curfew or rationing, which restricted life and made things generally miserable but could be endured. This was the uprooting of a hundred thousand—if not two hundred thousand—people from their homes. Not only the Jewish population but Christians as well. To be completed by the end of the month, less than three weeks away.

The loudspeaker crackled, then fell silent. The throng on the sidewalks roused to life again, and I walked on. The air bore a raw chill, low clouds hovering in the faded sky. But had it been the most golden of autumn afternoons, my heart would still have been gray.

Two German police strode down the sidewalk. I kept walking, neither making way for them nor ducking my head. This was my city, why should I cower?

But as the noose of occupation tightened, we had learned what it meant to be afraid. One found ways of bearing the rest. The aching void of hunger, the rising prices of goods while wages remained at prewar rates, the lack of coal, the reduction of the middle class to threadbare poverty. These were only physical miseries, after all.

Fear was another kind of occupation. Hunger and cold and privation did not steal from one as fear did. It wasn't fear as most imagine it, a worry that troubles for a time and then recedes, but the awareness that life had become cruel, and in the face of its machinations, one knew oneself to be small and insignificant. One couldn't calculate or rationalize this fear—terror, really. It was daily, constant.

The difference between whether one returned home at the end of the day and whether one did not could be as simple as what time one set foot out-of-doors. Or turning down one street rather than another, taking a tram fifteen minutes earlier or later. Sometimes one was doing no more than sitting in a café or in one's own home. The German police or SS would be there, suddenly, with their lorries, cordoning the street. We called the raids łapanki, derived from a verb which meant "to catch." If one had documents proving gainful employment, sometimes one could go free. But often the Germans forced people into the lorries at gunpoint, regardless of their papers, and took them away. This wasn't a hunt for criminals, for these people had committed no crime, just ordinary men and women who stepped out to buy a loaf of bread or left for their place of employment and never returned.

You could be arrested because of your social class or profession—professors or lawyers or priests, the intelligentsia, rounded up, some later released while others simply vanished. For being out a quarter of an hour past curfew or for smuggling goods from the country to sell in the city to earn enough to keep your family from starving.

They sent you to a concentration camp or deported you to the Reich to labor for the enemy. Sometimes they just shot you. No ceremony. A farce of a trial or none at all.

You were Polish. That was all. That was enough.

The Nazis made it a crime to be born.

None understood this so fully as the Jews. In addition to being Polish citizens, they bore the additional crime of being of Jewish origin. During the siege, Varsovians had shared in each other's sufferings, Jew and Gentile alike. Since the occupation, the Jewish people had been separated from those they'd lived alongside as neighbors by edicts and by so much more.

Perhaps what became of the Jewish people didn't much matter to others. Perhaps the weariness of their own existence left little room to concern themselves with misfortunes they did not share. Of course, there were plenty who stood by and laughed as German soldiers sheared the beards and sidelocks of Orthodox men. Plenty who didn't hesitate to join the occupiers in plundering Jewish property, pointing out the residences and shops with the best spoils, and helping themselves alongside the Germans. Polish thugs beat Jews in the streets, the violence only increasing since the armband decree.

The police did nothing, neither the German Ordnungspolizei nor the Polish "navy blues." Laws applied to the Jews but no longer protected them.

But what happened, what *was* happening, mattered to me. Because of Marek, it mattered. And I could not look away.

I read the announcements on advertising pillars and in the newspapers, the ceaseless restrictions and decrees. Marek and I could no longer meet at a café because Jews were barred from "Aryan" restaurants and cafés. Nor could we stroll together in the Saski Gardens because Jews could no longer enter the city parks or streets and squares marked "Entry Forbidden to Jews." For goodness' sake, we couldn't even sit together on a bench, because Jews had been forbidden to use public benches.

Insofar as the edicts affected the two of us, these limitations were trifling compared with what the Jewish people of Warsaw had endured since the start of the occupation—relentlessly stripped of their livelihoods, their possessions, their security, and indeed their very dignity.

Fischer's decree was only the latest. But it might prove the most shattering.

I reached our building and rushed up the stairs to Aunt Basia's flat. I withdrew the key from my handbag, twisted it in the lock, and pushed inside.

Without stopping to take off my coat, I went into the kitchen. Helena stood near the stove, doing the ironing.

I dropped the shopping bag on the table with a thud. "It's happening."

"What is?" Helena didn't glance at me as she ran the iron over a blouse.

"The Jewish district. By order of Dr. Fischer, all Jews in Warsaw living outside the designated area have been ordered to move by the end of the month."

Helena's eyes found mine. Understanding came slowly over her features.

"Only Jews are allowed to remain within the boundaries. Everyone else has to leave. They just announced it over the loudspeakers."

For a moment, Helena said nothing, just kept ironing. Then in a soft voice, she asked, "What does it mean?"

"They're putting them in a ghetto. All the Jews." I folded my arms over my chest and swallowed hard. "That's what it means."

ANTONINA
OCTOBER 13, 1940

We didn't meet often, Marek and I. How could we? It was too dangerous to be seen together, he said. Who could guess what torments German police or Polish thugs might devise for us? But since the announcement, I had thought of little else but the ghetto.

I took the tram to Mokotów and alighted at the stop nearest Narbutta Street. Several minutes later, I arrived at the building where the Eisenbergs lived, a creamy stuccoed brick residence with wrought-iron balconies at intervals. Occupying a flat in such a desirable building, it was a wonder they hadn't been forced out before now.

I climbed the stairs to the second floor. On the first door to the left, a gold nameplate read "Henryk Eisenberg."

Only then did I wonder if I oughtn't drop by unannounced, but the Eisenbergs had no telephone. Jews had been forbidden to own telephones, and few private homes in Warsaw had them anyway, even before the occupation.

I wrote to Marek to arrange our meetings, but I was too anxious to wait for his response, and it was Sunday besides. I'd told Aunt Basia I had a headache and slipped out of the flat as soon as she and Helena left for church. It wasn't wholly a falsehood. I'd slept little last night and awoke with a dull throbbing in my temples. But a headache powder wasn't the cure I needed.

I pushed the bell and waited. A moment passed before the door cautiously opened. Marek's mother stood inside. I hadn't seen her since the day he had been seized and I had come to tell the Eisenbergs. Marek had returned home late the same night, thankfully unharmed, after a day of forced labor for the Germans.

"Good day, Pani."

A faint tightening of her lips around the edges. "You've come to see Marek, I suppose."

"Yes, if he's in." I kept my voice pleasant. I hadn't come to call upon her, I reminded myself, and if it weren't for the Germans and their wretched edicts, I wouldn't be here at all. I would have met Marek at the broadcasting centre or the park, perhaps gone to a quiet café for coffee and pastries.

She moved aside, holding the door as I stepped into the flat. "If you'll wait here, I'll tell him you've arrived."

"Thank you." I stood in the entrance, my hands clasped around my bag.

She started down the hall. Voices emanated from the dining room, raised in heated discourse. "What, so you think they'll trap us behind the wall?" I recognized the voice as belonging to Marek's father. "What else could it be but an open ghetto?"

"Perhaps you ought to ask the people in Łódź." Cutlery clattered and a young woman's tone escalated. Marek's sister Rutka, I thought. "I heard a kilo of onions there costs ten złoty because the guards don't allow anyone out to buy food."

"But there are over 350,000 of us in Warsaw," Pan Eisenberg said.

"How can they expect 350,000 people to live in an area of what, a few hundred hectares?"

"There's to be an announcement about the boundaries of the district in a day or two." This, from Marek.

"And this is supposed to prevent the spread of an epidemic?" Rutka remarked in a dry voice.

Pani Eisenberg went into the dining room. The murmured exchange that followed was too low to catch. Chair legs scraped and, a moment later, Marek stepped into the hall. His brow furrowed as our eyes met. "Antonina."

"I'm sorry. I've interrupted your meal."

"No, no, it's quite all right. Here, let me take your coat." He helped me out of my coat, and I handed him my hat and handbag.

He hung my things on the rack in the entrance, then hesitated, glancing back at the room he'd just vacated. "Come, let's go into the sitting room."

I followed Marek and he closed the door behind us. Of the furnishings in the once-elegant room, only a worn armchair, a half-empty glass-fronted bookcase, and the piano remained. The sofas and armchairs and side tables, the paintings on the walls, the tall case clock in the corner, and the burgundy-and-gold carpet had all vanished.

"Sit, please." Marek gestured to the armchair.

I lowered myself to the edge of the horsehair cushion, and he pulled out the piano bench and sat, hands linked between his knees.

"So, how are you?" Marek's voice was as calm as though we were sitting down for tea.

"Fine, I . . . Oh, don't." The words broke from me. I couldn't bear it any longer. "I heard the announcement yesterday."

"Ah." He nodded. "So I owe the pleasure of this visit to the esteemed Dr. Fischer?" A smile hinted at his lips.

"It's not funny."

"No." He drew a long breath. "You're right."

I met his eyes, the shadows there unmistakable. "What will you do?"

"We have to find a place to live before the end of the month. I'm going out later to talk to a few people. See if I can arrange an exchange with a Pole in the Jewish district. Better for us to handle our own affairs instead of leaving it to whatever office they're setting up to deal with the transfer."

"Once you're settled, what then?"

He stared down at his hands. "We do as we have been. Live as best we can."

I pressed my lips together.

He raised his head. "It won't be the Hotel Europejski, but it won't be so bad. We'll still be in Warsaw. Living behind a wall, perhaps, but I feel certain it will be an open ghetto. There may be some restrictions. A curfew, maybe. But we already have that."

"Is there anything I can do?"

His gaze softened. "Your coming here is more than enough." He rose and went to the piano, rested his hand atop the fallboard. "It will have to be sold. We can't take it. Jews are not permitted to remove furniture when they vacate their residences. At any rate, how could I move it to the ghetto? A Bechstein." He shook his head, seemed momentarily lost in thought. Then he turned to me. "Would you take it? The piano?"

"Marek, I couldn't. It's your father's."

"I'd far rather know it would be your hands touching the keys than a stranger's. Worse yet, some SS officer who'll plunk out the 'Horst Wessel Lied' while his comrades toast to German victory. Father has heard you play. I believe he'd feel the same. Please, Antonina." He paused. "It would mean a great deal to me."

I hesitated. Would there be room in Aunt Basia's tiny flat? What would Marek's parents think?

But how could I refuse when he looked at me like that?

"If your family agrees, I'll take it for now. Keep it safe. Until you have a place for it again."

"Thank you," he said quietly.

"Your Guadagnini?"

"Will come with me. I may be able to earn by playing."

Silence fell. I wanted to say so much, but the words wouldn't form. I wasn't used to this scattered, uncertain feeling, not with Marek. The ghetto loomed, already a barrier between us.

Then he reached out and took my hand, drew me toward him. "Play with me?" The words were a whisper near my ear, intimate as a kiss.

How vividly I recalled the first time he spoke them. It had been only the second time we'd met. The first had been at the Café Adria in the spring of 1939. I'd gone to the nightclub especially to hear him play, the violinist and composer Marek Eisenberg whom I had often heard on Polish Radio. He and the small orchestra he'd appeared with had played tangos and other light music as my friend Jadwiga, her fiancé, and my current suitor, Julian, had joined the dancers on the floor.

Then Marek had performed one of his own compositions, a violin sonata. I'd sat, riveted to the stage, to the violinist who could draw such depth of feeling from the strings. Afterward Jadwiga's fiancé, who knew Marek, went over to speak to him, and then Marek had come to our table to meet Jadwiga. In an ebony tuxedo, strands of smoothed-back hair straying over his forehead, he'd congratulated the couple on their engagement. Jadwiga had introduced me, then added, carelessly, "Antonina is a pianist, you know. You two should become acquainted."

Blushing was Helena's specialty, not mine, but heat had flooded my cheeks. Jadwiga had obviously drunk too much champagne, telling Marek Eisenberg I was a pianist. Even Julian had laughed—he'd always been more taken with my pretty face than my playing.

But Marek had turned to me. "Really?" he'd asked, and I'd flushed still more before blurting out I was only a student.

"If you devote yourself to music, if you love it as if it were part of you, then you are a pianist, Antonina Dąbrowska." The words had been quiet, but the fervency of his gaze caught hold in my chest.

Before he left our table, he'd taken my hand and bent over my fingers. "If you'd ever like to come by the broadcasting centre, I'm there nearly every afternoon." Then his hand slipped from mine and he moved away, into the sparkling crowd.

Jadwiga had overheard and dared me to go. I made a point not to turn down a dare, so—heady from champagne—I'd laughed and agreed. But even without the dare, I would have gone anyway.

56

Two days later, I arrived at the broadcasting centre as Marek finished for the day. He showed me around, introduced me to a few colleagues. Last, we entered one of the empty studios, dimly lit, a piano in its center. I'd stood thre in my summer frock and hat, gripping my handbag with sweaty palms as Marek Eisenberg leaned casually on the piano, his gaze intent on my flushed face, chatting about music and my plans to study at the Warsaw Conservatory.

I wasn't wholly inexperienced when it came to men. I'd had my share of flirtations. They'd been little more than schoolboys, and I'd always been at ease, even a trifle superior because of their boyish ways, the power I held over them. But Marek wasn't like the others. He was twenty-seven, had studied violin and composition in Warsaw and Berlin, had composed orchestral works, as well as popular songs and scores for several films. He had achieved a success of which I could only dream, and I couldn't help but be a little in awe and more than a little intrigued. By not only his career but by him. Then Marek had looked at me, earnest, a slight challenge in his eyes. "Play with me?"

The past receded. Then, as now, I nodded. Marek left the sitting room, returning shortly with his violin case. I took my place at the bench, lifted the fallboard, brushed my fingers over the ivory keys, letting a few notes fall from my fingertips, releasing the rich tone of the Bechstein.

He withdrew his Guadagnini, then turned to me, a question asked and answered without a word.

I gave a nod and he leaned forward, placing the music in front of me.

Étude Op. 10, No. 3, in E Major

This étude, as with most of Chopin's works, had been composed for solo piano. But it had always been Marek's favorite of the études, and he had arranged it for piano and violin.

He lifted the instrument to his chin, and our eyes met in unspoken accord. I swallowed hard, though not from nerves as on that day at the broadcasting centre, but because my throat had grown tight. Because I did not know when this moment would be ours again.

I touched the keys. The first notes unfolded, soft, yearning. I played often now, both at the café where I occasionally provided light music in addition to my duties as a waitress, and as a student of the clandestine music school that had formed during the year of occupation.

But not like this. Not with Marek.

To play with Marek Eisenberg was not merely to execute the notes but to fill oneself with them as breath. To glimpse music beyond its performance, what it could be and what we could be when surrendered to its fullness.

And so we played, violin and piano coming together, our hearts meeting in the Chopin étude. It was forbidden now, Chopin. One could be arrested for public performances of his works. The occupiers had even torn down the monument to the composer in Łazienkowski Park, melted it down for its metal.

But the notes were still ours. The language we'd always spoken. Edicts and occupation couldn't take them from us, not here, wrapped in this moment, as the melody swelled with the sway and dip of his bow, the rise and fall of my fingers across the keys.

There was another note in the duet this time, one there had not been before.

The refrain of goodbye.

HELENA
OCTOBER 14, 1940

4 January 1940

My Dearest Ones,

How glad I am to be able to write to you at last. I have been ill, which is why you had no word from me sooner, though only since the end of November have we been permitted to send letters. I can picture your worried frown upon reading this, my kwiatuszek, always so concerned for my welfare. Rest assured I am in good health again.

███████████████████████████████████████

███████████████████████████████████████

Please tell me how you all are. How is Basia? Tell her I think of her often with great warmth and gratitude for the strength and support I trust she has been to my daughters. In her care for those I love best, she could render no greater service to me.

I long so much for news of you all. Often, lying at night on my bunk, I return in my mind to our cozy evenings together. I can still hear the notes of our favorite Chopin nocturnes, Tosia, and see your smile, Hela. The warmth of those memories gives me strength to meet each day.

Has it been very cold there this winter? Here the temperatures often reach -40° C. █████████████████████

Do not be anxious about me, only please write as soon as you can. A few lines from you would do a great deal to ease my mind. We are also permitted to receive parcels. If it would not be too great a burden, I would be grateful for warm socks and underwear, gloves, a thick shirt, soap, and writing paper and envelopes. If you can, something to eat also, perhaps dry sausage or some bacon, but please do not sacrifice anything you need for yourselves.

I am with you constantly in my thoughts. Be strong, my dearest daughters. There may be difficult days still ahead, but we must believe all will come right in the end. Know my love is with you, even though we are apart, and I pray to our Father in heaven to preserve you and keep you in His steadfast care. He has not forsaken me. Nor will He you.

Your Loving,

Tata

I traced his signature with my fingertip, the paper softened with wear and creased from the countless times I had read and refolded the letter. I scarcely needed to fix my eyes on the words, for my heart held them already.

At the bottom of the page, an address was written in Cyrillic script. Though he gave few details regarding his imprisonment, the address confirmed he was in the hands of the Soviets. I supposed we should be comforted he wasn't a prisoner of the Germans, but could one enemy really be preferred over the other?

Another letter followed in February. The last arrived in March. In it, he'd thanked us for our messages and the parcel of warm clothing and food. I'd prepared another parcel and letter and sent them to the address.

No answer came. Neither to that note nor any of the others in the weeks and months since. They had all been sent back stamped "Return to Sender. Addressee Gone Away."

The silence before the letters had been hard to bear.

The silence after the letters had emptied me inside.

At the tread of footsteps in the corridor, I quickly slipped the folded page into my handbag, shoved it into the bottom drawer of the desk, and bent once more over the typewriter. The other staff at Herr Bürkel's office usually left for their midday meal, but I preferred to eat at my desk, savoring a few moments of solitude.

The door opened. I didn't look up, glancing from the tablet covered with shorthand to the typewriter as I transcribed the morning's dictation.

"Fräulein Dąbrowska, any messages?"

I raised my gaze. My employer had come into the front office, accompanied by another man, a Wehrmacht officer.

"Just two, Herr Bürkel." Ordinarily I would detail their contents and the degree to which they required his attention, but I simply handed him the slips of paper. The usual memorandums that passed through the office of Hermann Bürkel, accountant and tax examiner for the Generalgouvernement. I didn't recognize the officer with Herr Bürkel, so I did not say more.

Herr Bürkel scanned the messages, a finger resting on his upper lip. The officer stood a few paces away, hands behind his back. He wore a field-gray tunic with a leather belt at the waist, high ebony boots, and a black-brimmed cap with a silver eagle-and-swastika insignia. Our gazes connected briefly and he nodded. I glanced away, uncertain whether to continue typing.

"Yes. Very good." Herr Bürkel looked up from the messages and turned to his guest. "Ah, Werner, this is my secretary, Fräulein Dąbrowska. Fräulein Dąbrowska, my nephew, Leutnant Reinhardt, newly posted to Warsaw."

Leutnant Reinhardt nodded again. "Good afternoon." The politeness of the greeting, his quiet tone, took me aback somehow, so I simply dipped my head.

"My office is through here." Herr Bürkel crossed the room, talking as he went, obviously eager to impress his nephew. "I had it redecorated when I arrived, the best furniture, carpets. Some Jews made me a fine present of them." He chuckled.

Agata, the typist, stepped into the office. On the way to her desk, she passed Leutnant Reinhardt. He gave her a polite nod before following his uncle.

The door to Herr Bürkel's office shut, the men's conversation an undertone behind the frosted glass.

Agata took her place at her desk. "Who was that?"

"Leutnant Reinhardt, Herr Bürkel's nephew." The clacking of typewriter keys filled the office as I resumed my work. Though Agata—who, like me, was Polish—did most of the typing, I handled Herr Bürkel's correspondence. I had not wanted to accept a position at a German office, but finding work of any sort was difficult these days, and we all had to earn or life's basic necessities would soon be beyond our means. The position required a command of German, as well as typing and shorthand. I'd learned German in school and had taken courses in typing and shorthand so as to be useful at Tata's firm. Herr Bürkel could be an exacting and temperamental employer, and I did my best to give him no cause for complaint, though at first, I often fought back tears at his tirades whenever I had to ask him to repeat a sentence during dictation. My proficiency in the language had been no match for his streams of rapid German. But with time, I improved and the work had grown easier.

Half an hour later, the door of Herr Bürkel's office opened and Leutnant Reinhardt stepped out, adjusting the brim of his cap. I glanced up briefly, then kept typing, returning the carriage at the end of the line.

The bootfalls stopped. I raised my gaze. Leutnant Reinhardt stood beside my desk. "Herr Bürkel asked if you could bring in the letters for him to sign." He bent slightly forward as he spoke.

"Thank you." My words came quiet. I collected the typed pages and rose. We stood, facing one another. He was taller than I by at least a quarter of a meter, his height only increased by his officer's cap. For the space of several heartbeats, his eyes held mine. They were gray, a soft gray like a winter dawn.

Then he gave a nod, swiveled on his heel, and strode toward the exit, the square of his uniformed shoulders disappearing as the door closed behind him.

ANTONINA
NOVEMBER 17, 1940

They'd sealed the ghetto.

I had been playing at the café when the news came. Two men had taken a table near the piano, and their conversation reached my ears as my fingers ran mindlessly over the keys, executing the light and lively notes.

I'd tried to convince myself it was only a rumor, one of dozens bred and repeated daily. Whatever event people thoroughly believed would happen or had happened turned out, half the time, not to be true.

If only it could have been so. But by evening, I'd heard the same report repeated twice.

The Jewish district had been officially closed.

Helena stepped into the kitchen as I placed a loaf of bread in a basket. She'd dressed for church, her navy coat—formerly Aunt Basia's, as were most of our clothes—buttoned, her hat in place.

She frowned. "Where are you taking the bread?"

I covered the basket with a cloth, weighing how to answer. If I told Helena what I intended, she'd only worry. Maybe even attempt to persuade me not to go, tell me it wasn't safe or some such. Whether she'd be right had yet to be determined.

Before I could form a reply, Aunt Basia came in, her coat and hat on, her handbag over her arm. "Coming, girls?" She stopped, gaze falling on the basket. "Antonina?"

"I'm afraid I won't be able to join you this morning. I promised to visit a friend." The words came smoothly. They weren't a lie, not really. Except the only person I'd promised was myself.

"I see." Aunt Basia paused. "Well then, shall we go, Hela?"

My sister looked at me hard. "This friend wouldn't by any chance live in the Jewish district, would they?"

And what if they do? I almost replied. *What concern is it of yours?* But I said only, "You'd best go or you'll be late for Mass."

Aunt Basia's brow creased. "I'm not certain you ought to go there alone."

"I'm out alone every day. It's no different."

"The gates are guarded by the German police. The district has been closed only a day. It's too soon to know what to expect. They may not even allow you to pass." Her frown deepened as though she were considering the implications if her speculation proved true.

"They're still letting Poles through. I heard it yesterday."

"It would be better if I went with you—"

"There's no need." I gave a reassuring smile. "I'll take care."

"Very well then." Despite Aunt Basia's assent, the crevice between her brows lingered. But she wouldn't stop me nor force her presence upon me. This was the woman who had not once failed to report to the hospital during the siege, even if it meant running through burning streets and dodging shellfire on her way. Resolute herself, she respected strength in others.

I told myself it was strength, not stupidity, that guided me today.

I waited until they left, then put on my hat and coat, picked up the basket and my handbag, and exited the flat. I'd studied the latest plan of the Jewish district printed in the *Nowy Kurier Warszawski*, so I knew how to find my way, though not what awaited me once I arrived at my destination.

The sky spat a thin rain and I kept a brisk pace. The streets were emptier this morning, the sidewalks less crowded. I hoped this was due to the rain and that it was Sunday morning, not because word of an impending łapanka had spread and everyone had fled inside. But those out didn't appear alarmed, no rushing to take shelter or slamming of doors, so I continued on.

Perhaps I marked the lack of commotion more in contrast to the chaos of recent weeks. The decree establishing the Jewish district had thrust the city into turmoil such as there had not been since the invasion. The greatest portion of misery had fallen on the Jews, though thousands of Gentiles had been affected too.

But in the frenzied exchange of dwellings, the Jewish person generally ended up the losing party. The ghetto had been established in an area mainly inhabited by the working class and the poverty-stricken. Even before the war, it had been known as the Jewish quarter, and a high population of Jews dwelt there already and had no need to move. In contrast, the Jews who had lived outside the area designated for the ghetto tended to be well-to-do, their social status reflected by their residences. The best flats in the Jewish district had gone for fantastic prices to those who could afford them. The rest scrambled for any lodging they could find.

The authorities had extended the deadline for the resettlement to the fifteenth of November. Likely they'd realized—or had been negotiated into accepting—the impossibility of completing such an undertaking in less than three weeks.

For days, a weary procession of horse-drawn carts and handcarts, rickshaws, and perambulators clogged the thoroughfares, every available conveyance pressed into service to bear the remnants of lives left behind. Despite the order, people took furniture, for how could they manage without it? They trundled through the streets like pack animals, pushing carts heaped with furnishings and household possessions, making the journey that began all across the city but ended in one place.

The ghetto.

On the fifteenth, the relocation concluded in accordance with the deadline.

On the sixteenth, police cordoned off the district. That same day, there had been a search in the rest of the city as Jews who remained outside the ghetto were rounded up and forced to move.

I'd gathered these scraps of information as I threaded among the tables at the café, serving coffee and clearing away plates. Some people expressed satisfaction, even relief, that the Jews would be confined to a closed district. "Let them keep their diseases to themselves," one man said. "We certainly won't regret their absence."

I'd had enough of rumors and reports. Today I intended to see the ghetto for myself.

My heart quickened as I neared the entrance. On either side ran a high gate of wooden planks, the gap blocked by two white-and-black beams, which could be raised and lowered. German police in greatcoats and helmets stood guard, along with a navy-uniformed Polish policeman.

The rumors were true, then.

I drew an unsteady breath.

Somewhere beyond the gates was Marek. I had come to find him and I would.

I lifted my chin as I approached, my steps firm, my basket in hand.

"Good day." I greeted the policeman in German.

Beads of rain clung to his steel helmet. His glance skimmed over me. "What is your business in the Jewish district?"

I kept my gaze level. "I'm visiting someone."

"Very well. Proceed."

I gave a nod and stepped through, glancing over my shoulder as the white-and-black beams lowered behind me.

Around me pulsed a crowd so dense it seemed but one mass. For the first time, I glimpsed the wall from within. A grim barricade, rising three meters high, shutting out whatever lay beyond, dividing the city. In the falling rain, the rust-brick wall and colorless sky blurred into a drab watercolor.

Rain pebbled my coat. I shivered. I'd been inside the ghetto less than five minutes, yet already I sensed what it was to stand on this side of the wall. No more than brick and mortar, yet somehow it seemed a physical force. Oppressive, powerful, impenetrable.

I gave myself a mental shake. This was an ordinary street thronged with traffic. It wasn't a prison.

Not mine, at least.

I'd left the newspaper at Aunt Basia's. I had intended to bring it but had forgotten with the two of them questioning me. I certainly wasn't turning back, not after I'd come this far. Marek had given me his address, and I had a vague idea of the way to Nowolipki Street. If need be, I'd ask for directions.

I strode onward, swept up in a living current. Never had I known a street so tightly pressed with people, not even Warsaw's busiest thoroughfares. Pedestrians choked the sidewalks and overflowed into the road, mingling with traffic. People trudged along, carrying luggage, some with bundles slung over their shoulders, as though the whole street were moving house. A boy balanced a chair above his head and men maneuvered handcarts laden with furniture.

Rickshaws with their low benches suspended between two wheels sped past, some empty, others occupied by a passenger or two, the driver pedaling away as the wheels grated over the stone cobbles, splattering mud.

Passersby brushed against me without apology, taking no regard for our closeness. In the gateways huddled little groups with suitcases and bundles. I passed a couple with two children. The small girl's head rested on the man's shoulder as he held her, the boy stood silently beside the woman, watching the throng flowing past. Their faces had a pale, pinched look from the cold.

Could no shelter be found for them?

Though an armband marked the sleeves of all but young children, no one paid my lack of one any heed as I wended deeper into the ghetto. I could not help but feel a little lost in such a crowd. No more than a grain of sand in an endlessly shifting heap. The clamor of voices in Yiddish and Polish, the rattle of wheels, a baby's cry, a man's shout, a hawker's chant, all merged together, forming a ceaseless din. The cadence of humanity struggling to breathe.

I turned down another street, then paused. Had I taken a wrong turn? I scanned my surroundings, unable to check an irrational surge of panic at the notion of finding myself lost in this labyrinth. Though I traversed Warsaw often enough on foot and by tram, I'd rarely frequented this part of the city.

I bumped into a man coming the opposite way. My handbag fell to the ground.

"I do apologize. The streets are so crowded."

"So they are. Dreadful, isn't it?" The elderly gentleman bent and picked up my bag, handing it to me with a slight smile. "Here you are, Pani."

"Can you tell me the way to Nowolipki Street? I may have taken a wrong turn."

"I'm afraid you did. If you continue down this street, then at the next . . ."

"Thank you very much," I said after he'd given me directions.

"Of course." He nodded. "Good day to you."

I continued on with more confidence. Two German police strode down the sidewalk. Pedestrians skirted them, stepping off the side-walk and into the gutter. I did the same, not wanting to attract notice.

"You, Jew. Come here."

I should have kept walking. If a year under occupation had taught us one maxim, it was "Concern yourself with your own affairs and let the rest alone."

So why had I turned today and there of all places?

On the sidewalk, cornered by the two Germans, stood the man who'd given me directions.

"Why did you not greet us with the proper respect? Take off your hat."

"I apologize." The man doffed his hat automatically.

"Down on your knees."

The man hesitated. One of the policemen struck him across the face. The old gentleman staggered backward, the loaf of bread he'd been carrying falling in the mud.

Muck soaked my shoes as I stood in the gutter, but I scarcely heeded it.

"Down on your knees!"

The man sank to the filthy sidewalk. The policeman drew his pistol.

Raised it to the man's temple.

I couldn't breathe.

Others scurried past, eyes averted, but I could not move.

"I swear I did not see you coming. I meant no disrespect," the man stammered, his hat clutched in both hands.

The policeman did not reply. But a cold satisfaction came over his face as he held the pistol steady, its barrel nearly pressed to the man's skull.

"Please . . ." The man's voice died away.

"Twenty-five push-ups." The policeman lowered the pistol but didn't holster it. "Don't make me repeat myself."

The man pressed his hands flat to the pavement in something like a push-up position. He lowered himself, then clumsily raised himself again.

"Two and down and three and down." The policeman circled the man, still holding the pistol. "Four and down. Faster now."

The man lifted his head, gasping for air. His gaze met mine.

I'd never glimpsed the eyes of an animal as the jaws of a trap snapped around its limb, but mute terror in a human gaze is a thing far more indelible.

"You." The other policeman grabbed an Orthodox man passing by, shoved him to the ground. "Join him."

With a glance at the pistol, the second man wordlessly assumed the same position. The two policemen laughed as they looked on at the spectacle.

I walked away, the policeman's voice following me, a rhythmic counting as the men raised and lowered themselves in the mud. "Eight and down and nine and down . . ."

ANTONINA
NOVEMBER 17, 1940

The hurried rap of my steps echoed as I crossed the courtyard, the cobbled expanse enclosed by four-story tenements, their decaying stucco facades in hues of unwashed gray or dirty sandstone. Not a single tree or blade of grass grew in the courtyard. Had it been the full bloom of summer, there still would have been none.

I went inside and mounted the steep stairs to the fourth floor. On the landing, I paused and opened my handbag to withdraw Marek's letter.

Though I very much hoped I'd found myself at the wrong building, a glance at the address penned at the bottom of the wrinkled page confirmed I had indeed arrived.

There wasn't a bell, so I lifted my fist and knocked, then waited on the dingy landing. A moment later, the door opened.

Marek's sister Rutka stood on the threshold. Her eyes widened, a slight frown crossing her features. "What are you doing here?" Her voice did not warm with welcome.

"I came to see Marek."

"He's not in right now."

"Do you know when he'll be back?"

"I couldn't say. He's out looking for work."

I stood there, tired and angry at myself for arriving unannounced instead of sending a note. Had I come all this way—not so much in kilometers but a distance somehow greater than the literal—for nothing?

I drew myself up. "Then I'll wait. If it's quite all right."

She opened the door without preamble, and I stepped inside.

From the furnishings and articles strewn about, the meager space appeared to serve as sitting area, bedroom, and dining room combined. On an iron-frame bed an elderly man sat reading a book while a middle-aged woman swept the floor. At the table, a boy sorted through a box of what looked like packets of cigarettes. To the left of the door stood the entrance to a kitchen, and I glimpsed a woman at the stove. The combination of musty staleness and the rotten odor of cabbage cooking made me faintly nauseous.

All eyes turned to me, the expressions of the room's occupants ranging from curiosity to disinterest. I recognized none of them. How many families shared this flat?

"Our room is through here." Rutka didn't bother with introductions. She crossed the floor, passing the woman with the broom, and I followed.

Rutka opened the door. "Mama, we have a visitor."

Pani Eisenberg set aside her darning and rose from the divan. "Such a surprise." She wore a navy cardigan over her blouse, her hair upswept as always in an impeccable chignon. "I did not expect . . . We did not expect to see you. Here, that is . . ." Her words trailed away, the usually dignified lady momentarily nonplussed. Then she drew herself up. "I'm afraid Marek is out at the moment."

"Rutka told me. I'll wait, if you don't mind."

"Of course. Please." She gestured to the armchair, the same one that had been in their flat. "Sit."

I settled onto the edge of the horsehair cushion and smiled at Marek's youngest sister, Chasia, who sat on the bed, an array of paper dolls scattered around her. She returned my smile shyly, her dark curls framing her face.

Rutka snatched her coat off a rack near the door.

Pani Eisenberg's brow creased. "Where are you going?"

"To see some friends." She knotted a kerchief under her chin.

"Must you?"

"They're expecting me." Rutka paused, met her mama's eyes. "I'll be back in plenty of time before curfew. Bye, Chasia." She turned to me. "Sorry to rush off," she said in a careless voice. She gave her mother a quick kiss on the cheek and slipped out.

The door clicked. Pani Eisenberg chafed her arms, lips pressed as she stared at the door. Then she resumed her seat on the divan.

For the first time, I took in their quarters. The walls bore yellowish stains, the pea-green paper faded and peeling. The space was cramped with the sum of their belongings—a carved mahogany bed, a bedside table on which sat a carbide lamp, an armoire beside it, a folding bed against the wall, the divan nearby. In one corner stood a screen draped with various articles of clothing.

So this was where they lived. This squalid room with a single window overlooking the courtyard.

I sensed Pani Eisenberg's eyes upon me, half-ashamed by the shock that had likely overtaken my features.

"How are you?" I modulated my voice, concern imbuing my tone. Though she'd never been particularly warm toward me, I'd never wish *this* upon her. What must this elegant woman be enduring, reduced to an existence in such a place?

For an instant, the tendons in her neck went taut, shock and humiliation, anger and fear, laid bare in her gaze before her features once again smoothed, an inward gathering of herself.

"I'm well, thank you." Her tone held the unapproachable poise it always had, her posture rigid, her hands in her lap. "And you?"

"Fine." I gave a half smile. Remembering the basket in my lap, I lifted the cloth. "I brought some bread and a jar of marmalade. My aunt made it. The marmalade, that is. It's only beetroot marmalade, I'm afraid, but I thought you might . . ." My voice faded at the look on her face.

"That's very kind." The words held unfailing good breeding, but the tightening of her tone set forth in no uncertain terms what she thought of taking anything from me. "But we couldn't possibly accept it. We manage perfectly well."

"It's hardly charity, Pani." I looked her in the eyes, my voice every bit as inflexible as hers. "I meant it only as a gift."

"All the same, it's entirely unnecessary."

Perhaps I should have understood what pride meant to a woman such as Pani Eisenberg, clinging to self-respect, the vestiges of the past, even as life in this place stripped both away. But pride did empty stomachs no good, and I'd meant the offering only as a gesture of support and sympathy. Surely I couldn't be the only person coming to the ghetto to visit friends. It wasn't as though I expected she'd suddenly alter her feelings about Marek and me just because she accepted a jar of marmalade.

Silence stretched. I shifted, wondering how long I'd be forced to wait in this prickling atmosphere before Marek arrived. Maybe I should go, come back another time.

"How old are you now, Chasia?" I brightened my tone. "Seven? Eight?"

"Nine," Chasia answered, voice soft.

"Nine. Goodness, you're getting to be quite a big girl."

She smiled, eyeing me like a kitten peeping around a doorway.

The door opened. Marek came in, his armband over the right sleeve of his overcoat, his hat in hand. "Mama, I'm back." He hung his hat on the rack near the entrance, then stopped, taking in the sight of me in the armchair. "Antonina."

"Hello, Marek." I rose, the basket in both hands, gaze holding his. It had been only a month since we'd last met, but somehow it seemed longer, the ache of absence deeper.

Pani Eisenberg stood. "I should prepare our dinner. Come, Chasia."

Chasia laid aside her paper doll. She glanced over her shoulder at me as she followed her mother from the room. I smiled at her.

The door shut. I set the basket on the chair, and we came together in the center of the room. He pulled me into his arms, and I clutched him, my eyes falling shut, drawing in his scent beneath damp wool and the faint odor of carbide.

Rarely had we been this close. Music had joined us far more than touch. I sensed he kept his distance out of honor, as if acknowledging what could never be between us. But it was him I wanted, not his honor, and perhaps for once he felt the same.

Finally, we drew away. "I came as soon as I could. I heard what happened."

He didn't answer.

"It's true, then? The district is sealed?" Why did I ask this? Hadn't I seen for myself the guarded gates? But part of me still clutched at hope or maybe denial.

"By all appearances, it seems we've found ourselves in a closed residential district." Irony tinged his words.

That was what they called it, a Jewish residential district. Like the Polish district or the German district. Only a few days ago, the newspaper had reiterated this.

It was a lie. Perhaps the ordinary streets and houses rendered the illusion of freedom, but none who entered the world bound by these walls could call its inhabitants free.

"There must be half a million people here."

"Not quite. Nearly four hundred thousand, if reports are to be believed, so not all that many." The last he said lightly, like a joke, but I couldn't laugh.

"It's a disgrace. How can you be expected to live like this?"

"We'll manage, if only to spite them. What?" Marek searched my face, concern knitting his brow. "What is it?"

"It's just . . . you . . . this place." Indoors, this bleak room and outdoors, streets teeming with humanity, on which police tormented passersby for sport, where one could never feel safe, not for a moment.

"It's not as bad as it looks." His lips slanted grimly. "Well, maybe it is, but it's a roof over our heads and one we were lucky to find at such short notice."

Had he thought I referred only to their living quarters, or had he simply chosen to ignore the rest?

"Don't worry about us."

"How can I help it?" I gave a little smile. "Have you found work?"

"I've spoken to several people, but there isn't exactly a great demand for violinists at the moment. Still, I'm certain to find something before long. The worst of it is the food situation. Now we're unable to leave the district without a pass, people are worried about supplies, buying up whatever they can. Prices are rising every day." He broke off. "Sorry. You didn't come to hear about all that."

I reached out, clasped his wrist, my eyes on his. "I came to see you." I turned and took up the basket. "I brought some bread and marmalade. I tried to give it to your mother, but she insisted you had no need of it. Now I see differently." I withdrew the round loaf from the basket, along with the small jar. "You can tell her you bought it. Maybe then she'll see fit to eat it." I couldn't keep the edge from my tone.

He took the food, set it on the bedside table, then turned back to me. "I apologize for Mama. She's—she's a very proud woman."

"She'd be glad if I never saw you again."

He drew a heavy breath, glanced away. "Times as they are, perhaps that would be for the best."

The words pierced my chest. For a moment, I couldn't believe he'd actually spoken them. Did I really mean so little to him?

No. He cared. Of course he did. He only spoke so because he thought it would be best for me. But how could we give one another up at a time when perhaps we'd never needed the other more?

I lifted my chin, my face tipped toward his. "If you're asking me to forget you, I'm not sure that I can. Can you?" The last words came soft.

His features constricted. He took my hand, cradled it in both of his, then bent, his lips grazing the inside of my wrist. He released a deep exhalation, the heat of his breath against my skin. I swallowed, my throat suddenly dry.

After a long moment, he lowered my fingers. "But I don't like you coming here. Not with the guards at the gates."

"As if I can't manage a couple of brainless helmet-wearing schoolboys." I laughed, even as ice scraped my spine with fresh remembrance of the policeman's chanting voice and the old man's gasping breaths.

74

Marek shook his head, a grin tugging at his lips. "You're impossible, you know."

"I know." I smiled up at him.

"Come. I'll walk you to the gate."

We left the flat. Arm in arm, we walked through the stifling crowds. We had so little time together, and urgency rose, a desperate need to hold every moment close, hoard our seconds the way the starving hoarded crumbs of bread. I tucked my hand more firmly into the crook of Marek's elbow, my shoulder brushing his as I looked into his face. For this moment, though the sky remained gray, I tried to catch hold of the sunlight.

ANTONINA
NOVEMBER 17, 1940

"What happened today?"

I glanced up from where I sat, brushing my hair. Helena had come into the bedroom in her nightdress, darkness long since fallen beyond the windows.

"What do you mean, what happened?" I said, though I knew full well what she meant. I continued smoothing the brush through my curls, my thoughts far from the familiar, mindless movements.

The mattress shifted as she joined me on the bed. The glow of the lamp illuminated her features, her honey-brown hair wound in pin curls. "You went to the ghetto today. Did you see him?"

I hadn't spoken to Aunt Basia or Helena of my time in the walled district and neither had asked. Until now.

I lowered the brush. Sighed. "Yes."

"And?" Her gaze probed my face. "Is he well?"

"He is well, but . . ." How to tell of it? "They can't leave to buy food or to visit friends or to do anything. They're trapped by the wall and the guards, and there are nearly four hundred thousand of them. Penned like rabbits in a cage."

"But the guards allowed you to pass?"

"They're still letting Poles through."

"Will you go back?" Helena asked, voice quiet.

"How can I not?" The words burst out. "I must help him, Hela. He's . . ." I pressed my fist to my mouth.

She frowned. "But is it safe?"

"Should that even be a question?" My words came sharp, and an injured look passed across her features. I drew a steadying breath, then reached out and placed my hand over hers. "Don't worry. What danger could there be for me? I can leave freely."

She nodded, but the worry in her eyes didn't recede. For a moment, neither of us spoke. Then softly, she said, "Marek means a great deal to you, doesn't he?"

Before the war, she had often teased me about "my violinist" as I fussed over my hair and discarded four dresses before settling upon one and came home from a picnic or concert with a flush in my cheeks and stars in my eyes.

How simple it all seemed then. Though even in those days, I had known the divide between us ran deeper than either Marek or I wanted to admit. But I had stubbornly refused to acknowledge it, living only in the present, as though reality had the power to be dissolved if I simply let it alone long enough.

"Yes." The memories returned. The way he held me as we stood together in that dismal little room, how his eyes fixed on mine for a moment that whittled the world down to the two of us before the white-and-black beams rose and lowered and I left him there. My chest ached. "He does."

7

ANTONINA
JANUARY 16, 1941

Riding a tram was nothing out of the ordinary. The familiar red cars, the rhythmic clacking of the wheels, the smooth wood of the seats, and the *clang-clang* of the bells had been part of growing up in bustling Warsaw. There had always been a skip of excitement in my chest as a child, boarding the tram with Tata or Aunt Basia, filing past the rows of passengers to take our seat, coaxing to be allowed the place by the window so I could watch the city pass.

As I boarded the tram on a piercing winter afternoon, my heart beat faster but for altogether different reasons. Following the plan I'd gone over in my mind as my fingers flitted across the keys of the piano in the café, I sidled through the crowd and took the seat nearest the rear exit. I settled onto the bench, my hands clasped atop a parcel wrapped in brown paper.

The bell clanged and the tram gave a jolt and lumbered forward.

As the tram trundled through the city, coming to a halt at the various stops, travelers boarding and alighting, I alternated between staring out the window and studying my fellow passengers. The latter seemed prosaically innocuous—a few weary-faced women with shopping bags or satchels, a man in an overcoat with a briefcase at his feet, an older man reading the *Nowy Kurier Warszawski*, a little boy sitting beside a middle-aged woman.

Doubtless, their private thoughts and daily cares so fully occupied their minds, they would take no notice of me. Or so I hoped.

I must do it. I would do it, and that was the end of the matter.

Two months had gone by since I visited Marek. When I attempted to return to the ghetto several days later, I found my passage barred, entrance now forbidden to Gentile Poles without a pass. The previous week, a policeman had shot a Polish man for tossing a sack of bread over the wall.

I'd sent the Eisenbergs a parcel of food—the Judenrat operated a post office inside the district—but no letter followed confirming they'd received it.

I had to find a way into the ghetto. I'd discovered which "Polish" trams ran through the streets of the walled district, a practicality sanctioned so as not to obstruct the functioning of the city's tramlines. The trams ran at full speed and without stopping, but they offered passage into the world on the other side of the wall. I hadn't told Helena or Aunt Basia what I intended. They would only worry. Probably with good reason.

The tram slowed as it neared the entrance to the ghetto, and a policeman boarded. All trams passing through the district had the escort of a Polish policeman, likely more to prevent inhabitants of the ghetto from attempting to board than to prohibit passengers from alighting.

With a grinding clank, the tram resumed its journey, increasing in speed as it passed the high wall, its top bristling with barbed wire and bits of broken glass that glinted like a crown of icicles. I kept my gaze on the window as the ghetto rushed past, its thoroughfares swollen with pedestrians, the dingy crowds blurred beyond the smudged glass. The yellow armband of a Jewish policeman stood out, a slash of color amid hues of brown and gray.

"Mama, why are there so many poor people?" the little boy asked.

"Hush," the woman said, tone sharp. "Keep still and don't ask questions."

In a moment, I'd slip from the car and jump off as the tram slowed at a bend. I sat stiffly on the bench as seconds slid by.

Boots thudded as the policeman came down the aisle.

I tensed. As he passed, his gaze fell briefly on me. I kept my face empty, eyes straight ahead.

Then he headed out to the rear platform. Where he wouldn't fail to catch sight of a woman alighting from the moving tram.

The tram made its way deeper into the ghetto, speeding through the teeming streets.

I darted a glance to the rear platform where the policeman still stood, his broad back a navy blue outline.

Should I go to the front of the car—reserved for Germans only? The driver would certainly notice if I jumped off. Or should I remain in my seat until we exited the ghetto, then board another tram and repeat the process?

Once the tram reached the gate at the other end of the district, my opportunity would be lost.

Minutes crept past. The policeman ducked into the car, blowing on his cupped hands. He took out a cigarette case, his back to the exit.

I rose as quietly as I could and slipped past as he lit his cigarette.

In an instant, I stood on the step, one hand gripping the cold metal railing, the other clutching my parcel and handbag to my chest.

Icy wind burned my cheeks, whipped my hair around my face. The cobblestones rushed past below me.

The tram slowed as it curved into a sharp turn.

I stepped off.

My feet struck the ground, the impact jarring my bones, yanking the breath from my lungs. I stood on the street, jolted and dazed, as the tram clattered past. I swung a glance around me. Had anyone noticed? But the crowd flowed on as before.

Drawing a steadying breath, I crossed the street. In the shelter of a gateway, I opened my handbag and withdrew a strip of cloth.

A white band with a blue star.

Since those who weren't Jews could no longer enter the ghetto without a pass, my lack of an armband would be far more conspicuous than before. Within seconds, I'd fastened it over the sleeve of my coat. I had fashioned the band from a scrap of fabric out of Aunt Basia's sewing box and stitched a star onto the cloth in blue thread. Likely I'd gotten the dimensions wrong. But it would pass inspection at a glance.

I strode onward in the direction of Nowolipki Street. Merging into the throng, becoming part of its collective mass, I ceased to be an individual. Perhaps it should have reassured, this shedding of distinction, but my chest tightened, as if there wasn't enough air to draw into my lungs. Here, within these walls, humanity beat its wings against bars of brick, fluttering and gasping. A vain and relentless struggle for freedom.

With a sudden wrench, a pair of hands ripped my parcel from my grasp. A small figure darted down the sidewalk, tearing the brown paper and cramming the bread into his mouth as he ran.

"Stop!" I raced after him, pushing past pedestrians. "Stop!"

At the corner, I paused, breathless, searching for the boy I'd glimpsed for only an instant. But he'd vanished, a pebble flung into a stream without so much as a ripple.

"A few groszy for a bit of bread. Please, good people. Just a bit of bread."

I turned. On the corner, a girl stood imploring the crowd. At her side, a boy crouched on his haunches, a tiny child huddled beside him, bundled in what at first glance appeared to be no more than rags.

I went to them, carried by a force almost beyond my consent.

"Just a bit of bread." The girl shivered in the wind, a ragged shawl cloaking her head, her cracked lips pale, her fingers fragile as a sparrow's wing. She couldn't have been more than twelve. "Please, Pani. Can you spare a few groszy for a bit of bread?"

I opened my handbag and took out twenty złoty, all I had.

"Take this." I pressed the banknotes into her palm. "It should buy you some food. Enough for a few days, at least."

Her gaze darted from my face to the złotys she now held. In a flash, she shoved the banknotes down the front of her dress. "Thank you, Pani."

"Where are your parents?"

"Mama sells buttons on Gęsia Street. Tata is too sick to work."
She swiped her hand under her dripping nose. "He coughs blood."
Her flat voice startled me.

I looked down at the two other children sitting motionless on
the slush-coated sidewalk, staring at the street as if in a stupor.
I bent beside them. Only now did I realize the smallest child
was a girl. Her skin had a blueish-gray tinge. Beneath the shawl
wrapped around her head, her hair hung in matted tangles, and
a rank stench emanated from the rags clothing her emaciated
little body.

I unwound my woolen scarf and placed it around her neck. She
blinked up at me, her eyes black hollows. The boy hunkered against
the side of the building, his knobby knees mottled with cold, his
face sunken and ancient.

What more could I offer? What else could I do?

I swallowed hard and straightened, turning sharply away.

"Please, good people. Just a bit of bread." The plaintive refrain
resumed, drifting on the wind as I walked on.

A woman sang in Yiddish, a cracked teacup outstretched to passersby, her thin voice lifting in mournful chorus.

I came to a halt. My stomach convulsed.

Near a gateway sprawled a woman's bloated body. She lay on her
side, one arm extended, her fingers clenched, her mouth a gaping
hole. Two sheets of newsprint had been draped over her frame, a
futile preservation of the dignity of the dead. Wind tore one away,
sent it skittering into the road, exposing her marbled flesh.

How old had she been? Middle-aged, perhaps. Or had privation
aged her prematurely?

Copper strands splayed against the snowy pavement. The sort of
hair a woman would take pride in brushing and arranging.

The singer's lament carried to me as I stood beside the woman,
my mind frozen and at the same time screaming.

What sort of mad universe was this where children begged for
bread and corpses lay like refuse in the streets?

And still, the multitudes rushed past, kept rushing past with
barely a glance at the living or the dead.

ANTONINA
JANUARY 16, 1941

Marek wasn't at home. He worked at a café on Leszno Street now, a job he'd obtained through the recommendation of a colleague of his, a former pianist for Polish Radio.

Pani Eisenberg told me this after greeting me with a look of shock. For the first time, her impassive exterior cracked as she rebuked me.

"Outside of this place, you could have your little game with my son. But now it's time for you to wake up and accept things as they are. Now you will go, and you will not come here again."

Her words echoed in my ears as I wended through the dense crowds. Rickshaws rattled over the cobbles, drivers ferrying passengers who occupied the slatted benches. A shop window displayed an array of pastries and cakes. I stared, such abundance incongruous with all else that surrounded me. Near the shop, a man played an accordion, a young girl accompanying in a high, childish voice. A woman passing by dropped a coin into the child's palm.

At last, I reached the Pod Gwiazdą café, announced as such by a sign above the door. I wondered if its name—Under the Star—had been chosen with a trace of irony.

Not far from the entrance slumped a skeletal old man, his head drooping to one side. Whether asleep or otherwise, I couldn't discern. Rags tied with a bit of rope bound his feet, blackened toes sticking out.

A woman in a fur-collared coat alighted from a rickshaw. She and her male companion passed the old man as if his existence had ceased to be seen, much less heeded. They approached the café, its door opened by an attendant. I followed them in, the doorman permitting me to pass after a cursory glance.

I hovered near the entrance, scanning the crowded interior. Staff bustled about, bearing trays, serving coffee. Groups dined at linen-draped tables, men in suits and ladies in comparatively elegant frocks. I could have stepped into any smart café in Warsaw and been met with the same scene, save for the armbands on the sleeves of the diners.

A woman sat at a piano in the corner of the room. Nearby stood Marek, his violin against his chin, the bow swaying as he drew it across the strings. Light music, the sort patrons would only half attend to as they sipped coffee and conversed with companions.

"Would you care for a table, Pani?"

I turned. A waitress stood before me with an inquiring expression.

I hesitated. But I couldn't interrupt Marek while he was working. "Yes. Thank you."

She ushered me to a table near the back. "There you are, Pani."

I sank into a chair, and she placed a menu in front of me. I couldn't very well sit and order nothing, so I requested coffee—ersatz, naturally.

"I'll be back in a few moments." The waitress started to turn away.

"Wait. Could you ask Pan Eisenberg to come to my table, please, when he has a moment? I came especially to see him."

A hint of a smile formed. "Certainly."

"Thank you."

After she left, I sat watching Marek, slowly growing warm again. Though midday, blinds cloaked the windows, the room dimly lit by the lamps on each table. To provide an atmosphere of intimate luxury or to shield the diners from the reality beyond the glass?

The strains of piano and violin mingled with the light clink of china and cutlery and the rippling notes of conversation and laughter.

It struck me, suddenly, the discordance of it all. Two musicians performing popular melodies to an audience of well-dressed patrons while a man lay in rags nearly on the doorstep. The bright tune converged with the memory of the young girl's clear voice as she extended her hand to passersby. Not a song so much as a dream of bread.

The score of the ghetto.

Violin and piano fell silent, followed by a smattering of applause. The waitress approached Marek, and he bent as she whispered near his ear. She gestured toward my table, and his glance followed. Across the bustling room, his gaze found mine. I gave a slight nod.

83

He turned to the pianist, a slim woman with swept-back dark hair, and said a few words to her. She nodded and he crossed the room, making his way among the tables until he reached mine. I rose, facing him across the table, drawing in the sight of him.

It didn't matter what it had taken for me to come here. I would do it a thousand times for a moment with him.

"Antonina." More expression of disbelief than greeting. "How—how did you get here?"

"I took the tram." I kept my voice light. "Once it passed through the gates, I got off."

The lines between his brows deepened.

"It's all right. See." I turned my arm to show him the band on my sleeve. "No one knows who I am." I resumed my seat.

He dropped into the chair across from me. For a moment, he simply stared as if unable to take in my reality. Outwardly he looked the part of the acclaimed violinist in a familiar charcoal suit and burgundy tie, his hair smoothed back. But he'd lost weight, a slackness to his once well-tailored coat. His features were tense and haggard, his eyes shadowed.

Since the war began, I'd glimpsed such an expression on many a face. On the streets of the ghetto, I'd seen it multiplied a hundredfold.

The waitress appeared, carrying a tray. "Here you are, Pani." China rattled as she placed a cup and saucer before me. Steam curled above the rim of the cup, wafting over my cheeks. "Shall I bring you something, Pan?"

He glanced up, but seemed barely to see her. "No. No, thank you."

She made her way to another table. Airy notes tinkled from the piano, expertly played.

"Marek, I—"

"Why have you come here?" The sudden words came as a jolt.

I frowned. "What?"

He leaned forward, hands folded atop the tablecloth. "This is no place for you."

"I—I came to see you."

Something flashed across his features, sudden and sharp. "Well,

84

you should not have." The words were low, hard. "Have you any idea what would happen if you were to be discovered here?"

"I know it was a risk, but I—"

"No. I don't believe you do. If you did, you would never have behaved so foolishly."

I drew a trembling breath, heat rising in my chest. "Listen to me," I said, voice a fierce whisper. "I sent you a parcel weeks ago, and I don't even know if you received it. Do you know what it's like, never seeing you, not knowing if you're safe, not knowing anything about what's happening here except rumors?"

He regarded me in silence, his steady gaze fixed on my face, yet somehow impenetrable.

"I came because"—my voice cracked—"because I care. Not only about you but about your family. The people here. You're so close and yet . . ."

He drew a long breath. "If you mean what you say, if you truly care . . ." He paused. "Then you'll do as I ask and keep away from here."

"You think it's too dangerous, or you don't want to see me?"

"I mean it, Antonina. This place—"

"I know. I've seen it. Children begging for bread, a dead woman lying in the street. I brought you some food, but a boy tore it right out of my hands. It's worse than anything I could ever have imagined."

"But you don't understand. This place, life here. Don't come here again." The last words he spoke in a tone I'd never heard before. Hard, dismissive.

How was it possible I could reach out and touch him, place my hand over his in a single movement, and yet the distance between us had never stretched so great?

No. I wouldn't let it happen.

I swallowed. "Then will you write?"

He hesitated, looking down at his hands, his lithe fingers clasped atop the tablecloth. Hands that once brushed mine in the dance of a Chopin duet, intricate and intimate, as we sat side by side at the piano. Hands that once cradled mine with tenderness as he turned my palm face up, studying my fingers, a half smile lingering about his lips.

"*You have beautiful hands.*"

"Perhaps it would be best if we didn't. For a while."

There had always been a tie between us, an invisible cord binding us together. Even when apart, I'd sensed its strength. Surely he had too.

How could it, then, be so easily broken?

Perhaps I'd invented it out of my own desperate craving for . . . what? A place in his life? The hope that he felt for me as I did for him? The dream of a love that had perhaps been futile all along?

I pulled in an unsteady breath. "You're right. It's probably best."

"You must see it's not that I don't want—"

Stop. I wanted to scream. *No excuses. I don't want to hear them.*

"No, no." I shook my head. "I understand. Truly. I—I should go."

"How will you leave?"

I gave a brittle smile. "The same way I came in."

"No, don't. I'll speak to one of the SP—the Jewish police—explain what happened. I should be able to arrange something at the gate."

"It's not necessary," I said quickly, gathering my handbag, wanting only to get away. Then I glanced at my coffee, still untouched. I unclasped my handbag, took out my little purse, reached inside.

The few remaining coins slipped through my fingers as, with a jolt of horror, I realized I had almost nothing with which to pay for my coffee. I'd ordered it, completely forgetting I'd given nearly every grosz I had with me to the children begging on the street.

How could I be so pathetically stupid?

Marek sat across from me, an inscrutable expression on his features.

"I—um—" I swallowed. "There were some children. They looked . . . I never saw anyone look so hungry. I gave them twenty złoty."

Understanding came over his features. Without a word, he reached into his coat and withdrew his wallet.

"I'll pay you back," I hastened to say. Could he afford even this small expense? His father had no work, and Marek had obviously shouldered the burden of providing for their family. From him, I'd expect nothing less.

He tossed a banknote on the table. "When have we ever dined together and I haven't bought your coffee?" Regret tinged his voice. Or perhaps I only imagined that too.

Chair legs scraped as I rose. I'd stayed long enough.

He stood too. "At least let me see you safely away from here."

I shook my head. "It's not necessary. You should return to your work." I paused, looking into his face. Searching his eyes a moment more. Willing myself to find . . . something. To glimpse I mattered to him still, in spite of everything.

He stood with his shoulders rigid, features taut, as though steeling himself for an unseen battle. I almost went to him. Put my arms around him and rested my head against his shoulder. Whispered that I would never let him go, could never give him up, no matter what he said.

Then his gaze hardened, the trace of pain receding.

I swallowed, drew my shoulders back. "Goodbye, Marek." I hated how fragile my words sounded. Hated even more how my throat thickened with the voicing of them.

He didn't reply. I turned away. If I did not, I would surely break before him, and that I wouldn't do.

I left the café with my head high. At the door, I paused. Turned. He stood, one hand resting on the edge of the table, his head bent.

What had I hoped? To find him gazing after me, as if this were some romantic film at the cinema?

I stepped outside, clutching my handbag, desperate to get away, to hide my eyes from the starkness of human suffering this place contained. Safety and home, that was all I wanted now.

The wind caught bits of falling snow. I shivered.

"Have mercy, Pani."

"A few groszy."

"Give me some bread."

A horde surrounded me, barring my way, grasping at my coat, voices rising in a babble of entreaty. Ragged children with wild eyes, a woman plucking at my sleeve with claw-like fingers, an old man who groped his way forward as if blind or nearly so. Faces all alike in their hollow, hardened mask of hunger. Driven by madness, despair, a visceral instinct to survive. A boy swayed, his glassy eyes rolling back as he crumpled to the sidewalk and lay limp. But the others didn't cease.

"A few groszy."

"My mama and baby sister are hungry, so hungry."

"You dine in luxury while we are starving." A woman seized upon my handbag, fighting to rip it from my hands.

"Please. Stop. I have nothing to give you." The clamor of the throng nearly drowned my words.

Panic clawed my chest.

They're going to tear me apart.

A Jewish policeman broke into the fray, beating the beggars off with his truncheon in a hail of indiscriminate blows. I jerked my handbag from the woman's grasp, shoved through the crowd, and ran.

My feet pounded the sidewalk. I ran as though madness had possessed me, heedless of whomever I jostled.

I slipped on the icy pavement, nearly lost my footing.

The effort it took to steady myself jolted me to my senses. I sagged against a gateway, gulping frigid air.

Then I left the shelter of the gateway and made my way down the street, swallowed by the press of the crowd. Hawkers called out their wares, beggars huddled on the sidewalks, the desolate strains of a child's song floated on the wind, snow swirled from the void of the sky, and I walked on.

8

HELENA
JANUARY 29, 1941

On the night of 27 January 1941, two German soldiers
on guard duty were shot from a pistol by an unknown
person.

One hundred hostages have been detained. The public and the relatives of these hostages are urged to co-
operate in the apprehension of the murderer.

If the name of the murderer is not disclosed to the
German authorities by 2:00 p.m. on Friday, 31 January,
1941, the hostages will be shot.

This order becomes effective on issue.

Dr. Fischer
Governor

The type blurred. I blinked, but the tear slipped free, trailing
down my cheek and landing on the page, a single droplet splotching
the newsprint, smearing the words *will* and *be*.

The notice had been posted throughout the city and printed in
today's *Nowy Kurier Warszawski*.

My hands trembled as I lowered the paper. I folded my arms atop
the desk and rested my head upon them. My throat swelled, the ache

pressing unbearably. Tears burned, trickled between my fingers. I could no longer fight them and so I cried. It didn't matter. I was alone in the office, and no one would know or see. By the time the rest of the staff returned, my tears would be dried, and I would be once more busily typing Herr Bürkel's correspondence.

But for these few moments, I allowed myself to feel.

For the death of two soldiers, the city would not go unpunished.

Aunt Basia.

They had taken her. Last evening, the Gestapo arrived at the hospital and arrested her, along with several other doctors. That the arrested almost certainly had nothing to do with the killing of the soldiers did not matter to the Gestapo. The incident had taken place not far from the hospital and so they plucked their hostages. Just before they led her away, Aunt Basia had managed to whisper our names to a colleague. "Tosia and Hela. Tell them." After the Gestapo left, the woman had come to Hoża Street, risking the curfew to bring us the news.

Antonina had cursed the Germans and vowed to go to Pawiak herself. Along with Gestapo headquarters on Szucha Avenue, Pawiak Prison had earned its place among the most feared addresses in Warsaw. Likely the hostages had been taken there.

Many who entered Pawiak never returned.

"They can't do this," Antonina had kept muttering as she paced the sitting room, shoving her fingers through her tangled curls.

But they could. For they had proven so.

What can we do?

What could any of us do?

Helplessness held a depth of pain far greater than the physical. To preserve the ones I loved, I would do anything, but in the face of the powers that ruled our lives, I was nothing. No matter the strength of my love, no matter the shattering of my heart, it wasn't enough.

I am nothing and I can do nothing.

Footsteps echoed against the floorboards. I started, lifting my head. I hadn't even heard the door open.

Leutnant Reinhardt entered the office.

"Herr Leutnant." I resisted the urge to wipe my damp cheeks

with my sleeve. It would only draw attention to my tears. "I—I didn't hear you come in."

He stopped a meter from my desk. Bits of fallen snow melted on his uniform, his cheekbones ruddy from the winter air. "I've come to tell my uncle I regret I will be unable to join him and my aunt for supper tonight as promised."

"Herr Bürkel is out at the moment, I'm afraid, but I'll pass on the message as soon as he returns." In spite of myself, my voice came out hoarse.

"Thank you." He seemed about to turn and leave, then paused, frowning as he took in my countenance. "You are not well?"

"No." I shook my head. "That is, I am fine."

"But you are crying." He took a step toward me. Then he reached into his pocket and withdrew a folded square of cloth, held it out to me. I didn't take it. What did I want with a handkerchief from him? Would he offer it still if he knew the acts of his countrymen were the reason for my tears?

"Allow me." His hand remained outstretched, his gaze steady on mine. "Please." The single word held an unexpected gentleness.

I could have turned away, not caring if I appeared rude. We owed the enemy nothing, least of all civility. That was what Antonina would say.

But I didn't. Perhaps because I was still the girl brought up to always be polite. Or perhaps I simply wanted him gone.

As I took the handkerchief, my fingertips brushed his. I jerked away as if a flame had seared my skin.

The pressed linen square held his warmth, and as I dried my cheeks, a hint of soap and bergamot rose from the cloth. I bent my head and blew my nose as quietly as I could, then raised my gaze to his. "I'll return it after I've cleaned it."

"No, please. That is not necessary."

Of course. He wouldn't want it back. Even once washed, it would still be soiled by me. A Polish girl. Inferior to his pure Aryan blood.

Beneath the desk, I curled my fingers around the handkerchief, crushing it in my hand.

He picked up the newspaper on my desk. Perhaps the stain from my tears guided him to the section, for he glanced up a moment later. "The hostages. It is . . ." He paused, a thoughtful frown crossing his features. "Terrible, is it not?"

"They arrested my aunt." The words emerged as a cracked whisper, slipping out before I could consider to whom I spoke.

For a moment, he said nothing. "I am sorry."

He was sorry? He, an officer in the army that had overtaken my homeland while its citizens suffered under oppressive edicts, lack of the most basic necessities, and above all, crushing fear for ourselves and the ones we loved. He, with his rank and his smartly tailored uniform, was sorry?

"She's a doctor at the Child Jesus Hospital. My sister and I have been living with her since our flat was bombed during the siege. She's a respectable, ordinary woman, innocent of any crime." The words poured out, my voice choked. "I don't understand. Why are your people so cruel?"

He crossed to the window. Clear winter sunlight slanted over his chiseled profile, the square of his shoulders in his gray-green uniform as he stood with his hands behind his back. I glanced away, pressing my lips together.

Why had I said it? The rare time I let my thoughts form into words without consideration, and now I had angered him. He would speak to his uncle, and I would be dismissed.

Somehow, though, I did not regret it. Perhaps I should and would later, when met with the consequences. But it was true, what I had said, even if he did not like to hear it. I would not regret the truth, not in this.

Silence collected, laden with the weight of words both voiced and unspoken.

"The desire to be master over other men brings out a cruelty that knows no measure." He spoke quietly, almost to himself, his gaze on the window. "Perhaps one justifies oneself with the belief that one's cause is right, one's aim is for the good. But there are some acts which are justified by no cause, despite what any man may tell himself. It is out of such things that wars are born, and it is the innocent whose suffering is laid on the altar of victory."

Never had I heard a German speak in such a way before. This wasn't the pride of Herr Bürkel and his friends, boasting about the victories of the Reich like they had won them themselves. Nor was it the satisfaction of the soldiers who strutted through Warsaw as if the city and its inhabitants were theirs for the subjugating.

I understood Leutnant Reinhardt's words and yet did not. Not what they meant nor why he spoke them to me. Not at all.

He faced me. "It may be that whomever is responsible for the murder of the soldiers will be apprehended and the hostages will be released."

I twisted the handkerchief in my hands. Speaking the words aloud only exposed their weightlessness, though I'd clung to such thoughts myself, no matter how cheap their reassurance. He glanced away, removed his cap, and ran a hand over his hair.

He took a step toward me, his cap under his arm. "With your permission, I will make inquiries on behalf of your aunt. My uncle knows a great many people. Perhaps something might be done."

My breath hitched. I stared at him. "You would do such a thing?"

"I can promise nothing, but I will do whatever is within my power."

Antonina hadn't even taken time for breakfast before setting out, determined to make an appeal on behalf of the hostages. I would have accompanied her if Herr Bürkel hadn't been expecting me. But we were far from the first whose relatives had been taken. They, too, had given all their strength to fighting for their nearest ones, writing letters, visiting offices, petitioning whomever they could. Only for an announcement to be posted that the reprisals had been carried out.

But if Leutnant Reinhardt, a German officer, intervened in Aunt Basia's case, perhaps there was a chance.

Such hope felt almost too fragile to grasp.

Why would he do this for me? His uncle's secretary, a stranger. What benefit would he gain from it? I'd considered approaching Herr Bürkel myself, begging if need be. If not for Leutnant Reinhardt's offer, I might have done so today, though I doubted my employer would take a great interest in my concerns.

Leutnant Reinhardt's reasons didn't matter. I was a girl who hadn't heard from her father in nearly a year. I couldn't bear another empty place.

Loss didn't make one stronger, only more desperate.

Before I could collect my thoughts to form a reply, the door opened and footsteps clicked across the floorboards. Agata glanced at the leutnant as she crossed to her desk. He nodded to her, then approached me, stopping beside my desk. "What is her name? Your aunt?"

"Dr. Barbara Dąbrowska." I kept my voice as quiet as his, aware of Agata's gaze on us as she inserted a fresh sheet of paper into her typewriter.

As his eyes met mine, it seemed they held wordless reassurance. "Good day, Fräulein Dąbrowska."

"Thank you," I said softly.

He gave a slight nod. Then he settled his black-brimmed cap on his head and pivoted, striding out of the office. A moment later, the door shut.

I still held the handkerchief, the fabric crumpled and damp from my palm. I slipped it into my handbag, then returned to my typewriter.

As I glanced at the tablet filled with dictation, my gaze fell on the folded newspaper. Lines of indifferent black type stared back at me.

"If the name of the murderer is not disclosed to the German authorities by 2:00 p.m. . . ."

HELENA
FEBRUARY 1, 1941

The second winter under occupation brought temperatures as unforgiving as all else seemed to be these days. Despite the scarf around my neck and the woolen cardigan beneath my coat, the cold bit through the layers of clothing and pierced to my very bones.

No matter how miserable the elements, we still had to queue with our ration cards for a few grams of bread or stand in front of the butcher's where we would be fortunate to receive our monthly allotment of two hundred grams of meat. Even when we did, it often turned out to be odorous, mostly bone, or generally inedible—though we ate it still. We'd grown used to eating horsemeat. It wasn't so terrible, really, as long as you didn't think about it.

The grueling struggle for the necessities of survival remained a constant in a life that offered few certainties.

Outside our building on Hoża Street, Antonina withdrew our ration cards from her handbag and passed them to me.

"Take these. See what you can get. I'll go to the Kercelak. I should be able to buy some potatoes, perhaps a little kasza." Illegal trade thrived at the market on Kerceli Square—the Kercelak, we called it—though the price of goods could be fantastically high. Better to travel to the countryside and buy produce and dairy products there, though the occupiers considered such activities smuggling and conducted searches in trains and on roads entering the city. The Germans would smash an old woman's basket of eggs or confiscate for themselves the milk a mother bought for her children. In such cases, the so-called criminals considered themselves fortunate. Far worse fates could befall smugglers. Even shopping at the Kercelak carried risks, for the police frequently raided the market square.

I stared at the cards in my gloved hands—pale pink, delineated into small squares which entitled the bearer to categories and quantities of food. Three cards. Mine, Antonina's, and Aunt Basia's.

"I'll try to find some coffee too," I said. "We have only a little left, and you know how Aunt Basia hates to do without it." Though the rich coffee of prewar days had been substituted for a brew of roasted acorns, chicory, rye, or even carrot root, Aunt Basia continued her practice of drinking a cup each morning. It was the one luxury she refused to give up, despite the necessity of carefully considering how every złoty ought best to be spent.

So many times I had come out of the bedroom to find her at the table, a steaming cup cradled in her hands, as darkness gave way to dawn. I would pour a small cup for myself and join her. Sometimes we talked, other times we simply sat together, savoring the stillness of the new day.

"Yes, that's a good idea." With my sister's voice, the memory dissipated. She seemed distracted, like whether I bought coffee for our aunt didn't much matter one way or the other.

We made our way along Hoża Street. Snow flurried from a colorless sky as a tram trundled past, its red body an outline against the gray morning.

A few people, dark-garbed in their shabby coats, clustered in front of an advertising pillar. I paused.

The notice had been plastered beside a faded advertisement for cigarettes. The reddish paper hadn't yet been streaked by rain or snow, the bold black letters still crisp.

Its existence as fresh as its reality.

ANNOUNCEMENT

As retribution for the atrocious murder of two German soldiers on the night of 27 January, 1941, one hundred detainees were shot this morning.

I stood dry-eyed and granite-still, the soft brush of drifting flakes against my cheeks.

Antonina stood beside me. I hadn't even noticed she'd stopped. She stared at the poster, frost emerging from her pale lips with every exhale. The brisk clop of hooves from a passing cart, the clang of a tram, and a man's voice nearby formed a vague din in my ears. Sounds of life.

Life.

Red paper and black ink blurred.

It wasn't tears. I wouldn't cry.

"Ah, my Hela."

It was so near, her voice, as tangible as her presence. I would come into the room, and she'd be sitting at the table with her coffee. She'd turn and the soft light of a smile would touch her lips. I found Tata in her face when she smiled at me, in the crevice in her right cheek, the creases stitching the corners of her eyes.

She would come back. She'd only gone to the hospital, that was all. I'd said goodbye to her, hadn't I? She'd be working the night shift and wouldn't be home till morning, that's what she told me. She'd been putting on her hat as she said it, then she picked up her handbag and rushed out the door.

She wasn't gone.

Leutnant Reinhardt had promised to help her. To obtain her release from Pawiak, that place of barred cells and vanished lives.

But not hers. They wouldn't take her.

I wouldn't let them take her from me.

I fought for breath, but my lungs weren't drawing in air. The pressure in my chest built, the tightness suffocating. I gasped, heaving in and out, but it wasn't enough. I couldn't breathe.

"Hela." Someone touched my arm. I turned, my sister's face hazy, pale like the snow wafting around us. "Let's go."

Go? Where did she think we would go? I shook my head. I couldn't stop shivering. I was cold, so desperately cold . . .

"Come, Hela," Antonina said, the hand at my back as firm as her voice. "Let's go home."

Mutely, I allowed my sister to lead me away.

This was only a dream. That was all. I would wake in the morning and everything would be as it had been. Aunt Basia would come home. We would be safe.

But somewhere in the fog of my mind, deep in the place that had once been my heart, I knew.

Morning wasn't coming.

9

ANTONINA
JULY 23, 1942

Time passed differently in a city under occupation. Once, the coming months beckoned with promise and there had been reason to anticipate their passage. Now, though the days varied, they remained changeless in their gray reality. Passing from one to the next, an unbroken chain of waking and sleeping, knowing the same burdens must be picked up and carried again no matter how weary our shoulders became.

In war, time became at once ephemeral and eternal.

It was summer again. Nearly a year and a half had elapsed since Aunt Basia's death, and it would soon be three years since the August day when we'd gone to the Main Station and watched our father board a train bound for war.

How little we knew then, that it would be the last morning we would spend in peacetime.

The café bustled in its usual manner that evening. I carried trays and served coffee, counting the hours until I could return to our flat to eat what little supper there was and fall into bed.

"It's said they're deporting them by the thousands. More every day." The man's words caught my attention amid the undercurrent of conversation and the clink and scrape of china and cutlery. The couple fell silent as I leaned in to set plates before them.

"Will there be anything else?"

The woman glanced up. "No, thank you."

I moved away, the tray under my arm, and began clearing a nearby table.

"But to where?" the woman asked.

I strained to catch her companion's reply. Why, I couldn't say, but something about the conversation made me purposefully linger.

"East, they say, to be resettled in labor camps or some such."

"Will they send them all, do you think?"

"This is only the second day since it began. I haven't the faintest idea what's coming."

My hands moved by rote, depositing plates and cups onto the tray, my head bent.

"All the better to have them out of the city," the woman remarked. "When I heard about the dreadful epidemic of typhus in the district last summer, I warned the children not to go anywhere near there."

My hands shook as I stacked dishes on the tray. There could no longer be any doubt they spoke of the ghetto.

"Yes, best keep away. Did I tell you my sister is coming for a visit?"

"Really? How is she these days?"

I lifted the heavy tray and carried it into the kitchen.

Had it not been enough to confine the Jewish people behind a wall? Now they would expel them from the city? Had Marek or his family been among those sent away?

Marek Eisenberg had ceased to be part of my life. He had taken something from me that day when he told me not to seek him out again. Long before then—perhaps when we'd met or the first time we played Chopin together—I had lost a part of myself to him which I hadn't regained. He had been the man who had shown me music in a way I'd never known before, the man I loved, or thought I did.

Sometimes I hated him for it. Hated him for my love of him. I hadn't returned to the walled district. Perhaps because my heart couldn't withstand his rejection a second time.

But I couldn't forget him. Nor could I forget the ghetto and what I saw there, though I spoke of it to no one, not even Helena.

Sometimes I passed by one of the gates for a glimpse beyond the barrier. Or wandered to the edge of the district and stood, staring at the wall, as if my gaze could sear through three meters of brick and shatter the barricade that divided a single city into separate worlds.

I sought what news could be had about conditions in the district—mostly rumors, none of them good. Last summer and autumn, typhus had ravaged the ghetto, its severity no doubt increased by the privations endured by its inhabitants. Thousands had fallen victim. When word of the epidemic in the Jewish district filtered through Warsaw, I'd broken the tear-choked promises I'd made to myself and wrote to Marek, begging him to tell me if he was safe, if I could do anything for him and his family.

Marek has the typhus but is recovering. There is nothing you can do for us.

Katarzyna Eisenberg

I still asked myself if Marek had been too ill to write or if he had requested his mother reply in his stead because he didn't want to correspond with me himself. It didn't matter. He was alive. That was enough.

Sometimes I wondered how it was possible to go on while hundreds of thousands of human beings languished on the other side of the wall and death proved without mercy.

Still I had. I did not know what else to do.

What could it mean—deportation? We had grown accustomed to łapanki, the rounding up of civilians for work in the Reich or—a far worse fate—incarceration in a camp. Such things happened in the rest of the city. Could this be more of the same, only this time it was the turn of the ghetto?

But thousands? How could it even be possible? Perhaps it would prove to be no more than rumors after all.

No. Something had shifted. I sensed it, instinctively.

And I could not turn from the shadow of my fear.

HELENA
JULY 27, 1942

Silence settled around me, the one quiet half hour of the day. No typewriters clattering or telephones ringing. No Herr Bürkel calling me into his office to take dictation, my pencil rasping as I scribbled in time to his guttural droning about financial matters of the Generalgouvernement.

Only the whisper of paper as I turned the page, my book in one hand, my bread and beetroot marmalade in the other. I chewed slowly, swallowing the dry bread and earthy-sweet marmalade. When I read Mickiewicz's poetry, I could think of nothing but the words, the way they spun epic tales of centuries past or burned with the passion and despair of youthful love.

When I read Mickiewicz, I could forget that, though I found solitude in these few moments, even when the office was filled with the conversation and gossip and commands of the others, I was always alone.

We had received no word from Tata, no word from anyone about his fate. I wouldn't stop clutching hope, wouldn't stop praying and fearing for him. But as time passed and the silence lengthened, forgetting became easier and it shamed me.

Last summer, in June 1941, Germany had invaded the Soviet Union. I supposed Hitler had wearied of his nonaggression pact and decided tearing up a piece of paper and ordering millions of troops to trample over the scraps was not so very difficult. There had since been several Soviet air raids on Warsaw. But despite our hopes, it didn't seem likely the war would end soon, at least not for several months, perhaps longer, though America had entered the fray last December. People had said Germany had gone too far this time and Hitler's decision to take on the Russians marked the beginning of the end. But how long would it take for the end to come and what would befall us in the meantime? Those were the questions that kept us awake at night.

The creak of the door brought my gaze up, and I hastily wrapped the remainder of my bread in a napkin.

Leutnant Reinhardt entered the front office.

I started at the sight of him. The last time we'd spoken beyond a brief greeting had been shortly after the execution of the hostages. His eyes held genuine sorrow and impotent anger as he told me how he had made every attempt to intervene on Aunt Basia's behalf, and his voice had faltered as he said how deeply sorry he was, but his words had been weightless to me. Then Herr Bürkel had come out of his office, and the conversation had been over before I'd even said a word.

Now Leutnant Reinhardt took in the room, empty save for me, and remained standing near the doorway. "Good day," he said, the low-spoken words at variance with the strident tones of Herr Bürkel and many of the officials who frequented the office.

"Herr Bürkel is at a meeting at present, but if you wish to pass on a message, I'll see he's informed as soon as he returns. He should be back within the hour." The stiffness of my voice could not be denied, despite the deference of my words.

"May I wait?" He worded it as a question, as if I—his uncle's secretary—could actually refuse.

"Of course. Sit, if you like." I indicated a chair against the wall to the left of my desk.

"Thank you." He took a seat, his boots planted on the polished floor.

I couldn't very well return to my bread and my book, not with him looking on, and I had already finished the morning's typing. By the time the office closed, I'd be even hungrier than usual, my midday meal only half-eaten.

Even as I busied myself with tidying the papers on my desk, I couldn't help but be painfully aware of his presence, the uncertain silence between us.

He removed his officer's cap and rested it on his knee, ran a hand over his smoothed-back hair. "The weather is fine today, is it not?"

"Yes."

He lapsed into silence again, and I continued straightening papers.

"What were you reading?"

The words startled me, despite his mild tone.

"Mickiewicz." The volume still lay on my desk. "He's Polish," I added, a little defiantly.

"I have heard of him, but regrettably, I am not well-enough acquainted with the language to read his work for myself. Unless, of course, I could obtain a German translation." He paused. "Would you read something to me?"

I stared at him.

"That is, if you are not too busy." He gave a slight smile.

I frowned. "You wish me to read?"

"I should like very much to hear one of his poems." His gaze held mine. "Please."

I almost refused. Perhaps I ought to have done so, out of pride. What right had he, the enemy, to the words of our beloved poet? But something in his quiet request—for it was no more and no less than that, a request, humbly spoken—made the words of rebuff dry up before they had even formed.

I picked up the volume. What should I read? One of Mickiewicz's rousing homages to his native land? Paper rustled as I turned to the place marked with a ribbon, the page I had been reading when he came in.

I glanced up. He sat, his head slightly tilted, one hand resting on his knee, waiting.

"'To the Niemen.'" I swallowed, my throat dry, and began to read.

> Where are the waters of those golden years
> That oft I dipped, as smoothly we would glide
> To some wild solitude where youth might hide.

My words came soft, my voice a little unsteady. I'd always dreaded recitations at school, all those eyes staring at me.

But here, now, there was only him.

I kept my gaze on the page, anywhere but his face, as I read on, translating the words into German as best I could.

Where are those sources, Niemen, that would fain
Bring me such happiness and hopeful dreams?
Where is my childhood with its varied themes?
Where are my friends? I sigh for them in vain.
Where is my Laura, mirrored by the streams?

I raised my eyes, met the quiet intensity of his. I drew a shuddering breath. "'Since all are gone, why do my tears remain?'" My voice faltered on the last words. I closed the book, staring down at the cover, my head bent. What was the matter with me? The words had not affected me so when I first read the poem.

Such longing they held. For innocence, for those one loved, for the past. The final stanza fading with the broken question. *Why? Why do I weep when there is no one left to hear my tears?*

The quiet tread of boots across floorboards. I didn't trust myself to look up. A faint fragrance reached me, the scent of bergamot returning me to a handkerchief once pressed into my palm.

"He writes . . ." He paused, swallowed. "He writes like a man who understands the emptiness of knowing that one can never return to what was and that what lies ahead is without light."

I did not know what to say, so I said nothing.

"You have known it too?"

I bit my lip, my hands clenched in my lap.

"I am sorry." The words came quiet. "For all you have lost."

I lifted my head. He stood beside my desk, silently regarding me, his officer's cap in his hand.

The door opened, men's voices carrying. Herr Bürkel entered, followed by his assistant, Herr Schultz.

"Werner, what a surprise." Herr Bürkel came forward, and the two grasped hands—the lean young officer in Wehrmacht gray and the thickset middle-aged man in an expensive suit and wisp of a mustache. "What brings you here?"

"Hello, Uncle."

"Come into my office and tell me what you've been doing with yourself." Herr Bürkel motioned his nephew forward. "Frieda was just saying it's been an age since you last visited."

The telephone on my desk jangled. I picked it up. "Herr Bürkel's office." Somehow my voice came out crisp and composed. The man on the other end of the line asked to speak with Herr Bürkel. "He's busy at the moment, but I'll be sure to pass on your message."

I glanced up as I jotted down the message.

In the doorway, Leutnant Reinhardt turned. For a fleeting moment, he looked back at me, then the door with HERMANN BÜRKEL lettered on the frosted glass shut.

The call ended, and I set down my pencil. A weight rested on my lap.

The volume of poetry. It had belonged to Aunt Basia. She loved Mickiewicz too. Tata had given her the book when they'd been young, the flyleaf playfully inscribed. *To My Favorite Sister, Basia. From Your Ever Devoted Brother, Staś.* I could hear Aunt Basia's bantering reply as her eyes sparkled, for they had often teased each other thus. "*So you have other sisters, do you? Just where have you been hiding them?*"

I picked up the book and placed it in the drawer where I kept my handbag. With a firm hand, I shut the drawer.

It had been more than a year, but how much longer it seemed.

Grief was a blade, slicing deep, cutting your heart to shreds. With time, the blade grew dull, your heart numb.

But you still bled.

10

ANTONINA
AUGUST 4, 1942

The shadow of the ghetto wouldn't leave me. By day and in the nights when I lay awake in the heavy summer darkness, Helena asleep beside me, questions and fears and speculations circled like birds of prey. Neither silenced nor shaken.

Below the surface of the city ran an undercurrent of rumors. You didn't go around asking about such things—or if you did, you chose carefully to whom you broached the subject, but still you heard. A scrap of news here, a chance remark there. It added up. The emptying of the ghetto hadn't ceased. Trains departed daily, transports of thousands of Jews.

The immensity of it made me shake inside.

Marek and his family must not remain in the ghetto. I would find them shelter, forged papers, whatever they needed. It would be dangerous, but I wouldn't let them be deported to the east, not if I could prevent it.

"Send word and I will do whatever is necessary. Please, Marek. I ask nothing but to help you."

No reply followed in the days after I posted the letter to him. I sent another, addressed to the Eisenbergs. If they had no need or desire for my aid, I asked only that they send an answer to that effect. None came.

I could write and keep writing, but letters that went unanswered would bring me no closer to Marek. I needed another way.

I wouldn't chance the trams again. Nearly all had been rerouted so they no longer passed through the district, and I had doubts about whether I'd succeed a second time at alighting from one and catching another on its way out without detection.

Then late one afternoon, standing as near the gate as I dared, searching for glimpses beyond the guard post, hoping for answers that did not come, I encountered Marysia Janowska.

She had been Aunt Basia's friend, had visited after our aunt's death, expressing both sympathy for our loss and fury at the murder of her friend.

I watched as she stepped briskly past the guards, leaving the ghetto behind. Our gazes collided. I nearly called out to her, but she strode onward as though she hadn't recognized me.

Aunt Basia's words returned to me. Early one morning, I had found her packing a basket. When I asked, she said she was taking it to her friend Marysia at the Department of Social Welfare and Public Health. Marysia had a pass to enter the Jewish district on matters of sanitation and epidemic control.

"The greatest epidemic behind the wall is hunger," Aunt Basia had said as she tucked a loaf of bread into the basket. Then her eyes held mine. Doubtless, she'd known about Marek. Probably Helena told her.

Days later, we lost Aunt Basia and never saw our aunt's friend following her visit. But before she left, Pani Janowska had turned to my sister and me.

"If you've need of anything, either of you, come to me."

Though likely what I intended to ask wasn't quite what the woman had in mind when she extended her offer so long ago.

The morning after my encounter with Pani Janowska, I hurried toward the Department of Social Welfare and Public Health on Złota Street, not far from the ghetto boundary. I reached the several-story office building and went inside. After inquiring of a woman behind a desk, I ascended the stairs to the second floor and continued down a corridor.

I drew my shoulders back and opened the door. In a middling-sized office, several women sat at desks, some busy at typewriters, one speaking into a telephone, the rest bent over papers.

"May I help you?" asked a woman from behind a typewriter.

"I've come to see Pani Marysia." I used her first name not from familiarity but from the need not to be seen as a stranger pushing her way into this industrious place of work.

"She's right over there." The woman gestured to where Marysia sat at a desk near the back wall.

"Thank you." I made my way among the desks until I reached hers. "Good day, Pani."

Marysia took off her spectacles and folded the temples. "Antonina, what a surprise." If the faint stiffening of her features gave any indication, it did not appear to be a welcome one.

"I'm sorry to disturb you, but I wondered if I might have a word?"

She gestured to the papers and stacks of files covering the surface of her desk. "As you can see, I'm rather busy—"

"It won't take long." I paused. "Please." Desperation and determination mingled in the single word.

She nodded and rose. "Follow me." She led me into an adjoining office and shut the door. She rounded the desk and took a seat, motioning to the straight-backed chair opposite.

I sat on the edge of the chair, my back stiff. Filing cabinets lined the walls, the space close, cluttered.

She folded her hands atop the desk. "Now, what may I do for you?"

Apparently there would be no exchange of preliminary civilities. Though, after all, I had come to her office rather than her flat, but only because I didn't know where she lived. I drew a breath. "I've come about the Jewish district."

She regarded me, expression unchanged.

I twisted my hands in my lap. "I saw you there yesterday, at the gate."

"Yes." Her tone remained professional, if guarded. "I'm authorized to enter the district on matters of sanitation and epidemic control."

"You've been inside the walls." The words rushed out. They hadn't been part of the speech I had rehearsed. "So you can tell me what's happening."

"What is it you wish to know?"

"About the deportations. How many are being taken? To where?"

"Six thousand a day, generally. Sometimes more, sometimes a little less. As for the rest, I'm afraid I cannot answer you, as I don't know. Is that why you've come? To inquire about the situation in the district?" A trace of impatience—or maybe tension—edged Marysia's voice.

"Not entirely. I'm . . . looking for someone. I wrote twice to his address, but I've had no answer."

"No letters are posted out of the district, not any longer," Marysia said calmly. "For a time, the postal service halted entirely."

Relief came in a rush. Marek couldn't have written, even if he'd wanted to do so.

"I hoped you might take a message to him. Bring me word of how he fares."

She glanced down at the papers cluttering the desk, then raised her gaze. "How do you know he isn't among those who've already been sent away?"

I swallowed hard. "Yes, but I can't go on . . . not knowing." I'd entered the office determined to remain in control, of both the situation and myself, but now my voice shook.

She tilted her head, her stare probing. "What makes this man of more import than any of the others? Who is he to you?"

I flushed. How pathetic I must seem, a rash and desperate young woman. Surely she had enough cares of her own without taking on mine.

"Merely a friend." I looked down at my hands, doubting she believed my flimsy explanation. "But I am concerned about him and his family. If you won't help me, I'll find another way." My words came bolder now.

Marysia rose and went to the small window. Droplets of rain painted the glass. She stood gazing out, a hand at the bow collar of her blouse, her features unreadable.

If Marysia didn't agree, what then?

She turned. "This letter, you have it with you, I presume."

I nodded and slipped the envelope from my handbag.

She held out her hand. "Leave it with me. I'll do what I can."

"Thank you." I handed her the envelope on which I'd penned Marek's name and address. "His name is Marek Eisenberg. He's a violinist. He works at the Pod Gwiazdą café. Or did once, at any rate. If—" I swallowed. *If he's already been sent on a transport.* "If you can't find him, please give the letter to his family. His parents are Henryk and Katarzyna Eisenberg. He has two sisters, Rutka and Chasia."

She nodded. Silence fell, save for the clacking of typewriters, the murmur of voices from beyond the closed door, and the thudding of rain on the roof.

"How are you and your sister?" Her features softened, a glimpse of the woman who had told her friend's nieces to come to her if ever in need.

"We manage well enough." For a moment I considered pressing her for details about the deportations, what she'd witnessed in the district, but thought better of it. She'd agreed to take the letter. That was all that mattered.

"Basia Dąbrowska was one of the finest women I've known." Marysia's voice was quiet. "She was a dear friend."

"Yes." Anger at the brutality with which her life had been stolen, the lack of her warm, capable presence in the moments I craved it most—in these ways, Aunt Basia's loss remained with me. But I did not feel it as keenly as I perhaps should have. Before the war, losses could be singly acknowledged. Now there were so many, it was difficult to separate them. They merged together, a void inside me, a hollow of absence and of emptiness.

Then Marysia straightened. "I must ask you not to come here again. Do you still live at the flat on Hoża Street? I'll bring you word there."

"No, don't." Though Helena certainly recalled Aunt Basia's friend, it would be difficult to keep the reason for her visit from my sister. At Marysia's questioning glance, I went on, "I work at a café in the city centre." I gave her the address and rose, sensing our meeting at an end.

Marysia started toward the door, then paused. She turned, the letter in her hand. For the first time, I glimpsed the shadows in her eyes. "I hope I find your Marek Eisenberg. For his sake."

11

ANTONINA
AUGUST 11, 1942

I was clearing dishes from a table when Marysia entered the café. My heart gave a little lurch as I searched her face for a sign as to the news she brought, but her features betrayed nothing.

I lifted a hand in greeting, then hefted the tray and carried it into the kitchen. I stepped into the proprietor's office to ask if I might take half an hour for my dinner. He agreed, and within moments, Marysia and I left the café. A tram rolled past and a whistle screeched as a policeman in navy blue directed traffic. Marysia walked beside me, a jacket over her blouse, an envelope bag clasped in front of her.

"Did you see Marek?" The question could wait no longer.

She gave a little shake of her head.

My steps halted. My heart stilled.

Marysia drew a breath. "I'm afraid you must be told. Marek was sent on a transport."

I stared at her. My ears rang as if I had been struck.

"How can you be certain?"

"I went to their address, spoke to one of the neighbors." Marysia hesitated. "I'm sorry."

"And his family?"

Marysia shook her head.

"All of them?"

Her silence was its own answer.

Marek's father, the distinguished orchestra conductor, whose aging years should have been ones of rest and contentment in his family and all he had achieved. His elegant wife, determined not to stoop to her circumstances, who had never been fond of me, but had loved her son fiercely—perhaps the former had been due to the latter. Rutka, whom I had never really known, and Chasia with her dark curls and shy smile.

Marek. The man who had shown me how the melding of piano and violin could bind one heart to another as indelibly as any kiss.

Into what unknown had they gone?

"I was told Marek managed to obtain employment cards for his father and himself proving they had work at a German factory, granting them exemption from deportation," Marysia said. "These employment cards were to have protected Marek's mother and sisters also, but they're taking people now regardless of their papers to fill the quotas."

"How long will it go on?" My voice emerged as a broken whisper. "If we could only know what was happening to them . . ."

Then I saw her face. And I knew.

Some moments, some truths, you can never return from. They sear the soul, changing you irrevocably.

I clutched Marysia's arm, pulling her into a nearby gateway, the clamor of the street receding in its shelter.

"Tell me." I pushed out the words, my voice a rasp. My nails clawed the flesh of my palms as I waited for her to speak. Even as I wanted to press my fists to my ears and shut out her words.

"A man has returned from the place where the trains are going. A camp called Treblinka. There, everyone who survives the journey is taken and"—Marysia drew a shuddering breath—"and forced into chambers where they are suffocated by poisonous fumes. The trains are always full when they arrive, and always, they return empty."

Words had meaning. This did not. Words were human. This was not.

The ground lurched. My legs gave way. Marysia steadied me, her grasp firm.

Somehow my lungs still drew in air, one breath after another. But how, I did not know. I pressed my eyes shut, my mind a void of silence and screams.

"I should not have told you." Marysia's quiet voice reached into the chasm.

"No." I shook my head. "It's—it's just rumors. Every day, there are thousands . . ."

Thousands herded onto the trains. Thousands bolted inside the cars. Thousands journeying toward one end.

They said the Jews had been sent to labor camps. Labor camps. I bit my lip fiercely.

"I heard it myself from someone who spoke to a man sent out to discover the destination of the trains. It is not known whether all the transports arrive at Treblinka, but most do. There is one reason for these trains. For this camp, only one purpose." Marysia spoke calmly, but her face had lost its color, become pale and tight as though from the effort of holding back her anguish.

The taste of copper trickled onto my tongue. I stood motionless, the sun on my face.

The soul can shatter in silence as well as in tears.

"Do they know?" My voice was dull. Time had passed between her words and mine. How much, I wasn't certain. "Those who remain in the ghetto?"

"Not all. Some do. Others refuse to believe. The Germans promise them bread, those who report voluntarily for resettlement. Three kilos and one kilo of marmalade. When one has known hunger as they have, what one will give for three kilos of bread . . ." Marysia's voice faded.

It was no use. There was no hope. Thousands had been consumed by the transports as if they were dry straw, worthless tinder easily burned. Those who remained had simply to wait in line. Whether a remnant would be kept alive for labor didn't matter.

Because the Nazis had answered the "Jewish question."

And it had a name.

Treblinka.

HELENA
AUGUST 11, 1942

Half past five had come and gone hours ago, and still, I remained at my typewriter. The front office was dim and shadowed, silent save for the staccato of typewriter keys imprinting freshly inked letters across the page. I paused to massage a knot that burned in my right shoulder, then continued typing, no longer bothering to fight the yawn that escaped.

Agata had fallen from her bicycle and sprained her wrist, and the doctor said she wouldn't be able to return to work for at least a week. Naturally Herr Bürkel wouldn't take into consideration anything so mundane as an incapacitated typist and still expected the functioning of his office to continue without interruption, so not only did I have my own duties to complete in a satisfactory manner but hers too. Herr Bürkel wouldn't trust a mere secretary to lock up, so Herr Schultz had to stay as well. At least once every half hour he came into the front office and asked, without bothering to hide his irritation, if I had "nearly finished," adding that he certainly hoped we wouldn't "be here all night."

Rapping came at the door. I started. Who could it be at this hour? I turned in my chair, about to call for Herr Schultz, but he wouldn't take kindly to being disturbed, and I wasn't in the mood for another round of his remarks.

I rose and left the front office, stepping out into the corridor. More quiet yet firm knocking.

At the door, I hesitated, one hand on the bolt. "Who is it?" I called, hoping my voice sounded forceful.

"Werner Reinhardt," came the muffled reply.

I drew a sudden breath, then unbolted and opened the door. Leutnant Reinhardt stood outside, his uniformed figure silhouetted against the fading daylight.

"I believe I left my cigarette case in my uncle's office this afternoon. May I come in?"

"Of course." I stepped aside to allow him entry, then closed and bolted the door. I turned, hesitated. "How did you know anyone would still be here?"

"My uncle mentioned some of his staff might be working late."

"Frau Lewicka has been unwell, so there were some things that needed to be finished."

"The typist?"

I nodded.

In the deepening shadows, he regarded me. "You are alone?"

"Herr Schultz is waiting to lock up. I'm nearly through." I led the way into the front office, stopping at Herr Bürkel's door.

"How will you get home?" he asked.

"Walk, the same as always."

He frowned. "It will soon be curfew. You must permit me to drive you."

"Thank you, but that's quite all right."

"No, please. I insist. My car is just outside." He paused. "I would not wish my uncle's lack of consideration for his staff to cause you to come to any harm."

Perhaps it had simply been an awful day and I was tired, worn from Herr Bürkel's demands and Herr Schultz's jibes. Or perhaps it was the sincerity of his tone, the concern with which he regarded me. It had been so long since anyone had cared. I hadn't realized or maybe acknowledged the measure of that lack until something touched it.

Whatever the reason, I couldn't find it in myself to refuse, though I ought to do just that. "All right." A hesitant smile touched my lips. "If you're certain it won't be too much trouble."

"Fine, then." He opened Herr Bürkel's door. "I'll fetch my cigarette case and wait for you outside."

Herr Schultz came out from his office. "I thought I heard voices."

I returned to my desk. "Leutnant Reinhardt left his cigarette case when he was here this afternoon."

"Really? I'd best see if I can be of any assistance." He gave me a sharp look as he stopped by my desk. "Have you quite finished?"

"I shouldn't be more than a few minutes."

"At long last."

Ignoring the comment, I resumed typing. A quarter of an hour later, I stepped out into the blue-black darkness, Herr Schultz behind me.

"Good night, Herr Schultz."

"Night," he muttered. At the sight of the leutnant standing beside his automobile, he stopped. "Leutnant Reinhardt, you're still here?"

"I waited to drive Fräulein Dąbrowska home as it's nearly curfew. You have a night pass, I presume, being Volksdeutsch?"

"Oh. Yes, of course," Herr Schultz said absently. "Well." He paused, glancing from Leutnant Reinhardt to me. "Good night." He started down the sidewalk, briefcase in hand.

Coolness tinged the evening air as I approached the automobile, carrying my handbag. Leutnant Reinhardt opened the door.

"Thank you," I said quietly as I settled onto the leather seat.

He closed the door, enveloping me in darkness. I placed my handbag on my lap and folded my hands atop it as he opened his door and slid inside.

He glanced at me, both hands on the wheel. "Where do you live?"

I gave him the address.

Silence fell as we drove, the sidewalks and thoroughfares nearly deserted, the dimmed streetlamps vaguely luminous in the night. I sat stiffly on the leather seat, awareness of his presence all the more acute for our silence. The interior had a scent of cigarette smoke and leather, underpinned by a trace of bergamot, a mingling that closed around me with every breath. What had I been thinking to place myself in this position, alone with a man—a German? Leutnant Reinhardt had acted nothing but the gentleman, but how could I feel safe with him? He said he didn't wish me to come to any harm, but why would he go to such trouble for a woman, a Pole, he scarcely knew out of kindness alone? Panic clutched my throat.

I should never have agreed to this.

"Your parents will be worried, no doubt, you being out so close to curfew."

I turned to look at him, the quiet words startling after several minutes had passed with neither of us speaking. "My sister will be, I suppose." Though Antonina had been so preoccupied of late, I wondered if she'd even notice. In answer to the question in his glance, I added, "My mama died when I was young and my father is . . . missing." I hesitated, decided not to elaborate. "What of your family?" I asked partly to avoid talking about myself and partly because I truly was curious. He'd had a life before all this. In that, he was no different than any of us, Poles and Germans alike. War had spared none of our worlds.

He kept his gaze on the street, his profile shadowed. "My father is still living, but we lost my mother some years ago. My sister, Inge, is two years younger than I am and has a little son, not quite four. Every day I await the post for news that my second niece or nephew has arrived. My younger brother, Helmut, is also in the army. We live near a village not far from the city of Mainz. Our family has owned a vineyard there for almost a century."

I wondered if he realized how his features softened as he spoke, the barest smile at his lips. What memories put it there?

"What does it grow, your vineyard?"

"We're known for our grapes of the Silvaner variety. A more subtle flavor than the Riesling, but in the hands of a skilled vigneron, they produce an excellent white wine."

"I'm afraid I don't know anything about wine," I said, a little abashed. "What is this Silvaner like?"

He paused. "How to describe it? It's dry. Delicate, fresh. There's a hint of apples, ripened by the sun. It tastes, to me, like home, I suppose."

"I think I would like that." My face warmed inexplicably. "Did you work in the vineyard?"

"Every chance I could, as a boy. There was an old man who'd been with us since the time of my grandfather. I was always tagging at his heels, asking a thousand questions." He gave a quiet chuckle, and I could glimpse that boy, wide-eyed and eager, finding wonder in everything that surrounded him. "My father and I planned I would manage the vineyard in his stead, but then, well . . ." He drew a long breath.

I caught regret in his voice, but I wouldn't pity him.

If your Führer hadn't aspired to conquer all of Europe, you would be there still. And I would be home, in my real home, not

Aunt Basia's flat. And she would still be alive, and my father would still be here.

The words came, but I didn't voice them. Leutnant Reinhardt didn't deserve them. Did he believe in his country and why they fought? Could a person believe in one and not the other?

I didn't know and I didn't ask. It didn't seem my place, and in the moment, somehow didn't seem to matter.

Silence slipped between us again, permeating as the darkness deepening over the streets. I stared out the window, lulled by the rocking motion of the car and the warmth surrounding me.

"I've been reading Mickiewicz. I managed to get hold of a German translation of *Pan Tadeusz*."

I glanced at him as he began to recite, his voice low, pensive almost.

> Bear thou my soul, consumed by longing, to
> Those wooded hills, unto those meadows green
> Broad stretching on the azure Niemen's shore;
> Toward those fields, rich hued with various grain,
> Golden with wheat, and silvered with the rye.

The words held a new cadence spoken in German. But their yearning remained, unaltered by language. For it dwelt within my own heart too.

I swallowed, my throat suddenly dry. "I live just . . . there."

The automobile drew up alongside the building on Hoża Street and parked. I reached for the door, about to slip out as quickly as I could.

"Permit me." He opened his own door, ducking his head as he climbed out. I sat, staring straight ahead as he came around and opened my door.

I alighted, and he reached past me to close the door. Standing on the deserted sidewalk, we faced each other. I could touch him, we stood so close, yet I did not turn away. The glow of a streetlamp illuminated his sculpted cheekbones, the insignias on his uniform, the black brim of his officer's cap and the soft, clear gray of his eyes.

Werner. How strange to think of him as such. Not as an officer in the Wehrmacht but as a man like any other. Though he had been born in Germany and I in Poland, though his country had wrought such destruction upon mine, did not something deeper lie between us? For did not our humanity bind all of us, no matter our birth or the divisions of our homelands?

I did not understand why I could not take my gaze from his. I did not understand why my throat ached as I looked into his face. I did not understand how loneliness could be so twined with longing.

None of it, I understood.

"I bid you good night." He gave a nod, but his eyes did not leave mine.

The click of footsteps made me turn. The lone figure of a woman hurried down the sidewalk, her head bent.

Antonina?

She glanced up. Her gaze slammed into mine. Her lips parted, and the tendons in her neck stood out as shock rushed over her face.

Then she strode past us and into the building without another glance.

I stared after her, realization slowly sweeping through me. Then I remembered Leutnant Reinhardt's presence. He wore a perplexed expression, as if he sensed something had happened but couldn't place what.

"Thank you for bringing me home," I hastened to say, my words stumbling. "Good night."

Without waiting for him to reply, I walked quickly up the sidewalk. I, too, did not look back.

I rushed up all three flights of stairs, stopped by the door and opened my handbag, fumbled with the key. The door gave way, and I stepped into the unlit entrance.

Lamplight emanated from the sitting room. Antonina faced the blacked-out window, arms folded. She didn't turn around.

I swallowed, standing in the doorway. "I'm sorry to be so late." I didn't know why I felt the need to apologize. She'd arrived home at nearly the same time and yet she wouldn't have begged pardon.

She didn't reply.

"Tosia, I-I can explain."

She turned. Spots of color stood out on her cheekbones. "Fine, then. Explain." Her voice had an odd, strangled sound. "Because I'm curious to know *what in the name of heaven* I just saw out there."

"Agata—you know, the typist—sprained her wrist. I had her work to do as well as mine, so I had to stay late. Leutnant Reinhardt forgot his cigarette case. He came back to fetch it and—" I wasn't making sense. Antonina's expression remained stony. "—and offered to bring me home."

"Who is Leutnant Reinhardt?" Her tone was lethal in its iciness.

"Herr Bürkel's nephew. He visits his uncle at the office from time to time."

"How can you do it?" She gave an incredulous laugh, a shake of her head. "I don't understand. It's bad enough you work for them, but to consort with one of them?"

"How could you think that?" I took a step forward, hands clenched at my sides. Something burst inside me, like a dam had cracked in my chest. "He did no more than drive me home. He isn't one of them."

She made a scoffing sound. "I suppose he dresses up in that uniform for show, then."

"You know *nothing* about him."

Her brow tilted. "Oh, and you do?"

"He's a decent man. He's kind and—"

"He isn't." Her eyes burned. "None of them are. People are dying, Helena, innocent Jewish people. They are dying by the thousands, and here you are carrying on with this man. This—this Nazi." She spat the words.

I stared at her.

"I thought I knew you, but not anymore. I don't know the sister who would betray me like this." She pushed past me and strode from the room. The slam of the bedroom door resounded through the flat.

I stood rooted in place, trembling uncontrollably. I sank to the floor and pulled my knees to my chest, wrapped my arms around them and lowered my head, pressing my eyes shut. Willing darkness to close over me and drown out the emptiness.

Such emptiness.

12

ANTONINA
AUGUST 16, 1942

"A camp called Treblinka. . . . The trains are always full when they arrive, and always, they return empty."

Sometimes the words were a crescendo, their mounting intensity resounding above all else. Other times they came in pianissimo, low yet pervading.

"There is one reason for these trains. For this camp, only one purpose."

Echoing scales, unending notes. A symphony of horror.

How easy it would be to dismiss the words, disbelieve them as mere rumors. It was incomprehensible. Unthinkable. The railcars awaiting the daily quotas, the herding of humanity like cattle, the train surging along the tracks until it came to the place called Treblinka. The unloading of the people from the wagons, the chambers with their fumes that choked, suffocated, extinguished.

Such an operation wasn't the work of a moment. For it to function as it did required orchestration. Someone administrated this, organized it down to the most banal details.

Why? Didn't the Reich have enough with which to concern itself on the battlefield? What justification could even the most depraved mind find in the systematic slaughter of innocent human beings by the thousands?

I had no answers. Nor did reasoning matter. Only reality. It had been nearly a month since the deportations began and still they did not stop.

What about us, the ordinary men and women who dwelt side by side with our Jewish neighbors, first as inhabitants of the same city and then with only a wall between us? Would we now turn our backs to their annihilation and shut our ears so we could not hear their cries? Many likely welcomed the removal of the Jews, counting it as one of the few favors the occupiers had done the Poles.

I knew such people and heard such talk. They didn't care where the Jews went, so long as they were gone.

I had never been one of them but had done little to prove otherwise.

I should have tried harder to aid the Eisenbergs. Hidden them in my flat, obtained documents so they could pass among the population outside the ghetto, whatever necessary. I would have risked everything, my life for theirs.

I loved you. Had I ever told you that?

I couldn't remember. I couldn't remember, and it didn't matter anymore because I couldn't say it now.

Even as my heart bled, a burning arose.

Tata used to say the only gain in regretting the past lay in the present. For only the present could be altered.

For Marek and his family, I could do nothing.

But I would not—could not—stand by while others remained.

Last night, I found Aunt Basia's address book. As I scanned the lines penned in her tidy script, my glance landed on the one I sought. Marysia lived in Wola, a district of factories and tenements west of the city centre.

But as I rode the tram to Wola that Sunday afternoon, it wasn't Marysia's words that reverberated with the clatter of the wheels, but my own. My tone so hard and cold, how could it possibly be mine?

"I don't know the sister who would betray me like this."

It happened so fast, a blur really. I had returned to the café after my meeting with Marysia, the hours until the end of my shift passing in a numb haze. Instead of going straight home that evening, I went to the outskirts of the ghetto. Driven by a restlessness devoid of purpose, I wandered in the shadow of the wall. I'd been hurrying along Hoża Street toward home, curfew fast approaching, when I caught sight of the automobile outside our building. My first instinct had been alarm. The Gestapo had come to search the block of flats, arrest one of the tenants.

Then I'd glimpsed the young woman and the man in uniform standing by the motorcar. There had been an intimacy in the way they stood in the light of a dimmed streetlamp, close enough to touch.

I had been so stunned—my sister with a German—that I simply strode past without a word. I'd barely entered the flat when Helena came into the sitting room. Her cheeks had been a little flushed, her gaze anxious as she stumbled over her explanation, guilt written across her features in unmistakable letters. At the sight, something inside me fell to pieces, and my words came in a vicious surge, sparing her nothing.

I'd watched it come over her face. The jolt of shock, the dawning of realization, the irrevocable wounding as my words found purchase. I glimpsed it only an instant before I shoved past her and left the room. But an instant had been enough to stain my memory with the look in my sister's eyes.

From childhood, I'd defended Helena, be it from a bully in the schoolyard or from our housekeeper's scolding. Always I sought to protect my sister.

How could I now do such a thing?

I didn't know why Helena had been with the officer. I'd seen the flush in her cheeks. What if it hadn't been as innocent as she claimed?

She worked in a German office, her contact with the occupiers closer than most Poles. She took the job because she had few choices, not because she liked it. That was what I told myself throughout her employment.

I thought I knew my sister. Now I was not sure.

Still, I never should have spoken as I had, nor maintained a frosty silence in the days since. Certainly I deserved an explanation. But I hadn't given her much of a chance to offer one, had I?

We needed to talk. When had we stopped? War had come between us, and its realities changed us. Of that there was no doubt.

It had been a long time since we'd shared our burdens and fears, secrets and hopes, turned to one another as sisters should. Too long.

The thoughts receded as I alighted at the tram stop. Minutes later, I arrived at the building matching the address in Aunt Basia's book. In the entrance, I scanned the list of registered tenants posted near the door.

Janowska. Number 5.

I ascended the stairs to the second floor, rang the bell, and waited on the landing.

The door opened. Marysia stood on the other side. She looked briefly taken aback by the sight of me.

"Good afternoon, Pani. I do apologize for calling uninvited." I hesitated. "I hoped I might speak with you. May I come in?"

"Very well." Her voice held a trace of strain, but she stepped aside.

I followed her into the sitting room. She motioned me to a chair and lowered herself to the sofa, clasped her hands in her lap.

"Now," she said, her tone as collected as her features. "Why have you come?"

I took a deep breath, trying to steady myself. "It's about what we spoke of when we last met."

Her expression remained unchanged, save for a slight inclination of her brow, a wordless invitation for me to continue.

"I can't stop thinking of it. The endless trains, the camp where they are . . ." I swallowed. "It's not terrible. *Terrible* is too common a word. So many things are terrible, but not this. I am not certain there are any words for this."

She drew a long breath. "I had not intended to tell you and regret having done so. The news was . . . fresh, even to me."

"How can you do it? Enter the district as you do, look into their eyes, knowing what is happening?"

Darkness drew its shutters over her gaze. "I do what I must."

"Surely something can be done," I said softly. "Surely it must be. Or else are we not, all of us who know the truth, complicit in this act?"

"It is a crime to offer shelter or aid to any Jewish person," Marysia said in an even tone.

"Yes." I kept my gaze level. "But perhaps there is yet a greater crime. One of which we are all guilty."

For long seconds, Marysia appraised me, her expression inscrutable. "What would you know of this?"

The fire caught fresh tinder, flickered into a blaze, red-orange and crackling, and I drew strength from its rising heat. "I know only that my father taught me if a man is drowning, you cannot simply stand on the shore and pity him. You must dive into the water and try to pull him out, even if you cannot swim, or else how can you call yourself a human being?"

At my outburst, Marysia gave a faint smile. "Ideals are rather like the bubbles in a glass of champagne. Rarely do they last longer than the first few sips."

"But where is determination born if not from our ideals?"

Unexpectedly, Marysia laughed. "Basia was right about you. She always said it was rather a good thing you never took up your father's profession."

"I want to help the people who remain behind the wall." My words came quiet but firm. "I'm willing to do whatever is necessary."

Her eyes sharpened. "And you think I know what be done?"

I swallowed, refusing to be daunted. "My aunt trusted you. That is why I've come. You are able to enter the district. I cannot, but I'm not afraid of risk."

"Well, you should be. These are lives you speak of. Theirs as well as your own. Do not handle them lightly." She paused. "Are you aware what this would require of you?"

"Perhaps no one ever really is until the moment comes," I answered honestly. "But I must do something."

She tilted her head, gaze assessing. For a moment, she remained silent. "If there came an opportunity for you to take part in such aid as you seem to believe is possible—and I'm not saying there will, mind—no one would be able to know of your involvement, least of all those you do not trust implicitly. What of your sister? Would you implicate her in your activities?"

I hesitated. "No. She mustn't be told." For her own sake, as well as the sake of the work. "I'd find another flat, if it came to it. Live on my own."

"You would leave your sister alone?"

Would I? But if it were the only way . . . "Helena would manage."

Finally Marysia nodded. "I'll see what can be arranged. If you're certain this is what you want."

The fire glowed with red heat and I let it burn away the doubt and fear, burn away everything but resolve. "I am."

Marek was gone, and the realization came with shattering loss and searing rage. Not only at his murderers but at myself for how little I had done.

For so long I had stood silently on the shore, but no more.

Who am I if I do not act? What is my life if it is only mine?

HELENA
AUGUST 22, 1942

"There's something I have to say."

I turned from the stove. Antonina had come into the kitchen. I was surprised she was home at all. Most evenings she spent at her clandestine courses and I knew not where else, sometimes arriving home with only minutes to spare before curfew.

We'd scarcely spoken since the night Leutnant Reinhardt brought me home. I expected the silence to last a day, maybe two. Antonina's temper might be quick to flare, but she didn't stay angry long. But though we'd had our share of sisterly squabbles, never had words such as we'd had that night been spoken between us.

"I thought I knew you, but not anymore. I don't know the sister who would betray me like this."

It took only the memory of those words to reopen the wound, the slash as fresh as when it had been inflicted.

I wanted to explain. About Leutnant Reinhardt and the way he made me feel things I knew I shouldn't for a man whose country was an enemy of ours, an officer in the army that had enforced occupation upon my homeland. Feelings I didn't know how to reckon with. About how lonely and frightened I'd been with no word from Tata, and with Aunt Basia gone. About how Antonina had seemed so withdrawn, different, these past weeks—longer, really—and I didn't know why. Sisters should be able to tell one another such things, should be able to tell one another everything.

But the words wouldn't come. How could they when she looked at me like I was a stranger? Worse than a stranger, for strangers, at least, didn't regard each other as she had me. The look in her eyes—the flare of anger, then the icy hardening of indifference—had been worse than any slap.

Since that night, we shared the same flat but little else. With both of us working during the day, we encountered each other only in the evenings and the early morning. The agreement to keep our distance mutual and unspoken.

Now hope sprung that maybe we could finally speak the words that needed to be said, maybe I could at last tell her all my heart held. Maybe whatever had been broken between us could be mended, made stronger even.

"What is it?" I kept my tone soft, wanting to show her I was willing to listen.

"I'll be leaving tomorrow. I've found another flat."

The words slammed into me like a fist to the stomach. I stared at her. "I don't understand. What do you mean you've found another flat?"

"I'm moving to Miodowa Street. I've already made the arrangements."

She'd made the arrangements? "Why?"

"I don't think we can live together anymore." Before, her words had come in an eruption of fury. Now, her voice was coldly, utterly composed. "It's better this way."

"But what will I do?" I hated how small my voice sounded. Small and a little desperate.

"You'll manage."

Somehow as panic rose, a swelling pressure in my chest, I found my voice. "If this is because of Leutnant Reinhardt, let me assure you, there is nothing between us, nor has there ever been. I hardly know him. If you'd listened to me the other night, I would have told you that."

Almost imperceptibly, her jaw tightened. "I simply think it's better we go our separate ways for now."

"Don't you believe me?" My voice broke.

"I don't know what to believe anymore." How calmly she said it, as if my words meant nothing to her, as if I meant nothing to her.

Suddenly it wasn't only panic mounting in my chest; it was anger, red and raging. For once, I wouldn't tamp it down or reorder it into an emotion that wouldn't wound. For once, I would speak my mind.

"Do you remember what Tata said before he left? To take care of each other for him, hold the other close. What would he think of this? It would break his heart, I know it would. That because of some ridiculous notion I'm carrying on with a German, you're—you're leaving me?"

She'd turned pale, her gaze a fissure revealing a sudden glimpse of pain. My words had found their mark. Good. I wanted them to hurt. To leave her as broken as she had me.

"It's more than that."

"What then? What is it?" I was nearly shouting now and didn't care. Better that than to dissolve into tears.

"It's . . ." Then she shook her head. "I need to pack," she said, voice weary.

Silence stifled the air as we stared at each other. The smell of scorched potatoes grew stronger. Supper would be ruined. It didn't matter.

How could it be possible to look into the eyes of someone once as close as your own heart and realize you no longer knew them at all?

Antonina turned and left the kitchen.

I almost went after her. But I couldn't make her stay, couldn't make her care. So I just stood there as the potatoes burned and my heart crumbled into dust.

ANTONINA
AUGUST 23, 1942

The quiet snap of the suitcase latching sank into the pit of my stomach.

I gave one more glance around the small bedroom, once shared by the three of us—Aunt Basia, Helena, and me. I hadn't much to pack, only what I'd accumulated since moving to Aunt Basia's, my life easily confined to a single case. A few clothes, some sheet music, a brush and hairpins. Little else.

The oval-framed photograph of Tata and Mama on their wedding day rested on the bedside table, a spidery crack marring the glass. I remembered how Helena dashed up to our flat to fetch it and how I'd gone half-mad with panic, running through choking smoke, finding her lying on the ground, bright red trickling from the wound on her temple. How we'd raced hand in hand down the burning street and how I'd grabbed her trembling fingers and held them fast as we sat pressed together in the crowded cellar.

We'd been sisters still. Neither of us had fully understood what war would bring, all it would take from us.

I drew a breath. I'd made up my mind. I wouldn't turn back now.

Marysia had come to the café a few days after I visited her. She'd spoken to her associates. They would be willing to make use of me as soon as I had a flat—she'd been most particular about my having a flat. She didn't fully explain the nature of the work, but what it would be didn't matter. Only that I'd finally be doing *something*.

I'd found a single room and a kitchen to let on Miodowa Street. I would need to count every grosz and eat only twice a day to afford the rent, but I'd manage.

This wasn't about Helena and the German officer. She'd likely been telling the truth and there wasn't anything between them, at least on Helena's side. I saw that now, the first rush of anger giving way to clarity. She shouldn't have allowed him to drive her home, but perhaps he'd given her little choice.

I didn't yet know what Marysia's associates would ask me to undertake, but the punishment for violators of the decree prohibiting Jews from leaving the ghetto and anyone else from providing them refuge or aid could not be stated more plainly. Whether you were caught giving an escaped Jew a crust of bread or a month's shelter, the sentence remained the same.

Execution.

If the police arrived at my door, I doubted they would believe my claims that Helena had no knowledge of my activities. I'd made the choice to risk my life, and whatever consequences came, I would accept. For myself, but not for my sister.

So I would do what must be done. Even if it hurt her. Even if she came to hate me.

Someday, this would all come to an end, and I would explain everything. Whether she'd forgive me when—*if*—that day came was a question I couldn't answer.

I stepped into the sitting room, carrying my suitcase and handbag. Helena sat on the sofa. Part of me hoped she'd be at church by the time I left. I could leave a note and avoid the goodbyes. But that was a coward's way out.

I set a scrap of paper on the table. "My address. In case you need anything."

Needed anything . . . like a sister who cared.

"What about the piano?" Her voice was soft, the Helena I knew. Not the one full of fire and fury who'd shouted at me when I told her I was leaving. The worst of it hadn't been the words themselves but the knowledge that I deserved every one.

Against my skin, under my blouse, lay the cool metal of the medallion.

If he could see us now, see me now, Tata's heart would surely break.

But what if I told him the truth? The real reason I had to leave. I didn't know.

I glanced at the piano, Pan Eisenberg's Bechstein. Marek had entrusted it to me. Not himself. Not a part in his life. This instrument.

None of the Eisenbergs would return to claim it now, but I couldn't leave it behind.

"I'll arrange for its removal to my flat."

Helena nodded. How young she looked in her worn navy dress, her honey-brown hair loose and uncurled.

She would be all right. But I couldn't make myself believe it.

Always I'd tried to protect her. Now I was leaving her alone in a city overrun by the enemy, rife with danger at every turn. Even if she didn't hate me, I hated myself for what I would do.

I didn't have a choice. Though I had.

And I hadn't chosen my sister.

She didn't speak, only stared at me, looking wounded and confused and so very lost. My resolve nearly cracked. It would be easy to tell Marysia I had changed my mind. She'd been right about my ideals, after all.

But I wouldn't, of course.

I stood, holding my bags, wondering what else to say, what else I could say. "I should be going."

Somehow I couldn't bring myself to voice my goodbye. Easier to pretend I was only leaving for the day.

Helena said nothing, just lifted her chin a little, pressed her lips tight.

I turned and left the room, stopping in the entrance long enough to put on my hat and drape my coat over my arm. Then I left the flat, shutting the door behind me and hurrying down the stairs, heels clicking fast.

I stepped outside and started down the sidewalk. Toward Miodowa Street and the purpose I would find there.

Then I paused, glanced over my shoulder. Back at the place I'd come to as a girl reeling in the wake of war and now left as a woman, older, harder, broken. But perhaps never more determined.

I lingered only an instant before walking away, my shoulders straight, my throat tight, trying to shut out the memory of all I left behind.

13

HELENA
SEPTEMBER 1, 1942

A week had passed since my sister packed her suitcase and left our flat on Hoża Street. In that time, there had been nothing—no messages, no knock on the door, not so much as a word. She'd forgotten to take her flannel nightdress and her lipstick, but either she hadn't noticed the lack of her belongings or had decided she wasn't coming back.

No matter what she'd left behind.

I noticed her absence less than I expected—or told myself I did. We'd come a long way from the days when we shared everything. That terrible night when it all fell to pieces had been the first time—since when?—we'd had a conversation about more than everyday tasks or something else equally meaningless, the sort of exchanges you had with a colleague or neighbor with whom you weren't on particularly intimate terms.

How had it happened? In the days since she'd gone, in the echoing spaces of solitude, the question had risen. Once we'd known each other better than anyone, the nuances and unspoken thoughts, the best and the worst of the other.

Nothing had been the same since the war. It had come between us, formed us into strangers, both to the people we used to be and to one another.

War left everything in fragments. Even bonds that should be unbreakable.

More than once I had picked up the scrap of paper with her new address and imagined going to Miodowa Street, then and there. Saying how sorry I was for whatever I had done or failed to do. Telling her I missed her. Asking her to come home. Helping her pack her suitcase.

But she'd made it clear she no longer wanted me in her life. So I didn't.

I rolled a fresh page into the typewriter, then started on the next letter. The strike of the keys combined with the droning of Herr Bürkel's telephone conversation from his office and the *thunk* of Herr Schultz dropping a stack of papers on Agata's desk.

"See to it these are filed away promptly," he said.

The door opened. I glanced up.

Leutnant Reinhardt entered the front office. Even as I fixed my eyes on the typed lines, awareness of his presence overwhelmed me.

"Leutnant Reinhardt." Herr Schultz's tone instantly went from supercilious to agreeable. "Pleasure to see you this morning."

"Herr Schultz." He nodded, then stepped past Herr Schultz and went into his uncle's office. The door shut.

I returned to the task at hand as the muted tones of male voices reverberated from beyond the closed door. Sometime later, a quarter of an hour perhaps, the door opened and Leutnant Reinhardt emerged, closing it behind him.

"I have just taken leave of my uncle." He paused. "I've been ordered to the eastern front. I'm returning home to spend a few days with my family before my departure. My train leaves Warsaw this afternoon." His tone was quiet, stiffly formal. As he spoke, he looked at me, only at me.

You're leaving now? Today?

The words caught in my throat.

"Goodbye, Herr Leutnant," Agata said.

I said nothing. I did not trust myself to speak.

He approached and placed a volume upon my desk. "You were so generous as to lend me the words of your poet. Allow me to return them to you."

I kept my eyes on the typewriter.

"Goodbye." He turned abruptly and exited the office.

It should not matter to me that he was leaving. It should not matter to me whether he returned or if he fell there, somewhere on the eastern front.

He should not matter to me.

Suddenly I rose, snatched up the book, and heedless of Agata's startled glance, walked quickly from the room.

I pushed open the door, rushed out onto the sidewalk.

"Herr Leutnant."

He turned.

I stood motionless as he came toward me, my breath coming fast. Wind tugged wisps of hair into my eyes. So much I wanted to say to him, this man who had met me in my loneliness. Shown me that a kindred heart could be found in the face of an enemy.

"Thank you," I whispered. The simple words could not convey my heart, but they were all I had to give.

We both knew I could offer nothing more.

"I . . ." He swallowed, his eyes holding mine.

Then he turned and strode toward the waiting automobile. Ducked into the back. The door shut. The engine started.

I remained on the sidewalk as the car pulled away, tires scraping the cobblestones. It continued down the street, a dark shadow passing from view.

My gaze fell on the volume in my hand. Mickiewicz's *Pan Tadeusz* in German. I opened the book. The page had been marked with a ribbon.

> When we first met each other, you and I,
> One evening, and 'twas there you said goodbye.
> In some strange way the memory of you
> Within my heart like autumn seedlings grew.

Heat rose to my eyes, blurring the stanza's final line.

> And so I knew, that if I loved at all, it must be you.

Standing on the empty sidewalk, I covered my mouth with my fist and cried, for no one was left to hear my tears.

ANTONINA
SEPTEMBER 7, 1942

"Smuggle children out of the ghetto and shelter them on the Aryan side." That, Marysia explained, was the aim she and her associates undertook.

We could not extend help to everyone. To save some, others must be left behind. But we could snatch away a few, the most vulnerable, from the abyss of the death trains.

Child or adult, it made no difference so far as I was concerned. I had failed the one who most mattered to me, now I would render aid to strangers in his place. Once I would have thrilled at the chance to defy the occupiers, now I simply did it because I could not do nothing.

Today I would begin.

I would collect a child—newly extricated from the ghetto—from a woman in Bankowy Square. I would take the child to my flat, and they would remain with me until a more permanent place could be found.

Emergency care units, Marysia called them. She'd questioned me about the block of flats to which I had moved, which floor I lived on, the various places where someone could be concealed inside my rooms. Then, after all that, she asked, "Will you use your flat for this purpose?"

I had given my yes without hesitation.

With clipped steps, I crossed the square, its expanse humming with traffic and pedestrians. A youth hawked the *Nowy Kurier Warszawski*, his hoarse voice carrying on the morning air. On the corner, a man smoked a cigarette as he loitered with his rickshaw, waiting to be hired. People hastened across the square. A tram rolled past.

But no woman with a child.

I lingered by an advertising pillar as if absorbed in reading the posters plastering the column, even as I kept the throng in the square in my periphery.

DEATH PENALTY FOR AID TO JEWS
WHO HAVE LEFT THE JEWISH RESIDENTIAL
AREAS WITHOUT PERMISSION.

The letters shouted from a newly posted notice.

The edict had been issued two days ago. To remind the city's population of the consequences should any of them dare to violate the decree by extending decency and compassion to another human being.

My stomach clenched. I was glad I hadn't eaten breakfast before leaving my flat.

A woman in a brown coat approached, a little girl hurrying at her side. I waited for them to pass, just a mother with her child on their way somewhere.

The woman paused, her gaze traveling the square.

I hesitated, the advertising pillar between us, giving her time to continue on if she wasn't here to meet me after all.

Once I approached, there would be no turning back.

I took a breath, then rounded the pillar. The woman glanced in my direction. Nothing about her diminutive height and unremarkably pretty features suggested she was engaged in anything less innocuous than buying a loin of horsemeat from the butcher's.

"Have you seen a boy in the square selling Mewy cigarettes today?"

The woman took me in, her eyes china-doll blue but piercingly astute. "He sold his last packet not ten minutes ago," she replied as Marysia said she would. "Antonina?"

I gave a nod.

"Jolanta," the woman said. She turned to the little girl standing silently beside her. "This is Danka."

The child couldn't be more than five. Her dark hair hung in two plaits, and a worn, too-small coat was buttoned over her dress.

"Hello, Danka." I offered a smile.

"Go to your auntie now, Danka."

The child lifted her eyes questioningly to the woman. "Go now, Danka," Jolanta said again, her calm voice firmer this time.

The little girl stepped forward, and I took her small, clammy hand.

"We'll send word once arrangements have been made."

I nodded.

"Take care of her." The woman's words came quiet. Then without a goodbye to the child, without another glance or word, she stepped briskly away. Likely she'd left in a hurry to avoid a scene. Still, Danka's wide eyes followed her retreating figure as she disappeared into the crowd.

I swallowed, my throat chalky. "Come now, Danka." I started across the square, keeping a firm clasp on her hand.

It wasn't far to my flat, but as I hurried the child along, her little feet in their scuffed black shoes trotting to keep pace, it seemed the route had expanded to twice the distance.

I was leading a Jewish child by the hand through a bustling thoroughfare in a part of the city inhabited by a great number of Germans, not far from the square they'd renamed Adolf-Hitler-Platz.

Despite the autumnal morning, I started to sweat.

I wanted to scoop up Danka and run until I'd reached my rooms and bolted the door behind us, but I forced myself to stride, no more in a hurry than any other housewife going about her morning errands.

The door of a shop opened and a boy hurtled out, a package under his arm, jostling into me and Danka before darting down the sidewalk without so much as begging pardon.

Clutching Danka's hand, I continued on.

"Wait." A man's voice. German. "You there, halt!"

I didn't so much as pause, keeping my head down, gripping Danka's damp little fingers.

Keep walking. Keep—

A hand grasped my elbow. My heart stopped.

I swung around.

A Wehrmacht soldier stood directly beside me, so close I smelled the cigarettes he had smoked and the waft of coffee on his breath.

Ice swept my veins.

I am on my way to the shops. The child is my niece. She is my niece and—

"You dropped this." He held out my well-worn handbag.

"Oh." The word came shaky. I took the bag. "Thank you."

His gaze fell on Danka. "What a pretty little girl." He gave a genial smile.

Danka stared round-eyed at the man in the gray-green uniform. Could he detect the mute terror on her face? How could he fail not to?

Somehow I forced my lips into a demure smile. "Thank you. Come along now, child." I kept my tone brisk, tugging Danka after me. It wasn't until I put several meters between us and the soldier that I finally glanced over my shoulder.

Only when I ascertained he wasn't following us did I suck in a breath.

I looked down at Danka, her legs pumping automatically, her breath coming in pants. I loosened my hold on her fingers. I must have been hurting her.

Time elongated into slow agony. The clamor of traffic melded with the thudding of my heart. Finally we reached the block of flats on Miodowa Street.

Through the gateway and across the courtyard. Into the building, gaze skimming the entrance before I ushered Danka after me.

If I encountered the caretaker or one of the neighbors, what then?

Rarely had I taken four flights of stairs faster. Danka stumbled at my side. We reached my flat and I rifled through my handbag for the key, the metal slick in my damp fingers as I shoved it in the door and twisted hard. The back of my neck prickled in the stillness. The door swung open. I pushed Danka inside, casting one more glance at the dim landing, as if expecting to see old Pani Nowak peering around the edge of her door watching the childless Antonina Dąbrowska ushering a little girl into her flat. But only two closed doors stared back at me, silent sentries.

I followed Danka inside, shut the door, bolted it fast. I dropped my handbag on the shelf above the rack, shrugged out of my coat and hung it up, then I took off my hat.

When I turned, Danka no longer stood beside me.

My gaze swept the room. The bed against the wall, the armoire, the piano, the table in the corner. But no child.

Panic surged.

I looked in the kitchen, found it empty, rushed back out.

"Danka," I called softly.

I knelt and checked beneath the bed, opened the armoire.

My chest hammered.

She couldn't have slipped out. I'd bolted the door.

"Danka." I wanted to shout but didn't dare raise my voice so much as an octave.

I bent and lifted the tablecloth. There, under the table, crouched Danka, her arms wrapped around her knees.

Relief washed over me.

"What is it?"

"Danka must hide from the bad men." Her voice scarcely lifted above a whisper. "Mamusia says 'Danka, hide.'"

"Did you hide under a table in the ghetto?"

She bit her lip, then nodded, her round face small and scared and lost. The fears of childhood no longer meant a dark room or a creature from a bedtime story but the daily routine of death itself. Knowing you were hunted. Knowing it was waiting.

"You're a very brave girl, Danka. But it's safe here. You don't have to hide." *At least, not right now.* The thought came grimly. "Come." I held out my hand.

She studied me, her soft eyes wary, before she crawled out from under the table.

"There now. That's better." I smiled as I knelt beside her. "Do you want some kasza?"

She tilted her head, then nodded.

Less than half an hour later, she was sitting at the table, spooning the milky porridge into her mouth. When she finished, her bowl scraped clean, I wiped away the dribble of milk at the corners of her mouth.

I carried her bowl to the kitchen. When I returned, I found her clutching her stomach. "I need to go to the toilet," she whispered.

She couldn't use the communal lavatory on the landing, but I'd anticipated this need and brought a pail. "I'm afraid this will have to do."

She perched over the pail, her features twisted in pain.

I turned away to give her privacy, but from the smell that soon rose from the pail, the child's gastric suffering was painfully apparent.

Was she sick? Or had I simply fed her starved little body too much, too soon?

When she finished, I took the pail and slipped out onto the landing. Thankfully the lavatory was unoccupied, so I ducked inside and emptied the pail.

Back inside the flat, I checked my watch and nearly groaned.

I had to be at the café in twenty minutes.

I went to Danka, who sat quietly at the table. I drew a breath. "I have to leave you here for a little while, but I'll be back before dark. You must stay in this room and not make a sound, do you understand? Don't go near the window and don't answer the door, not to anyone."

"Will the bad men come?" she asked in a soft voice.

"No." I shook my head. "But there are people who would be very angry if they knew you were here, and they would take you away, so you must be as quiet as a mouse. Can you do this for me?"

She regarded me, eyes solemn, then nodded.

"Good." I gathered up a tablet and pencil, along with a ladies' periodical from before the war, left behind by the previous tenant, and brought them to her. "You can look at this and then you can draw me a picture, all right? If you need to use the pail, it's right over there." I paused, smoothing a hand over her hair. "I promise I'll be back before dark."

I crossed the room with hurried steps, put on my coat and hat, and collected my handbag. At the door, I turned.

Danka sat at the table, watching me.

I swallowed hard. I had to go to the café. I needed the wages, and I must do everything exactly as always to give no one cause for suspicion.

I managed a smile.

Then I left the flat. On the landing, just as I did each time I went out, I locked the door.

As I hurried through the gateway and onto the street, my mind repeated a single, fervent petition.

Take care of her.

Whether I spoke to God or myself, I did not know.

ANTONINA
SEPTEMBER 7, 1942

That evening, three SS came to the café.

As a rule, the occupiers kept to their own restaurants and bars. "For Germans Only" read the signs marking the finest establishments the city had to offer. But they could, and occasionally did, dine or drink anywhere they pleased. I'd been at the piano when they entered the café and a waitress showed them to a table.

Immediately I flourished my fingers across the keys and ended midpiece.

I would play for my fellow Poles. But—call it patriotism or pure stubbornness—I refused to perform for the occupiers. They could issue their edicts and let terror do its work to coerce us into submission, but I would not give them my music.

Then one of the SS came over and asked me to play something cheerful.

It was one thing to rise quietly and retreat to the kitchen, yet another to look a German in the face and flat-out refuse.

To do exactly that would have given me no small satisfaction.

But in that moment, Danka's frightened eyes came to me, and I simply bent my head and began to play.

Midway through the piece, I realized the song I'd chosen. A popular melody made famous by Poland's darling, Hanka Ordonówna, "Love Will Forgive You Everything."

For two hours, I played while the SS ate and drank and harried the waitresses with their demands. When they finally staggered out the door, the usual time for closing had come and gone.

Alongside the other waitresses, I hurried through the tasks of clearing away the soiled tablecloths and stacking the chairs atop the tables. At last, we finished and I rushed out the door, into the night.

By the time I reached Miodowa Street, my breath came in gasps, pain twisting sharply in my side. When I stepped into the darkened flat, I took in the room with a glance and couldn't check the rise of alarm when neither table nor bed showed any sign of Danka.

I dropped to my knees and raised the tablecloth.

Under the table lay the small girl, curled up and asleep.

I touched her shoulder. "Danka. Danka, I'm back."

She stirred and opened her eyes.

"I'm sorry I'm so late, but I came as soon as I could." I kept my voice quiet. "Were you frightened?"

She sat up, her hair tangled. "I thought you would not come."

At her matter-of-fact tone, something wrenched in my chest. "I know. But I'm here now. Would you like some supper?"

I prepared potato soup and served her a small portion, hoping it wouldn't be too much for her stomach. Then I set the metal tub in the kitchen and heated kettles of water on the stove.

"Let me help you off with your things and then you can have a nice bath." I unbuckled her cracked shoes and slid off her socks, drew her dress over her head, dropping it in a pile on the floor along with her threadbare underthings.

It was painful to see the outline of her ribs against her taut skin, her arms and legs like bony little twigs.

She stepped into the bath and a tiny smile stole over her face as she trailed her fingers through the water. I combed through her hair, checking for lice as she sat in the tub. Thankfully I didn't find any. I lathered her hair and scrubbed her scalp, washed her arms and legs.

While she dried herself with a towel, I retrieved one of my blouses and a pair of woolen socks from the armoire. The blouse would fit her better than a nightdress.

Then she sat on the bed while I brushed her damp hair, careful to section the strands and tug the comb gently through each tangle. I'd tended to Helena's hair in much the same way when we'd been small. Our housekeeper had been a busy woman and had not the time or patience to bother whether we winced at her handling, so

I brushed Helena's hair myself, determined no one would hurt my sister.

"How did you get out of the ghetto?" I asked in a gentle voice as I worked the comb through Danka's strands.

She didn't answer. Perhaps she didn't understand. I wouldn't press her. It would be better, safer, for her to put the past from her mind.

"I put my feet in Uncle Chaim's boots, and he wrapped me in his coat." The words came soft. "We walked for a while and I heard the bad men, but I held tight to Uncle Chaim's belt like he told me. Then Uncle Chaim put me down, and a lady came and we went away."

From Danka's description, I gained a picture of a man, likely leaving the district as part of a labor brigade, smuggling a child in his coat past the guards at the gate. Then the woman named Jolanta waiting nearby, taking the little girl's hand, hurrying her through the streets.

I set down the comb, and she turned to face me, her freshly washed hair loose around her cheeks. "You were very brave," I said. "But you must never tell that story, not about Uncle Chaim or the ghetto or anyone you knew there. You must pretend it never happened. It's very important, Danka. Do you understand?"

Danka nodded.

"Now you must learn some prayers so you can be like the other children." Marysia had put special emphasis on this, the necessity of schooling each child in Catholic rites. When the time came for a child to be placed elsewhere, their unfamiliarity with what most learned from birth could lead to questions, and questions could lead to grave consequences.

It felt wrong, training an unformed young mind to practice a religion they had not chosen. But the alternative, the ghetto and the death trains, did not bear considering. Life mattered above all else. Someday, when this ended, they could choose for themselves which faith to embrace.

"Kneel here beside me." I knelt before the bed as I had not done since my own childhood, Danka at my side. "Now cross yourself, like this." I demonstrated, touching my forehead. "In the name of the Father." Sweeping my fingers to my chest. "And of the Son."

Then from my left shoulder to my right as I finished. "And of the Holy Spirit. Amen."

Danka gingerly mimicked my movements.

"No, like this, see." I repeated the gestures. "Yes, that's it. Now fold your hands and repeat after me. 'Our Father, which art in heaven.'"

Lamplight framed the little girl kneeling by the bed, her hands clasped under her chin as she softly repeated each line of the prayer.

If one of the guards had noticed the bulge in her uncle's coat, if she had been discovered . . .

Thinking it made me shake inside and my amen came a bit unsteady.

"Very good." I rose. "Now into bed."

She clambered onto the mattress, and I tucked the eiderdown around her, her hair dark and silken against the pillowslip. "I'll be only a moment."

I extinguished the lamp and undressed in darkness. As I approached the bed, a faint sniffling reached me. I crawled into bed and rested my head on the pillow beside her.

"Danka?"

She didn't turn around, the only sound her soft hiccupping cries.

I raised myself up on my elbow and brushed a hand over her hair. "Sweetheart, what is it?"

"I want . . . Mamusia."

"Come here." I sat up and gathered her in my arms. "Shh. It's all right." I rubbed her back, my cheek against her damp hair as her little body shook with sobs. For long minutes, I held her. "I miss my mamusia too."

Danka lifted her head, her cheeks wet. "Where is she?" she asked, suddenly curious.

I wiped her face with the back of my hand. "She died when I was little."

"My tata too. He had the red spots and then he didn't wake up anymore, and Uncle Chaim carried him out into the street and Mamusia cried."

A pang went through me, but I nodded as if she had just told the most commonplace of childish anecdotes. "You must forget all about that," I said quietly. "Shall I tell you what my tata did when I couldn't sleep? He would sit on my bed and he would sing to me, and it always made me feel better. Shall we try it?"

The years had not completely stripped her of the trust that makes children surrender their cares into older hands, and she nodded, nestling under the covers. I sifted through the layers of memory to a time when the cadence of a lullaby could set my fears to rest, when so long as my father was near, I could drift to sleep trusting I was safe.

"Ah-ah-ah, ah-ah-ah, there were two kittens." I smoothed her hair as I sang, voice soft. I hadn't heard the song in years, but the words returned as though I'd been a child only yesterday. "Ah-ah-ah, kittens two, gray and brown, oh both they are. Oh, sleep, my darling." As I sang, she quieted, her eyelids falling shut. When I finally settled beside her, she snuggled close, her body small and warm, her breath brushing my cheek.

Who was she, the woman who had given this child life, first at birth and then again when she placed her daughter into the hands of strangers? Entrusting her child to others, for they could give what she could not. Was she even now lying in a dingy room somewhere in the ghetto, her thoughts carrying her to her little one, wondering if her child slept in safety, asking herself if her choice had been right, shedding tears over the sacrifice she'd made in silence?

I had never been a mother. I didn't know what it meant to love a child so deeply you would give your very breath for theirs.

But I vowed for as long as I could, in the best way I knew how, I would give all of my life for these children.

14

HELENA
SEPTEMBER 12, 1942

Life, I had learned, is as relentless as a river's tide. It flows on, an inexorable current, and we can either huddle in a corner and weep over what has been dealt us or steel ourselves as its coursing waters carry us and save our tears for when no one can see.

I chose the latter. By now, I knew it well. People left and I went on without them. The mother whose face was only a hazy image in a photograph, Tata, Aunt Basia, Antonina.

Werner.

For so long, I had clung to people and needed them, afraid they would leave me, then watched them do just that. No more. I was through with being a little girl, always searching for someone to hold my hand.

From now on, I would stand on my own.

On a Saturday afternoon in mid-September, a knock came at the door. I dried my hands and left the kitchen, crossed to the entrance, checked the peephole. I didn't recognize the woman on the other side, but I unbolted the door.

On the landing stood a young woman about my age, her coat unbuttoned over a simple blouse and skirt, her auburn curls slightly windswept.

"Yes?"

"Are you Helena Dąbrowska?" At my nod, she went on, "I'm Jasia Konarska."

I must have given her a blank look, because she added, "My cousin, Agata Lewicka, said you were looking for someone to board with you?"

"Oh, yes." I'd happened to mention my search for a boarder to Agata, and she told me her cousin was looking for a place and offered to pass on my address. "Won't you come in?"

"Thanks." She gave a friendly smile. "I hope you don't mind my dropping by unannounced."

"Not at all." I led her into the sitting room.

She took in the space with its sofa and armchairs, the small table and chairs. "What a comfortable flat."

"It belonged to my aunt."

She raised a brow.

"She was executed more than a year ago in reprisal for the death of two German soldiers." It ached, speaking the words, even after so long.

At that, the young woman muttered an obscenity under her breath.

Well, then.

"Where were you living before?" I supposed I ought to try and learn something about the girl before agreeing to let her share my roof.

"I grew up in Praga. My family is still there, but I work in the city centre, so I wanted to find a room nearby."

It made sense. The district of Praga was on the east bank of the Wisła River, and crossing the bridge that linked it with the city, even by tram or bicycle, would take extra time.

"The bedroom is through here." I showed her out of the sitting room and opened the bedroom door, motioning her to precede me. "I thought this is where you might stay. I'll clear out my things."

She surveyed the little room with a look of satisfaction. "Where will you sleep?"

"In the sitting room. I'll be quite comfortable on the sofa, or I'll see about finding an old folding bed."

"I don't want to turn you out."

"I don't mind." Really, I didn't. I would simply be glad to find someone to help with the rent.

"You've lived alone, then? Since your aunt died?"

"My sister was living with me until recently, but she moved away." I didn't say more, and the young woman didn't ask. "There's a kitchen, so you can cook whenever you like, and the lavatory is the door just to the left." I motioned in its direction.

"How much per month?"

I named the price, half the full rent. Hopefully the two of us would be able to manage without taking in anyone else. "I'll introduce you to the building administrator so you can make arrangements to be registered as a tenant. That is, if you think it will suit."

She folded her arms, casting an assessing glance over the room. Then she faced me. "Yes." She gave a nod. "I believe it will."

"Good." Better this young woman than someone less agreeable. "It's a pleasure to meet you, Panna."

"Please. Call me Jasia." A dimple flashed. "Might as well dispense with formalities straight off, since we'll be living together."

I found myself smiling too. "I'm Hela."

"I think we'll get on just fine, Hela." Jasia grinned. "Well, how soon can I move in?"

ANTONINA
SEPTEMBER 13, 1942

The day came, as I knew it would. A false baptismal certificate had been arranged and a place found for Danka elsewhere.

I would not be told where she would be sent. My chapter in Danka's story had come to a close.

She had learned to cross herself and recite Catholic prayers. She no longer spoke of her family or the ghetto. She ate her meals without being sick afterward. She had been schooled in her part—as much as a child could be in barely a week's time—and must now play it.

But she still spoke little, her eyes etched with a somber knowing despite my efforts to make her smile. I still returned home each night to find her hiding under the table.

Now I would give her into the care of others. Not knowing how she would be looked after or if they would be kind. Would there be someone to sing her to sleep or comb the tangles from her hair?

Such things did not matter, not in a country under occupation where hunters sought their prey and betrayers waited in the shadows.

I had undertaken this role with an urgency driven by guilt, seeking to preserve lives so they might somehow stand in the place of others. I had expected to provide care, not to feel it.

But as I knelt and buttoned Danka's brown wool coat, my chest squeezed.

"Where are we going?" she asked.

I finished doing up the buttons. "To meet someone who will take you to your new home."

She tilted her head, eyes searching mine. "Why do you not want me?"

No child's eyes should hold such a look. No child should ever need to ask such a question.

I didn't need to do this. I could care for Danka, ask that whatever place had been found for her be given to another.

No. Because others still needed my aid, children like Danka who would suffer, perhaps die, if I did not give it.

"I do want you. But I can't keep you here. You must go where a place has been found. Can you understand that?"

"Mamusia sent me away. Now you. Was I not good?"

I swallowed, my throat suddenly tight. "It's not because of you. You must never think it's because of you." I reached up and touched her cheek. "Your mamusia loves you so very much, that's why she sent you away. I know it's hard to understand right now, but she did it only because she wants you to be safe."

"So the bad men don't take me away?"

I nodded, both grateful for and hating how well she understood, this child who had been taught too young that the world was not innocent and men were not kind.

"Listen to me, Danka. You must never tell anyone who you are, but you must always remember." The words came with unexpected fervency. "Keep your memories close. They are your secret. And no matter who you become, no matter what happens, no one can ever take them from you. Will you do this for me?"

Danka nodded. Whether she recognized the importance of my words now didn't matter. Perhaps one day she would return to them and they would help her to remember.

"Good." I brushed a strand of hair behind her ear, found a smile. "Now come."

We left the flat without detection. Falling rain cast sky and street in dingy shades. On we walked, Danka's hand in mine, two in a nameless throng.

Though alertness hummed, if later I had reason to remember that walk, I would not recall the risk of the moment. Instead, I would recollect the way Danka's fingers folded into mine, the tap of her little shoes at my side, the clutching in my chest as I prepared to do what I must.

We reached Ujazdowski Park, and I hurried Danka along its paths. On this inclement Sunday morning, the park had few pedestrians. Perhaps this made our presence more conspicuous than it ought to be.

Near a bench stood a woman in a dark coat and hat, her back to us. As if alerted by our footsteps, she turned.

Marysia. I had not known she would be collecting the child.

We greeted each other briefly.

"This is Danka." I glanced down at the little girl.

Danka's fingers curled tighter around mine as she looked up at Marysia, following our conversation attentively.

Marysia nodded. "Shall we go, then, Danka?"

Danka raised her face to mine, eyes unblinking. Trusting.

What is love if not tenderness? What is war if not brutal?

Sometimes both are brought together. Sometimes to be tender, love must be brutal.

I released her hand, her small fingers slipping from mine. "Go with this kind lady now, Danka. She'll look after you."

Danka hesitated, looking up at me.

"Go on." I made my tone firm, as Jolanta had done, and somehow my voice did not crack.

Danka stepped forward to stand beside Marysia, who took her hand.

There could be no other goodbye. This must be done quickly, and Danka must be kept calm.

"You'll receive another package in two days' time," Marysia said, voice quiet.

I nodded.

Then she stepped past me, leading Danka away. Danka paused, her hand in Marysia's. She looked solemnly back at me, her small face framed by her dark plaits.

Somehow, I smiled. Smiled so she could be brave.

They walked down the path, a woman and a child side by side, as rain fell from the empty gray of the sky.

I drew a shallow breath.

The first of the children. There would be others.

And I would remember them all.

15

ANTONINA
JANUARY 26, 1943

Winter stretched on, gray and grinding, the łapanki and reprisals and deportations of Poles to labor in the Reich or far worse conspiring to teach us that life under occupation could indeed stoop to new depths of misery. Despite what they printed in that rubbish they called a newspaper, the Germans were facing defeat on the eastern front, and they vented their rage on us.

In its fourth winter of the war, Warsaw had become a city of striving desperation, where even the once-decent no longer hesitated to trample over another in the struggle for sustenance and survival.

But it was the shots that resounded on the other side of the wall that stunned me more than anything else that tumultuous January.

No one really knew what had happened, but it appeared the Germans had commenced another Aktion in the ghetto, and a number of Jews, instead of allowing themselves to be rounded up for resettlement, had resisted. Word was there had been casualties among the Germans—could it be true, casualties?—and though deportations had been carried out, they ceased after only a few days.

They fought back.

How? How had they managed such a thing? How had they obtained weapons?

I didn't need to understand how it had been achieved to inwardly

152

rejoice at whatever vengeance had been meted out upon the murderers.

In the midst of it all, there were the children. Children who cried
for their mothers in Yiddish. Children who spoke not a word, cowering in the corner of my flat like small terrified animals. Children
with fair hair and blue eyes, who easily slipped into the world of the
Aryan side; others with dark curls and distinct features, whose faces
had to be bandaged when they traveled in daylight, for fear their so-
called bad looks would betray their heritage. Little boys frightened
of being bathed, perhaps told by a parent never to undress in front
of anyone lest they be betrayed. Children who hid food under their
pillows, having known nothing but hunger. Children smuggled out
by way of cellar passageways that linked a building in the ghetto to
one outside, while others passed through the gate unnoticed among
adults in a labor brigade. I usually learned this from the children,
as they recounted scattered details of their flight, just before I told
them they must never again speak of their past.

Children. Nineteen of them now.

Marysia and her colleagues could no longer enter the district to
bring children out. Their passes had been canceled in the aftermath
of the January revolt. Now we could help only those who crossed
to the other side on their own, and many did, somehow.

I learned to deal with the unexpected—a sick child who needed
to be dosed with codeine so they wouldn't cough or a neighbor
who caught me coming up the stairs with a little girl. In a flash of
inspiration, the unknown Jewish child became the daughter of a
friend who had asked me to tend her little one for a few days.

I played the piano, drowning the wails of a hysterical four-year-
old with the first movement of Beethoven's "Sonata Pathétique" or
Chopin's "Revolutionary Étude"—better the neighbors hear forbidden Chopin than a crying child. The piano intrigued the children.
For some, it brought a hazy memory of a time before the ghetto; for
others, the music calmed as the notes of Brahms's "Wiegenlied" or
Chopin's "Prelude in E Minor" slipped from my fingers.

Sometimes the child couldn't be left alone, so I rushed to the corner shop to telephone the café—I had a fever, my cousin had taken

ill. I resorted to excuses only when no other alternative presented itself. To do so too often could lead to suspicion, not to mention my dismissal. When I had to leave the flat, I passed the working hours in a state of perpetual tension, relieved only when I returned and found the child safe and undetected. Each time I left, I locked them in. I had no choice.

Soft voices lisping the Our Father and the Ave Maria. Emaciated bodies huddling in the metal tub as I boiled their threadbare garments to kill lice. Little hands clinging to mine.

I had become a mother. A mother to children who would never know my name. For a day or two, perhaps a week, I held a small life in my hands, balancing with them on that fragile, fracturable edge between survival and discovery.

Then word would come that a place had been found, followed by preparations and explanations and attempts to soothe fears, the brief encounter with a liaison, and then the child disappeared, ferried to an unknown refuge by another link in this chain of life, the length and breadth of which I did not know and was not told.

A few days, a week later, another child would be ushered into my tiny fourth-floor flat.

The daily operation of an emergency care unit.

Dusk crept over the sky as I hurried home, the sidewalks crowded with figures garbed in shabby coats, hunched against the bitter wind as they trudged with mechanical weariness. We were all weary. Of winter and privation, of occupation and endless fear.

A woman strode down the sidewalk, head slightly bent, a woven shopping bag over one arm. Something about the thin figure in a rather ill-fitting black coat gave rise to a vague sense of familiarity. Maybe I would have dismissed it, hastened on my way without another thought.

But then she raised her head.

Breath fled my lungs.

Rutka Eisenberg?

If I hadn't been certain already, the sudden recognition that flared across her own features would have confirmed it. Rutka hid it well, for in the next instant, her face again smoothed into impassive lines.

Rutka, whom I thought swallowed by the death trains, along with the rest of her family. Rutka, Marek's sister.

How could it be possible? How could she be here, outside the ghetto?

We passed each other, so close I could catch hold of her arm, force her to stop. She wouldn't meet my eyes, but her spine stiffened with an almost undetectable tension.

For months, I'd lived believing she and her family had perished in Treblinka. I couldn't allow her to walk away, not now.

I turned and started along the sidewalk, searching for a glimpse of her among the throng. She could have ducked into a shop, slipped into a gateway, anything to put distance between us.

I sent frantic glances left and right. How could I lose her so quickly?

A tram clanked to a stop and several passengers disembarked. The coat-clad figure of a woman hurried across the street, toward the waiting tram.

I quickened my pace, icy air rasping my lungs, my worn soles slipping on the snow-slick cobbles.

She'd nearly reached the tram when I stepped in front of her. Now she had no choice but to face me.

"What a surprise." I didn't say her name. She might be using another now. "It's been so long." I kept my tone light, as befitted a chance encounter between friends.

She gave a forced smile. "I suppose it has." She cast a furtive glance at the street and the people boarding the tram, then took a step forward, cutting her voice low. "What is it you want?"

"To talk, that's all."

Wind tugged chestnut tendrils around her chapped cheeks. "Please, let me alone."

Then she turned and walked away.

I should do as she asked. Rutka wasn't the only one whose existence had slanted toward the edge of danger. I had my own secrets.

But Marek's sister was the one person who could tell me what had happened to him and the rest of his family.

I had to help her or at least try. I could use my contacts to provide her with the right documents, safe lodging. Marek would not want his sister to struggle alone and without friends as she navigated the perils of the Aryan side.

I caught up to her. "Wait, please."

She paused.

"I want only to talk." Desperation crept into my voice. "I heard . . . about your family."

Finally she looked at me, and her carefully controlled features could not conceal the wasteland of her gaze. Only a flicker of time, the lapse, but it told enough.

"Come to my flat." I couldn't have extended such an invitation with a child in my care, but I had no one staying tonight. "I'll make some coffee. After that, I won't trouble you again."

She hesitated, her features obscured by falling darkness, her breath emerging like tendrils of smoke. Then she nodded.

Half an hour later, Rutka wrapped reddened hands around a steaming cup, as if to draw its warmth into herself. I took a sip from my own cup but could barely swallow the roasted acorn brew sweetened with a little saccharin.

Lamplight touched her features. There could be no doubt she was her mother's daughter with her thick chestnut hair and the same sculpted elegance to her cheekbones. But she had her brother's eyes, deep brown and piercing.

She'd been a girl, perhaps seventeen, when I visited the Eisenbergs in the ghetto.

In the years since, the spark in her gaze had turned to steel.

"How long have you been on the outside?"

She took a swallow of coffee. The cup rattled as she returned it to its saucer. "Not long."

"And Marek?"

"Still there."

I frowned. They made no sense, her words. "But—but wasn't he . . . ?"

Rutka didn't reply.

Everything within me stilled. "I tried to send a message. They said he'd been taken away. They said all of you had."

Seconds unraveled into lengthening silence before she spoke

again. "Mama and Chasia were taken when our street was block-aded. Marek went to the Umschlagplatz as soon as he heard. He offered his violin to an officer as a bribe, but they were taken directly into the trains. The next day, Tata reported voluntarily." Her voice was hollow. "He said Marek and I could manage on our own, but he and Mama had never been parted in all the years of their marriage and she needed him. So he went. A few days later, there was a raid at the factory where Marek and I were working. Marek passed the selection, but I didn't, and he wouldn't leave me. But somebody in our car had a file, and this man and I made an opening in the bars. Marek didn't want to jump. He didn't care about anything then, but I forced him and we threw ourselves out. After a couple of days, we managed to return to the ghetto."

I stared. It wasn't possible. I'd buried him, flung shovelfuls of earth over his memory, embedding it so deep the grief wouldn't break me. At first, I had cried, at night mostly, so many tears I thought my body would shatter with their rending.

I didn't weep anymore. I fought for other lives while carrying the loss of his and trying to forget.

Now, Rutka sat across from me, her words gathering in the air, in my chest, in the very marrow of my bones.

"We must find a way to get him out." My words came low, fast. "I can arrange lodging, papers, whatever you need, but it must be done as soon as possible."

"That's very generous, but—"

"But what? The deportations won't stop, not until the ghetto is empty. That is why we must act now before—before it's too late."

Rutka shook her head. "He won't go."

"He must. Now while there's yet a chance. The people on the transports, what has become of them . . ." I could not voice the words, not to Rutka. "I will help you." I paused. "Please, let me help you."

Rutka sighed. "You do not understand. But then, how could you?" She leaned forward. "Armed resistance is being organized in the ghetto. I've come to the Aryan side only for a couple of days. Then I'm going back. We'll stay and fight."

Even with what had recently transpired in the ghetto, hearing the words spoken aloud still struck like a thunderbolt. "But how? With what weapons?"

"We're using the reprieve to organize what we can. Our ranks have grown and we are unified. The Jewish Fighting Organization." A trace of pride came into her voice. "When the Germans resume deportations, we'll be ready. And we will meet them with force." How simply she spoke the words.

"But it's . . . such a fight, how can you possibly win?"

"Do you think that matters anymore?" she said, voice choked. "Our families are gone, the Allies are silent in the face of the destruction of our people. We have stood by and watched as thousands upon thousands of us have been led like sheep to the slaughter. None of us expect to survive. But we will choose how we live until we die, and our actions will be a voice to the world that the Jewish people did not silently accept their annihilation. That is how we will be remembered." She paused, her eyes like sparks of flint in her sharply boned face. "And there will be honor in our lives and in our deaths."

"And Marek?" I asked quietly.

"He is not the man you remember, Antonina. There is only the fight for him now." She pushed a strand of hair behind her ear. "He's one of our best. I'm proud of him."

For the inhabitants of the ghetto to come against the might of the German military . . . it was impossible. Nothing less than madness.

But what was the alternative? The transports? Numberless lives cast into the void of Treblinka, their cries consumed by deafening silence?

Outside the ghetto there remained a chance of life, however friable.

Dwell in secret and in silence, conceal your identity, take on another self entirely. Do whatever you must, but live.

I wanted to say it, to force Rutka to understand. I would do all I could for them, if they would only take this chance. Let others stay and fight. What purpose could there be in these two sharing the fate of the rest?

But in the wake of Rutka's words, my own dried up on my tongue. She had not chosen the ghetto, the starvation and degradation and terror, the fate of her family and countless of her people. So much she had not chosen.

Perhaps there could be no prison so binding as existence without free will. Perhaps there could be no greater freedom, no greater act of humanity, than in choosing for what one would fight and for what one would sacrifice one's very self.

Rutka had made her choice.

"Is there anything I can do?"

"Not unless you know where to find a supply of rifles and hand grenades." She gave a weary smile. "What about you? I thought your sister lived with you."

I shook my head. "Not anymore."

Rutka finished her coffee and rose. I offered her a bed in my flat for the night, but she said she was expected elsewhere. I went into the kitchen, crouched, and pried up the loose floorboard under which I kept my wages and the funds I received for the children. I wouldn't give what was meant for them, but I would give the little I had.

I took the loaf of bread I had bought that morning and returned to where Rutka stood.

"Here. Take this."

For an instant, I expected her to refuse, remembering the way her mother bristled at the prospect of accepting anything from me when I first visited the ghetto. But Rutka tucked the bread into her shopping bag. "Thank you," she murmured.

I pressed the few złoty into her palm. "However it can be of use. For what you are doing."

She hesitated, then slipped the banknotes into her handbag.

At the door, I paused, touched her arm.

"Will you tell Marek—" I swallowed. "Tell him I won't forget him."

For a moment, her eyes held mine. Then she nodded. She turned to go, then reached out, our hands clasping briefly. "Goodbye, Antonina."

I squeezed her hand, gaze steady, and told Marek's sister goodbye.

ANTONINA
MARCH 30, 1943

The quiet *rap-rap* reached into the hazy depths of sleep.

I started and opened my eyes.

The knock came again. Muted yet urgent.

Raising myself up, I blinked in the almost-darkness.

I didn't remember dozing off. I'd intended to rest for only a moment upon returning home that evening, but I'd been up until the early hours, scrubbing and mending the garments of a little boy before the liaison came to collect him. Afterward I'd had to hurry to the shops and then to the café. Was it any wonder I fell into a leaden sleep while still in my clothes?

I rose from the bed and crossed the room, swiping my tangled curls away from my cheeks. It must be nearly curfew. Who could it be at this hour? Maybe a liaison bringing a message, perhaps accompanied by a child urgently in need of shelter.

I slid back the bolt, eased open the door.

The outline of a man stood in the shadows.

"Antonina." One word, a rough whisper, bound with a thousand memories.

My breath caught. I pulled him inside, closed the door, drew the bolt with trembling hands.

His arms came around me, mine around him, my cheek against the curve of his neck, the scratchy wool of his coat under my hands, the solid warmth of his body against mine. I couldn't hold him tight enough, couldn't be close enough.

How long did we stand, drawing in the other like breath?

Time enough did not exist to hold a universe of longing.

Finally, I drew away. "Why are you here?" I could barely trust my voice.

I heard him swallow. "I needed to see you."

I led him into the room and lit the lamp, its dusky glow eradiating through the glass. Then I turned and took him in.

It had been more than two years since we sat across from each other in the Pod Gwiazdą café and he'd barricaded his life from mine. Time had hewn his features and hollowed his cheeks, but his gaze had become that of another man. Once there had been light, the kind that flowed from the cherishing of life, but it had gone out. Flint had hardened in its place, a dark and unyielding glint.

But as his eyes held mine, they lay bare the hidden places of this man whom loss had crushed and then reforged. They softened as they rested on my face, a kind of wonder in them, as if he marveled at my reality as much as I did his.

Marek had come back to me, and in that moment, nothing else mattered.

Part of me—a desperate part—wanted to hold him and ask no questions, though they rushed through my mind, pressing to be spoken.

"You left the ghetto." I did not voice the rest, the real question. *For how long?*

"I'll return tomorrow morning."

So that would be the way of it. I had lost him once only for him to now leave me again.

"I brought you these." He laid a satchel on the table, then unfastened the buckles. I came to stand beside him as he withdrew a portfolio. I opened the worn green cover. Within lay sheets of music, the staves filled with notations in Marek's hand.

The pages rustled as I turned them over. Some of the works I recognized; others were unfamiliar to me. He stood at my shoulder, looking on silently.

I raised my eyes to his. "Your compositions?"

"Yes." For an instant, his jaw tightened. "I would be grateful if you would keep them for me. They will be safer here."

"Of course." How could I refuse such a request? "If that is what you want."

He nodded. "Thank you." His glance went to the piano against the wall, and his features changed as he crossed to it. He raised the fallboard, his fingers soundlessly brushing the keys with a kind of reverence, his shoulders taut, his head bent.

Then he turned, facing me. More than two years and countless unspoken experiences lay between us, making us strangers to each other. There wasn't time to bridge such a distance.

There wouldn't be time.

There had never been, not for us.

Something cracked inside me at this loss. So much of our love had been loss layered upon loss.

Life and love, how they break us. But if I could know love, no matter its frailties and failings, or live empty of its fullness, I knew what I would choose.

"Would you like some coffee?"

At that, he gave a faint smile. "That would be good."

My own smile unfolded. "All right."

I went into the kitchen, lit the stove and filled a kettle with water, reached for the tin of ersatz coffee. I twisted the lid and realized my hands were shaking.

How could he be here, in the next room? This man who had long been a shadow invading my days and my dreams—even when I thought him gone, no matter how I fought to forget.

The creak of footsteps. I glanced up. Marek stood in the doorway. He'd taken off his overcoat and hat, his dingy shirt open at the collar, his dark hair slightly stringy and in need of a trim, though it appeared he had recently shaved.

"Rutka told you of our meeting, then?"

A nod. "She told me what you did for her."

I busied myself with setting out cups and saucers. "I did nothing." Silence lingered as the kettle heated. "How are things in the ghetto?"

He hesitated. "You know, then?"

The water came to a boil, and I took the kettle off the stove. "Rutka told me."

"We're continuing to acquire weapons, prepare our fighters."

I faced him across the tiny kitchen, the dresser at my back. "And then?"

"Deportations will resume, perhaps next week, perhaps a month from now. When they do, we will respond with armed resistance." Like Rutka, he spoke in a calm but firm voice. What they undertook had not been born in a moment, for I knew well the heat of impulse.

They had carefully considered and organized. Now they prepared, awaiting the appointed hour.

"Will you not let me help you? I could arrange papers, a place for you somewhere in the city." The words would not be held back; desperation pushed them out.

"My place is there. With the others."

"What of your life? Your music? You're so gifted—"

"That life is gone."

"But there will be an end to this one day, a future after this madness. There will be music again and—and Chopin." My voice cracked.

He shook his head. "There is no music anymore." His voice was weary, empty. "There is nothing for me but silence. For so long, we thought only about how to survive, how to preserve ourselves and our families. We told ourselves if we did not resist, we had a hope of saving some. Because of it, the innocent went to their deaths. But now we will settle accounts, bullet by bullet. Jews fighting as human beings, with dignity. With our last breaths, we will avenge this slaughter. It is our only hope," he said quietly. "Now do you understand why I must go back?"

I could only nod. The old light had gone out of his eyes, but they kindled now with another kind of fire. The saving of his own life had ceased to have meaning, but he had found a way to live, and in giving himself fully to this fight, he found a way to grieve.

Had I not done the same when I thought him gone? I had found a purpose greater than my own losses and had thrown myself into it with all of my being. Would I not do the same again? If not for the children, I would go with him, fight at his side, love him as long as I could. But I couldn't.

He did not hope for his own survival; how could I hope for us? We would never again sit by the lake in Saski Gardens, tossing bits of bread to the ducks and talking of our dreams. Never again would the notes of his violin soar while I sat in the audience, marveling that the man who could draw such aching wonder from the strings would be waiting to take me home. We would never again stroll arm in arm under streetlamps that winked like starlight.

Never again would we play "Étude in E Major" together, our Chopin.

Our future would be our memories. For us, there would never be more.

The truth pierced with sharp and certain clarity.

I would never fall asleep in his arms, never wake each morning beside him. I would never know what it meant to be his.

Morning would come and we would meet it alone.

But this night was still ours.

I went to him, my pulse beating fast in the hollow of my throat. "I thought you'd forgotten me."

He looked at me with a tenderness that made me ache. "I could never forget you."

In his eyes, I found what I had always been searching for. I had never been certain before. Sometimes I wondered if all along I'd simply been chasing him.

Now it lay exposed. His love.

And it was enough.

So I kissed him. As my lips touched his, he went still. I kissed him softly but with sureness, my last uncertainties falling away.

In the next instant, his mouth met mine with a desperation born of loneliness and longing.

We'd kissed before, but never like this, searching and urgent, clinging to the other as if to solid earth in the center of a storm.

My fingers slid down his shoulders, lingered at the buttons of his shirt.

He froze, disentangled my hands, drew away. "I should be going."

"Stay with me," I whispered. "Only tonight."

He swallowed hard.

"Just once, I want to be held." My voice broke.

He didn't say anything, just kissed me again.

"Tell me you never stopped loving me." The words came soft, a breath against his lips.

"I have always loved you."

I gave myself over to his kiss and told myself we had more than goodbye.

ANTONINA
MARCH 31, 1943

Beyond the blackout curtain, dawn stole across the sky.

Don't leave me.

The words pressed as my throat constricted, my bare arms prickling in the chill. But I didn't speak them. Not while the mattress shifted as he rose. Not while his fingers jerked the buttons of his shirt through their holes, his back to me.

If I'd pleaded or wept or accused, he might have stayed, out of decency or penance or maybe even love. I could have tried at least. But it would have been low and cheap. Though I supposed I was already both.

Even if he stayed, even if he chose safety, it would always be between us. Perhaps he wouldn't blame me or at least acknowledge he did, but it wouldn't change the guilt. His guilt, his failure. My guilt and my failure. I couldn't live with that.

He dressed quickly, as if there couldn't be enough distance between himself and this room, what we had done.

"I'm sorry."

It was the last thing he said. He looked it too, his features taut, pain raw in the depths of his eyes.

But in the end, the door closed behind him, its click sinking into my chest, hollowing me to my bones.

I curled up among the tangled sheets and pressed my eyes shut, there in the silence of my regrets.

16

HELENA
APRIL 14, 1943

Typed letters on a newly inked page. So simple yet so intangible. Nothing to grasp hold of, to grapple against, save cheap newsprint.

Even if I tore the paper to bits, even if I burned the shreds in the stove, watched them dissolve into ash and turn gray and cold, it would not change the reality of the words.

I sat on the sofa, the newspaper limp in my hands. I did not need to fix my gaze upon it, for the headline had been seared into my brain.

> **Graves of Polish Officers Discovered by the German Army at Katyn Near Smoleńsk**

It couldn't end like this. How could it end like this?

"Hela?" A familiar voice vaguely penetrated the rushing in my ears. Jasia. I thought she'd been out somewhere. When had she returned? "What's the matter? What's that you're reading?" She reached for the paper, and my lifeless hands gave way.

I knew what she would read. The discovery by the Germans of mass graves in the Katyn forest. The exhumation had revealed these to be the corpses of Polish officers captured by the Red Army.

Appended to the typed words were grainy black-and-white im-

166

ages. One of a ditch, the other of bundles laid out alongside one another.

Bodies. They were bodies.

The rustle of newsprint. Then Jasia's half-whispered voice.

"Abczyński, Jan, lieutenant. Abratowski, Tadeusz. . ."

Stop! I wanted to scream. To press my fists against my ears and shut out that soft, terrible recitation of names and ranks. But I could neither move nor speak, so I just sat.

"Czajkowski, Wiktor, captain. Dąbrowski, Stanisław, second lieutenant reserve."

Dąbrowski, Stanisław, second lieutenant.

How could four words consume a life?

A shifting of the cushion, then Jasia's warmth beside me. "Who is he?" A pause, which I did not fill. "Your father?"

I gave a dull nod.

"Oh, Hela," Jasia said softly.

Suddenly I raised my head, turning to her, desperation raking its talons across my chest. "Is it true? What's in the paper?"

The German report claimed the Soviets had murdered the officers in early 1940. When the two countries had still been allied. Now the Soviets had become their enemy and consequently our ally.

The Germans barraged us with propaganda and then expected us to believe this?

Tell me they're lying. Tell me Tata will come home.

She drew a long breath. "It's possible, I suppose. Or the Germans did it and decided to blame the Soviets to sway public opinion. No one has forgotten Stalingrad, nor will they. Roundly defeated and the Germans are still swallowing it." She paused. "There's also a chance it's entirely propaganda. The Germans certainly have enough bodies at their disposal to produce whatever evidence they want."

"It's been three years," I whispered. Three years since the last letter fell away into a chasm of silence. Three years of not knowing, of wondering, of reading three letters penned in cramped, precise script until I carried every word like pebbles in my palm. Three years of living without him, of losing the texture of his voice and the steadiness of his touch, of forgetting the way his eyes softened when he called me his kwiatuszek.

This wasn't like the news about Aunt Basia. Then all was blade-sharp, a knife-thrust of horror, followed by an icy severing.

This was night pressing around me, dark and heavy, but somehow more present. Maybe because its approach had whispered to me in the years of nothing, even as I tried to stifle it with hope.

"Three years and I didn't know. *I didn't know.*" The last words mangled by sobs, hard and raw and wrenching.

Arms came around me. Jasia didn't whisper soothing words, and if she said anything at all, I didn't hear. She just held me fast as the force of my gulping sobs nearly made me vomit.

I cried because I didn't know, and because I did, deep in that place of irrevocable certainty. I cried because I wanted to tell my father how much I loved him and because I wouldn't be able to again.

I cried because, right now, I couldn't be brave.

When I'd spent all I had within me, Jasia rose. I hunched forward, swiping tears with the back of my hand.

"Here." A glass pressed into my hand.

I glanced up. Jasia sat again on the sofa, cradling another glass. "It doesn't bring them back, but it helps." She gave half a smile. Jasia's older brother had been deported to the Reich last winter. That night, she'd had more than a few glasses, crying and cursing the Germans. Then, I had been the one to sit beside her.

I held the glass gingerly for a moment, then swallowed half. It scorched my throat, liquid fire sliding down. I coughed, wondering only briefly what Aunt Basia or Tata would say, before gulping the rest. Jasia bolted hers, then we sat, silence collecting as twilight bled into night.

For the first time since I took in the typed words—*Dąbrowski, Stanisław, second lieutenant*—I thought of my sister.

Surely in this, the loss of the man whose life had linked ours, we should be united.

Had she read the paper yet? If she didn't know, she must be told.

Most weeks, I saw Antonina at church. She'd come for Christmas Eve, but though we both made an effort, there had been a brittleness to the way we attempted to carry on as if nothing had come between us. When she'd left after we'd broken the opłatek and exchanged small gifts, loneliness had swallowed me, all the more enveloping with remembrance of what had once been.

I hadn't visited her flat on Miodowa Street, but I would go tomorrow.

I leaned back against the sofa, the glass loose in my hand, Jasia silent beside me. My eyes slid shut as hazy warmth purled through my veins. Jasia was right. It did help. I felt less.

But the pain would be in my heart until the very end.

ANTONINA
APRIL 15, 1943

Pale broth flecked with bits of potato splashed into the chipped bowl as I ladled out the soup and carried the two bowls to the table where Piotr waited. The six-year-old had been with me four days and would soon be placed elsewhere, another child passed into the hands of strangers in this perilous game of hide-and-seek.

We crossed ourselves and said the usual mealtime prayer. Piotr ate, swallow after swallow, but I had to force down every bite of bread and spoonful of soup. I ate because I knew I must, for I'd barely had anything all day, my stomach gnawing despite my lack of appetite. Finally I handed the rest of my bread to Piotr and pushed aside my bowl, unable to manage more.

"The remains of Polish officers murdered by the Bolsheviks are being exhumed from the Katyn forest . . ."

Tata was on the list. The Germans or the Soviets—one our enemy, the other our so-called ally only because our enemy had become theirs too—had killed him, my brave and steady father. For years, he had been dead while we had gone on living, the lack of certainty leaving us a thread of hope just long enough to clutch—someday he would return to us, the ones who'd never stopped waiting for him.

Last night, I'd curled up on the bed and wept, the newspaper crumpled in my hand. Piotr had laid down beside me, touching my hair with his small fingers as if to comfort me. I sobbed hot, choking tears, then rose and splashed my face with water and dried my eyes because I must. I had allowed myself to crack, but I could not shatter. Not even for such a loss as this.

The rap of knuckles against wood broke into my thoughts. Piotr's spoon clattered against his bowl as his eyes flitted to the door like a startled fawn.

"Into the armoire."

Piotr responded instantly to my whispered command, his feet pattering across the floorboards as he hurried to the armoire, just as we'd practiced. He opened the door and crawled inside, scooting to the furthermost corner and pulling up his knees. I closed the armoire, snatched Piotr's bowl, cup, and plate from the table and rushed into the kitchen, opened the dresser, and thrust the dishes inside.

My glance swept the room once more, catching the green cover of a children's storybook lying on the bed. I shoved the book under my pillow, then crossed to the door with measured steps. Drawing a slow breath, I unbolted and opened the door.

My sister stood outside, her features drawn, pale.

"Hela?"

"Hello, Tosia."

I had only to look into her eyes, the depth of emptiness they held, to know why she had come.

"Do you want to come in?"

She nodded and stepped inside. I led her into the flat. She took in the room—the bed covered in a shabby eiderdown, the small table with its poorly mended leg, the Bechstein looking out of place where it stood against the wall, the armoire nearby.

My neck prickled. The armoire drew my gaze, even as I dared not give it more than a glance.

"It's a nice room," Helena said in a strained sort of voice.

It wasn't. It was sparse and dingy. I'd never been the domestic sort. Helena had been the one who could put a room to rights with all the little touches that lent an atmosphere of home. She'd done it when we'd been girls in a house absent a mother's presence, always tidying or arranging. "To make it nice for Tata," she'd say when I teased her about putting on airs as the lady of the house.

Tata.

"I came because . . ."

"I know," I said quietly.

We looked at each other, and Helena blinked like she might cry. I wanted to say more, but what words could fill the void when your father was gone? If she cried, I wouldn't be able to keep from drawing her close and letting my own tears fall, but her eyes remained dry.

"They say"—Helena hesitated—"Jews from the NKVD are the ones who—who did it."

"The Jews aren't to blame." I hadn't meant to sound so sharp. If it had been a neighbor or someone at the café, they could say what they liked and I would say nothing. But not my sister. "As for the NKVD, that much may be true, but the rest is nothing but fallacy and propaganda."

I'd read the headline as Helena had likely done: "Horrible Crime Committed by Jews from the NKVD." The paper had contained another list, more columns, snuffed-out lives reduced to black type.

The Bolsheviks and the Jews. Both enemies of Poland, according to propaganda. Indeed, according to many Poles themselves. Certainly the NKVD—the Soviet "People's Commissariat for Internal Affairs"—counted Jews among their number, but to suggest the Jews had been the ones to murder the Polish officers . . . well, the German propagandists knew what we would be eager to believe.

"I know it is." Helena's voice was soft, a little ashamed. "It's only . . . all this time he's been . . ." She blinked hard. "I don't know how to believe it."

A noise, stifled. Like a child's sneeze.

Somehow, I kept my features empty, my eyes on Helena. She glanced toward the other side of the room—she'd heard it too. But her gaze didn't linger before returning to me. She'd been saying something about Tata. I needed to answer. Then she needed to leave.

"It's hard to think of it, I know." Did my words sound genuine? I couldn't tell with how my pulse pounded. "If there's anything you need."

A flicker of hurt, then something slipped across her features, a curtain falling over the loss she had exposed. "No," she said, her tone stiff. "There's nothing I need."

"I'm afraid I'll be late for a lecture." I hadn't attended the clandestine courses in months. I had apologized to my professors when I told them I couldn't continue my studies. *After the war*, I promised. They had been disappointed, disapproving even, telling me not to waste my talent, but I had been firm.

I forced an apologetic smile. "Some other time, perhaps."

She nodded. "Yes, another time."

I showed her to the door, our goodbye brief. Just before she left, I started to reach out, to pull her close for a moment, but she drew away and took her leave.

I closed and bolted the door. Then I rushed across the room and opened the armoire. Piotr turned his head, peering warily through the thicket of hanging garments.

"Come." I held out my hand.

He didn't take it.

"It's all right. You can come out. It's only me."

Slowly, he climbed out of the armoire, bent like an old woman.

"I sneezed." I had known Piotr four days and hadn't once heard him speak above a whisper. "I tried to keep quiet. I tried . . ." His chin quivered.

I wrapped him in my arms. "Shh," I murmured as he cried into my chest. "It's over now."

Only it wasn't.

I wasn't certain it would ever be.

17

ANTONINA
APRIL 19, 1943

The darkness splintered.

I woke with a start, my heart pounding.

Again, a piercing crack. Two, three, four, five.

Shots.

My breath came unevenly.

From where and how near? I sat, bedclothes tangled around my limbs, listening. The shooting wasn't in this building or below my window. The staccato bursts came from a distance but still near enough for their reverberations to carry.

The blackout curtain darkened the room, so I wasn't certain if night had yet given way. I fumbled with the lamp, the rush of light childishly welcome.

My watch lay on the bedside table. I picked it up.

Just after seven in the morning.

I rose and began to dress. My fingers stumbled over the buttons of my blouse as the shots went on. I ran my fingers through my curls and drew them away from my face, pushing in pins with little care. Then I slid into my coat, picked up my handbag, and left the flat.

On the second-floor landing, Pani Nowak stood talking with Pan Grabowski, the caretaker. His shirt hung untucked over his paunchy middle, and Pani Nowak still had a turban over her hair.

"Good morning, Panna Antonina." Pani Nowak greeted me.

"Good morning." I didn't usually seek out encounters with the other tenants, keeping my participation in the prattle among the neighbors to the minimum of politeness, but now I stopped on the landing. "Do you know what's happening outside? I heard shots."

"It's the ghetto," Pani Nowak said, obviously eager to encounter someone who hadn't heard the news. "The Germans entered the district early this morning, and the Jews are fighting their troops. Pan Grabowski heard it from a newsboy."

It had begun.

Even as the reality gripped me, I kept my features blank of anything but the most indifferent look of surprise. "Really?"

"I can't see why the Jews should want to defend themselves," Pani Nowak said in a peevish voice. "What can they expect to achieve by it? Do they think to force the Germans to retreat?" She laughed, as if nothing could be more preposterous.

"What does it matter?" Pan Grabowski rubbed the back of his neck. "If they manage to rid us of a few Germans, they've more mettle than I'd have credited."

"However did they get hold of weapons? Of course, *some of them* have gotten out." One would think Pani Nowak had been speaking of vermin that had managed to infest the building.

"We'll see what comes of it, I suppose," I said offhand, like it didn't much matter to me one way or the other. "I'd best be on my way."

I hastened downstairs, the echo of their voices as they continued their speculations trailing after me.

I walked quickly through the gateway and onto the street. Night had receded into a soft, clear dawn, the city stirring as it did every morning.

Monday. The second day of Holy Week.

"We will settle accounts, bullet by bullet. Jews fighting as human beings, with dignity."

Marek. Surely he fought at the forefront of the battle.

The German forces had been trained for combat. Marek was a musician. Did he even know how to fire a weapon?

How many weapons did the fighters in the ghetto actually have?

Shots resounded.

My breath shuddered. I walked faster.

174

Within minutes, I reached Krasiński Square. Near the square rose the wall, a drab barricade backdropped by a cloudless sky. Here a throng had collected, gazes turned toward the ghetto, as though the square were a cinema, the wall a silver screen, and they the ticketholders waiting for the film to begin.

I joined this cluster of the curious, edging my way nearer the wall where helmeted SS stood guard at intervals.

"What's happening?" I asked the young man at my elbow.

He turned to me. "Some Jews are exchanging fire with the Germans. I guess they think they can teach them a lesson." He gave a knowing smile, as if we shared some private jest.

I smiled too, though it ached. "Is anything known about how the fighting started?"

"German forces amassed outside the ghetto well before dawn. Marched in like troops going into battle, they say. Tanks, armored cars, cannons, the whole lot. The Jews must have been ready for them."

Dread sank into my stomach with every fresh detail.

"Likely our underground organized the whole operation. They can't have done it on their own, not the Jews."

How sure you are. You didn't hear the fire in Rutka's voice as she spoke of choosing how to live until you died. You didn't see the flash in Marek's eyes. These are the pathetic Jews you so easily dismiss. Perhaps they will surprise you yet.

But I said only, "Maybe so."

Shots spattered.

At my side, my fingers clenched into a fist. What I wouldn't give to cross the wall, to grip a rifle in my hands, to meet this battle with them shoulder to shoulder.

I must go to Marysia at once. Not all in the ghetto could fight, some were too old or too frail or too young. They would be safer in hiding places on the Aryan side.

On the other side of the wall, I vowed I would not stand by.

As I stood among the onlookers, as gunfire ripped the dawn, my heart beat with a single refrain.

Fight. Settle accounts, bullet by bullet. Light a match, so the spark of your resistance will kindle into flame, so it will burn so bright none can turn their eyes from it. All of you, fight.

ANTONINA
APRIL 25, 1943

How would I remember those days, the days when the battle raged and the smoke of the ghetto rose into the silence of the sky?

Would I recall the defiance and desperation of the fighters as they met the enemy with force, day after day? The solitude in which they waged their struggle as the city looked on, looked on and did so little to give aid? "Today them, tomorrow us," some remarked with grim faces, expecting that once they'd finished off the Jews, the Germans would turn on us next. Still, those on the other side of the wall cheered the battle—it gave them satisfaction to see ambulances ferrying wounded soldiers to the hospital, and rumors flew about the scale of the losses inflicted on German forces. Some even praised the courage of the Jewish combatants. But if one had come to their door and asked for a night's shelter, a loaf of bread, how many Gentile Poles would have provided it? How many would turn them away or turn them in?

> **THE FIGHT IS BEING WAGED FOR
> YOUR FREEDOM AND OURS!**

The appeal had been posted near the wall, a message from the Jewish Fighting Organization to their fellow Polish citizens.

> **BUT KNOW ALSO THAT EVERY CORNER OF THE GHETTO,
> JUST AS EACH HAS BEEN UP TO NOW, WILL REMAIN A
> FORTRESS; THAT MAYBE ALL OF US WILL DIE IN THE
> FIGHT, BUT THAT WE WILL NEVER SURRENDER.**

Would I recollect the lack of news and the rumors that swirled in the void? Marysia had more definitive information. On the first day, the Jewish insurgents, under a thousand men and women, had forced the Germans to retreat. Twice SS troops fled under a barrage of fire. Likely they entered the ghetto expecting the rounding up of its population to be accomplished with the usual efficiency, any resistance easily subdued.

How gloriously wrong they had been.

Would I remember the hours I stood by the wall in Krasiński Square, a solitary woman in a crowd of bystanders often dispersed by the police? Daily I went there, to learn what I could, to witness what could be seen of the battle as it unfolded, to be near Marek.

What would I remember? I knew only what I could never forget.

Easter Sunday. Church bells pealing. A perfect spring day.

I went to church—out of habit, I supposed—but I barely heard the Mass. I sat stiffly in the pew, gripping my hands in my lap, and knelt alongside everyone else, but I could not pray. I had stopped believing God listened, and if He did, it would not be to me, a woman who lied without shame, who hated the occupiers with a vehemence that ate at my chest, and who had committed fornication because I'd wanted to be held more than I'd wanted to be pure.

After Mass, I wandered through streets thronged with families turned out in their holiday finest—women in spring hats, little girls with ribbons in their hair. On this bright April morning, it would be easy to slip away from the present and its realities. To imagine myself in another world, the Warsaw of before.

I bought a bunch of flowers from a stall, marsh marigolds, and I went to Krasiński Square.

Maybe later I would ask myself why I bought the flowers. The lady selling them had called out to me. A pretty girl needed such a bouquet, she said. I'd handed her a few coins and accepted the blooms in a daze.

A festive crowd had gathered in the square. On a carousel, children and young couples spun round and round to the merry strains of a barrel organ's tune. Hawkers sold cigarettes and sweets, for with the multitude in such holiday spirits, this was a profitable place to peddle their wares.

There were field cannons too, manned by helmeted soldiers, but nobody minded them.

I went as near the wall as I dared, carrying my bunch of flowers.

The ghetto was burning. Smoke darkened the air on the other side of the wall. The flicker of fire tinged the sky red. I drew a breath and tasted ashes.

Maybe I was mistaken, maybe my mind invented what wasn't there, but it seemed a scream carried on the wind. A tearing cry, a woman screaming.

"Look." A man pointed toward the sky, his voice slurred. "The Jews are frying."

His female companion laughed, and they sauntered toward a man selling pastries.

Petals of ash floated on a haze of smoke as the organ played and the carousel spun and the people laughed.

And I stood by the wall and hid my face in the bright yellow blossoms so no one could see my heart breaking in my eyes.

The wind turned and another scent drifted, charred and strangely sweet.

My stomach convulsed. I pushed through the throng, jostling passersby. Somewhere along the way, I dropped the flowers, but I didn't stop.

Away from the press of the crowd, I bent double and vomited onto the cobblestones.

Finally, I straightened and swiped the back of my hand over my lips, bile sour in my mouth.

I returned to the wall while the revelry went on.

Marek is there. Marek and Rutka and untold others.

Battling in the flames, rising against forces that would not relent until their cry of defiance had been consumed. For they would give their last breaths to this fight, Marek and his comrades.

I blinked against the sting of smoke.

For more than two years, the Jews of Warsaw had dwelt in forced isolation, the truth that lay beyond the wall unseen, their struggle for survival rendered invisible. The invisible had become the forgotten, by the city and perhaps the world.

The carnival melody and the laughter of the crowd formed a blur in my ears, and I could only watch from the other side of the wall, watch as the ghetto burned.

HELENA
MAY 11, 1943

The instant my gaze landed on the eagle stamped in ink, I knew the truth about Jasia Konarska.

I knelt, collecting the scattered papers, working too fast to read them. I had no need. Among the typed sheets, the bold emblem of the Polish eagle could not be mistaken.

I had suspected for a long time. Jasia said she visited her parents on Sunday afternoons, but I'd gone to their flat in Praga on Sunday and Jasia hadn't been there. I'd met Jasia's family when she invited me to join them on Christmas Day, and she must have told them about my aunt and my father, because as I thanked them for their hospitality, Jasia's mother had smiled kindly and said I could visit whenever I liked. When I called, I asked if Jasia had visited recently, and Pani Konarska said they hadn't seen her since Easter. "She comes when she can," Pan Konarski had interjected gruffly, as if to deflect his wife's words.

That evening, I asked Jasia how she'd spent the day, and she told me she'd been with her parents. I didn't confront her and I certainly didn't tell her I'd been sipping tea at her mother's table that very afternoon. I figured it wasn't my business how she spent her time, but combined with her frequent absences—often she returned late, brushing the edge of curfew—and the vague answers she gave whenever I asked where she'd been, I decided either Jasia had a secret romance, was engaged in smuggling, or was in the underground.

I hadn't been sure which, but I doubted her entanglements were of the clandestine romance variety. I'd met Jasia's boyfriend, Bronek. He'd come to the flat a few times, and from the way they nestled on the sofa with their arms around each other, I doubted she'd be false to him.

That left smuggling or the underground.

My hands shook as I stuffed the papers back into Jasia's brown leather handbag. Typewritten documents, others covered with handwriting, copies of the underground publication, *Biuletyn Informacyjny*—

Footsteps.

"What are you—give me that!" Jasia snatched the bag. "What do you mean by rifling through my things?"

"I wasn't." I rose. "I knocked your bag off the table."

Jasia checked the clasp on the handbag, which I hadn't had time to fasten. It hadn't been secured before, hence why its contents had spilled. She probably didn't realize she'd gone pale. She also didn't realize I'd handled the papers—they'd all been returned to the bag by the time she came in.

"Sorry." She smiled, sheepish. "I didn't mean to fly at you like that."

"It's all right." I gave her a no-harm-done smile, then she left for her job and me for mine, and neither of us said another word about the matter.

Until that night when I knocked on the bedroom door.

"Come in," she called.

I drew a breath, straightened my shoulders, and stepped inside. Jasia lounged on the bed, winding her auburn hair into pin curls by lamplight. With her tumbling locks and vivid hazel eyes, she looked like a girl with her head full of fashion and admirers. Certainly not someone who'd carry a handbag bulging with underground documents. Perhaps that was why she was good at it. And I had no doubt Jasia was good at it, whatever she did. After all, we lived in the same flat, and she'd hidden her activities from me for months.

"Hela, why aren't you in bed?" She selected a hairpin from the scatter on her bed and pinned a curl in place.

"It's time I told you something." I swallowed. "On Sunday, I went to visit your parents. While I was there, I asked about you, and your mother said they hadn't seen you since Easter. Later, when I asked how you'd spent the day, you told me you'd been with them."

"Oh, that." Jasia calmly twisted a lock of hair. "I'm afraid I wasn't quite honest with you. I was with Bronek. The old lady he lets a room from was out, so we had the whole afternoon to be quite alone, if you know what I mean. I would have told you before, but you don't seem the sort who would approve."

She almost convinced me. But I caught the slight falter as she reached for another hairpin.

"I saw the papers in your bag."

Jasia stopped twisting, and the coil of hair fell limp.

"I know what you're doing." Instinct made me drop my voice, though none but us could hear what we spoke. "I want to join you."

My breath gave a little hitch once the words were out. How long had it been there, a desire buried in the deepest reaches of myself? Perhaps it had been born that first day, as I stood on the sidewalk while ranks of helmeted soldiers marched past, the unified stamp of their boots reverberating in my ears and in my heart that beat with love of my homeland.

The yearning—the visceral need—to rise up and resist.

Jasia stared at me without saying a word.

"I want to join you," I repeated, firmer this time, standing at the foot of the bed with my shoulders drawn back and my chin lifted, like a soldier at attention in my navy dress and wooden-soled sandals.

"You're not already involved?" Jasia finally asked in a careful voice.

"Not yet." Of course I knew of the existence of the conspiracy— what Varsovian didn't? I'd passed the buildings daubed with the emblem of the underground, a P twined with a W to form an anchor. P for *Polska*, W for *Walcząca*. Fighting Poland. Defiance embodied in sweeps of paint, its message broadcast throughout the city, no matter how soon the occupiers ordered the defacement scrubbed away. I'd read a few copies of the *Biuletyn Informacyjny* passed around discreetly by the caretaker, and of course, I heard of actions carried out by the conspiracy when the Germans posted a notice of reprisals.

My inactivity wasn't for lack of will but lack of initiation. No, that wasn't quite true. If I had been asked a year ago, before Antonina left, when I still clung to the hope of Tata's return, would I be so eager to fling myself down a path of shadows, where the ground on which one trod might give way at any turn?

I could not give an answer for the past. Only now mattered.

And I was ready.

"So many are, but it's best not to ask questions." Jasia tilted her head, studying me. "Why do you want to do this?"

I frowned. "Is it not apparent?"

"That's not what I'm asking. Why do you want to join?"

"Because I want to fight," I said simply.

War and occupation had ripped from my hands all I once held close. I had borne every blow but dealt none of my own.

No matter how great the forces against us, I had to believe they had not rendered us powerless. No matter how little we gained and how much we lost, I had to believe we could strike back.

"I wonder if you know what that means."

Did I? Maybe Jasia was right. What did I know of the realities of resistance, what it might ask of me? For so long, perhaps always, I had sought safety, for myself and the ones I loved. But just because a child shuts their eyes against the dark doesn't make it turn to day. I'd spent far too long cowering in the corner with my eyes shut.

Come what may, I would face the night.

"I can learn."

"If you are caught, you will learn something else. They are very good at what they do there, at Szucha Avenue, you know," she said, her tone hard, almost brittle. "They break your body and, slowly, your will. And they do not stop until you talk or they kill you. I know this because my fiancé, the man I was with before Bronek, they took him there." Her voice caught. My breath did too. I hadn't known Jasia had been engaged. "He didn't talk."

182

She picked up the packet on the bedside table, extracted a cigarette, put it to her lips, and flicked the lighter, her eyes falling shut as she took a long pull. She exhaled smoke, then plucked the cigarette from her lips, eyeing me as she held it between her fingers. "Still want to fight? There's no shame in saying no." Her words came quiet. "Wanting life."

Maybe this wasn't only about defying the occupiers. Maybe I wanted to believe I could be more than the frightened girl standing by helplessly as an unrelenting current dragged the ones I loved into its undertow. Maybe I wanted to prove I wasn't just the woman who gave a piece of herself to a man in Wehrmacht gray because she was achingly alone.

Maybe I wanted to believe I could give something that mattered. Maybe I wanted to believe I could be tested and not fail. Maybe I wanted to believe I could be brave.

"Yes." My answer came without hesitation, my voice stronger than I felt. "What certainty or safety is there for any of us now? To live without hope of freedom is not to live at all." I could not help but think of the ghetto, the outnumbered and poorly equipped Jewish insurgents who had battled German forces for nearly a month. I had heard the bursts of gunfire and the thunder of artillery, had witnessed smoke billowing into the sky as flames devoured the ghetto.

I had heard and felt powerless, separated from their struggle by an impenetrable wall. I did not know what had become of the thousands of Jews deported last summer, but they had been taken away by force, the resettlement carried out with cruel efficiency. In the years of occupation, none had suffered so greatly as the Jewish people.

In joining the underground, I would be fighting against the occupiers who had persecuted and oppressed all of Poland's population, but especially the Jews. However I could resist, I would.

The seconds ticked, heartbeat after heartbeat. I waited, expectation and questions and the fear I couldn't entirely check tangling in my chest.

Then Jasia nodded. "Fine, then. I'll make inquiries. Don't look so elated, and no, I don't know when you can start."

I did my best to school my features into an expression less *elated*.

"The first lesson of conspiracy, Helena Dąbrowska"—Jasia took another puff of her cigarette, its tip a flaring coal—"how to wait."

ANTONINA
MAY 12, 1943

In the shadows that painted my dreams, the ghetto burned. Only now I was within its walls, instead of beyond them. Buildings blazed against the night, fire a greedy beast. Several figures pounded down a street, all of them filthy, soot-darkened, desperate.

Marek. There was Marek. Leading the group.

I started to run, but it was as though I had been turned to stone. If I could only reach him, he would be safe. But my feet refused to move, no matter how I fought.

I screamed his name through the smoke and the flames. I kept shouting, my throat hoarse, but he pushed onward, as if he couldn't hear me, as if he wouldn't.

Suddenly he stopped, his eyes on mine, his frame silhouetted against the firelit darkness.

I stretched out my hand, shouting for him to take hold. He reached toward me, but he was too far away, a chasm between our fingertips.

A shot exploded.

I woke, shaking, my face wet.

And then my stomach heaved and I had barely enough time to stumble to the kitchen before being sick. I rinsed my mouth, crawled back into bed, and squeezed my eyes shut. Not from a wish to return to sleep but to banish the vividness of the images.

The reality that even in my dreams, I couldn't save him.

Three weeks had passed since the first shots crackled across the dawn, yet the revolt in the ghetto had not ceased. No longer was it a battle as it had been in the early days, but an annihilation. A fight where there could be only one victor and one end.

The Germans had failed to subdue the revolt through ordinary fighting tactics, had been unprepared for the resistance of the Jewish insurgents, so they turned instead to another kind of weapon and proceeded to set the district ablaze, street by street, building by building.

Life by life.

Fire succeeded where the Germans could not.

With the district surrounded, and the wall guarded day and night by patrols, now the only way out was underground, through the treacherous catacombs of the sewers. Somehow a few fighters and civilians managed to escape, emerging from manholes, covered in filth and on the verge of collapse after the grueling journey through the canals.

On the other side, the circle of associates who had been providing aid and shelter for months sought to do what we could. The flat on Miodowa Street became a "safe address" not only for children but also for those who had fled. They arrived without warning, remaining with me a day or two before moving on.

Though I never failed to ask, no one knew anything of Marek and Rutka. They had vanished among the defending and the dying as the ghetto rose up and the sky above Warsaw burned red. The spark of their resistance had kindled to flame, and its burning had consumed them.

I stood, movements wooden, and began to dress. Faintness washed over me, and I swayed, clutching the back of the chair, pressing my eyes shut against the spots that blackened my vision.

What was the matter with me? I had been sick nearly every morning for two weeks. I'd accounted it to strain or illness or the beef the butcher had probably sold to me so cheaply because it was rancid.

But it hadn't subsided. The dizziness, the exhaustion, the nausea, not only in the morning but at the scent of food or for seemingly no reason at all.

The nausea.

Oh.

I knew little about such things. But Aunt Basia had told me a bit. Enough for me to frantically try to recall . . .

It had been weeks since my last monthly. I hadn't thought anything of it, hadn't even realized until now.

Panic coated my throat.

My stomach roiled, and I clamped a hand over my mouth as I rushed to the kitchen. There wasn't anything left in my stomach, but still I retched, my body shuddering with dry heaves. I stayed there, drawing shaky breaths, my hands braced against the sink, my head bent, my tangled hair falling around my face.

It could be illness. I could be mistaken.

In my room, I lowered myself to the edge of the mattress and stared at the wall, reality as fragile as the life growing within me.

How much I wished I were mistaken.

HELENA
MAY 25, 1943

How did one prepare for their first meeting with the underground? I still wore the simple navy dress I had donned before going to Herr Bürkel's office, along with my one pair of painstakingly mended stockings. I touched up my hair in front of the bedroom mirror, securing a few pins and smoothing stray tendrils into place.

The girl staring back at me looked nervous, eyes too wide, cheeks a bit flushed, younger than my nearly twenty-two years. No one had ever taken me for the older sister; without fail, they guessed Antonina to be a year or two my senior, though we'd been born the same day.

I never admitted as much, but I'd always hated that.

I drew a steadying breath, smoothed the bodice of my dress, and left the bedroom. Jasia had given me the address when she informed me of the meeting she'd arranged. They would meet me, she said, and then we would see. That was all she told me.

I took the tram to Żoliborz and alighted at the stop, my shoes clicking with little, determined taps as I hurried along the sidewalk, hazy wisps of twilight brushing the sky.

I reached the address—a tasteful residential building, the sort repeated a hundred times in the district of Żoliborz. Had I found myself knocking at the side entrance of a building that resembled

187

the abode of a suspect in a detective novel, I would have been less surprised. The reality was somehow more unexpected.

I went inside and mounted the stairs. Third floor, first door on the left, an ordinary entrance to a flat.

I hesitated, my throat suddenly dry, then I swallowed hard and pushed the bell.

The door opened a moment later, a lanky youth on the other side. A pair of round spectacles slanted down the bridge of his nose, and brown strands fell over his high forehead. "Yes?"

"I'm . . ." The password Jasia had instructed me to give stuck in my throat. "I'm here about the drapes you're selling."

"Only curtains today," he answered and opened the door wider. "Come in."

I followed him inside. From the adjoining room came an undercurrent of voices. When I entered, accompanied by the young man with spectacles, the conversation died.

At a table in a modestly furnished room sat Jasia and a man I didn't recognize.

The youth who'd answered the door rounded the table and dropped into a chair. "This the girl you were telling us about, Nina?"

I glanced around. Nina? There wasn't another woman in the room.

"That's her." Jasia flicked ash off her cigarette.

I stood awkwardly near the entrance, my handbag clasped in both hands. "I'm—"

"No introductions." The other occupant of the table, a wide-shouldered man somewhat older than the others, spoke up, voice brusque. Chair legs rasped as he rose, facing me. "For now, you're just Nina's friend. Understood?"

I gave a wordless nod. Here Jasia must be known as Nina. I wouldn't reveal my ignorance by asking for confirmation.

"Sit, please." He motioned to a chair, waiting until I took it before resuming his seat. I perched on the edge of the chair, hands folded atop my bag, shoulders taut, like a schoolgirl at her desk the first day of a new term.

The man reached into his coat, took out a battered silver case.

He opened the case and offered it to me, the row of thin white rolls only half full. "Cigarette?"

"No, thank you." I'd never smoked and certainly had no intention of starting now and making myself sick in front of these strangers.

Calmly, he extracted a cigarette, tapped it against the edge of the case, put it to his lips. He withdrew a lighter, flicked his thumb across the wheel and lit the cigarette, cupping his hand around the flame. He took a steady pull and exhaled smoke. All the while, he watched me. Not directly, not staring in the sort of way that drew notice, but I sensed his observation nonetheless.

He had a sharp-hewn strength about his features, his jaw sturdy, the tight ridge of a scar bisecting the tan of his skin just above his left eyebrow, his gaze incisive and startlingly clear.

He took the cigarette from his lips, appraising me. "So Nina tells me you want to join us?" It wasn't really a question, but his voice made it one.

"Yes." I almost went on about how much I wanted to be of use, how I was ready to do whatever necessary so long as I could fight, but he hadn't asked for my reasons, so I didn't give them.

"She said you share a flat?"

"She lives with me, yes."

"In your flat?"

"Mine now. It belonged to my aunt," I added.

A faint lift of one brow.

"She was executed because two German soldiers were found dead. It happened near the hospital where she worked, so they took her."

The crease between his brows deepened as he took another pull of his cigarette. "Are you employed?"

"I'm a secretary."

"At a German office, Nina tells me."

I frowned. "Does that matter?"

"Your papers must serve you well in the event of a łapanka." One corner of his mouth edged upward. "Ever belong to the Scouts?"

Many of my schoolmates had been part of the Girl Guides while the boys of our acquaintance had been members of their own scouting groups. Antonina had participated briefly but had ceased attending to devote more time to music. I'd gone to meetings a couple of times as a young girl, but my shyness had been at its worst at that age and Tata hadn't forced me to continue.

"No. I was"—*too shy and awkward, so I cried and my father let me stay home*—"never interested."

He nodded, leaning slightly forward in his chair as he smoked. "Nina gives you a good recommendation. The real test is how well you perform. I'm sending you on an exercise this Saturday, starting at 10:00 a.m. You will be given three routes throughout the city. I'll write them down and you'll memorize them here, tonight. To confirm your completion of each, you'll collect items, such as writing paper from a certain stationer's. On one of these routes, you will be trailed by someone unknown to you. It is your task to detect the person following you and shake them off before reaching your destination." He paused, fixing me with his penetrating stare. "If you complete this exercise successfully, you will be sworn in."

My heart skipped a beat. This was what I had been waiting for. The chance to prove I could be useful. To earn the right to join this fight so I would no longer look upon the suffering of my homeland as I stood with bound hands.

Resolve burned as fervently as any vow.

This would be a test. I would not fail.

"May I ask," I ventured, voice quiet but steady, "to what I will be sworn in?"

Another shadow of a smile. "The army of the Polish underground. The Armia Krajowa."

HELENA
MAY 29, 1943

The sun bludgeoned my bare head, my blouse stuck to my clammy skin, and with every step, my left shoe rasped against my heel, chafing it raw. Longing for a glass of cool water consumed both my throat and my mind, but stopping for a drink wasn't part of my orders, so I didn't stop.

I had been traipsing across Warsaw for over three hours. How many kilometers I'd covered, I could only guess. Had I been setting out on these errands for my own purposes, I could have completed them far more efficiently, for in following the routes I had been given, I would traverse a street only to cross it again half an hour later in the opposite direction.

Every so often, I paused beside the window of a shop or café, using the reflection of the glass as a mirror to check if anyone slowed when I did or if I recognized anyone in the crowd from previous glances. Jasia had told me to do this, just as she'd told me to take a series of unlikely turns if I suspected I was being followed.

Once, barely half an hour after I began, I thought I spotted the person trailing me, a middle-aged man in workmen's overalls. I took a few erratic turns, my heart jumping, but when I stopped and checked my surroundings beside the window of a photographer's shop, he was nowhere to be found. I had been more disappointed than relieved.

It wasn't until after I set out that I wondered how this person—if, indeed, there would be anyone—would recognize me. The man said they'd be unknown to me, but surely they had to know me or else how could they follow me? The question remained unanswered as I had no one to ask, so I simply continued on.

I stopped beside an advertising pillar on Nowy Świat and wiped my sweaty forehead with the back of my hand, feigning interest in the weathered advertisements and notices as I scanned the throng on the sidewalks.

An old woman limped past, carrying a shopping bag. A ruddy-faced man ambled by with his coat slung over his shoulder. A boy hauled a bundle of newspapers across the street, the heel of his shoe flapping with every step.

I filed away each face like papers in the office cabinet, neatly, precisely.

On the other side of the street, a man leaned against a lamppost, a cap tipped over his eyes as he read the *Nowy Kurier Warszawski*.

Wait.

He'd been there before, when I stopped last beside a pharmacy. He had the newspaper under his arm then.

A little jolt went through me.

I continued along Nowy Świat. My spine prickled. I could be mistaken or maybe just worn out and eager for my shadow to reveal themselves, but a slowly wakening sense told me I wasn't.

I paused by a gateway, reached into my handbag, and withdrew my compact. It opened with a little snap. Slowly, I raised the mirror, patting at my sweat-damp curls. Just a girl fussing over her appearance before she met her boyfriend. I angled the compact, individual snapshots passing in the small circle. A couple arm in arm. A pair of middle-aged women. An old man tapping along with his cane.

I continued to pat inanely at my hair as I slanted the mirror to the right.

There.

He'd stopped in front of a young cigarette seller, counting out coins as he purchased a packet.

Maybe I'd been mistaken. Maybe he wasn't trailing me after all.

Then he glanced up, pocketing the cigarettes. And aimed his gaze directly at me. Only an instant, a flash in my little mirror, but I caught it.

I clicked the compact shut and dropped it into my handbag. Then I walked onward at the same even stride as before.

At the next intersection, I crossed the thoroughfare. With enough distance between us, I could slip away. If he lost sight of me, even for an instant, he'd have to guess which direction I'd gone, and if he was wrong and if I kept moving, I could evade him.

A tram clattered along the rails at full speed, a fleeting barrier between us. I snatched my moment and turned into a bystreet, hurrying along, one among only a few pedestrians. Hopefully the passing tram had prevented my pursuer from following my diversion.

Near the end of the street, I paused. Swung a glance over my shoulder.

A glimpse of the familiar cap as he rounded the corner.

I ground my jaw. I could keep walking, make any number of turns, and he would only follow. If I ran, he would simply give chase.

This isn't real. He isn't a true threat.

But he could be.

Fury rose to a boil in my chest.

No. I would not end this game as the mouse, trapped by the cunning feline. He would not best me.

I swiveled around and started in the direction from which I had come. Toward, not away from my pursuer. I set my eyes straight ahead, kept my steps steady. When we passed each other, as I knew we would, I didn't give him so much as a glance.

He would have to slow, to maintain distance between us so as not to break anonymity. I kept walking, returning to bustling Nowy Świat.

A tram came rolling along the thoroughfare, slowing as it neared an intersection.

I didn't think. I just ran, hurling myself toward the approaching tram, stretching out my hand as I grabbed for the rail. My shin cracked against metal with sparks of dazzling pain, but I clung to the rail, hauling myself aboard.

Wind swept my hair away from my cheeks as I turned just in time for a glimpse—one gloriously vindicating glimpse—of the startled features of my pursuer as the tram carried me away.

HELENA
MAY 29, 1943

"Jerzy says you did well this afternoon."

With those words, spoken in a tone of mild approbation, every second of the day's misery became something forgettable, easily borne. The purpling bruise on my shin no longer mattered, nor did my blistered heel or lingering headache.

Nothing mattered except those words, sparkling through me like just-poured champagne.

"You did well."

And I would again. And again and again, as long as it mattered. So long as I could do something.

Give me the next task, I wanted to say. *A real task this time.*

I only smiled in answer to the man who'd given me my orders. I was too flushed inside, spilling over with relief and quiet exultation.

"I had quite a time keeping up with you." Jerzy gave an easy grin. Upon entering the room a few minutes prior, I'd been startled to come face-to-face with my shadow. This close, I discovered he was simply a young man a few years my junior, tawny-haired and handsome in the sort of way that promised few members of the fairer sex immunity to his charms. Certainly not the intimidating figure my mind had conjured. He'd been there the other night but had remained in the kitchen, hence why I hadn't recognized his face before. "You do that sort of thing often?"

"No. Never."

"Well, I take off my cap to you."

At his frank admiration, my cheeks warmed.

The man to whom I had reported turned to me. "Are you ready to take the oath?"

My heart quickened. "Yes."

The lanky boy with the spectacles whom they all called Sowa—Owl—brought a small crucifix, which he handed to his superior.

"Prepare for the oath." The man before me wore a rather threadbare suit coat over a shirt open at the collar, and his dark hair was rumpled. But when he gave the order for me to stand at attention, he did so with the bearing of an officer.

I drew myself up, posture rigid, gaze straight ahead. I had never saluted before and likely did so clumsily, raising my forefinger and middle finger to eye level, the other fingers bent inward.

"Before God Almighty, I hereby put my hand on this Holy Cross, the sign of the Passion and Salvation, and I pledge allegiance to my Fatherland, the Republic of Poland."

I echoed the oath, my right hand raised, the other touching the crucifix he held.

"I pledge to steadfastly guard Her honor, and to fight for Her liberation with all my strength, even to the sacrifice of my life."

As I recited the words, standing in an unremarkable flat in Żoliborz, a heaviness came to rest upon my shoulders. I did not make this oath only before these men, I made it before my country and before God. Would I be prepared to sacrifice my very self for this cause, to keep this pledge I now made?

I did not know what it would require of me, but I knew I would give all I had.

Jerzy and Sowa stood near the table, faces solemn in the lamplight as they looked on.

"I pledge unconditional obedience to the President of Poland, the Commander-in-Chief of the Republic of Poland, and the Armia Krajowa Commander whom he appointed. I pledge to resolutely keep secret whatever may happen to me. So help me God."

I repeated the words, my voice quiet but strong.

"I hereby accept you into the ranks of the Polish Army, fighting its enemy in conspiracy for the liberation of the Fatherland." The man's words settled into me as he went on. "Your duty shall be to fight with arms in hand. Victory shall be your reward. Treason shall be punishable by death." He paused. "At ease."

I lowered my hand.

"I'm Andrzej, commander of this platoon. Now what will you be?"

I frowned.

Jerzy spoke up. "Your pseudonym. You must choose one."

"Oh." I hesitated. Always I had been Helena or Hela, the shy Dąbrowska sister, or Fräulein Dąbrowska, the dutiful secretary.

Here I could choose the woman I became.

"I'm Emilia," I said simply.

Emilia. What Polish schoolgirl had not heard the story of the noblewoman who fought to liberate her country from Russian domination during the November Uprising? She cut her hair and donned a uniform, rising to command an army of volunteers hundreds strong. Mickiewicz had written a poem in tribute to her, and she lived on in the history of Poland as an almost mythical figure.

I had no visions of myself as Emilia Plater, but I hoped in taking her name I might find a measure of her courage. Perhaps she, too, had once been afraid, but in knowing for what she fought, for whom she fought, she had become brave.

"Welcome, Emilia." Andrzej held out his hand, enveloping my fingers in a firm, warm clasp. Creases deepened around the corners of his eyes as they met mine.

"Congratulations." The young man called Sowa shook my hand, his spectacles sliding down his nose, his smile crooked.

"I'd say we got to know each other pretty well this afternoon." Jerzy gripped my hand, laughter dancing in his eyes. "Let's hope I won't spend the whole of our time together chasing you, eh?"

I smiled as I took in these earnest young men, my newfound comrades.

I would keep Helena with me. Take her out when needed.

But from this moment forward, there would always be Emilia.

20

HELENA
AUGUST 2, 1943

Don't ask, don't repeat.

The first maxim of a liaison girl for the Armia Krajowa.

If you don't ask, you won't be told. What you aren't told, you can't repeat to a Gestapo officer on the other side of a desk at Szucha 25. You quickly grew used to not asking—at least, you did after an innocent remark to a superior earned you a sharp look and even sharper words about following orders and the role of a liaison, the risk of even the simplest information and what happened at Szucha Avenue. Just like you grew used to not knowing, to being a single cog in a machinery of undisclosed breadth.

And the second maxim of a liaison?

Accustom yourself to walking.

Because you will be doing it every day, for hours. Certainly you can take a tram, but it's more difficult to escape a łapanka on a tram than on foot, and trams are often subject to searches by the police and you will be carrying things, a great deal of them, that must under no circumstances be discovered.

I supposed the third maxim of a liaison must be: *Become skilled in concealing and transporting.*

There were several ways this could be done. Some were simple. A handbag or shopping bag could become a receptacle for all sorts of papers or small parcels. Who would guess a young woman would be carrying anything less innocuous than a handkerchief? Hiding places could be designed within these items: a false bottom in a shopping bag, a hidden compartment in the lining of a handbag. We dealt in weapons too, the risk of their transportation perhaps greater than the rest, though a liaison soon learned the fruitlessness of tallying danger. A pistol could be wrapped like a parcel from a shop, ammunition or explosives bound in grease paper to resemble foodstuffs. If a policeman looked inside a woman's basket and noticed such a package, he'd assume she'd just come from the butcher's or the market. The worst he'd suspect her of was smuggling.

Other times we carried the material on our person. Tiny pockets stitched into a brassiere proved excellent for concealing bits of cigarette paper on which messages had been written. We had only to ask our male colleagues to turn their backs before we could deliver whatever we'd brought. One morning, I came into the bedroom and found Jasia binding strips of cloth around her torso. At first I'd been alarmed, thinking she'd been injured, but she'd cheerfully shown me the packets of banknotes and documents secured inside the binding. I helped her finish wrapping herself like a mummy, making certain not a single bulge could be detected, before she put on a loose-fitting dress and coat and set off on the day's deliveries.

I'd grown up in Warsaw, knew its thoroughfares and bystreets, the districts encompassing its sprawling patchwork, but it could be said I didn't truly know the city of my birth until I became a liaison. We needed to learn its streets thoroughly, carry a map in our minds, not only our own routes or the fastest way to travel from one part to another but its nuances, for a knowledge of those could be the difference between whether one slept in one's own bed that night or in a Pawiak cell. The gateways and bystreets where we could slip in the event of a łapanka. The tram routes and their stops. The streets on which we would be least likely to encounter a patrol. She could be a faithful ally, our Warsaw, if we took the time to know her.

Two months had passed since I took the oath and I'd fallen into the routine of it all—as much as involvement in the underground in an occupied country could be called routine. Though, truth be told, many of a liaison's activities were far more prosaic than an outsider might imagine.

For our work, we received training, undertaken in addition to our duties. Jasia and another man gave me and a few others instruction in such subjects as how to identify insignias on German uniforms and the various models of vehicles used by the military and police—all very useful if the Armia Krajowa intended to take action against (which meant a bullet) a certain Gestapo or SS officer. We learned how to observe an area without attracting notice and studied radio communication and Morse code, topography and firearms. For, according to Jasia, what good did it do to smuggle weapons if we hadn't the faintest idea how to use them? At present, our education was limited to assembling and dissembling a weapon, as well as basic drills, but in the seclusion of the Kampinos Forest, we would learn to shoot.

I rose early to rush around the city on liaison errands before hurrying to spend the day as Herr Bürkel's inconspicuous secretary. No sooner did the door to his office close in my wake than I became Emilia again, collecting and delivering the day's messages and reporting to my commander or attending training courses until curfew forced us to separate. Then I returned home for supper and to perform the household tasks I'd thus far neglected before studying for the courses late into the night. Such a schedule meant I managed on precious little sleep, for when I fell into bed, thoughts flurried through my mind of what the day had held and what the coming one would bring.

According to Jasia, the role of a liaison was twofold. To uphold the secrecy of individual cells and to maintain communication with the wider organization. Both were essential, not only for current operations but also in preparation for the uprising. For one day, our unseen army would step from the shadows and take up arms. We would fight and we would reclaim freedom for ourselves and for Poland. When the battle would take place and where, none of us knew, but for that day, we planned and waited and hoped.

The present duties and future preparations were the purpose for which we rose each morning, for which we trekked across the city in all kinds of weather, carrying materials that, if found, could lead to our immediate arrest and the certainty of torture and probable execution. I was almost always tired, but it was the kind of weariness that came with purpose—after existing so long in a void of meaninglessness, at last I had purpose, and I welcomed it. More than that, I flourished.

Darkness cast its net over the streets as I hurried toward Andrzej's flat. His promotion to platoon leader in the Błysk—Flash—Battalion had been nearly as recent as my initiation into the conspiracy, and I had become his liaison.

Every liaison had their intermediary points, known as postboxes, where we collected and delivered orders, money, documents, the underground press, and parcels containing items required for certain purposes. There had been more stops than usual today, and I'd twisted my ankle that afternoon when I'd jumped off a tram after a newsboy called out a warning about a łapanka on the next street. I should have waited until the driver stopped the tram, as he'd likely been about to—for among the greater part of Varsovians, the solidarity forged by occupation ran deep—allowing the passengers to disembark and evade the raid. But all I could think of was the papers in my handbag and what would happen if they were discovered. So I had jumped off before the tram had slowed and ended up sprawled on the cobbles. My ankle wasn't badly injured, only swollen, and I refused to be hindered by the result of my own stupidity.

The steady thud of boots.

A pair of German police emerged out of the shadows of the blacked-out street. The third patrol I'd encountered in a quarter of an hour. Apart from their presence, the streets were nearly deserted.

There were too many of them. They must have been preparing for a raid to begin right after curfew. They did that, raided houses when they knew their inhabitants would be home, forced off the streets by the curfew hour.

The sense had become innate, so much so that I had ceased to pay it conscious heed—always glancing over my shoulder, listening for footsteps on the stairs or the grate of tires over the street, never free of the awareness that danger was a face I might stare into at any moment. Sometimes my body betrayed me and my throat went dry and my pulse sped, but I had learned how to swallow panic and keep it down, how to lock away the fear and give it orders in my mind.

I quickened my pace. Hopefully they would think me anxious to reach home before curfew and pay me no heed. I hobbled along as fast as I could, my ankle throbbing.

In moments I'd be climbing the stairs to Andrzej's flat, gladly taking any reproof he'd mete out about my lateness, if only to be off the streets.

A firm hand grasped my shoulder.

I jerked around, heart slamming. The outline of a policeman stood out in the blue-black darkness. He was young, his jaw smooth-shaven.

He held out his hand, a wordless demand for my identity card.

My identity card. In my handbag. Which currently bulged with the orders and reports I had collected that day, as well as several copies of the latest *Biuletyn*. To attempt to find my identity card among all that illegal material in the dark without the policeman noticing, well, I already knew how it would end for me.

So I did the only thing I could think of.

I slapped him. Not hard, just a quick smack of his outstretched hand. The slap of a schoolgirl to a boy making advances.

For an instant, I glimpsed his pop-eyed stare.

Then I lifted my chin in prim schoolgirl fashion and continued down the sidewalk.

He would shoot me. He would draw his pistol and aim, and the sharp report would reach my ears in a flash of time before I went down.

I'd *assaulted* a German policeman. There could be no other conclusion.

Every nerve in my body screamed at me to run. But I kept walking with my chin up.

Seconds stretched.

I tasted my heartbeat.

Why wouldn't he just have done with it? The delay gave me time to think and I didn't want time. I wanted it over.

I continued on my way, spine erect, steps even.

Minutes passed. Surely it had been minutes.

Still no bootfalls pounded in pursuit, no crack of gunfire.

Before I reached Andrzej's building, I paused, glanced over my shoulder. If the policeman had followed me, I wouldn't lead him to my commander.

But the street stretched dark and silent.

I went inside and limped up the stairs. At Andrzej's door, I knocked.

A moment later, the door opened. I stepped past Andrzej without a word. He followed me into his single room.

"It's late."

"I know," I replied a bit more sharply than a liaison ought to speak to her superior. I unshouldered my handbag, pulled out the papers and envelopes, and deposited them on the table where a carbide lamp sat amid half-drunk cups of coffee, scattered crumbs, and an overflowing ashtray.

Low footsteps across the floorboards. "Anything the matter, Emilia?"

I shook my head, not looking up. "I passed several patrols on the way. I think there might be a raid near here tonight. We should make certain the flat is clean." All the papers I'd brought would need to be hidden or burned. I turned to face him, trying to hide a wince as pain stabbed and pulsed. "The time and place for tomorrow's briefing has been set. It's—"

"You're limping."

The abruptness of the statement made me start.

His brows lowered. "What happened? Did you hurt yourself?"

"I'm fine. It's foolish. I jumped off a tram this afternoon to avoid a łapanka. I rather missed the step." I tried to laugh.

In the lamplight, the crevice between his brows deepened. "And you've been walking about all day with your ankle like that?"

"It's all right. It doesn't hurt much." I stepped to one side and winced again. Of course he noticed. His perceptive stare rarely failed.

"Sit." He drew out a chair. "I'll make up a compress."

"There's no need to trouble yourself on my account." I was his liaison, not a child. He didn't need to tend to me.

"When did you eat last?" He scrutinized my face. Just then, my stomach gurgled. My cheeks warmed. "Then we'll have supper too," he went on easily. "I haven't had mine yet."

"I should be going. Curfew won't be long now."

He glanced at his watch. "Even if you left now, you wouldn't reach home in time. You'll sleep here tonight." He paused, considered. "I'll take the divan."

I stood, wobbling a bit on my swollen ankle, too weary to protest and dully relieved I wouldn't need to venture the streets. At least, not tonight.

His broad hands settled on my shoulders, guiding me into the chair. My legs gave way like boiled cabbage leaves.

"There, that's better." He stood, fingers in the belt loops of his trousers, looking down at me. "You rest while I see to these"—he gestured to the papers—"and then I'll make supper and that compress. I warn you though." A grin hinted at his lips. "I'm a very bad cook."

Briefly I wondered what Antonina would say if she knew I'd agreed to spend the night with a man. Not that what I did mattered to her, at least anymore. Before the war, before the conspiracy even, my scruples would never permit such a thing and with good reason. But I was a member of the Armia Krajowa now, and Andrzej was my commander. We trusted each other with our work and with our lives. Surely we could sleep on opposite sides of a room without impropriety. It wasn't as though curfew left us much of a choice. In the past years, we'd all grown used to making up a bed for a friend if they found themselves in a tight spot.

I sagged in the chair as he leafed through the papers. Later, safe under the covers, I would relive the encounter with the policeman. I always lived those moments again, danger's breath against my skin, and sometimes I shook a little, my body trembling and my eyes pressed tight. For now, I would put it out of my mind, and if I ever told any of my comrades what had befallen me, it would be as an anecdote, given with plenty of flourish and laughter.

Because that was the way of it.

The everyday life of a liaison girl in the Armia Krajowa.

21

ANTONINA
OCTOBER 20, 1943

If four years of occupation had taught us anything, it was this: never think misery has shown all it is capable of. Sometimes, in the midst of edicts and privation and fear's daily shadow, I told myself things could not possibly become worse than all we had already borne. Each time, I was proven wrong.

There was always something worse.

In the middle of October, the streets became a hunting ground. We'd grown accustomed to the arbitrary ruthlessness of the occupiers, come to expect it even, but the łapanki that swept the city and the fate of their victims left few unshaken, hardened though we had become to the commonplace of terror.

Warsaw boiled over as the police seized hundreds in the streets, on trams, in shops and cafés. Even our homes offered no more than a semblance of protection. No one remained immune; sex, age, or documents proving employment made no difference to the snatchers. Only those who labored for the German war machine went free. Everyone else—the young, the old, the ailing—boarded the lorries. They drove straight to Pawiak.

Two days after the first łapanka, a voice broke over the loudspeakers announcing the names of seven men who had been shot in reprisal for attacks on Germans. The names of a hundred hostages followed, with the warning that if any further attacks took place, ten of the hostages would be executed for every German. The next day, they broadcast a list of twenty more who had been put to death for the killing of two German soldiers, the sentence carried out in broad daylight on a blockaded street.

Days passed with more executions, more names read out in a monotone as Varsovians listened while our hearts turned to ice.

I needed to see Helena. To know she was all right, at least in that moment. So, after leaving the café—another day with few customers, everyone casting frequent glances toward the window overlooking the thoroughfare—I walked quickly toward Hoża Street as dusky twilight surrendered to darkness. I reached the familiar building and ascended the stairs to Aunt Basia's flat. Somehow I still thought of it as hers, even after so long.

On the landing, I paused, pressed a palm to my midsection, my coat open to accommodate its swell. I drew a slow breath.

I hadn't told Helena. I'd seen her last at the end of June, when it had still been possible to conceal the truth. Only in the past few months had my condition become evident with a glance and I'd discarded my constrictive girdle, for fear of causing harm to the child.

On the hand resting atop my middle, a thin band glinted. I preferred to let my condition and the ring speak for themselves, but when pressed for details, I told how my husband had returned to Kraków directly after our marriage to arrange a flat for us before I joined him. Days later, he'd been caught in a łapanka, and I'd had no word from him since. A husband somewhere in the Reich generally received sympathy. Of course, legally, I remained Antonina Dąbrowska, but it helped, having a story. Better to be a young wife alone and with child than an unmarried woman carrying shame. Maybe some of the neighbors doubted my fabricated account, perhaps whispered that I wasn't a "nice girl" and "wasn't it dreadful how the war had corrupted the morality of the young?"

Only with Marysia had I been honest. I hadn't given the truth, but I hadn't invented fiction. She hadn't pried, only asked if I wanted to continue my work—using my flat as an emergency care unit—and I assured her I did. I would not abandon it now.

It wasn't fear that kept me standing outside my sister's flat, at least not the kind that had become so ingrained I could carry it with little conscious attention to its presence. This tremulous pressure in my chest wouldn't be forced back so easily.

I couldn't go on keeping this from Helena. Though it would be far from the only secret that had come between my sister and me.

Before lifting my fist, I twisted the ring off my finger and slipped it into my handbag. Then I rapped twice and waited.

The door opened. Helena's boarder—Jasia, was it?—stood inside.

"Is my sister here?" Did I have the right, still, to call her that? I doubted it.

I didn't miss the slight widening of Jasia's eyes, and she didn't miss the way my skirt pulled taut over my belly.

"She's inside," was all Jasia said as she opened the door. She didn't offer to take my coat, so I didn't bother taking it off as I followed her into the sitting room.

Helena sat on the sofa, sedately mending a stocking.

She was here, safe. The Germans hadn't caught her in their snare.

My eyes pricked and I blinked. If anything had happened to her . . .

She glanced up, setting aside her mending as she rose. "Tosia?"

"I had to be certain you were all right. I've been so worried with the łapanki."

"I'm fine . . ." Her voice died as her gaze took in what could not be concealed.

Instinctively, I placed a hand over my rounded midsection. To shield myself or the child, I did not know.

"I'll be in the kitchen." Jasia's smooth voice entered the silence.

Helena gave an absent nod as Jasia left the room.

We looked at each other, the unspoken choking the air. Helena's lips parted, but she didn't speak.

"I didn't know how to tell you," I said softly.

"Is there . . . you're not married?"

I shook my head.

Helena lowered herself to the sofa. "Who is he?"

For so long, I'd held secrets close—some by choice, others by necessity—never free from the burden of knowing other lives depended on my ability to succeed at the part I had chosen to perform. I had ordered my life around it, and only for one night, with Marek, had I allowed myself to forget.

I was weary. So terribly weary of untruths and concealments and allowing no one to glimpse beyond the roles I played—innocuous tenant, dutiful underling at the café, the woman who stood briefly in a mother's place for each child who came to me, and now the pitiable young wife. With others, I would keep the facade in place.

With my sister, I would give the truth.

Even if only in part. Even if only about this.

I joined her on the sofa, drew an unsteady breath. "You remember Marek Eisenberg?"

Shock dawned on her face. I had never told her how I'd gone once more into the Jewish district and how it had wounded me when Marek told me not to come there again. Nor had I spoken of the ravaging loss after Marysia gave me the news that he and his family had been sent to Treblinka. Perhaps Marek had been the first real secret between us, the first of many.

"He moved to the ghetto." Her voice was quiet.

I nodded. "He was there with his sister during the revolt. The rest of his family had already been sent on a transport. Not long before the fighting broke out, he came to my flat to—to say goodbye. He—we . . ." I swallowed, remembering the way Marek had kissed me, softly first, then like a drowning man gulping in air. How he had whispered my name into my hair.

"I have always loved you."

I did not want to think of him. In loss, perhaps, we are none of us as brave as we believe ourselves to be. A better woman would know how to bind grief and love into a single strand of memory.

I was not a better woman.

"He left and—and he died in the revolt." I looked down at my clasped hands, my eyes burning. Even after the battle ended, I waited, hoping somehow Marek had been among those who escaped as the Germans laid waste to the ghetto. But only a few, so few, had survived.

For a long moment, Helena didn't speak, and I didn't meet her eyes. I waited, a knot in my throat, willing her to say something.

What did I expect her to say? *I understand*, maybe. Or, *I'm sorry*. What should a sister say?

But we hadn't been sisters to each other in so long, not really. If I had, I would never have left her. I still remembered how she looked that day, her eyes asking the question her words did not, asking how I could leave her.

I had and she had found her way alone.

For that, as with so much else, I had no one but myself to blame.

HELENA
OCTOBER 20, 1943

I couldn't stop staring at the swell of Antonina's middle. I knew little about the way of things when a woman was expecting, but from the look of it, she appeared several months along. The battle in the ghetto had broken out in the middle of April. I mentally made the calculations.

At the least, she would be six months along.

She'd been with child for six months—if not longer—and hadn't told me.

Because she'd been afraid of what I would think? Because she feared revealing the truth about her child's father?

I knew she and Marek Eisenberg had once been close. If I'd thought about it then—which I admittedly hadn't—I supposed I would have assumed Marek and his family were among the thousands who had been, as the Germans called it, resettled. Reports from the underground told the truth about their fate. They'd been sent to a camp, and there they had been forced into chambers and gassed.

I wondered if Antonina knew that.

But Marek had remained in the ghetto, among the men and women who fought on for nearly a month. The ghetto had become a vast plain of rubble. A monument to the obliteration of the Jews.

"What will you do?" Perhaps I should have other words, better ones, but I didn't.

Antonina raised her gaze. "I've told everyone my husband was deported to the Reich."

I nodded. It could be no other way. The Nazis intended to hunt and exterminate every last Jew. I doubted being half-Jewish and an infant would matter to them.

"Why didn't you tell me?" I asked quietly.

She drew a long breath. "I didn't know how."

Would I have done differently? If I had found myself pregnant, would I have gone to her?

What if it had been Leutnant Reinhardt's child?

The thought came unbidden. It had been a long time since I had thought of him. Though I had little time to think of much besides the conspiracy these days.

It could have been me. Achingly lonely with Tata gone and Antonina absent, how much would I have given for someone to hold me?

I didn't like the answer.

"I know what you must think of me." Her voice was scarcely more than a whisper.

"No, it's not like that." I stumbled over the words.

It was only a flicker, the pain that passed across her features, but I caught it still.

"I should be going." She rose. "It will be curfew soon."

I rose too.

"Be careful," she said. "Don't go out unless it's necessary. It doesn't seem the łapanki will stop."

Neither will the Armia Krajowa.

I could almost hear Jerzy's voice.

"I will." Of course I would go out, and frequently. Because nothing could be more necessary than continuing my work.

What would Antonina say if she knew what I undertook, the purpose that flowed through my veins and, in spite of the weariness of it all, filled me with life?

"I'll show myself out."

"I'm sorry, Tosia." My words came soft. "If there's anything you need, you have only to ask."

She nodded, pressed her lips together. With one hand resting on

209

her rounded middle, she looked suddenly vulnerable, frightened almost. I wanted to reach out, clasp her tight, tell her she wasn't alone, because a sister's love is forged in steel. Though the fire may rise, though it may bend, may even crack, at its heart, it endures unbroken.

But before the words could come, she left. A moment later, the door shut.

I crossed the room. Standing at the window overlooking the street, I drew back the curtain. For long moments, I stood, watching my sister's slight, hurrying figure fade into the night.

ANTONINA
OCTOBER 20, 1943

"A moment, Antonina."

I started, turned midstep at the voice. The half-open door of her flat partially hid the shadow of Pani Nowak's figure, the landing dimly murky at this hour.

How had I not noticed her standing there?

"What is it, Pani?" I asked, the ache in my head pounding like a pulse.

"Come in. I want a word."

I nearly said I was very tired, but her tone gave me pause. There was something not quite right about it. Unease traveled my spine, so I stepped inside.

Pani Nowak shut the door—deliberately, it seemed. The entrance of her flat had an odor of damp wool and the garlicky fumes of a carbide lamp.

"What was it you wanted to speak to me about?"

Pani Nowak faced me, loose-jowled features sallow in the feeble light, graying threads of hair wisping from her chignon. "I'm not one to listen to idle gossip, but there's been *talk*"—she put a knowing emphasis on the word, let a pause stretch a few seconds longer—"among the other tenants, and I thought you should be told."

"Talk about what?" I kept my voice even.

Pani Nowak cast a furtive glance around us, then took a step toward me. The sour waft of cabbage on her breath made me faintly sick. "They say you're keeping cats."

Keeping cats.

Everyone knew what it meant. Just like everyone knew what happened to people caught hiding Jews.

"Really?" I gave a laugh. How did I do it—laugh as my blood turned to ice? "That's funny, they say that about you too."

Pani Nowak looked mildly nonplussed. Likely she'd been waiting for me to give a vehement denial or stumble over my words, prove my guilt by my own actions.

"Such talk has a way of getting round and could easily reach the wrong ears."

"It's no more true of you than it is me, but people will say what they like." I kept my voice light, even as my clammy palms dug into my handbag.

"I merely thought I ought to tell you. In your condition, you must take care to avoid . . . unpleasantness."

"That's very good of you." I forced a brief smile.

"You must be missing your husband a great deal with your child expected so soon." Pani Nowak's brow pinched with concern—real or feigned, I couldn't say, but I wagered the latter. Probably every tenant in the building suspected my husband was nothing but a fabrication. Doubtless, they had a dozen stories about the identity of my child's father, and doubtless, Pani Nowak had heard and repeated every one. "Still no word?"

"No." I made my voice catch a little. "Not yet."

Pani Nowak hmmed from the back of her throat.

"I should be on my way now. Good evening, Pani."

She opened the door, and I stepped onto the landing. Though I wanted to run, I mounted the stairs slowly, and though the back of my neck burned, I didn't glance over my shoulder to check if Pani Nowak remained standing in her doorway. Somehow I sensed she did.

In the semidarkness of the fourth-floor landing, I rifled through my handbag and withdrew my key. My hands shook as I moved to insert it into the lock.

The key slipped and *pinged* onto the floor.

I bent to retrieve it, movements ungainly. I unlocked the door and went inside, then drew the bolt and checked it once more, because what if it wasn't secure?

I placed my handbag on the shelf, took off my hat and coat. I couldn't stop trembling.

Then I stepped farther into the room, its darkness permeating. I never let them turn on the electric light or have a lamp because someone might notice, and I wasn't supposed to be home.

Even in the pitch-dark, I could make out the form on the bed.

I crossed to the window and closed the blackout curtain, then I fumbled to light the lamp. There had been no electricity on this side of the street all week. The occupiers had once again cut it off. Of course they never went without in the German residential district.

I turned, shaking out the match.

Zygmunt sat up with a yawn. "Hello, Pani."

So long as the light held, he read, then once it grew too dark to make out the words, he slept. He read every book I could bring him, no matter the subject, always with an appetite for more. The books brought color to his otherwise blank existence, for in hiding one did not live so much as mark time. In the weeks the ten-year-old had stayed with me, he'd consumed some volumes three or four times.

I couldn't smile. "I'll make our supper."

Minutes later, I stood in the kitchen, slices of potato falling away under my knife as thoughts crashed one after the other.

Did they know or only suspect? How had it happened? What had started the whispers? Footsteps during the day, a voice, a cough, a child's crying?

How didn't matter. People had begun to talk, and idle talk could lead to someone taking matters into their own hands. Telling the caretaker he had better deal with the situation or they'd go to the police themselves. Or I could be approached by a blackmailer who'd threaten to denounce me if their palm wasn't satisfactorily greased.

Someone—it didn't matter who—would turn me in, and the police would come for Zygmunt . . . and for me. Boots slamming up the stairs, rifle butts battering the door. They would ransack the flat as Zygmunt cowered in the armoire, and such a hiding place would offer little protection.

If Pani Nowak had been convinced by my performance, she might drop a few words into the ears of the neighbors and put an end to their ruminations.

I doubted that. I'd seen her face. She had her suspicions and approached me to discover if they held any weight. Perhaps she'd turn me in herself.

My knife blurred as I chopped faster.

Was it safe for Zygmunt to remain here tonight? But curfew had set in, so I could do nothing until tomorrow. Then I would telephone Marysia at her office, tell her I had a package that needed to be collected without delay.

Since the revolt, children no longer came to us from the other side of the wall. Though much of the barrier still stood, beyond it stretched only ruins and desolation, a city condemned to silence. The adults and children who had managed both survival and escape had been scattered throughout the city and its environs, hiding in cellars or attics or flats or living "on the surface" with false papers, betrayal as close as an inadvertent remark, unconscious gesture, or unexpected inspection of an identity card. Children had been placed with families or in convents and orphanages.

Few guests arrived at my emergency care unit now. When they did, it was usually because their previous hiding place had been compromised—"burned," we called it—and they needed to be moved as soon as possible. Zygmunt had been among them. His "bad looks" made it difficult for him to pass on the Aryan side, so he'd remained hidden with a family until an acquaintance happened to catch sight of him. After that incident, the family concluded they could no longer take the risk, so one of our liaisons had brought Zygmunt to me.

"They say you're keeping cats."

Fear flashed along with my knife.

For when you live at the edge of a precipice, it takes only one step to fall.

22

ANTONINA
OCTOBER 21, 1943

"They've arrested Jolanta."

At Marysia's low words, a chill swept my skin.

My contact with the fair-haired woman called Jolanta had been as fleeting as with all the liaisons. The less we knew of the others, the better. But she had been one of us. I shivered in the autumn twilight.

"How?"

"The Gestapo came to her flat. There was a search. They took her away. What they know, I am not certain."

We stood in Krasiński Garden, not far from the square where the carousel had spun last spring, nearly on the border of the field of rubble that had once been the ghetto.

"Where has she been taken?"

"Pawiak. They're interrogating her at Szucha."

My stomach wrenched. Behind the barred and guarded door of Szucha 25, interrogations unfolded, the viciousness meted out spoken of in hushed tones, a kind of sacred horror.

I swallowed. "Will she . . . ?"

Betray us.

"How does one know what one will do in a place like that? When I think what those animals are doing to her." She pressed her lips together, the tendons in her neck taut. Marysia—who'd faced the strain of the past months without so much as a fissure in her control, at least none she allowed me to glimpse—had been visibly shaken.

"What do we do now?"

"Your flat can no longer be of use to us. The situation with the other tenants is too much of a risk. If you wish to continue, you must find another, well away from your current lodgings."

I nodded.

"Inform us of your address once you're settled." Marysia paused, gaze resting on my rounded middle with something akin to pity. "Look after yourself."

"I will."

Marysia approached Zygmunt. He sat on a bench nearby, bent over a book, his boyishly gawky features partially concealed by a cap. "Come," she said.

Zygmunt raised his head and rose, tucking the book under his arm. He had absorbed my explanation of why he could no longer remain at my flat with the weary wisdom of one who had long known the realities of the hunted.

The boy gave me one last glance, eyes wide, looking at once older and younger than his years, before Marysia hurried him away. I stood, gazing after them, a palm against the swell of my child.

My heart twisted.

Goodbye, Zygmunt.

I knew no more what would become of him than I did any of the children who had passed through our hands. Just as I did not know what would become of us, the ones who had given the whole of ourselves to care for them.

I had long ago ceased to pray, but if I had, my petition would surely have been, *God, help us all.*

ANTONINA
OCTOBER 22, 1943

Pounding.

I lurched awake.

Heavy footfalls on the stairs. Distant but near enough . . . near enough.

I lay motionless, my mind hazy, my breathing uneven.

Blows against a door. My door.

I raised myself in bed, blankets tangled around my legs.

My throat squeezed.

This couldn't be happening. How could this be happening?

The slam of a fist or a boot or a rifle butt against the door grew louder.

I rose. The chill of the floorboards bit into my bare feet. In the darkness, I fumbled for my dressing gown at the foot of the bed, slid my arms through the sleeves, and drew it around me as I crossed the room.

"Open the door!" Words in heavily accented Polish, muffled by the barrier of wood.

My legs moved by rote, my pulse filled my brain.

It could be a raid on the entire building, a search for illegal weapons or members of the underground. It could be nothing to do with—with . . .

Stay calm.

I unfastened the bolt, opened the door.

A figure in a dark coat and fedora bludgeoned past me, another right behind him. A third in uniform followed. Behind him stood Pan Grabowski, a wrinkled shirt half-buttoned over his undershirt. I caught a flash of the old man's stricken face before the door shut.

One of the men jerked aside the blackout curtain, the room washed in the gray light of dawn. The uniformed Gestapo agent rounded on me. He had a pistol, its barrel a toneless black. "Papers."

Wordlessly, I moved to the rack by the door and reached for my handbag. I unclasped the bag and rifled for my Kennkarte.

I handed my papers to the one who'd demanded them. He opened the small gray identity document, scanned my photograph and details while I stood, my dressing gown gaping to reveal my worn nightdress, my hair in tangles, my throat papery.

Boots tramped across the floor as the other two ransacked the flat—opening the armoire, tossing my dresses and skirts in a limp pile, throwing back the bedclothes.

They would find nothing in their search, for I had nothing.

Zygmunt is safe. The children are safe. Zygmunt is—

The Gestapo agent glanced up from my Kennkarte, his sharp eyes narrowing on me. "Antonina Dąbrowska?"

"That is correct." I forced out the words, choking on fear.

"You are registered in this flat?"

"As you see."

From the kitchen, cupboards banged, china shattered.

"You live alone?"

"Yes." In the folds of my dressing gown, my fingers curled inward.

The Gestapo agent tossed my Kennkarte on the floor, took a step toward me. "You're lying!" His face pressed close to mine, his hand grasped my upper arm. "We know there are Jews hiding here."

I swallowed. "Your men may search all they like, but there are no Jews here."

Men like these could smell fear the way a wolf catches the scent of blood on the trail of a wounded animal. To show any would only draw notice to my vulnerability and render me even more defenseless.

"You may beat about the bush now, but we have ways to make you talk."

My eyes watered at the clench of his grip.

"Look at me." Indignation flared in my voice, even as I shook inside. "Can you actually believe I would involve myself in that sort of business?"

His gaze slid from my disheveled curls to the bulge of my midsection. I stared evenly back at him.

One of the other Gestapo agents—the shortest of the three— jerked my suitcase from beneath the bed. He emptied it, leafed through the green portfolio.

"Where is your husband?"

I wet my lips. Marek's compositions cascaded to the floor in a storm of paper. "My fiancé was taken in a raid a few months ago."

"Ah." The agent interrogating me nodded, a slight curve to his lips. "A whore as well as a Jew-lover, is that it? Who knows? Perhaps you found a way to be both at once."

I turned my face away, overpowered by the stench of cigarette smoke and pomade. The short Gestapo agent shoved the armoire away from the wall with a shuddering rasp of wood. My interrogator glanced in that direction, as if expecting the removal of the armoire to reveal a hidden entrance. But all it exposed was a dark spot where the wallpaper hadn't faded.

If the Gestapo had come two nights ago, Zygmunt would have been here. He would have hidden in the armoire, and they would have found him already.

"If you take any care for what becomes of you, you'll tell us where they are. Don't think we won't find them ourselves."

"How many times must I tell you? There are no Jews here. I am alone and expecting a child and have barely enough to live upon. What would I want with Jews? Heaven knows I've no fondness for them." I might feel a pang for such a remark had I been less afraid, but I could barely think for the terror thrashing in my chest.

"They could be paying you to keep them."

They would arrest me and I could do nothing to stop them. They would interrogate me and either the torture would kill me or they would.

"May I sit down, please?" I asked in a quiet voice. I needed to think and I couldn't with my head reeling, the man's fingers digging into my bones, the crashes from the kitchen.

"Not now."

The short Gestapo agent snatched my handbag and upended it, scattering my handkerchief and little purse, my ration card and compact. He picked up the little purse and leafed through the wrinkled złoty notes before stuffing them into his coat.

"If you are not hiding Jews," said the agent interrogating me, "you must know someone who is. Tell us where to find them, and I might be convinced to leave you in peace."

"Why should I know of such a thing?"

"Stop lying." He grasped me by the shoulders and shook hard. My teeth rattled. The edges of my vision blackened.

I would faint. I would collapse to the floor and what then? They would probably take me anyway.

"It's a crime to know of Jews in hiding and not inform the authorities. If I knew of any, don't you think I would have reported the matter? I don't want trouble."

My interrogator flicked a glance as the third agent came out of the kitchen. By now, their colleague had begun pounding on the walls.

"Well, Holz?"

"There's no one in the kitchen. Only this." He held out the sock in which I kept the funds for the children hidden under a loose floorboard. I tried to remember how much had been inside—it couldn't be more than a hundred złoty. Not a large enough sum to be incriminating.

Without warning, the Gestapo agent released me. "Sit there." He motioned to a chair by the table.

I crossed the room, the floor littered with rumpled garments, strewn sheet music, and bits of down. My legs nearly buckled as I lowered myself into the chair.

The men conferred in an undertone. I strained to detect what they spoke but could make out little of the rapid exchange in German. I braced my hands against the edge of the chair and bent my head, drawing slow breaths to ease the faintness.

What more could I do to convince them of my innocence?

Innocence didn't matter these days. The names of several women and a boy of twelve had been on the list read out over the loudspeakers yesterday. Such incidents had become expected, almost ordinary. People no longer inquired of one another if there had been a łapanka, they simply asked what streets it had been on that day.

These men needed no proof to do what they would with me.

At the small, sudden jab, my breath shuddered.

I pressed a hand to my midsection. I still remembered the first time I felt that faint but unmistakable flutter within me. The tangible presence of another life. Vulnerable and part of mine.

My throat constricted.

Dear God, punish me for my sins. But my child is innocent.

Could I withstand torture or would I crack? I had to be strong, but what if I wasn't strong enough? When they took me, I must never forget two things. Tell them nothing about the others, no matter what happened.

And tell them nothing about my sister, not so much as her name.

This was why I had left Helena, that day long ago. Because if the Gestapo had come to the flat on Hoża Street and she had been there too, they would have taken us both.

Bootfalls clunked. I lifted my head.

"Consider yourself fortunate we found no one or it would have gone most unpleasantly for you."

I said nothing. Time stretched as the uniformed Gestapo agent's stare rested on me. I sat without moving, neither ducking my head nor meeting his eyes. I scarcely breathed.

Then he swiveled and strode toward the door. His colleagues followed at his heels like obedient dogs.

The door shut.

The reverberation of boots and harsh tones grew distant. Silence descended, a voice all its own. I stayed where I was, staring dully at the detritus around me.

You're safe now.

How often I had repeated those words to the children in my care. But my reassurances did nothing to alter the truth, and many, even the youngest, knew it to be so.

They did nothing to alter the truth for me either.

23

ANTONINA
DECEMBER 15, 1943

Time became a haze of white walls, hands touching me, and firm but gentle voices. And pain. Wave upon wave, swallowing in its grip, rending me from within.

"Push now." The midwife's voice. "Push."

I bore down against the unrelenting pressure, pushing as hard and as long as I could, tasting blood from my bitten lip.

"The head has crowned." The voice of the Sister assisting. "Nearly there now."

I fell back against the pillow, panting, soaked in sweat. I couldn't keep doing this. I couldn't—

Another surge of pain built, tearing through me, and I could do nothing but push. I screamed, pushed, then a flood of release. I collapsed against the pillow, breathless. The midwife bent over the bed, the Sister at her side. I raised my head. What was happening? My baby?

Then a tiny vigorous cry.

The Sister turned, her face framed by her snowy wimple, her smile broad. "You have a little girl."

A girl. I had a little girl.

"Is—is she all right?"

221

"She's fine." The midwife glanced up. "You shall see for yourself in a moment."

I rested, waiting while the women bustled about. Soon the Sister came forward, carrying a swaddled bundle. I reached out as she carefully passed my baby into my arms, the small, warm weight settling against my chest. I gazed down at the face peeking out from the blanket. My breath caught.

"Hello, little one," I whispered, tracing the curve of her cheek with my fingertip. She looked up at me, eyes wide and velvety. Her hand curled around my thumb, and I marveled at the grip of those little fingers, so perfectly formed with their dimpled knuckles and tiny pale pink seashell nails. So fragile and yet so whole.

I hadn't known what it meant before, a mother's love. Perhaps it isn't the sort of thing you truly understand until you know it in the depths of yourself. Like breath, its force fills every part of you and gives you life. Maybe it breaks you in a way, loving like this, because it has the power to wound you like nothing else, and once touched by it, you can never return to who you once were. But it also fills you with more strength than you've ever known, for there are no limits to what you would give for the life in your arms.

It doesn't end, this kind of love, and it doesn't begin. It simply is. Fathomless and immutable.

Marek's face rose to my mind, smiling in that slow and tender way. He would have held his daughter with such gentleness, and how small she would be in the cradle of his arms. Small and safe and treasured.

My daughter's face blurred as I blinked back heat.

She would be safe and treasured.

Only it would be in my arms alone.

If Marek had known, would he have chosen a different battle? Fought for life instead of vengeance?

I would never know the answer.

I raised my head as the baby nestled against my chest. "Is my sister here?"

The midwife nodded. "She's been waiting for hours."

I had asked them to telephone the shop near my sister's flat and ask someone to pass a message to Helena. I didn't deserve to expect her to be what a sister should when I had done nothing but fail her for so long, but I wanted her to know and to be waiting, if she chose.

She had. She'd come and she'd waited.

"May I see her?" I asked the midwife.

"In a little while, yes. But not for long. You need to rest."

When Helena entered the bed-lined ward where I had been moved, I lay, supported by pillows, my baby asleep. My sister looked spent, her face pale, but she had a hesitant smile at her lips as she approached.

She searched my face. "How are you?"

"I'm fine. It was . . . well, it's over now and"—I drew back the blanket slightly, my smile tremulous—"she's here."

Helena bent, taking in the face nestled in the blanket's folds—the gentle roundness of her cheeks, her slightly scrunched eyes, the downy wisps of dark hair on her tiny head.

"She's beautiful, Tosia." Awe softened her voice. "Have—have you chosen a name?"

"I'll call her Katarzyna." I could give my daughter so little of the father whose face she would never know, but I could give her his mother's name. "Katarzyna Maria."

The name of Marek's mother. With it, that of my own.

Our mother's name.

Helena smiled, reaching out to brush a fingertip over the baby's cheek. "Hello, Kasia."

How well the diminutive fit. My little Kasia.

"Would you like to hold her?"

Helena's eyes went wide. "Me?"

"You were always better with our dolls." I passed the baby into my sister's arms. "Watch her head. There."

Helena gazed down at the bundle she cradled. "It's a thing of wonder, isn't it?" she said softly. "The beginning of a life. We've come so well to know its end, and yet it doesn't only end. There's hope in that. Knowing there's more than the ending." She touched Kasia's head. "Knowing there's this."

Our gazes held. Much still lay between us, but for the first time in so long, it seemed our eyes met as sisters.

Life. How ephemeral it was. Only a breath separated one from its ending.

I lay, watching them, the two whose lives would always be stitched with mine.

And yet it begins.

And yet we begin.

24

HELENA
JULY 29, 1944

Who among us would ever forget the summer of 1944? Those momentous days when the air sweltered with heat and unspent breath, when the very wind seemed to carry the message that all we had waited so long for was coming to pass. Gone was the city that bowed its head and trudged with stooped shoulders under the burden of occupation. Warsaw strode with her chin high, and though she walked in silence, she did so with a newfound gleam in her eye, with defiance tugging at her lips. And so did we, the men and women who had lived those years, nearly five now, of bitterness and suffering and oppression.

Germany would not admit its own defeat. Oh, no, for them, officially at least, final victory still waited around the next corner—or the next strategic maneuver. But the frequency with which phrases like "planned withdrawal to prepared positions" or "straightening out the lines" appeared in their press told the truth, as did the *Biuletyn Informacyjny*. The Allied landings in Normandy the previous month, the long-awaited invasion, only gave us greater reason to hope. Then, mere days ago, word reached us of an attempt on Hitler's life by some of his own officers. Regrettably, they had failed, but if those in the highest echelons had begun to turn against their Führer, surely that must be a sign of the imminent collapse of the Reich.

The Red Army had crossed the prewar Polish border. As the summer passed, they continued to advance. Now we could hear the distant rumble of Soviet artillery. In a matter of days, they would reach Praga, the district on the eastern bank of the river, separated from the rest of Warsaw by only a bridge.

In those hot July days, German soldiers streamed through the city. This was not the procession of 1939, when ranks of shining troops paraded with the swagger of victors. This was a march of the beaten, the chaotic flight of an army in defeat. They crossed the bridges over the Wisła, withdrawing from the east, columns of soldiers trudging with vacant stares and filthy uniforms.

Civilians joined the exodus. Panicked German officials and their families packed their belongings and flooded railway stations, paying exorbitant sums to secure any means of transport out of Warsaw. No German wanted to be trapped in the city when the Soviets arrived. Poles, on the other hand, had been forbidden to board departing trains lest they take up a seat required by a German. The majority of German offices and government buildings closed. Frantic workers loaded vehicles with all manner of goods, the occupiers eager to be on their way but nearly as eager to take their ill-gotten property with them.

I had arrived at the office Monday morning to find an automobile waiting outside and Herr Schultz and even Herr Bürkel feverishly emptying drawers and filing cabinets, packing crates. "There will be no letters to type today, Fräulein Dąbrowska," he'd said by way of greeting. "We've no time to lose. The Bolsheviks will be in Warsaw any day." He cursed the Soviets while his stubby fingers fumbled the files, scattering papers all over the rich carpet he'd long ago stolen from Jews who could not protest then and would probably never return to claim it now.

I had not pretended sorrow at his leave-taking. I no longer had work, but that did not matter as much as it would have once. Now I could devote myself fully to the preparations of our army at this crucial hour.

For it was coming. The battle for which we had prepared and trained and waited.

The day when the city would rise.

For so long we had not known how it would come, whether Warsaw would be part of the insurrection, if its outbreak would happen elsewhere in the country or even occur at all. We, mere foot soldiers in an army that upheld secrecy as an imperative, knew little of the decisions of our highest commanders, save when orders reached us. We could see for ourselves the retreat of the German army, the weakness of the enemy we had readied ourselves to come against for so long.

It wasn't only about ridding ourselves of the hated occupiers but about establishing the independence of Poland and ours with her. By our actions, we would declare to the Germans, the Soviets, and the world that the citizens of Poland were prepared to sacrifice for their freedom, to take it back with both hands.

And we, the soldiers, were ready for the fight.

I strode down the sidewalk, my handbag over my shoulder, a flush in my cheeks from the heat. I had spent most of that Saturday morning traipsing across the city, and my feet hurt in my old brown oxfords, but I'd grown used to the ache. I sometimes thought of the wide-eyed girl I had been that long-ago morning, Jerzy trailing me as I roamed Warsaw on nonsensical errands. Remembering my innocence with a bit of a grin when I dragged myself up the stairs after a particularly tiring day.

The whole of Gryf Company had been placed on alert yesterday. Andrzej's platoon had spent last night concentrated in designated quarters throughout the city, waiting for orders, for the fight to begin. The day before, Thursday, the loudspeakers broadcast a proclamation of the governor of the Warsaw district ordering all men between the ages of seventeen and sixty-five to report to dig anti-tank trenches. The announcement stated that a minimum of one hundred thousand men must assemble at gathering points by 8:00 a.m. the following day. The mobilization of men for the construction of defenses, if heeded, would cripple the ranks of the Armia Krajowa in Warsaw to the point that it would be impossible to mount a revolt. Posters soon appeared, produced by the AK, urging Varsovians not to comply, and few presented themselves to dig the trenches. Fischer's order and the uncertainty regarding the consequences if the men failed to report had likely precipitated the alert.

Reaching the building, I climbed the three flights of stairs, out of breath and sweating in my light dress. I gave three sharp raps on the door. I doubted this group would welcome my arrival any more than the others after they heard the news I brought.

Sowa opened the door and I stepped inside. From the sitting room came voices.

"What a showman."

"Come on, Ryś. Let me have a go."

At the table three young men looked on as their comrade danced a knife between his splayed fingers on a slab of wood, the blade tapping as it darted around his flattened palm.

Coop up a group of boys, leave them to their own devices, and what did they do but start playing with knives? Meanwhile I'd been wearing my heels to tatters running all over Warsaw.

The others glanced up as I came in. Ryś caught sight of me and stopped.

"Where's Jerzy?" I'd expect him to be the one showing off with a knife, but the squad leader was nowhere in sight.

Ryś slid the knife into his belt. "He went out awhile ago."

"To a briefing?" The squad leaders' briefing took place this morning. Jerzy should have been back by now.

"He didn't say."

Sowa pulled out a chair, saying quietly, "Sit, Emilia. I'll bring you some water."

"Do you have orders for us?" Ryś leaned forward, voice eager.

"Not the ones you want." I drew a long breath. "It appears it was a false alarm. You're to remain here until further notice. The platoon is still on alert."

Ryś slammed a fist on the table. "These blasted delays. What do they wait for? Can't they see the Krauts are in retreat? Every day we waste sitting idle is a day we could be fighting."

Sowa returned and handed me a glass of water.

I gave him a grateful smile. "Thanks."

One corner of his mouth tipped upward.

I swallowed the water in two gulps, the coolness easing my parched throat.

"Surely our leaders must see the hour to act is now." A knock at the door interrupted Ryś's fuming.

Sowa rose. A moment later, he returned, accompanied by Jerzy.

"Afternoon, everyone." He wore a cap at a jaunty slant and a belted trench coat and appeared none the worse for whatever had befallen him.

"Where have you been?"

Had Ryś not spoken first, I would have asked the same question.

"Is that any way to address your squad leader?" Jerzy said with mock severity, then he grinned. "Look what I've brought." He set the long, thin package he carried on the table.

Chairs scraped as the young men clustered around. Even Sowa came over for a look. Brown paper rustled as Jerzy drew back the wrapping, revealing the glossy stock and ebony barrel of a rifle. I tilted my head for a closer look. A Mauser—a Karabiner 98k, I guessed. Standard-issue for the German army, bolt-action, highly effective.

Ryś gave a low whistle.

"What a prize."

"Where did you get it?"

"Bought it off a Kraut," Jerzy said, clearly pleased with himself and his acquisition. "He was happy to part with it for a few bottles of bimber."

What had Jerzy been thinking, bartering moonshine for a rifle from a German? Word had circulated that among the defeated troops one could find those amenable to such exchanges. But for Jerzy to set off on his own, without orders, was nothing less than sheer recklessness.

The soldier could just as well have shot him as given him the weapon and kept the bimber in the bargain.

Since the Kraut hadn't, I might very well do the job myself.

"If you can bear to tear yourself away, Jerzy"—I raised my voice to be heard above the exclamations of admiration interspersed with Jerzy's tale of his encounter with the soldier—"I'd like a word."

"Certainly." Jerzy followed me into the kitchen, leaving the others still gathered around the rifle. "Well?" He leaned against the dresser. "Do you have orders for me?"

"You have been instructed to leave this flat only to attend briefings or carry out specific directives." Fury leaked into my low-voiced words.

"Haven't you heard? Fischer has ordered us to dig trenches. I had to get my spade." Jerzy mimed a shoveling motion, then winked. On another day, I might have let his charms cajole me, but not today.

I folded my arms. "I should report you to your commander." Andrzej would no doubt have Jerzy by the collar by now. Jerzy was a good squad leader, respected by the others, but he had a streak of daring clearly made worse by restlessness.

At that, Jerzy sobered. "And will you?"

"No. You will tell him yourself." I sighed. "Now, of all times, you ought to show some discipline."

"We need weapons. We haven't nearly enough to arm our platoon."

"Unless you're given orders to procure them, it's not up to you. This is not the time for heedlessness. The fight will come soon enough."

Jerzy swallowed, his frank stare holding mine. "Will it?"

Silence lingered, heavy with the questions and fears we did not speak. We waited, nerves and patience fraying, none of us knowing when the hour would come. *If* it would come.

Nor what it would mean for us if it did.

"Come," I said, voice brisk. "I have something to show all of you too."

He pushed away from the dresser. "Charming the Krauts out of their Walther P-38s? Or an MG-42 in exchange for a kiss? Really, Emilia, a nice girl like you? I'm shocked."

I laughed. "You're incorrigible, you know."

"But you adore me anyway." His eyes crinkled as he grinned.

In the sitting room, I opened my bag. The men watched as I drew out the white-and-vermilion bands of cloth, the colors of our flag that for nearly five years had been replaced by the swastika of oppression. Each band had been stamped with the letters WP, the symbol of an eagle between them. Wojsko Polskie. Polish Army. It had been the task of the women to stitch and stamp the armbands, and Jasia and I had sat up late into the night imprinting each with the insignia of our army. The exultation of those sleepless hours, preparing uniforms for the future day of battle.

The men reached out, taking the strips of cloth, turning them in hands ready to hold weapons.

Ryś immediately slid one over his shirtsleeve, angling his upper arm to admire the white-and-red band. "Dashing, isn't it? The patriotic young ladies of Warsaw won't be able to resist the charms of such a uniform."

Jerzy chuckled. "In your dreams maybe."

"Hey!" Ryś gave him a shove.

"Under no circumstances are these to be worn until the order has been given," I said amid the exuberance. "Understood?"

Jerzy nodded, serious now. "Yes."

"Good." I slung my bag over my shoulder. "Daily briefings as scheduled. I'm off, then."

"Dzień się zbliża," Ryś called after me.

I turned, glancing back at the young man with earnest eyes and the white-and-red emblem on his sleeve. "Dzień się zbliża," I repeated with a little smile.

I'd heard the words in recent days, used in greeting or farewell.

Dzień się zbliża.

The day is coming.

HELENA
JULY 29, 1944

The light in Jasia's eyes had left me in no doubt of the truth even before I caught sight of the glint of gold on her finger.

"Bronek finally asked me," she said, a grin spreading across her face. We'd hugged like giddy schoolgirls, for a bride-to-be's joy is contagious whether in war or peace.

In a burst of enthusiasm, I had declared that we must celebrate. A party, tonight.

"Shall we invite Andrzej?" Jasia asked with a sly smile.

I replied it was her party and she could invite whom she pleased, but my cheeks heated. I told myself it was only natural, the closeness that had grown between Andrzej and me. For after all, my role as his liaison necessitated our frequent meetings.

But it was more than that. Despite the rational voice in my head telling me there must be only one purpose now and to leave personal relationships for someday, I couldn't deny how often I caught myself thinking of him, remembering how it felt so right to slip my hand through his arm when we walked through the city on some errand or another. Or how when I arrived at his flat at the end of a long day, he noticed when I seemed tired or shaken and would pull out a chair. I'd sit while he made coffee, often sharing what little supper he had prepared. I teased him about his cooking—if his abilities as a platoon leader had been equal to his skills in the kitchen, he would not have kept his rank very long. Sometimes we talked. Sometimes we didn't. It was enough either way.

With Andrzej, it was always enough.

That evening, the six of us gathered in the flat Jasia and I shared. Jasia and Bronek, who I knew in the AK as Irek, commander of another platoon in Gryf Company, as well as a liaison called Władzia and Jerzy, whom I suspected had been invited only because Władzia begged Jasia. Jerzy collected admirers at an astonishing rate.

Ordinarily, such a gathering—members of the conspiracy meeting socially in one another's homes—would be prohibited, at least officially. But the slack behavior of the Germans meant we need not be as strict as we had once been. For an hour or two at least, we could put duty aside.

I bustled about, handing around glasses of wine.

Jasia and Bronek stood side by side as Jerzy clapped Bronek on the back. "Congratulations. But I must say you took long enough about it."

Jasia laughed, her hand tucked through Bronek's arm. "Finally someone says it."

"I had to get up enough courage." Bronek grinned, stealing a kiss.

"Thank you," Andrzej said quietly as I handed him a glass. Only recently had I learned he and Bronek had more in common than their roles as platoon leaders in the same company. They were brothers, though few among us knew, not even Władzia and Jerzy. Jasia had told me, though she'd been cross with herself afterward. I had decided it would be best not to mention to Andrzej that I knew. After the liberation of Warsaw, there would be no need for secrets and pseudonyms and we could all meet freely.

"I'd like to propose a toast," Bronek announced once everyone had a glass. "To my Nina, the bravest and most beautiful." He looked at her, his gaze tender. "With such women as are among us tonight, how can victory fail us?"

"Hear, hear," Jerzy said.

"And to the coming of the day when we will take up arms at last." The fervency in Bronek's voice swelled within my chest as we stood in a circle, glasses in hand. "So we and our children may again know what it is to live in freedom."

"To Irek and Nina." Jerzy raised his glass. "And to victory."

"To Irek and Nina," I chorused along with the rest. "And to victory."

Amid the clinking of glasses, my gaze found Andrzej's. Though he toasted with the others, his eyes were grave. I knew his features too well not to mark their strain. What troubled him? Was it simply the tension of waiting, the uncertainty stretching before us all?

Władzia put on a record. The rasp of the needle, then Mieczysław Fogg's rich baritone rose from Jasia's record player. Bronek set down his glass. "Would you care to dance, my love?"

Jasia nodded and claimed his hand with a smile. He led her into the center of the room to a smattering of applause, drawing her close as they swayed to the music. Jerzy bowed and took Władzia's hand. Bronek dipped Jasia, and I smiled. It was good they had found happiness together. Jasia had already lost one man to whom she had given her heart, but she had not shut herself away from the chance to give love and to be loved. If I had stood in her place, would I be brave enough to do the same?

To know what it is to be shattered by love and yet take hold of it again with all that is tenuous and vulnerable . . . perhaps few acts of courage are so great.

Andrzej crossed the room. "Well?" He held out his hand, the corners of his mouth softening. "Shall we?"

"Why not?" I slipped my hand into his, and we joined the others. The firm warmth of his palm settled at my waist, and our fingers entwined as we stepped slowly to the music. His nearness and the scent of soap that clung to his freshly combed hair enfolded me.

"Is something the matter?" I asked as we danced.

A pause. "Not right now," he said quietly, his gaze on my face.

There will be time enough for all the rest tomorrow. For tonight, let there be only this.

Jerzy spun Władzia and drew her close again, Jasia rested her cheek against Bronek's shoulder, and I moved closer to Andrzej, his cheek against my hair. We danced as twilight fell and the record spun and Mieczysław's baritone crackled from the record player, singing about love and autumn roses and goodbyes.

When the last notes faded away, we were still dancing.

25

ANTONINA
JULY 30, 1944

On a drizzling Sunday, I opened the door and found Helena standing outside.

I had made certain the others were hidden first. For Róża and her seven-year-old daughter, Łucja, taking shelter at a knock on the door had become a way of life. They had been on the Aryan side eighteen months, the flat in Wola to which I had moved the fifth place they had hidden. They'd been forced to leave the last place after their funds had run out and the man who'd agreed to keep them for a certain sum each month decided it wasn't worth the risk to harbor the woman and her daughter when they could no longer offer sufficient inducement.

Such were the stories that played out with myriad variations for the surviving Jewish population of Warsaw.

Somehow Róża had made contact with my associates and all had been arranged. She and her little girl had been with me two months now. Having a baby made it easier to shelter invisible houseguests. Kasia's crying could cover suspicious noises, and few made a more inconspicuous impression than a woman with an infant. Only during the day when I left Kasia with a neighbor while I worked did my guests need to maintain complete silence.

"Hela, how good to see you." I shifted Kasia on my hip, her

favorite rattle crammed into her mouth. "Come in." I shut the door behind us.

"Hello, Kasia." Helena bent to smile at the baby.

I looked down at my daughter. "Can you say hello to your Auntie Hela?"

"Why, how you've grown since I last saw you." Helena fussed over the baby as Kasia blinked wide brown eyes. My sister turned to me. "She's getting so big."

"Every week, she does something new. She's begun to kick off one of her booties. Always the right one. I never can seem to keep it on her, no matter how I try."

We both laughed, and Helena chucked Kasia under the chin. "Are you stubborn like your mama, my little Kasia? Oh, yes, you are."

Kasia gurgled and waved the rattle in her tiny fist.

We went inside and sat at the small table. I settled Kasia in my lap. Helena glanced toward the window. Her hands were clasped, and she rubbed her thumb against her forefinger, the way she often did when preoccupied or troubled. I doubted she even realized she was doing it.

I was about to ask what was the matter, but she spoke before I could. "It's time you left the city, you and Kasia. Just for a little while."

I frowned, startled by the suddenness of her words. "Why?"

Helena's eyes fixed on mine. "You're not to speak of this to anyone." Never had my sister's voice held such command. "There's going to be fighting, perhaps even in Warsaw. It won't last more than a few days, a week at most, but it's best you and Kasia are safely away."

"But the Germans are retreating . . ."

"That is why we intend to take Warsaw. Once the battle begins, the Soviets will cross the Wisła and aid us in liberating the city."

"Us?" The word was barely more than a whisper.

Helena nodded, very serious.

Of course I knew what she meant. I wasn't involved in the underground—at least not the organization that had for years carried out all manner of sabotage, printing of posters and publication of newspapers, even executions of members of the SS and Gestapo. Still, I couldn't fail to be aware of its existence, and I read the *Biuletyn* whenever I had the chance.

But never had I imagined Helena among its members. My sister who had always been timid, who had never sought danger or even adventure outside of books, who had endured the occupation and its losses with her head down.

"How long have you . . . ?"

"Since last summer," she said simply.

Maybe that was how I'd chosen to see her, the sister I had known, or thought I did. Perhaps it's one of the ironies of family: the ones we know best become those we truly see the least.

"Do you know when it will be?"

"There are no orders yet, but we expect them any day now." Controlled urgency permeated her voice. "I have a friend whose family is leaving tomorrow for the countryside. I've asked them to take you and Kasia. They have room in their cart. You can stay with them until it's over."

After having been dealt so many blows of shock, it would seem I'd no longer be shaken by anything. But there I sat, Kasia in my lap, my thoughts unraveling.

One remained clear.

I couldn't leave. Not because I wanted to stay for the coming battle, though had I not been a mother, there would be no question about whether I would defend my city or abandon her.

But Róża and Łucja had no papers. They had remained in hiding rather than living on the surface, because though both spoke excellent Polish, Róża's looks would surely draw notice. This was the world in which we found ourselves, and to survive meant to understand its realities.

Even with the Soviets so near and the German army in retreat, Róża and Łucja couldn't leave. Not this flat, much less the city. Not until Warsaw had been well and truly rid of its occupiers. Until then, it wouldn't be safe for any Jewish person.

Helena watched me expectantly, as if waiting for me to agree or maybe to start packing my bags.

Always I had tried to care for her. Even when I left her, it had been because I wanted to keep her safe. Now her gaze held a new force of will and she sought to protect me.

Maybe we'd both been trying all along. Maybe that was what had broken us. The secrets war had forced between us, kept to protect the other.

But this one would remain, for now at least. Róża and Łucja couldn't leave and neither would I.

I had usually been able to convince my sister to come around to my way of thinking, but I didn't recognize this new Helena. I doubted she'd be so easily persuaded. I swallowed. "It's good of you to arrange this, but I don't want to leave. Others are staying, why shouldn't I? You said it won't last long."

"But it will be quieter outside the city. Better for you and Kasia."

"The Soviets have been bombing us for months and I haven't left yet. I won't flee now, not with the end so near. Perhaps I can be of some use." I hesitated, unable to check my guilt at the disquiet in her eyes. "Don't worry. I'll take care."

Slowly, she nodded.

"And what about you? Shouldn't I be the one worried?"

"We've been preparing for this day a long time. We're ready."

"You could stay with Kasia and me, you know." My words came quiet. If she agreed to stay, I could tell her about Róża and Łucja. My sister would never betray them. We could face the days ahead together.

"You may not understand, but I am a soldier now, Tosia." The quiet resolve of her voice stilled me inside. "This fight is mine, and I will not turn my back on it."

I could press her, beg her even, but it would do no good. If I somehow succeeded in convincing her, she'd only resent me later. Try as I might, painful as it was, I couldn't protect my sister any more than she could me. Not this time.

She had her fight and so did I. It was for each of us to see it through, so when the end came—if it came—we would be able to meet our own eyes in the mirror and know we had done what we must.

"What does a woman do in such a fight? Surely they won't give you a gun." I kept my voice light, even as I wondered what part Helena would have in the coming battle.

"If necessary." She was utterly serious. "But there are many kinds of soldiers."

I did not fully understand who my sister had become, but the strength of purpose in her gaze . . . that I could not fail to recognize. It had lived in muted black-and-white in the eyes of the man, earnest and painfully young, as he'd sat for his photograph before leaving to join his unit, and it had dwelt in his gaze again as he'd packed a rucksack and boarded a train on the verge of yet another war.

My fingers reached instinctively for the chain that lay under my blouse where the medallion rested against my skin.

In that moment, she'd never looked more like our father.

And as it had been that distant August day, there was nothing I could do but let her go.

HELENA
JULY 30, 1944

I had gone against the order for secrecy and anyone who liked could fault me. I wouldn't blame them. But if they did, then they knew nothing of loss as I had come to understand it. How the need to keep close what remained turned one desperate, almost feral.

For myself, I had no fear of the fight to come. But I wanted to meet it knowing my sister and her child, my only family, would be safe. Even if the battle lasted no more than a few days, as everyone said.

I had made arrangements with Jasia's family, who'd agreed to take Antonina and Kasia when they left the city tomorrow. But Antonina seemed to think the idea of leaving cowardly, a kind of desertion.

I knew my sister well enough to be certain that once she'd made up her mind, there was little hope of changing it.

So I would protect them another way.

By fighting.

"I doubt much will happen in Wola," I said as we sat in her flat.

239

"You should be all right here." I didn't know for certain where the battle would break out. But it wasn't likely the industrial district of Wola would be at the forefront.

Antonina nodded. She tried to ask about our plans then, how great a force we could muster, the supply of weapons we had, but my answers were evasive. I had told her too much already. The decisions rested with our commanders, I said. Then I said I ought to be going, and she showed me to the door.

"Come to your Auntie Hela." I lifted Kasia into my arms and cuddled her close, her body small and warm, fragile yet sturdy. I nuzzled her cheek, breathing in her fresh, milky scent.

It's for you, my sweet Kasia. We're fighting for you. For the land in which you will grow. For the freedom that will be yours.

Kasia's tiny fingers tugged at the ends of my hair, and I laughed.

"Soon Auntie Hela will take you to the park and we'll feed the little ducks."

"You'd like that, Kasia." Antonina's voice was bright, but I caught the shadow of strain. "Feed the ducks and then have ice cream."

My smile turned wistful. "Just like with Tata."

"We'll take her together." Antonina's eyes found mine, and suddenly my own burned.

It won't always be like this. Soon there will be strolls in the park and sweet vanilla ice cream. Soon there will be more than the fight.

I kissed Kasia again, then moved to pass her into Antonina's arms.

"Wait."

I watched as Antonina reached up and fumbled at the back of her neck. Then she drew out the small silver oval. My breath caught. Tata had given it to her before he left, and I knew she wore it always.

The medallion dangled as she held the chain by its ends and slid it around my neck. I turned and she brushed aside my hair, her fingers cool as she fastened the clasp.

I glanced down, touching the tarnished silver engraved with the image of Christ where it rested against the navy bodice of my dress.

"Keep it safe," she said softly. The same words Mama had spoken to Tata all those years ago. I hadn't known Antonina remembered.

I nodded. My gaze held hers. In that moment, all that separated us, all the words we'd spoken and hadn't spoken, all the ways we'd wounded each other . . . none of it mattered.

Because she was my sister.

They were everything, those words. That bond. In the end, it all whittled down to that.

But no matter how strong a sister's love, it couldn't hold back the tide of a world at war.

She pulled me close then, Kasia between us, and I clung to her as I hadn't for so long. In that moment, I wasn't a soldier. Only a sister. Desperate and afraid and wishing it all would put itself to rights without me.

Knowing it wouldn't.

Because this fight was mine, and I would not turn my back on it.

Just before she drew away, she whispered something into my hair.

Later I would tell myself it was *I love you*.

Later I would wish I'd said it back.

AUGUST 1, 1944

SOLDIERS OF THE CAPITAL!
I HAVE TODAY ISSUED THE ORDER WHICH YOU DESIRE,
FOR OPEN WARFARE AGAINST POLAND'S AGE-OLD
ENEMY, THE GERMAN INVADER. AFTER NEARLY FIVE
YEARS OF CEASELESS AND DETERMINED STRUGGLE,
CARRIED ON IN SECRET, YOU STAND TODAY OPENLY
WITH ARMS IN HAND, TO RESTORE FREEDOM TO OUR
COUNTRY AND TO METE OUT FITTING PUNISHMENT
TO THE GERMAN CRIMINALS FOR THE TERROR AND
CRIMES COMMITTED BY THEM ON POLISH SOIL.

BÓR, COMMANDER-IN-CHIEF, ARMIA KRAJOWA

26

HELENA
AUGUST 1, 1944

W-Hour.

The news had come in the afternoon, just before one.

"Today at 17:00. Assembly at 16:00. The order has gone out."

How calmly Jasia had said it, but oh, how bright her eyes had been. How we had caught our breaths, looking at one another with a mixture of anticipation and elation and perhaps a little fear deep in our stomachs, hidden to all but ourselves.

For so long we had speculated. The day, the time. Would we strike at dawn, or would midnight be our hour of initiation?

Now it had been set. No more wondering, preparing, waiting.

W-Hour. W for *wybuch*. Outbreak.

Then we sprang into action. Tiny cogs in a vast machinery, whirring to life. Climbing too many flights of stairs to count, delivering orders, mobilizing the men. Crossing the city by tram, bicycle, on foot, traversing the streets mapped into our very bones.

Carrying the message, the stirring, glorious, at-long-last message. Sending forth the rallying cry.

W-Hour.

Four hours away.

How could a battalion, much less an entire army strewn throughout the city, be mustered in under four hours? We needed time. The thought flickered through my mind as I rushed from group to group of restless men who hailed my news like young colts on the verge of being freed from the stables.

Time to assemble our ranks, to distribute weapons, to absorb this reality.

But there was no time. Only action now.

I delivered orders to the squads gathered in various flats and back rooms. And then I flew home to change my clothes. In the little bedroom Jasia and I now shared, I dressed hurriedly in a gray skirt, a navy jacket over my blouse, and my oxfords. I picked up the rucksack that had been packed and waiting for days. It held a blanket, two changes of undergarments, a woolen cardigan, a clean blouse, a cake of soap and a towel, a toothbrush, and some rusks and tinned food. I slung the rucksack over my shoulder and paused, catching my own eyes in the mirror.

Reflected in the glass was a young woman with a rucksack on her back, dark blond curls swept back at the sides, cheeks flushed from heat and excitement.

Eyes a bit wide but kindled with a flame I had glimpsed before. In that moment, I found my sister's face in my own, stubborn, undaunted Antonina. Upon learning we were twins, people often remarked how little we resembled one another. What they really meant—or so I always thought—was how Antonina could be so much prettier, so much more vivid.

But that was in the past now and perhaps we were not so unalike, my sister and me.

The cool silver of the medallion lay against my skin, under my blouse. It steadied me somehow, knowing it was there. A piece of Tata and my sister both, to carry with me into this fight.

Just before I left the room, my gaze fell on the bedside table where the photograph rested. Mama and Tata on their wedding day. I crossed the room and took up the oval frame. Holding it in my hands for a moment, I gazed down at the faces of my parents in timeworn black-and-white. Mama elegant, almost ethereal, in her filmy veil and embroidered gown. Tata, so dashing and young, eyes only for his bride.

Then I tucked the frame into my rucksack and left the flat.

The air simmered, not only with heat but with a kind of electricity, an undercurrent pulsing just beneath the surface of the hurrying crowd. There were more pedestrians than usual, and in a city where able-bodied males tended to limit their movements for fear of łapanki and deportations to the Reich, there were more young men than I'd seen on the streets collectively in months, years maybe. If one took the time to look, one might notice similarities, almost uniformities, in their appearance and manner. Despite the sweltering day, many wore trench coats or windbreakers. Likely an arsenal of weapons was even now being conveyed through the city in broad daylight, smuggled under the innocuous garments.

Almost everyone carried a rucksack or suitcase or parcel, as if the whole of Warsaw had decided to set off on holiday. A young man strode purposefully past, and I noticed with a start of horror that the brown paper concealing the object he carried had ripped, the protrusion of a rifle barrel unmistakable. Scarcely had I taken in the sight than he melded into the throng, and I had no time to run after him.

Though we barely exchanged glances, an unspoken accord passed between us as we hurried to our posts, numberless and solitary, yet moving with one purpose. Soon our army would be invisible no longer. Soon our enemy would learn the measure of its strength, the strength of Polish men and women who had suffered too long under a merciless occupation, and we would wrest back our city and our freedom.

Perhaps someday we would remember the atmosphere of exuberant youth, how a breathless expectancy pervaded the air, as in the moments before a summer storm. How victory was not only possible but at our very fingertips. How that day, the first day of August, we grasped hold of it and gave all our strength to winning it for ourselves.

There were German patrols on the streets too, but we continued on our way in spite of them, and as far as I could see, they stopped no one. Could we really be so inconspicuous and they so oblivious to the heightened atmosphere, our quasi-military garb, bulging rucksacks, and resolute stride? If they detected our plans before

W-Hour, if they informed their superiors who then ordered troops to be on alert, we would lose the advantage of surprise. If only we could have mobilized quietly instead of en masse.

A middle-aged lady coming out of a gateway glanced at me with a knowing smile. I returned her smile with a faint one of my own and walked on, uncertain what to make of this.

We wore no uniforms, not even our armbands. No outward sign of the insurgents—the soldiers—we would soon become. How many in the city knew what would happen today? We'd been instructed not to speak of the imminent uprising, not even to our families, lest word circulate and find the ears of the enemy. I had disobeyed this order by telling Antonina, and likely others had also confided in wives or parents or sweethearts, so their closest ones would know what would come, so they could say a proper goodbye rather than give a flimsy excuse and slip away. On the eve of the unknown, the heart prevails over reason.

An armored vehicle drove along the street, bristling with a machine gun. It wasn't the first I'd glimpsed that day. The presence of German military and police in the city seemed greater than a week ago, when the panicked chaos of their flight in the face of the Soviet advance had been evident to all.

I tried to shake the rising unease. There were still Germans, yes, but that was to be expected. Had the situation been unfavorable, our leadership would not have issued the order.

It won't last more than a few days, a week at most. Then the Red Army will reach the city and this will all be at an end.

I took a tram to Wola, again noting a number of passengers garbed in coats, wearing military boots, carrying rucksacks and mysterious parcels. It was nearly four by the time I reached the concentration point for our battalion, a factory on Mireckiego Street.

In front of the factory gate stood a young man wearing a beige trench coat. I doubted he'd donned the garment merely because it made him look dashing, though I could detect no bulges indicating a weapon.

I gave him the password and he gave me a grin as I passed, the boyish gesture belying his sentry stance.

For a moment, my steps stilled, and I simply stood, taking it all in. In the factory yard, men and women, mostly young people, milled about, greeted one another, strode past as if on urgent business. Some carried weapons openly, a Błyskawica—lightning—submachine gun manufactured in one of the AK's clandestine workshops slung across the chest of one while a cluster of young men stood admiring a pistol.

My chest fluttered from the atmosphere of freedom, so many men and women, at once purposeful and exultant. From the realization that this wasn't just a figment anymore, a secret hope nourished in the depths of ourselves, spoken about with comrades in that half-anticipating, half-disbelieving way in which people ruminate about the future, painting it in the colors of their choosing, prepared for with never-ending weapons drills and first aid courses, which at times had felt so very pointless as day after day passed in the clutch of occupation.

No. This was real. *We* were real.

And my heart fluttered from fear, because of that very thing. The actuality.

I drew a steadying breath and wended through the crowd, searching for familiar faces.

Two girls nearly bumped into me as they hurried out of the factory, arms full of boxes containing an array of bottles and dressings. "Sorry," one murmured.

I made my way through corridors and rooms echoing with bootfalls and called-out greetings and a dozen conversations. Ours wasn't the only company assembling at the factory, nor the only battalion, it seemed. For so long we'd had contact with only a few of our number, and so the conspiracy had seemed slight somehow, in contrast to the might and prominence of the enemy, though we knew full well we stood alongside unseen ranks. But the days of lonely struggle were behind us. Judging from the enthusiasm spilling over around me, others felt it too.

We were all comrades here.

And we would fight as one.

"Emilia."

I turned, catching sight of one of the men from Andrzej's platoon. He led me to where the others waited.

Ryś and Jerzy and Sowa. Jasia and Władzia and Malina. I recognized more familiar faces, noted the absence of others.

Maybe they were elsewhere on the factory grounds or simply hadn't arrived yet.

"Emilia, it's so good to see you." Malina gave me a quick hug.

"And you." She and Władzia and I had been in the same training courses, and the sight of her, of all of them, sent a glow spreading through me. Sowa's shyly awkward grin unfolded, and I smiled back.

"Decided to join this sorry lot at last?" Jerzy grinned.

Ryś gave my hand a hearty clasp, as if we were meeting again after an absence of weeks instead of hours. "What a day, isn't it? Someday we'll tell our children about this. That we were there on the day Warsaw began to be free."

The words settled into me with shining solemnity. I could only nod, unable to form an answer to convey the swelling in my chest. The mingling of promise and expectation and hope.

"I didn't know the two of you had an announcement." Jerzy smirked. "Have you chosen names for these children yet?"

Ryś punched his shoulder. "Shut up, Jerzy."

"Where are the others?" I asked.

"Andrzej and Irek are in a briefing," Jasia replied. "I've met others from our company. Some haven't arrived."

"I wonder how long before we're issued orders," Sowa said.

"*I* wonder how long before we're issued weapons," Jerzy said. "Naturally, I already have mine"—he gestured to the Mauser, its sling over his shoulder—"but a grenade or two wouldn't be amiss."

"Do you have your armband?" Władzia asked me.

I opened my rucksack and took out my armband. Held it in my hand for a moment, the cloth smooth under my fingers, then slipped it onto my arm and secured it over my jacket.

Featherlight, but oh, the weight of that white-and-red band.

Andrzej and Bronek made their way toward us. Andrzej's armband stood out against his charcoal-gray coat. He wore a leather belt at his waist, his trousers tucked into officer's boots, a military cap with a white-and-red ribbon atop his dark hair. I had stitched the emblem onto his cap only a few days ago. Jasia had done the same for Bronek.

At the sight of their platoon leader, the men, even Jerzy, straightened their stance. Andrzej's gaze connected with mine, and he gave a brief nod, an even fainter smile.

"Assemble the other squad leaders." Andrzej issued the order, his voice firm but steady.

"Yes, sir." Jerzy strode away.

"On the day Warsaw began to be free."

This was our city. With her we would rise or fall.

HELENA
AUGUST 2, 1944

On the first day of August, the clock struck five, and the city erupted.

Men and women in white-and-red armbands burst upon the streets, a storm of soldiers and liaisons and nurses. The air echoed with the crackle of single shots and the rattling stutter of machine guns, mingled with grenade explosions. The sound of it . . . like a magnificent display of fireworks in the city streets.

The battle for Warsaw had begun.

The freshly minted soldiers surged upon their objectives, armed with newly issued pistols—or better yet, a rifle or submachine gun. Many carried only a single hand grenade. Not for lack of willingness, for all would have taken a weapon—any weapon—gladly, learned how to fire it in moments, if necessary. But there simply weren't enough. Because of this deficiency, none of the women in the Błysk Battalion—liaisons and nurses, all of us—had been issued arms. I imagined it was much the same everywhere, weapons scarce, so many eager to take up arms, to join the battle, to wrest the city out of the hands of our enemies.

Wrest it, we did.

Oh, the glorious reports. The AK had gained control of swaths of territory in the Old Town and the city centre. From the sixteen-story

Prudential Building, the tallest structure in Warsaw, the white-and-red flag of Poland flew, fluttering proudly above the city for the first time in five years.

We had our own victories in Wola. Andrzej's platoon, along with Bronek's, had captured the area of the Jewish cemetery and seized a former school on Okopowa Street, which the Germans had converted into a barracks. The platoons took both prisoners and weapons, along with the bountifully stocked pantry, which caused nearly as much jubilation as the rest. We called our newly acquired quarters "the Fortress."

Other AK units captured a German storehouse where they discovered substantial reserves of flour, sugar, rye, tinned meat, and uniforms—boots, helmets, and thousands of Waffen-SS camouflage smocks. Though no cache of weapons had been found, as had been hoped, our fighters would make good use of the supplies. Boots, helmets, and even the smocks would outfit many who'd begun the battle in civilian garb.

That day, our battalion had its first wounded. Its first casualties. Women had been among them, a nurse and a liaison from another company. I didn't know their real names, only their pseudonyms. Danuta and Irka. Danuta had been hit when she'd attempted to rescue a wounded comrade under fire. Irka had been struck by machine-gun fire as she'd tried to retrieve a weapon from a fallen German.

I hadn't been there when they fell. I had not been close with either. But still, they were part of us.

The deaths of those girls—for that was what they were, girls, neither above twenty years of age—touched us all, pierced the euphoria.

Our first losses.

They could only be our first.

By nightfall, smoke hung over the city from burning buildings, the sky cast in an amber glow despite the falling drizzle.

Long into the night, when all had been quiet, we'd put up barricades with furniture, sandbags, garbage cans, boards, whatever could be found. Inhabitants of nearby flats came out to help, willingly giving whatever we asked, eagerly giving without being asked. "What do you need? Bandages, blankets? Some bread for your boys?" Had we the weapons, we could have added many to our ranks, but we hadn't even enough to arm our soldiers, so most spontaneous volunteers had to be turned away.

An old woman, her eyes a faded blue in her lined face, had pressed something into my hand, her knobby fingers briefly clasping mine. "You must keep up your strength, my dear." Her voice had been a mother's, and her eyes had glistened as she looked at me, as if in us, young men and women with white-and-red armbands, dwelt hope itself.

When I later unwrapped the paper, I found a roll and a bit of sausage. In our quarters, while others slept around me, tears started to my eyes. This was why we fought. Not merely against the hated occupiers, but for each man, woman, and child who'd carried their own furniture to our barricades, for the old woman who'd sacrificed to give nourishment to a liaison. For our parents and brothers and sisters, our sweethearts and friends.

For all true Varsovians.

It was now the second day of the battle. Droplets of rain prickled my neck as I crouched behind a tramcar that had been overturned as a barricade. Over my jacket, I now wore one of the SS camouflage smocks. Though I'd searched for the smallest, the garment certainly wasn't tailored, despite the belt I'd fastened around my waist. Andrzej had ordered us all to don the captured garb. Most eagerly changed, even as they joked about looking like sons of the Führer, though a few protested, saying they didn't want to dress like a Kraut. I found a pair of boots that almost fit and wore a steel helmet over my pinned-up hair. Andrzej had placed it on my head and adjusted the strap, a furrow in his brow as his callused fingers grazed my chin. Though he didn't speak of it, the loss of Danuta and Irka had left him shaken. I expected I wouldn't be here at all if he had his way, though he hadn't asked me to leave. He was a commander and I was his liaison. Nothing else mattered now.

One of the squads from Andrzej's platoon manned the barricade while others occupied the grounds of an adjacent factory. Opposite the factory rose the wall of the Jewish cemetery where Bronek's platoon had their positions. The report of gunfire echoed in the cool of the morning. I had been sent out not with orders this time but with hot coffee and bread, which had been gratefully received by the men at the barricade.

On the air came a low rumble, a grinding creak of steel.

The men exchanged glances, trained their gazes on the street, weapons at the ready as they hunkered behind the barricade. Andrzej squinted through his binoculars, his profile hard-set.

Then it appeared. The lumbering sandy-hued outline of a tank.

Not far behind the first tank, another followed.

My breath froze.

Great mechanized beasts coming straight toward us.

"Strange they're without infantry support." Sowa's forehead creased, his eyes behind his round spectacles riveted to the approaching tank.

The grating of its tracks filled my ears.

"Jerzy, a petrol bomb." Andrzej's voice, firm, low. "Wait till it's closer."

Behind the barricade, Jerzy readied one of the petrol-filled bottles.

Fire spurted from the mouth of the beast.

"Now."

In a flash of movement, Jerzy leapt up from behind the barricade, hurled the bottle at the first tank, then ducked down.

The air shattered.

The smoke cleared. The tank remained unscathed.

Bursts of fire ripped from the first tank's gun. An eruption of glass and metal. They would blow the barricade to bits.

Jerzy threw a second petrol bomb.

"To the cemetery," Andrzej yelled. "Go, go!"

We sprinted toward the cemetery in a blur of pounding footfalls. Through the gate, we dashed. Andrzej scrambled to the top of the wall.

"Get me a Gammon bomb."

Ryś passed up one of the pear-shaped anti-tank grenades. Atop the wall, Andrzej twisted off the cap. In a single motion, he drew back his arm and lobbed the grenade.

Seconds later, a blast.

"Another one. Throw everything you've got at them."

Time slowed, or maybe sped, as we crouched in the cemetery, as fire surged from the tanks and explosions resounded.

A slamming crash of steel.

"We've got it. Come on, boys." With that, Andrzej slid down the other side of the wall and vanished.

Then the men were on their feet, pouring out of the cemetery. I followed the others through the gate, past the barricade, hanging back a bit.

Flames leapt from the first tank. The other had crashed into a steel tram pole, the hulking Panther at a swerved angle near the intersection of the street. The great beasts now impotent.

"Hände hoch!" Andrzej shouted, his MP-40 raised. "Hände hoch! Schnell!"

Men emerged from the hatch, faces and uniforms blackened with soot, hands in the air. Encircled by our soldiers and their weapons, the bedraggled crews stood in the middle of the street, the tank in flames at their backs.

Andrzej turned, glancing in my direction. Our eyes met and he gave a nod, boots planted in a stance of alertness, a camouflage-covered SS helmet on his head. He held his submachine gun with a soldier's unconscious ease.

"We've captured the Panthers. Hurrah!" Cheers erupted as the men thronged the tanks.

Later that day, I clambered atop the tank with a few others, all of us eager for a closer look.

The third and last Panther in the convoy had turned to escape the onslaught and been captured not far from the other two. Though one had been burned out, its salvaged parts could be used to repair the others. The crews had been taken prisoner.

Once the tanks had been repaired, they would be put to good use by the newly formed armored platoon of the Błysk Battalion.

Standing below us, Ryś squinted, holding a camera to his eye. "Look this way, everybody. One, two, and smile."

The wind blew my hair, and I grinned as the camera clicked.

In my mind, I captured the memory, tucked it away, all of us sitting atop the Panther, young and proud and smiling.

"Can I have a copy?" I asked with a laugh, swinging my legs as I perched atop the tank. "I want it for my album."

"At the moment, I doubt there are many photography shops open for business. But don't worry." Jerzy grinned at me. "After victory, I'll give you a hundred copies."

27

HELENA
AUGUST 4, 1944

Amid the settling weariness of soldiers at evening came song.

Ryś sat at the piano in the dining room of the barracks that had become our quarters, a group of others gathered around. Young and exuberant, voices blending and rising.

I glanced up with a smile from where I sat mending a pair of trousers for one of the men in my platoon. On the next chorus of "Hey, boys, fix bayonets," I joined in, singing along to the rousing tune already so popular among the fighters. Many in our battalion had once been scouts who gathered for weekend excursions to the countryside, singing scouting songs and patriotic melodies by firelight.

But in war, scouts had become soldiers.

Perhaps we found strength in song or perhaps we lifted our voices to drown out our fears. Still, we sang, our spirits rising with the words.

Nearby, somewhat apart from the rest, sat Andrzej. He leaned forward slightly, boots planted on the floor, his submachine gun on his knees. He'd been cleaning the weapon, but his hands had stilled and he wasn't singing, simply looking on at the youthful circle as they triumphantly chorused the last verses to Ryś's hearty accompaniment. Despite the quiet steadiness of Andrzej's stance, his features had changed, darkened, a restlessness in his eyes.

Our gazes caught, briefly held, then he went back to cleaning his weapon.

Several songs later, Ryś closed the instrument. I bit off a loose thread and smoothed a hand across the trousers as Jerzy said, "Hey, Sowa, what've you got there?"

"Nothing." Sowa closed the little book he'd been scribbling in, began to tuck it away.

"Let me see." Jerzy rose, snatched the book in a flash. "Well, well, well, what have we here?" He leafed through the pages. "Looks like poetry."

Sowa stood. "May I have my notebook, please?" His usually mild voice had gone tight.

"Our Sowa is a poet." Jerzy continued to skim the pages. "Listen here, everybody. 'I wonder—'"

Sowa lunged for the book, but Jerzy ducked, swiftly sidestepping.

"Come on, Jerzy," one of the others called. "Give it back."

"Why don't you read us something, Sowa?" Ryś spoke up.

"Go on, Sowa."

"I could use some poetry to put me to sleep."

At this barrage of eager voices, Sowa shook his head. "It's nothing, really." Red crept into his face. "I didn't write it for anyone to read."

"I should like very much to hear one of your poems." Malina's voice came soft and clear. "That is, if—if you would share one."

Sowa turned. Malina looked up at him from where she sat, her young face flushed, pale blond wisps framing her cheeks, her eyes earnest.

"If you wish it," he said quietly, his gaze on her alone. Paper rustled as he flipped through the book. He adjusted his spectacles and cleared his throat, raising his gaze to take in the faces around him.

> I remember the Augusts of yesterday
> The earth sated with sun,
> Boys strolled with sweethearts
> Girls twined flowers in their hair.

Silence descended over the room save for Sowa's voice, faltering at first, almost too quiet to hear.

Another August
Boys marched to their posts
Girls twined bands of crimson around their arms,
Youth rose up, spirits as one
Boys with grenades and girls with proud hearts,
The sun shone then too
Or perhaps it was only a memory.

To the fight, they went
Steadfast and shining in their youth,
They went in Old Town and Wola
In Żoliborz and Mokotów
The air erupted with a thousand bursts of fire
Every street, a barricade
Every house, a fortress.

Why did they go?
Why do I?
Why raise my weapon, sever breath?
No soldier's heart is mine
Nor does my flesh burn with hate for any man,
Only love do I seek
Its knowing and its being,
Yet I will not shirk this fight
Not by order of any man,
Nor in hope of any prize.

For the boys who will stroll with sweethearts
For the girls who will twine flowers in their hair
For the Augusts of yesterday,
For the Augusts of tomorrow.

And if we should fall, let it be as the leaves,
With their last, giving themselves to the earth.
The soil nourished by their fading,
Their memory kept by the stars
Though dust, through them, the world reborn.

Sowa closed the book and swallowed, strands of hair falling over his high forehead, spectacles slanting down his nose as he stood before us. But no longer was he the shy, gawky youth, but a man who had formed into words what the rest of us felt in our depths.

"Well," Jerzy said, for once seeming at a loss for a ready quip. "I think you chose the wrong pseudonym. We should call you Poet instead of Sowa."

Sowa flushed and ducked his head.

"Thank you," Malina said softly.

Sowa's eyes held hers. He gave a nod, the smallest of grins at his lips.

Andrzej rose suddenly and left the room, his bootfalls receding. As the others talked among themselves or dispersed to their quarters for a few hours of rest, I stood, laying the trousers aside.

I found him on the roof, the square of his shoulders an outline in the darkness. He glanced at me as I approached but said nothing. For several moments, we stood, gazing silently out across the stretching forest of rooftops and spires, the smolder of fire a halo in the sky.

There had been a German air raid that day, in Wola and elsewhere in the city. The first since fighting broke out. I had feared for Antonina, who lived to the south of our positions, but I could not abandon my duties to go to her. Now stillness enfolded the summer night. I inhaled through my nose, caught the bitter waft of smoke. The quietude a gentle deception.

Strange, the absence of sound. Why did I mark it? Then I realized what I instinctively sought and lacked. Not the tumult of battle but the distant thunder from across the Wisła that had reached our ears for days. The artillery that heralded the advance of the Soviets.

Had the Germans halted the Soviet offensive? I swallowed a rise of panic. Or had there merely been a lull in the fighting?

For a moment longer, I strained for the far-off rumble, but it had gone silent.

"Will there be a drop tonight, do you think?" We needed weapons and ammunition, desperately, if we were to hold the city until the

Soviets arrived. The leadership of the AK had been calling on the Allies to drop supplies to our soldiers. The nearby cemeteries had been designated as a drop zone, and squads were sent there nightly to await the delivery and unload the containers of precious armaments. I had gone yesterday with the others, crouching all night in a grave dug up by looters, Władzia huddling beside me as bullets whistled above us, for the enemy had anticipated the drop too. But there had been no drop, no supplies.

"It's expected, but so it was last night too." He glanced at me, the features I knew as well as my own half-obscured by the night. "There's been an order from headquarters. We're to proceed with active defense, but offensive action is to be undertaken only in cases of tactical necessity, to conserve ammunition."

The capture of objectives, the victories of the past four days, would be significantly checked by this directive. *Preserve what is already yours, but claim no new ground. Cling to your raft, but do not swim.*

I swallowed hard. "How much longer can we hold out?"

He stared out across the city where the glow of fires painted the horizon, his profile shadowed. "Under the present circumstances, no more than four or five days."

"The Soviets will come," I murmured even as a chill bled into my bones. They must come. In the last days of July, Radio Moscow had broadcast a call to the "sons of Warsaw" to take up arms. They had as good as pledged their support. Until then, we would hold the city.

He nodded, as if coming back to himself. "Of course, you're right. It's only a matter of waiting."

"You are a fine leader, Andrzej." My voice was soft. "We could not ask for a better man to stand with us."

He shook his head, exhaled a heavy breath. "I'm no different than the rest. No less afraid. They all are, you know. Even Jerzy. So young, all of them."

"Yet none would choose another path if it meant going on as before. And perhaps what matters is not if we are afraid." I hesitated, gathered the words. "Perhaps courage is to be afraid, but to hold on still until the end."

He regarded me as I faced him on the roof, still wearing my bulky camouflage smock. "You should be commander of this platoon. From the first time I saw you, I knew . . ." Whatever he'd meant to say faded unspoken. "You ought to get some rest." The words came low, almost rough.

"Good night." I turned to go, then paused. Brushed my lips against his cheek. It wasn't meant to be a kiss, not a real one. Just a fleeting impulse, acted upon in an instant. Perhaps I meant to give him courage, to show this man who bore so much that he was not alone.

It lasted barely more than a breath. But it was enough. For though, heaven help me, I had imagined what it would be to touch him, to kiss him, now my memory would ever hold the warmth of his skin, the salt of his sweat on my lips. Now there would ever be a lack inside of me for having known it once.

He remained motionless, an intensity in his stillness as he gazed down at me in the almost-darkness. I drew away, pressing my lips together, heart beating fast.

"I'm sorry. I shouldn't—"

He leaned in and his lips met mine. A single kiss at first, slow and gentle. Then I was kissing him back, and he was kissing me, urgent and breathless, drawing apart only to come together again. None of my imaginings had prepared me for this. How a kiss could be an unraveling and a binding, a chasm and the steadiest place I would ever know. How, in it, I could be at once shattered and never more whole.

I would always remember that kiss, my first, there on a rooftop as Warsaw burned.

ANTONINA
AUGUST 5, 1944

We built barricades. In those first days, when the battle was fresh, we tore up cement slabs from the sidewalk with crowbars and pick-axes, uprooted cobblestones from the street, stacked them one upon another. A string of men, many old, women in light dresses, young boys in short trousers and caps, passed the heavy blocks of pavement from one hand to the next—hurry, hurry, hurry. People carried out their own furnishings. These, too, were added to the barrier. A table, its surface worn from countless meals. A chest of drawers. A child's pram.

Block German tanks, defend the street, fight for the city. The refrain beat in our chests as the barricade rose high.

No one ordered us to put up barricades, at least not on our street. The civilians decided it themselves, willingly, spontaneously. Civilians . . . but was there really a difference anymore? We had all been civilians, and we had all become soldiers. Whether we'd donned a white-and-red armband mattered little, though those who wore the emblem of the Armia Krajowa were treated with deference, lauded for their bravery, if not universally, at least by many.

The air pulsed with the dry clatter of machine guns, bursts of gunfire, the muffled tremor of detonations. The instruments of battle performed in orchestra. Our street remained peaceful—at least there had been no fighting outside our building—nor had we glimpsed any German troops, but Wola had become a battleground.

I rarely ventured outside. If I weren't the mother of a seven-month-old, if I hadn't Róża and her daughter to consider, I would follow the example of an adolescent boy in our building and go off in search of a unit to join. Or make my way to a nearby hospital, where I heard wounded fighters had been brought, and offer my services. But I wasn't certain what I would encounter if I tried to reach the hospital or if it could even be reached at all.

How I hated the waiting, the way it left room for unrest to gnaw at my mind with tiny, razor claws. It would be easier to be in the midst of it all, to be given some task to throw myself into, no matter how menial. To know my city—my beloved, familiar Warsaw—was fighting for her lifeblood and I did nothing to come to her aid filled me with shame. To know my sister fought among the others racked me with fear. I should be with her. Instead, I didn't know where she was, what she was doing, if she was safe.

One of the tenants had gotten hold of a copy of the *Biuletyn Informacyjny*. Now it could be distributed openly and we read the reports of AK victories. Surely the Soviets would soon cross the Wisła. The arrival of the Russians was not an event anticipated with great eagerness by most, but to see them now would be a relief, if only to hasten our deliverance.

A vague drone broke the early morning stillness.

China rattled as I lowered my cup of coffee.

I'd heard that sound too many times not to know what it meant.

I rose, pushing back my chair. Rushed into the next room. Róża and Łucja weren't even dressed, Róża's blouse still unbuttoned. Łucja's feet bare.

The throb of engines grew louder.

Stukas. Their diving shriek unmistakable.

In her cradle, Kasia began to cry.

We could stay here, as we'd done during yesterday's air raid. Or we could seek shelter elsewhere, though it would be madness to go into the open now.

"We'll go to the cellar." I lifted Kasia from her cradle. "Come. Quickly."

Róża hesitated. "What about—"

"That doesn't matter now. I'll say you're from another district—refugees." Surely everyone would be too crazed with fear to speculate whether a woman and her daughter might be Jewish.

A shuddering blast. Not here. Not us.

Not this time.

Róża fumbled to fasten her blouse. "Łucja, put on your shoes, quickly."

Engines roared overhead as Łucja pushed her feet into her shoes. I snatched Kasia's blanket and my handbag, and we left the flat, merging into the frantic crowd, Kasia's high wails joining the din.

In the stuffy dimness of the cellar huddled a mass of women, children, men. I ushered Róża and her daughter to a vacant place, then lowered myself beside them, patting Kasia's back, humming a lullaby as explosions reverberated, striking unknown targets.

Then came the waiting.

ANTONINA
AUGUST 5, 1944

In the cellar, time narrowed to grimy walls, pressing bodies, and the heaviness of the unknown.

A woman clutched her rosary, a small boy his stuffed dog. Kasia slept, her body slack against my chest. Łucja rested against her mother's shoulder. No one had questioned Róża's and Łucja's presence. Terror overpowered all other concerns. The musky rankness of sweat and the foul odor of a carbide lamp pervaded the air. Perspiration trickled down my back, a dull pounding in my head from thirst.

Gunfire resounded. Screaming, somewhere nearby.

A splintering crash. Closer than anything else.

I jolted. Łucja raised her head. A woman gave a stifled cry.

"Hush." An old man stood sentry-like near the entrance, his whisper sharp. "Keep still."

Heavy boots above us.

"Raus, raus!"

Róża and I glanced at one another. No one spoke.

The cellar door was bludgeoned open.

My breath came shallow from my parted lips.

Uniformed men burst into the cellar, weapons raised, yelling, "Raus, raus! Schnell!"

For an instant, we sat frozen.

In a flash, a shot discharged. People screamed. The old man fell with a heavy thud. Kasia began to cry. I clutched her against my chest, my heart pounding.

One of the soldiers lowered his pistol. "Raus!" he bellowed.

The crowd pushed to their feet. I rose, trembling, Kasia in my arms. Róża pulled Łucja close.

"Hände hoch! Raus!"

I shakily raised one hand, the other supporting Kasia.

Herded at gunpoint, we stumbled out of the cellar, hands in the air. Out of the building, across the courtyard, into the street.

I squinted against the sun, its glare dazzling after so many hours belowground.

Around us, an inferno. The street teemed with women, men, and children, driven from the surrounding buildings, a few clutching bundles or suitcases. Men in green-gray uniforms swarmed the street. One of the soldiers lurched from the opposite building, carrying two bottles. He took a long swig from one and swiped the back of his hand across his mouth.

Another soldier pushed into the crowd, grabbed the wrists of a girl with golden plaits, jerked her away from the woman she stood beside. The girl fought, sobbing as he dragged her toward a gateway.

"Zosia." The woman's garbled scream ripped the air. She ran after the girl—her daughter, maybe—but made it less than a meter before a shot rang out and she crumpled.

Róża's face blanched. Terror shone out of Łucja's eyes, her hair limp around her flushed cheeks, her hands in the air. Kasia wouldn't stop crying, adding to the pandemonium.

"Shh," I murmured, adjusting her blanket, rocking her in my arms.

The soldiers shoved among us, separating men from women and children. Wives clung to husbands, children to fathers, but the soldiers showed no pity, dividing the throng with orders, blows, shots.

"What will happen to us?" breathed a woman near me.

No one answered her.

"Schneller, schneller."

Forced onward by the soldiers, we started down the center of the street, a group of about forty women and children with our hands in the air. I glanced over my shoulder.

One of the soldiers hurled something through the window of our building. Glass shattered and flames erupted.

I turned away from my burning house, following the others.

On Wolska Street, the main thoroughfare, fires raged, the sky dark with smoke from structures set ablaze. Corpses littered the street and sidewalks, their blood glazing the ground. I passed the sprawled body of a man with a white-and-red band on his arm.

How could this be happening? What of our soldiers?

Where are you, Helena?

The soldiers herded us past the detritus of what had once been a barricade. Whether blown up or dismantled, I couldn't tell.

I'd helped raise a barricade. Hadn't I?

Out of the corner of my eye, I caught a sudden, darting movement. A woman slipped from the column, toward a gateway.

My heart quickened. I glanced at Róża and Łucja.

Could we get away? We had to try.

I leaned closer, about to whisper to them, when a shot exploded. The woman fell and we trudged onward.

28

ANTONINA
AUGUST 5, 1944

Outside the gate of the Ursus factory, SS men patrolled a cauldron of humanity. Mostly women and children, a few men among them, the crowd surely numbering into the hundreds.

At the end of the ragged column, snaking toward the gate, our group halted. I stood, holding Kasia, my head still pounding from thirst.

Then came the shots.

The staccato report of gunfire from somewhere on the other side of the gate.

It did not pause. If it did, the lapse lasted no more than seconds, a minute maybe, before the shots resumed again.

One after the other after the other.

But the air was filled with more than shooting. I could not absorb these other sounds. Weeping, screaming, pleading.

Human. And inhuman.

All ended the same way.

Cold sweat soaked my skin.

Soldiers emerged from beyond the gate, driving those at the head of the line through. It happened so fast, the herding. Women, children, men passed by, moving like shadows, swallowed by the gate.

Some fought or wept, but the soldiers paid no heed, pushing them through by force.

The gate closed. Maybe a hundred, maybe less, had been forced inside.

Silence.

Then shots.

Round after round.

I looked at Róża. Sweat glistened on her neck and forehead, but her face was pale. Like ash.

"Mama, Mama, what's happening?" Łucja's frightened young voice.

"I don't know, darling."

Soldiers roamed the crowd, casting their gazes about for valuables, robbing people of watches or jewelry, whatever caught their fancy, with the casual ease of passersby browsing market stalls. One girl hesitated when a soldier with high cheekbones pointed to her earrings. He ripped them out with two swift twists before pocketing the baubles, now sticky with blood.

It was midafternoon, the heat sweltering. Kasia's mouth gaped like a tiny fish, her skin clammy. I had nothing else to give her, so Róża helped me drape the blanket, and I unfastened my blouse and fed Kasia while Róża and Łucja shielded me with their bodies.

How did I do it, hold my child to my breast while the air shattered with shots?

How do mothers do such things?

The soldiers drove another group through the factory gate.

Once more, the gate shut.

Once more, shooting.

My head swam, my surroundings hazy, fading.

The glittering sky. Corpses discarded where they had fallen. Forgotten trifles, a man's hat, a child's doll, a bread roll.

Puddles of blood congealed in the heat, swarmed by fat blue flies.

Wailing. Screaming. Gunfire.

The pull of my daughter's mouth against my skin, her soft gulps.

Clarity jolted.

My baby.

Kasia finished suckling, and I adjusted my clothes and her blanket. The column now stretched ahead and behind us as others had been brought to the factory. My gaze traveled the area, searching for a way out. Guards surrounded the perimeter, cordoning it off, hemming us in.

"Róża," I whispered. "Listen to me. We must keep to the end of the line."

She stared, eyes unfocused. "Why?"

"Perhaps they won't take everyone. Perhaps something will happen. I don't know."

Róża nodded slowly.

But the sense grew stronger, and I grasped it.

I began to edge my way backward, the crowd an undulating mass around me. Róża did the same, Łucja clinging to her skirt.

Somehow we kept near the end of the line, hanging back as soldiers herded the ranks of people. The closer we drew, each time the heavy gate opened, what lay beyond flashed in a glimpse.

Sacks or maybe bundles of cloth spread over the ground.

How could it be anything else?

Again, the soldiers returned.

Róża's eyes met mine.

No others remained before us.

A slow numbing seeped through my limbs.

The gate creaked.

"Schnell. Schnell." Rough voices and rougher hands pushed us inside.

A wasteland. Corpses piled in a tangled mass stretching on both sides of the broad yard. Glassy patches on the pavement.

"Mama, what's happening?" Łucja's high-pitched voice. "I'm scared, Mama."

"Hold tight to Mama's hand, darling." Róża's voice did not shake. "Hold very tight."

The soldiers led us through the yard and down a narrow passage, flanking our ranks.

Run.

Where? How?

I couldn't make my legs work, my limbs heavy, wooden. The crowd closed around me, its current dragging me along.

Crying, praying, wailing. Hysteria. Feral terror.

A man bore a crippled old woman on his back, a woman and a small girl at his side. A middle-aged couple walked silently, holding hands. How many were among us? Thirty? More?

We came into a second courtyard. Corpses lay in heaps. Near the end of the yard, uniformed men stood. Dark spatters stained the wall behind them.

Time faded. The soldiers pushed us into groups of four.

"Please, I beg you." A woman fell to her knees before a young soldier. "Have mercy on us."

The soldier dragged the woman to her feet. She spat, cursing him as he shoved her back into line.

Forced by the soldiers, the first group stepped forward. Two women, a man, and a boy. The boy wore short trousers, and with every step, the loose heel of his shoe slapped the ground.

A blink. A volley of gunfire.

Four bodies crumpled among the mound.

The pounding in my chest surged until surely my heart would burst. Kasia was screaming.

"Shh." I pressed my lips against her sweat-damp curls. "Mama's here."

The next group approached. This time only three walked, for the man carried the crippled woman on his back.

Another volley.

I did not watch. I could not breathe.

Some of the soldiers passed flasks and bottles, talked with comrades. One did not. He put a cigarette to his lips, stood apart from the rest. A crease deepened between his brows as he exhaled a stream of smoke.

I glanced at Róża. She held her daughter, stroking her hair, the clasp of her arms shielding Łucja's eyes from the scene. Her gaze caught mine.

"I'm sorry," I whispered. For what did I say it?

Then I edged out of line.

The soldier turned slightly as I approached.

"Please." My voice shook. I'd spoken in Polish. I sifted through the jumble of words in my mind, searching for ones in German. I couldn't think. "My baby. Spare my baby."

He regarded me, smoke trailing from the blackened end of his cigarette.

"Please." My voice cracked. "Do you not have a child?"

Kasia was crying without tears, her cheeks blotchy. I shifted her onto my hip, twisted the simple gold band from my finger. I held it out to him. "Please. For my child. Spare my child."

He hesitated, his eyes on the jewelry in my hand, the baby in my arms.

Then he dropped the cigarette, crushing it under his boot, and pocketed the ring.

"Come." He took my arm, started to lead me away.

Abruptly, he stopped, releasing me.

"Why is this one not in line?" a brusque voice demanded.

I turned. An officer stood behind us, boots planted on the pavement. "Put her back with the others."

"Please." I could barely force out the word, my throat like ashes. "You are an officer. You must have some honor—"

The shove threw me to the ground.

"German women and children are dying because of you, so you must also die." The officer gritted out the words as he stood over me.

The other soldier hauled me to my feet, forced me into line. As he left me there, a look passed across his features. Pain? Pity?

I stared at him mutely, my crying baby in my arms.

Shots spattered. Strength ebbed from my limbs.

"The LORD is my shepherd; I shall not want . . ."

Dully, I turned my head. Beside me a woman stood, eyes closed, lips moving with the murmured cadence of her words.

"Yea, though I walk through the valley of the shadow of death, I will fear no evil: for thou art with me."

For Thou art with me.

How could He be here?

Róża and Łucja stepped forward, holding hands. As they passed,

I heard them reciting softly in Hebrew. "Sh'ma Yisrael, ADONAI Eloheinu . . ."

Seconds wrapped in stillness.

A burst of gunfire.

I did not watch them fall.

They led us forward, me and three others.

Time slowed to heartbeats. My vision blurred.

The soft weight of my child in my arms, my cheek against her hair. The taste of metal. A woman's strangled weeping. My own shuddering breaths.

Somehow I took one step after another, walked so the soldiers would not drag me. Somehow I held Kasia close.

Near the end of the yard, the gray shadows stood. Waiting.

In the seconds that stripped all else away, my sister's face rose. Lifting her hand in farewell as the train carrying our father drew out of the station on a rise of steam. Cradling my newborn daughter in her arms. Holding my gaze just before she left, the medallion around her neck, resolve bright in her eyes.

I'm sorry, Hela.

I'd never said it to her. There was so much I had never said. So much I had done and failed to do. I'd told myself we would have time, after all this, after the war.

But time had slipped away from us, and now she would never know.

"Be Thou with us, Lord," the woman whispered as we walked side by side, one step after another. The gray shadows waited. "Be Thou with us."

Be Thou with us.

Did I say it out loud?

A bolt of fire.

Falling, falling.

Then there was only the darkness, cold as midnight, closing around me like water over my head.

29

ANTONINA
AUGUST 5, 1944

That sound. I knew it. It reached for me, drew me out of the bottomless darkness even as the blackness beckoned with its heavy enveloping warmth, so easy to fall into.

A terrible staccato. It meant only one thing, that sound.

With it, other sounds. Groans of pain. Male voices. Weeping.

Heaviness pressed me down. Though I didn't open my eyes, I knew I lay under fallen bodies, pinned by their lifeless weight, one among a heap. As consciousness grew, so did pain, a fiery pulsing in my head.

The shooting went on as I lay without moving, unable to shut out the sounds that made me wish only for oblivion.

More bodies collapsed, tumbled onto the mound, the weight above me crushing, suffocating.

I opened my eyes, turned my head ever so slightly. Dark shapes above and around me. Splinters of light. I wet my lips and tasted metal, brackish and sticky. My blood or another's?

I couldn't move my left arm. Trapped by my own weight, it had gone leaden. I moved the fingers of my right hand slowly downward. They touched warmth, skin, a face.

I was lying beside the body of my child.

In that moment, I knew I would never rise from this pile of the dead, for I would never leave my baby.

It would be only a matter of time before death found me. I hoped it would not be long.

Against my fingers . . . a stirring, like a wisp of wind.

Kasia.

The gunfire had fallen silent. Now the space echoed with the heavy tread of boots, harsh voices.

"Here's one still moving."

The air fractured. A single shot.

In this field of the dead, they yet sought the living.

Beside me, a soft snuffling. Kasia was beginning to stir. She lay on my stomach in a cocoon of space, half-hidden by the corpse lying across me. I couldn't tell if she had been injured.

Moments ago, I thought only of death.

What coursed through me now might not be called strength, but with the flutter of my daughter's breath against my skin, a visceral force rose up within me.

I had to keep her still and quiet. If they heard her crying . . .

I traced my finger over her face until it brushed her lips. Gently, I slipped my fingertip into her mouth. I could think of nothing else to do. Within seconds, her mouth began to tug at my finger.

More pairs of footsteps, voices pleading in Polish, women and children screaming and sobbing amid the relentless drilling of gunfire.

They'd stopped killing at the pile where I lay, though they couldn't be more than a few meters from us. As the shooting went on, I slid my finger from Kasia's mouth and drew her closer with my free hand, praying the soldiers would be distracted by the new arrivals and not notice any movement from the heap where we were.

I lay, touching her, feeling the warm slick of blood against my skin. Was it hers?

Sometime later, the shooting stopped. Booted footfalls. Slurred laughter. Raucous singing. Through a crack in the pile of corpses, I glimpsed one of the gray shadows. He stood no more than two meters away, tipping a bottle to his mouth.

They were drinking as they moved among the bodies, kicking and trampling them with their boots. An exclamation about a diamond, for it seemed they looted from the bodies as they searched them. Every so often, a shot rang out.

Somewhere among the mound where I lay, someone was moaning. Thudding boots. Drawing nearer.

I pressed my hand to Kasia's mouth.

Shifting. Above me. I lay on my side, motionless, eyes shut.

A shot erupted, deafening.

My fingers tightened over Kasia's mouth.

Hands moved the corpses. A draft of air passed over my face as a body rolled off of me.

The presence of the soldier hovered above me.

Seconds expanded.

I did not breathe.

The bootfalls faded. As a drunken chorus resounded, I pried my fingers from Kasia's mouth. Her breath touched my skin. She hadn't suffocated. Again, I slipped my finger between her lips.

Please. My baby. Please.

The words became a prayer. I had no others.

I lay among the dead, my breathing shallow, my ears filled with a horror from which there could never be any escape.

ANTONINA
AUGUST 5, 1944

Silence.

Some time ago—maybe an hour, maybe less—the clack of boots and the voices of drunken men had grown fainter, receding, and a hush descended.

Kasia had fallen asleep. Every few minutes, I put my hand near her face to be certain she still breathed, but I dared not make any move beyond that lest I alert the soldiers to my presence. I couldn't tell where they had gone or if any remained on guard in the courtyard.

So I waited, the minutes unraveling. Through gaps in the mound of bodies, the sky extended vast and navy-black above me. I clung to that sky, a shard of the universe I knew, as I lay beneath corpses.

When Kasia began to stir and fuss, I knew I needed to move. I had managed to shift, so my left arm was no longer pinned under me, but the limb remained heavy and numb. It took all my strength to push aside the leaden weights that covered us, shoving the corpses so they rolled away from where Kasia and I lay, so they did not crush her as they fell. I closed my mind off from what I did, thought only of Kasia as I fought my way out. Slowly, painfully, I broke through the surface of the tangle that had trapped—and shielded—us.

Somehow I clambered off the pile, carrying Kasia. Faintness swamped me. I sank to the ground, the pavement under my knees puddled with blood. My skull throbbed fiercely. I had been wounded. How badly I wasn't sure.

For seconds, I huddled, listening for voices or footfalls. Then I pushed to my feet, gritting my teeth against the rush of dizziness.

Cast in pale moonlight, the courtyard stretched, an expanse of peaks and valleys backdropped by the outline of factory buildings, a landscape of the dead. They lay everywhere, singly and in masses. Thousands of bodies.

Stillness encircled me as I stood among the moonwashed heaps. No words could render the terror of that silence.

Find a way out.

I groped my way across the courtyard, stumbling over bodies. A hill of corpses at least a meter and a half high blocked the passage between the courtyards. I hesitated.

Voices. German.

I dropped, hunkered behind the mound, my hand pressed to Kasia's mouth. The sounds came from the first yard, or maybe beyond it, near the gate. For long minutes—or was it only seconds?—I crouched, listening.

I needed to move.

I rose, my head reeling and my vision blackening. Crept back across the courtyard, crawled onto a smaller pile of bodies. I stayed there, straining for any movement or sound before crossing into the third courtyard. This yard held fewer bodies. I made my way deeper into the yard, my footsteps quiet taps against the pavement.

Kasia's fussing grew louder. My heart raced.

There, against the side of a building, leaned a ladder. High above, the dark square of a window vent. It was open.

For an instant, I stood at the foot of the ladder, staring up. Then I started to climb, supporting Kasia with one arm, casting glances over my shoulder for any sign of the soldiers.

At last, I reached the top and crawled through the window. I balanced on the sill and slid down, my body jolting with the impact of the drop, my head pounding. I sucked in a breath, dizzy from the effort and the pain. Kasia was wailing.

I lowered myself to the cold floor. Moonlight slanted through the high window as I ran my fingers over my daughter's body, checking for injuries, soothing her with quiet words. Panic tightened my throat at the blood matting Kasia's hair, smearing her face and dress. But my probing fingers found no sign of a wound. I unfastened my clothes and leaned against the wall in the murky darkness as Kasia suckled. Would I have enough milk? I couldn't remember when I'd last had anything to eat or drink.

Just before the bombing forced us into the cellar, I'd been sipping a cup of coffee. How many days ago had it been?

Less than one.

I couldn't think anymore. About any of it. I could only slump against the wall, my child in my arms, the night silent and suffocating.

ANTONINA
AUGUST 6, 1944

The first rays of dawn fell across my face as I huddled on the floor of the factory. Kasia slept against my chest. I'd tried to force myself to stay awake, to keep watch, but sometime in the night, my body succumbed to exhaustion. When I woke, the darkness had not broken, and I sat, shivering in my flimsy blouse and bare legs, waiting.

For what, I did not know.

Morning brought illumination, if not clarity. I found myself in an abandoned factory hall, surrounded by machinery. The air smelled of metal and oil, overlaid by the reek of Kasia's soiled diaper and the sickening waft of death.

My head ached, a hammering that pierced my skull and left me woozy. Last night I'd thought only of Kasia, first too frantic, and then too spent, to consider my own injuries. I gingerly touched my scalp, drawing a sharp breath as my fingers found the blood-encrusted wound. I couldn't discern its severity, but I was still alive, so I supposed that told me something.

Kasia woke. She was fitful, fussy. In the morning light, I again examined her for injuries. Somehow she was unharmed. I fed her, then changed her soiled nappy, using my own underthings for lack of anything else.

Carrying her, I crossed to a window, careful to keep out of sight. The vacant yard stretched below me in the gathering daylight, a field of paving stones strewn with corpses. I leaned against the window frame to steady myself, head throbbing in time with my pulse, trying to think, to form a plan.

Dogs barking.

Voices. Distant, vague, coming from the next yard. The yard I'd escaped only hours ago.

The crack of a lone shot.

My breath trembled.

The gray shadows had returned.

I sank to the floor again, my back against the wall, choked by a rise of desperation.

Trapped.

ANTONINA
AUGUST 6, 1944

Twice the soldiers went over the yards, inspecting their handiwork, any professional blunders righted with a single shot.

When night fell and silence once again settled, I knew I needed to move. I'd already explored the building, searching for the exits.

In my wandering, I'd come upon a bucket of water, likely for use in case of fire. Dead flies drifted in the liquid, a film of grime clouding its surface, but I drank anyway, scooping handfuls into my mouth, gulping greedily, though the water stank. Then I washed the blood from Kasia's face and hair as best I could. I didn't dare give her any to drink, nor did I use the water to clean my wound, for fear of infection, though I bandaged my head with a strip of cloth torn from the bottom of my blouse.

I'd hoped to come across an exit that led directly onto a nearby street, a safe passage out of the factory complex, but found none. I fed Kasia and waited until she slept, then made my way to the door that led into the yard. I cracked it open, sifting the night, my shallow breaths marking the seconds.

Then I slipped out, into the deepening shadows.

I flitted across the expanse, my baby in my arms. Alertness honed my senses, eclipsing all else, even the pounding in my head. I came into the second yard.

I went still.

Less than two meters away stood a man. He could barely support his own weight, obviously wounded. Rusty blotches stained his coat.

Seconds passed as we stared at each other.

I stepped over bodies, approaching him. "The guards?" I whispered.

He nodded, gaze flicking back and forth.

"Do you know a way out?"

He shook his head, his eyes not on me but Kasia. "Is she . . . ?" The first words he'd spoken.

"My child." I paused. To encounter another living soul in this hellish landscape . . . how could it be possible? But this wasn't the time for questions. "We need to move."

The instant after the words came, I wondered if I'd be better off on my own. But how could I desert him, knowing what would happen if the soldiers found him? Beyond that, the draw of another human being after so many hours of near solitude could not be denied.

He pointed in the direction of the first courtyard and the factory gate beyond, then gave a shake of his head. *Not that way.* I nodded to show him I understood, then we set off.

How long did we wander? Trying doors and finding them locked, roaming the fenced-in grounds in the moonlit darkness as we searched for a way out. My companion wasn't young, his breathing labored with pain. Twice we heard German voices nearby and crouched low, barely breathing, until they moved on or we risked continuing.

Beside the fence bordering the factory, he drew me to a stop.

"The street is just on the other side. We'll climb it."

I stared up at the metal barrier looming alongside us. On my own, maybe I could manage, but with Kasia?

"I'll help you." When I hesitated, he added firmly, "It's the only way." He glanced at the fence, then back at me and Kasia. "Wait here." Without another word, he melted into the shadows.

I stood by the fence, wondering where he'd gone, if he'd be returning. Maybe he'd decided his chances would be better without a woman and a baby. He'd likely be right.

At footsteps, I tensed, then the man reappeared.

"I'll tie this around you." He had a man's shirt and belt in his hand and soon began fastening a sling of sorts. "You'd best carry her. With my arm . . ."

I nodded. Together we bound Kasia to my front. I couldn't allow myself to think about from where—from whom—the garments came.

He tightened the belt around my waist, checked to make sure all was secure. "I'll help you up. Go."

I drew a ragged breath. Metal gouged my fingers as I pushed myself up, fighting to gain a foothold, Kasia's weight heavy against my chest. The man boosted me from behind as I clawed and scrambled, the rasp of metal and my gasping breaths all too loud in the stillness. My wound pulsed, but I did not stop.

Somehow I gained the top of the fence, clinging to cold metal, the ground far and terrifying below me.

Then I swung my legs over, sliding, falling.

I landed hard, the air yanked from my lungs, bruised and scraped and aching. Kasia began to cry. I pushed to my feet.

Grunting and scrabbling came from the other side of the fence. The high barrier glinted in the moonlight.

Bootfalls.

I froze.

The outline of two soldiers. One had a cigarette, its tip an ember in the night.

My companion appeared at the top of the fence.

The soldiers spotted me. "Halt!"

Pale brightness, a swath of light.

I flashed a glance at my companion. He hadn't moved, features chalky in the glare of the soldier's electric torch as he perched atop the fence.

"Run." His whisper pierced the air. "Run."

"Halt! Hände hoch!"

I hurled myself into the night. The crack of gunfire, a whistling near my ear.

My heart slammed against my chest.

Clutching Kasia, I ran.

30

HELENA
AUGUST 6, 1944

Our boys stormed Gęsiówka yesterday. Two platoons from our battalion and Pudel, one of the tanks we'd captured, newly repaired and crewed. Somebody had the idea to christen it in honor of a fallen comrade—with each passing day, the number of the lost grew. The tank broke through the gate and barraged the watchtowers. Our platoons attacked, and the Germans surrendered. The seizure of the concentration camp in the ghetto ruins had been as much a tactical decision as it had been about the inmates at the mercy of their captors, for the watchtowers gave the enemy an ideal position from which to fire upon us with their machine guns. Inside the camp, three hundred and forty-eight Jewish prisoners remained. Upon gaining their freedom, many immediately volunteered to fight in our ranks.

The capture of Gęsiówka, the liberation of men and women who would surely have been murdered in a matter of days, and the victory with our recently acquired tank boosted our spirits in spite of our losses. "The daring lads from Błysk," Jerzy called our battalion. "Send in the daring lads from Błysk, and the Krauts will soon take flight. Write that in your next poem, Sowa."

Then Jasia had retorted, "And if the *ladies* of Błysk but had the weapons of the lads, they'd drop twice as many Hitlerites, and don't you ever doubt it. You can write that too, Sowa," she'd added with a flash of a grin.

Despite our successes, the fighting in Wola the past two days had been heavier than any we'd yet come against as German reinforcements mounted a fierce counterattack. Elements of our battalion had been positioned in the area of the cemeteries. Enemy troops attacked our positions, sometimes captured them, then our soldiers counterattacked and retook the positions, as if our two armies were children, one grabbing a toy, claiming the prize only for the other to snatch it back again a moment later. As one of the sites designated for weapons drops, which we'd finally begun to receive, it was vital the cemeteries remain in our hands.

Darkness drenched the rows of gravestones, a jagged forest stretching into the night. Tombstones slanted at sharp angles, others lay broken and discarded, the desecration of the Jewish cemetery evident even in the dark. Nearly all who lay beneath the ornate monuments had been interred before the war. But the dead from the ghetto had also been brought here and buried in pits when the ghetto had still existed, when the Jewish population of Warsaw had still existed. Or so I had heard.

I huddled behind a massive gravestone, the chill of fading daylight seeping into my skin. All day, I had carried orders to the line—whether they should withdraw, where they should direct fire, if German forces had increased from a certain direction. Now I leaned my cheek against the cool marble slab, my eyes drifting shut. For now, all was quiet, save for a sporadic flash of machine-gun fire from enemy lines. Under orders to conserve ammunition, our soldiers did not answer the fire as they hunkered among the tombstones.

My stomach gurgled, though my hunger was no more than my body's physical need for sustenance. I reached into a pocket of my smock and pulled out a paper-wrapped caramel. One of the nurses in the battalion had bestowed a handful of the sweets upon Jerzy, who cheerfully accepted the admiration of all, and he'd given one to me. Slowly, I unwrapped the candy, used my thumbnail to slice the caramel in two, nudged Malina.

She glanced at me. I held out my palm, showing the two halves of candy. She shook her head, her arms wrapped around her knees, her back against the stone.

"Malina, what's wrong?"

For a long moment, we sat in silence. "They shot the patients at St. Lazarus Hospital." Her words came soft, small. "The patients, the doctors, the nurses." Her voice caught on a hitch of breath.

I stared at her, my chest tightening. "But how—how do you know this?"

She swallowed hard. "I heard it from the doctor at the dressing station. They're forcing our soldiers to retreat, slaughtering civilians in their wake."

The words slammed into me with the force of a bomb blast, leaving me dazed, the world muffled. Striking me before I fully realized I had been shaken.

I crawled between the monuments and the men crouching behind them, keeping low, a soldier's instinct all that permeated the howling in my brain.

Andrzej turned as I dropped beside him. He'd positioned himself with his MP-40 behind one of the smaller tombstones. He gave me no more than a glance before his eyes again fixed on the line.

"What is it?" he asked quietly.

I sat, my shoulder pressed against his, and for a moment, I could not form the words. Perhaps because deep down, the irrevocable had already reached me.

"Malina told me they shot the patients at the St. Lazarus Hospital, that they're"—I swallowed—"that they're killing civilians."

He stared out at the line and did not speak.

No.

Before W-Hour, I told myself Wola would be safe, that there wouldn't be much fighting in this district west of the city centre. In the first days, as we seized objectives, drove out the enemy, and captured the tanks, I told myself it wouldn't last long. We would hold out until the Soviets arrived.

Then I didn't know what I told myself.

Before the district became a tattered patchwork of barricades and shifting lines, I could walk from the cemetery to Antonina's flat in less than an hour. Now I wondered if I could even reach her without crossing German lines. The enemy thrust across Wola had been met with strong resistance but also retreat. The fires in other parts of the district swept smoke across the sky, the wind carrying its acrid scent. But lack of communication with other units made it difficult to gather the breadth of the situation, each battalion forced to fight as a separate element rather than a unified force.

"How . . . bad is it?"

"It's not only ours who are being slaughtered, and it's not just the work of a few soldiers. They're rounding up civilians for execution, forcing women and children to walk in front of their tanks, so our men won't open fire."

I sat, enveloped by darkness, in the ruins of a cemetery, on a stranger's grave. And I shook. Not only my hands but my entire body. Shivering as if in a January wind, my teeth clattering.

"Tosia." The single word emerged, papery.

"What?"

"My sister. She lives here. In Wola."

"The one with the child?"

I nodded, fingers digging into the folds of my smock, clutching the fabric as if it were an anchor. I had no other.

For an instant, Andrzej took his gaze from the line. "I didn't know."

"No," I said softly, more to myself than him. "You wouldn't, would you?" I'd told him I had a sister, a niece, but we'd been schooled not to disclose personal information to comrades in the conspiracy, especially about our families. "We'll attack, force their troops to withdraw." My words spilled out, frantic, babbling. "We must fight for them."

For the civilians. For Kasia with her round cheeks and wondering brown eyes and wide gummy smiles.

For Antonina.

A long pause. Then finally, he said, "Our orders are to hold the cemeteries."

"Others can defend this sector. We're among the best. Tell the commander to send us there, tell him to send the whole battalion."

I was talking madness and I knew it, my voice breaking with desperation.

He drew a heavy breath. "I can't do that."

I wanted to ask why not, but I already knew the answer.

Because we had our orders. Because here, in this wilderness of crumbling tombstones, the enemy had pinned us down. We had to hold the cemeteries or retreat.

If we retreated, if Wola fell, then nothing remained to stand between the Germans and the Old Town where thousands more civilians dwelt.

"I told her she'd be safe," I whispered, staring dully into the night. "I told her it would be over in a few days."

He put a hand on my shoulder, his touch firm, steadying. In the moonlight, his eyes held resolve but also raw powerlessness. "You need to rest. One of the men will take you back to the Fortress."

"No, I'm fine."

I expected him to argue. Instead, he turned back to the line.

If I let myself absorb this reality, I would scream and I could not scream. I would run toward Antonina's flat, run as the Germans shot at me, and I would not care.

If I let this touch me, it would break me.

I drew a serrated breath, wishing I could curl up on the cold ground and sleep, just close my eyes and forget the rest.

"They'll counterattack." He gazed out across the field of tombstones. In the distance, a burst of machine-gun fire pierced the night. "If we fail to hold the cemeteries . . . Wola may very well be lost."

"She is my sister." The words escaped as a breath, exhaled and borne away on wind that carried the bitter waft of burning and destruction. "What does the rest matter if she is lost?"

ANTONINA
AUGUST 7, 1944

All night, I cowered in a burned-out building. Hiding from the gray shadows. Waiting for them to find me.

The patrol hadn't pursued me as I fled from the factory. They'd fired several rounds in my direction, then the shooting stopped. Hunters giving up as a wounded animal bounded into the forest, letting it go free so they might seek after other quarry.

They'd found my companion though, the man who'd bound my baby to my chest and helped me scale the fence. Of that I had little doubt. I didn't know how he'd survived the massacre in the factory. I didn't even know his name.

By his actions, he had saved my life. My child.

He had been a stranger to me. Still I mourned him.

Once again, I was alone.

Never had I felt the burden of my solitude more than now.

Morning arrived, and with it, the need for a decision. I couldn't stay here, for this place where life had dwelt only days ago had become a shell that might crack and give way around me at any moment.

I knew nothing about the situation elsewhere in the city. If Wola was any indication, it hardly mattered where I went. But I needed to leave. To attempt to reach safety, if only for Kasia's sake.

Debris and broken glass crunched under my feet as I scanned the blackened walls and ceiling. I didn't dare venture beyond the ground floor, but in a room that had perhaps belonged to the caretaker, I found several tins, a spoon, and a knife. I managed to cut open one of the tins and discovered—of all things—tomatoes. I ate the entire contents of the tin, crouching on the ash-strewn floor as I shoved the pulpy mixture into my mouth.

When I finished, the gnawing in my belly had eased, and I'd gained a bit more strength. I loaded the remaining tins and cutlery into the bundle I fashioned out of the shirt the man had used as a sling for Kasia. I fed her and changed her nappy, using a piece of cloth torn from the shirt. It had rusty brown stains on it, like Kasia's dress and my clothes. I noted them abstractedly.

Then I left my hiding place.

The burnt carcasses of buildings stood stark against a sky bright with sun, the street littered with rubble and tangled wires and corpses sprawled in the dust. Paving stones and battered furniture lay in a heap, remnants of a barricade.

Instinct made my senses sharp as I picked my way along the ruined street, keeping close to the shelter of buildings. Gunfire reverberated, distant.

Even under occupation, this could still have been called an ordinary city. Now it had become a field of battle.

I wasn't a soldier. Only a mother, frightened and alone. But that did not matter in war.

It did not matter to the German patrol at the corner of Wolska Street. I tried to evade them, to dart unseen into the rubble. I tried to fight. But they surrounded me with weapons and rough orders. They had no pity for my pleas.

I stood under the hot August sky, staring down a tunnel of cold black steel, my baby in my arms.

Strength bled from my body, my child's cries strangely far away. It didn't matter what happened to me. It no longer mattered what they did.

I had nowhere left to run.

31

HELENA
AUGUST 8, 1944

Among ivy-clad monuments of aged stone, men brought forth a glimpse of hell.

Time dissolved into smoke and chaos and sound. Deafening, unearthly. The tearing crackle of small arms fire, the drumming spurt of machine guns, the shattering blast of grenades and shells. The shouting of orders. The screams of the wounded. The silence of the dead.

The last forced its way in, but the rest drowned it out. In the cacophony of battle, there wasn't time or space or peace to die, but that did not matter.

Death made room for itself.

That morning, our battalion commander had issued an order from the commander-in-chief, Bór himself—positions in Wola must be held as long as possible to allow time to strengthen defenses elsewhere in the city.

A few hours later, I carried the urgent summons for our platoon to relieve the Parasol Battalion in the Evangelical cemetery where the Germans were attacking with force. The yet-unarmed among our ranks took weapons from the wounded and dead of Parasol and straight away put them to use against the advancing enemy infantry.

The living fighting for this place of the dead and falling as they fought.

Here, in the cemetery, I wasn't a liaison, not really. I was just one of the unarmed girls, ducking and crawling as bullets ricocheted among the tombstones, as I ran madly, blindly, to reach a wounded comrade and drag him to the makeshift dressing station we'd set up in an old tomb.

"Hold tight, Żbik." I plunged forward, hauling him on my back while he used his feet as much as he could. I would've dragged him by his legs, but fragments from a grenade explosion had embedded in his buttocks, so I had to do it this way. "Not much farther now," I gasped, doubting he could even hear me over the din of gunfire. When we'd learned to shoot, we'd fired one weapon, one round at a time. Now there were dozens of weapons, hundreds of rounds, and they just *kept going*. I wanted to run as far as I could, hide under my bed like a little girl, cover my ears from the terror of it all. But even if I did, it wouldn't end.

So I kept moving.

I reached the dressing station in the old tomb, and Malina relieved me of my burden, helping me ease Żbik onto a stretcher, lying on his stomach. We lowered the stretcher into the tomb and shifted him onto the metal coffin where, sheltered from falling debris, his wounds could be dressed.

"Grenade fragments." My voice sounded tinny above the ringing in my ears.

The nurse cut away Żbik's trousers, revealing the tattered flesh of his buttocks and lower back. As they rushed about tending him, I clambered out by way of the makeshift steps that led down into the tomb.

In the open again, I stood without moving, strangely lulled by the dreadful cadence around me.

Through the haze and chaos, Sowa darted from behind a tombstone, raised his Błyskawica. I didn't hear the shots he fired or maybe I did, maybe all the distinct sounds had simply become one great sound, one single horror.

The seconds slowed. Sowa was standing there and then he wasn't. Then he swayed, fell, crumpled.

Screaming.

The agony of the sound jolted through me.

Get to Sowa.

I ran at a crouch, ducking behind battered marble monuments as bullets whined and the air splintered.

In moments like that, when a comrade lay, meters away, needing help, needing you, all of your existence narrowed to a single purpose.

Get to Sowa.

An explosion. I dove, barely conscious of the jolt as my body struck the ground. The earth shuddered. Fragments of masonry and fallen branches rained. I tasted grit and gun smoke. I raised my head, adjusted my helmet, and crawled the remaining meters to Sowa. He turned his head as I reached him. He wasn't screaming anymore.

"Emilia." He struggled for breath, eyes wide behind his spectacles. Blood darkened his smock.

"I'm here. Everything will be all right." Keeping low, half-crawling, I dragged him by the legs, out of the cross fire. He cried out as I moved him. Somehow I got us both behind a tombstone near where he'd fallen.

I reached into the bag over my shoulder, took out scissors, cut away his smock and his shirt, revealing the pale skin of his torso. The hole just below his breastbone, slightly to the right.

Blood spurted from the wound. I pulled out a dressing, wiped away the blood, but it flowed faster than I could mop it up, seeping through the dressing, spreading warm and sticky between my fingers. I took out my canteen, unscrewed the cap with trembling hands, splashed water over the wound. Panic tasted metallic.

Sowa lifted his head. "How . . . how bad is it?"

"You'll be all right." I fought to keep my voice steady. "Just lie back."

I pressed a fresh dressing hard, held it in place. I'd had only a few courses in first aid. I wasn't a doctor nor even a nurse.

I had to fetch help. But I couldn't move him, not as I had others whose wounds had been less severe.

He started to shake, his body tremoring like he'd been too long in the cold.

What could I do? I didn't know what to do.

"Help!" The staccato of gunfire all but drowned my hoarse shout.

Sowa was gulping, coughing on blood. "I don't want to die." His breath made a burbling sound, blood sputtering from his lips. His eyes . . . they were so frightened.

"I promise, you're not going to die." I swallowed dryly. "Help!" I shouted again.

I had no morphine to give him, nothing to ease his pain. I reached up with my free hand, brushed his hair away, smoothing his forehead. "Shh."

"My poems. In my smock." He drew a struggling breath, his voice agitated. "Give them"—he swallowed—"to Malina. You've gotta give . . ."

"I will." My voice was soothing. "Don't worry."

"Mama." He shivered violently, gasping, choking on blood. "Mamusia. I'm . . . scared. Mamusia."

"Shh," I murmured, crouching beside him, stroking his hair. Blood saturated the dressing, but still I held it fast.

Someone screamed, a distant yell. In German. Someone was screaming in German. Not a shout of battle but an animal cry of pain.

"Ah-ah-ah, ah-ah-ah, there were two kittens," I sang softly, as Tata had often sung to me, as Sowa's mother had perhaps sung to him, rocking him to sleep, her brown-haired baby boy. His features eased, even as he fought for breath. Fought for life, even as it ebbed away, slipping so fast, too fast. "Gray and brown, oh both they are. Oh, sleep, my darling." My voice cracked, fading.

His breath gurgled, then . . . nothing.

I drew away my hand, leaving the soaked dressing behind.

The shooting didn't stop. Nothing stopped. No one noticed that a man had died, men were dying all around us, on both sides. I, too, might die by the next blast, the next bullet, and still, it would not stop.

I told him he'd be all right. I promised him.

I should have done more. Should have tried to bring him to the dressing station, carried him there. Should have . . .

Malina dropped beside me. "Sowa, Sowa!" She glanced at me. "We have to take him back to the dressing station."

I met her eyes, her heart-shaped face drained of color. She pressed her fingers against his neck, movements frantic, checking for a pulse.

I fumbled through the pockets in his smock until my fingers found the item I sought. I withdrew the little notebook, my fingerprints staining the battered cover. I slipped it into my bag. Malina knelt, motionless, cradling his head in her lap, touching his face.

"You never told me your name," she whispered, voice broken. "Tell me, Sowa. Just tell me your name . . ."

"Malina." Panic made my voice firm. "Malina, come."

When she didn't respond, I pulled her to her feet.

For a heartbeat of time, I stood in a haze, looking down at him— the bloody dressing, his face turned to one side, his skin chalky, his lips dark, his eyes open.

Then we ran. Bullets whizzed and slammed, electrifying the air. I shoved Malina down, flung myself on top of her as a grenade burst. My ears buzzed, sound muffled. I staggered to my feet.

At the dressing station, two of the nurses loaded a man onto a stretcher. One glanced up. "Sowa?"

I shook my head. She pressed her lips together, then said quickly, "Take this one back to the Fortress."

Malina and I went to the stretcher. A young man lay atop the canvas, the field dressing on his leg stained with blood. I took the head, Malina the end. We started off, bearing the stretcher between us. The wounded man groaned from the jostling, but we didn't slow our pace.

When carrying a stretcher under fire, you're lucky if you can find cover for the wounded, even if it's only your body shielding theirs. If not, I had learned there were two choices. Either drop the stretcher and take cover yourself or keep going, praying the bullets will miss both the wounded and you, expecting in the next second, you'll fall, not knowing and yet knowing that it's finally happened to you.

"I am a soldier now, Tosia."

I hadn't known what it meant then. I hadn't run with orders amid the crack and surge of bullets. I hadn't listened to stories of women and children driven in front of enemy tanks, of patients herded from their beds and shot in the street.

I hadn't stroked a boy's face as he bled to death, crying out in agony and fear, calling for a mother who would never answer.

With dogged grimness, I put one foot in front of the other, my shoulders burning under the weight, my palms sticky—with sweat, with blood—as I gripped the handles of the stretcher.

I hadn't known. About any of it.

ANTONINA
AUGUST 9, 1944

They marched us to St. Wojciech's Church. Maybe thirty of us altogether. All civilians, haggard, dazed, frantic. The soldiers searched the crowd for valuables, robbing us of whatever they found, including my tins of food. Before we reached the church, they separated men from women, forced the men into a half-burnt building.

Bursts of gunfire, then silence, and we moved on.

Next it would be our turn. I took in this probability with dull acceptance. To fight or run would only hasten the inevitable.

In front of the majestic Gothic edifice, soldiers stood guard, herding us inside.

St. Wojciech's Church had become a holding pen. Where Latin litanies and the soaring tones of the organ once echoed, now a chorus of human misery rose to the vaulted ceiling—the moans of the wounded, the weeping of the hysterical, the cries of frightened and hungry children. Where the fragrance of candles and incense had wafted, now hung the stench of waste, sweat, and the smoke of burning.

Hundreds of civilians had been brought to the church, mostly women and children. For what purpose, I wasn't certain, though talk had spread of a transit camp outside the city. How long could we remain here, with little water and even less food, penned in the nave like cattle awaiting slaughter?

Darkness coated the huddled forms covering the marble floor, others lying on pews. Some had blankets or eiderdowns, but I had nothing. I fed Kasia, cradling her warm weight against my chest. Somehow, despite the scant nourishment I'd taken in, my milk continued to come. Yesterday an old woman pressed a small hunk of dry bread into my hands, perhaps out of pity for a wounded woman with a baby. I'd taken the food, not for myself but for my child. Because of Kasia, I ate.

Because of Kasia, I tried to live.

After I fed her, she continued to fuss, so I rose, gently bouncing her as I stepped around the slumped figures. The vastness of the church surrounded me as the quiet click of my shoes echoed against the aisle. Coughing, moaning, and whispering filtered through the cavernous sanctuary; apart from this, all was silent.

I paused before a high window, stillness a chasm around me. Faint light emanated from the tapestry of the stained glass. At the center, Christ gazed down from the height of His cross, arms outspread, feet bound, the panes around His figure in vivid hues.

There You stay.

The thought came bitterly. That had always been His way, it seemed, viewing humanity from above, if He bothered to look at all. If He even existed.

A fragment of memory. The horror of the courtyard. The woman beside me. She'd been reciting something. Only now I realized it had been the twenty-third psalm.

"Yea, though I walk through the valley of the shadow of death, I will fear no evil: for thou art with me . . ."

She'd walked at my side as the gray shadows waited against the backdrop of that wall. Even then, she had prayed, her last breaths given in entreaty to Him.

In the next moment, she had fallen, as had I.

"For thou art with me."

How could He be? How could we be anything but alone in a world where men slaughtered children in a courtyard, a world that held a place like Treblinka, a world devoid of hope?

Perhaps He regarded our suffering and deemed it justice for our sins. But how could He find justice in this and be anything but cruel? If justice He sought, then why hadn't the woman who'd beseeched

Him so fervently been spared instead of me? For my sins were plain. In my eyes, and surely in His.

Maybe I had simply been spared by chance. Maybe God had turned His eyes away from that courtyard, seeing and hearing none of it, neither the woman's pleas nor my own.

For most of my life, I had neither denied nor sought Him. He had always been a shadowy figure, distant and intangible. As a child, our housekeeper told me God had taken my mother because He'd wanted her for His own. I'd decided God must be cruel, a king for whom subjects were playthings to be chosen and discarded on a whim, and I had lived in dread of the day God decided He wanted me too. I grew into a woman who dismissed those fears as childish nonsense and relegated religion to an antiquated tradition. Life had spread itself before me in those days, so full of possibility and expectation, it crowded out all else.

Now I did not know what I believed.

"He has not forsaken me. Nor will He you."

I bit my lip hard. I heard the words in Tata's voice, though he had written them in a letter, one of the few we'd received from the prisoner of war camp.

But He has, Tata. How could you be in that place and not see it?

How could I be in this place and not see it now? The indifference of fate and our powerlessness at its hands. The irrevocability of my own helplessness.

Why look to You if You abandon us? Why believe at all?

I gazed at the figure of the suffering Christ.

For Thou art with me.

The words whispered through the barren corridors of my soul. With them came a certainty I did not understand. With them, in the depths of myself, inexplicably, came peace.

It did not remove the fear, the anger, or the questions. It did not banish the darkness.

But gentle light filtered through stained glass, and I was not alone.

32

ANTONINA
AUGUST 13, 1944

Durchgangslager 121.

A sprawling complex of industrial buildings that once had been a railway works, less than twenty kilometers west of Warsaw, encircled by a high wall mounted with watchtowers. Thousands filled the transit camp, civilians from Wola and Ochota, brought here in transports as the SS advanced and overtook the districts.

Durchgangslager 121.

From one holding pen to another.

When they marched us from St. Wojciech's Church, I had been certain we were being taken to our execution. Even when we arrived, queuing outside the gate for hours, I'd prepared myself for the inevitable, though we heard no shots from within. Inside the camp, they herded us into a vast hall for "processing." German doctors and Gestapo officials sat at tables, Poles acting as translators, and we stood before them in turn. I could do nothing but look on as they separated an old woman from her daughter, a mother from her nearly grown son, a man from his wife and children. Pleas and tears had no effect. They led away the sobbing daughter and the stricken father, and the selection went on.

Durchgangslager 121.

From one hell to another.

In another cavernous industrial building, hundreds huddled on the filthy concrete, a blanket of misery so tightly woven, there remained little space between one body and another. The hall had no beds or cots, not even straw pallets. People covered themselves with whatever they'd brought—a blanket or coat—or lay on the bare ground. The stench of unwashed bodies and waste consumed the air, the long inspection pit formerly used to conduct repairs on train carriages now swimming with urine and excrement. In this hall were mostly the elderly and women with young children.

A doctor in a white coat and a nurse with a Red Cross armband made their way among the crowd, seeing to those in need of medical attention. The seriously ill and wounded had been separated from the rest during processing, but I hadn't been among them.

At last the wound on my scalp was cleaned and dressed. While the Polish nurse tended to me, I questioned her about the fate of the people here. Transports left from the camp almost daily, she told me. She wasn't certain of their destination—though she knew they were selecting the young and healthy for labor in the Reich. On other transports, she'd heard they simply deposited the people elsewhere in the Generalgouvernement. Some of the severely wounded and ill were being admitted to nearby hospitals, and the camp administration issued release papers to a small number of others, allowing them to leave freely. But—here she hesitated and I pressed her for the truth—she'd overheard a conversation between two Gestapo officials about other transports. Transports bound for the camp near the town of Oświęcim. Auschwitz.

The woman said she'd speak to one of the Polish doctors and ask him to add my name to the list of the ill to be discharged, which would then be approved by the German administration, upon which I would receive official release papers. She made it plain this could not be done for everyone, but she would do what she could for me and my child. Tears started to my eyes as I thanked her, and she rested a gentle hand atop Kasia's curls, her smile tinged with sorrow.

Days passed as we remained penned in the hall. Then came the third morning. The guards entered the hall and forced hundreds of us out to the siding. On the tracks pocking the wide expanse, a column of railcars waited.

I stood in a mass of others, Kasia in my arms. The nurse had promised to arrange for my release. But I had no official papers. Was this how we would depart the camp, in these wagons? Would they really allow so many to leave at once? Each day, new transports arrived, crowding the Durchgangslager, so perhaps . . .

No. Whatever was about to happen, this wasn't our release. Not to freedom, anyway.

I stared at the cars. Coal wagons, roofless to allow for the loading of cargo.

That's all we are to them. Cargo.

I drew a shaky breath. My wound pulsed.

"Do you know where they are sending us?"

I turned at the woman's voice. A kerchief covered her gray-white hair, her shoulders stooped. She had no one beside her.

"They say"—I swallowed—"people are being sent to other parts of the Generalgouvernement. At least, some of them. I don't know, really." I forced away thoughts of what the nurse had said about transports to Auschwitz.

"No one knows." Her words came quiet.

Our turn came to board. I had no luggage, not even a handbag, only my child. Supporting Kasia with one arm, I clambered inside, then reached down to help the woman, her knobby fingers clutching mine as she climbed aboard unsteadily.

"Thank you."

I managed a faint smile in reply.

Once the wagon could hold no more, a guard bolted the door. I sat, leaning against the side of the car, drowsy with the heat of the sun on my face. Finally, they coupled the engine. A whistle shrilled.

Kasia started to cry. I rocked her, pressing my lips against her damp cheek. "Shh."

The train drew out of the siding, slowly gathered speed. Wind tugged at my hair. I drew a long breath, the air warm and scented with late summer, the sky a clear, endless blue.

How could it be? This untarnished landscape, this peace, while Warsaw burned and her children fought and corpses lay in heaps, thousands upon thousands? *No, don't think of it—don't remember Wola.*

I turned my head. The old women sat by me, the ends of her kerchief fluttering in the breeze.

"My son," she said, voice almost a whisper. "He is fighting. Warsaw is not lost yet."

The words carried the echo of our anthem. "Poland has not yet perished, so long as we still live. What the foreign force has taken from us, we shall with sabre retrieve." I'd heard an old man whistling the notes as we built the barricade and had smiled at the rousing melody, forbidden during the years of occupation. I didn't want to think of what had likely become of him.

I nodded, but couldn't find the words to answer her. Wola had fallen. Ochota too, if the stories its inhabitants had repeated during the days at the transit camp were to be believed. How long could the remaining districts hold out? If the Soviets crossed the river, rendered the aid we had expected, perhaps a chance remained.

Meanwhile the soldiers fought on, an army alone.

Helena with them. My sister, shy and wide-eyed, younger by only minutes, but always seeming the little one, in need of care and protection.

"I am a soldier now, Tosia."

And there had been fire in her eyes.

She was still there, still fighting. I wouldn't allow my thoughts to form any other possibility.

Please, God. Protect her.

Hours went by. Several times, the train lurched to a stop to allow a military transport to pass. Kasia slept, her tiny fist curled around the collar of my blouse. The old woman did too, her head drooping.

I didn't know our destination. But anywhere would be better than in the hands of our captors. There might be no opportunity for escape once our journey ended. The longer I waited, the farther the train would carry us from Warsaw.

When we stopped next, I would take the chance.

I sat, crammed alongside dozens of others in the open box of the car, waiting for the train to slow, preparing myself.

The train came to another jolting halt. Not on the tracks but at a station.

Bolts clanked as the doors opened. Along with the others, I stumbled out of the wagon, legs shaky. I stood beside the car, cradling Kasia in the midst of the teeming crowd.

On the station building a sign read "Łowicz."

HELENA
AUGUST 14, 1944

Memories came jagged, like broken china strewn across a floor, fragments too myriad to ever hope to collect, much less fit together.

Our last day in Wola, the eleventh of August, when the cemeteries had fallen, German forces striking our weary remnants in a ruthless onslaught with losses on both sides.

We had spent ourselves for Wola. Our comrades had spilled their blood to hold this district of factories and blocks of flats inhabited by working-class families, this bastion between the enemy advance and the Old Town. And then the order came.

Withdraw. Retreat.

Leaving the remaining civilians in the hands of a pitiless enemy.

But the command had been given. It was for us to follow it, to forsake that which we had fought for bitter days to defend.

How easy it would have been to slip off my armband and make for the street where Antonina lived. To search for my sister and her child, to be with them in whatever lay ahead.

But I would almost certainly have been captured by the Germans and then I would be no use to either my sister or my comrades. It was said civilians were being held in St. Wojciech's Church, and from there, sent to a transit camp outside the city. I could have tried to reach the church, but in the end, I remained with my platoon.

Because I had sworn an oath that bound me to the defense of my homeland, bound me to the men and women I fought beside. Because this had become more than a battle for the liberation of

Warsaw. We, the soldiers, defended not only the city but also the civilians who dwelt there, the thousands who may not have been armed with weapons but had nonetheless been thrust onto the front lines. Because I had a duty—to my fellow Varsovians, to my brothers and sisters in arms, to my country, and to my family.

For us, the soldiers of the Armia Krajowa, this became everything.

Other memories. Our retreat through the former ghetto, its ravaged landscape an echoing reminder of how our occupiers dealt with defiance. We fled over the ruins as shots cracked and projectiles from grenade launchers exploded, often in the very place our feet had touched but a moment before.

Our tanks had been lost. Our staunchest soldiers in Wola— without whom we would never have captured Gęsiówka, nor held the district for so long—had taken wounds in the battles and had to be abandoned. Before the crew fled, they'd set Pudel on fire. Better to destroy the Panther than leave it for the enemy to use against us.

The shards of memory would remain embedded in my mind, always there, always broken. I could sweep them into the corners, out of sight, but I would never be free of them so long as I remained among the living.

Sowa lying on the ground, his vacant eyes staring into the blue endlessness of the sky. The seven from our platoon who died with him that day. Władzia, who fell on our final day in Wola.

On the day of W-Hour, there had been thirty-nine men in Andrzej's platoon, along with three women. I'd stopped counting our losses. The other platoons in the company, the other companies in the battalion, the whole of the Radosław Group had all suffered heavy casualties. We'd buried as many of our dead as we could in Wola. There had been only a few mounds of fresh earth at first, but they had grown in number as the days passed, each marked by a humble cross.

They, too, had been left behind.

We were left reeling, stripped by our losses, but there was no time to acknowledge them. No chance to absorb their pain. There was only the fight before us, and to that, we must give all our strength.

No rest awaited us in the Old Town. Our battalion had found itself among those assigned to the area of Stawki Street, which had become the advance defense of the Old Town. More had been wounded and lost in the fight to hold Stawki. Jasia had been carrying orders to Bronek's platoon when she'd been struck in the elbow by a bullet and had to be taken to the hospital.

In the end, after two days of heavy fighting, Stawki had fallen.

The Old Town is trapped.

The truth lay deep in the pit of my stomach. We were encircled. The enemy had secured their noose of fire—heavily armed troops and artillery and armored trains—and now had only to tighten the rope. Constricting the medieval streets of the Old Town and its citizens within. Cutting off its oxygen. Suffocating it slowly, inescapably.

I knew little about the situation in the rest of Warsaw, only what we read in the *Biuletyn* or heard from someone who had come to the Old Town. Each district fought its own isolated battles, each grappled to hold what scrap of the city they still possessed.

But I couldn't think about that now. Nor about anything except the message I had to deliver to the headquarters of the Radosław Group.

Our platoons and battalions had no radio links, no telephones, no means of communication on the lines of battle, save us.

We were their radios, their telephones, their links. Girls without weapons.

And we would get them through, the orders and reports and messages. So help us, we would get them through or give ourselves in trying.

In the days since W-Hour, Varsovians had built a city beneath a city, knocking openings through the cellar walls of neighboring buildings to create a warren of passageways through which people could travel without risking the dangers of a journey through the streets. They'd even painted signs on the walls so pedestrians didn't lose their way. The ingenuity of necessity.

Sweat trickled down my back as I wended among the mass of people cloistered in the cellar, fortifying themselves in the recesses of the building against the terrors aboveground. I'd been in the Old Town only three days and already I had learned you died just as easily below as you did above. Buried under the rubble of a collapsed building or struck by a sniper's bullet while walking down the street. It was simply a matter of detail in the end.

The air was close, oppressive. A musty dankness emanated from the cellar as if from its very pores. In the dingy light of a small carbide lamp, a woman rocked a crying baby. Two children quarreled over a toy. A man dozed in a corner. An old woman fingered the beads of her rosary, chanting, "Hail, Mary, full of grace . . ."

From somewhere above came the crump of an exploding shell. The sound no longer made a great impression on me, for when you heard the hit, that meant the shell hadn't found purchase where you stood. Somewhere else, somewhere close, but not there. Not in that instant, at least.

But the moment always came when I had to leave the shelter of the cellars and emerge into the light again. I blinked, the sun startlingly bright after the dimness belowground, as I hurried across a vacant courtyard, passing the place where a cross marked a newly dug grave.

I paused in the gateway. Men hunkered behind a barricade of mounded sandbags just beyond the entrance of the courtyard. Shots echoed off the buildings. The soldiers at the barricade fired, reloaded. From my vantage point, I couldn't deduce where the Germans were firing from.

"I'm jammed," a young soldier yelled, cursing the shoddy workmanship of his Błyskawica as he tried to clear the magazine.

One of the men turned in my direction.

"I need to get across," I called, my words caught in the clatter of gunfire.

"Well, you can't do it now," he shouted back, as if the mere fact of my presence was somehow a personal inconvenience. Perhaps my *female* presence might be closer to the truth. "Wait for my signal."

Having nothing better to do and no real choice in the matter, I sat down in the shelter of the gateway to wait. The shooting went on, a drumming blur in my consciousness. No longer did I jump at every burst of fire. I supposed I had grown used to it. Not heedless, not unbothered, not fearless, just accustomed. To what else could I grow accustomed, if given the time?

Footsteps crunched over glass and debris. I turned. A woman approached, the armband over the sleeve of her blue jacket all that identified her as a member of the Armia Krajowa. She wasn't as young as most who served as liaisons, perhaps in her thirties. Her frame slight, her hair mousy brown. She crouched beside me, clasping her arms around her knees as she took in the street.

"We have to wait for the signal to cross."

She nodded. "They're whistling quite a tune out there," she remarked in a seasoned sort of way.

A particularly unpleasant tune.

We sat in the gateway, not speaking, like two strangers waiting at a tram stop. I might have attempted conversation, asked what battalion she was from, but the gunfire made it difficult to speak as well as to hear.

When the signal came, who would cross first? The first to attempt the dash had the advantage of surprise; the enemy would not be expecting them. Life and death hung on the infinitesimal—the space of a breath, the tick of one second into another, the breadth of a centimeter.

I had arrived before the woman. By rights, I ought to be first. The importance of the message each of us carried should really decide the matter, but to sort that out would not be so easy.

She kept her gaze ahead, lips moving soundlessly. I couldn't make out whether she was counting, praying, or simply muttering to herself. She was older, frailer.

Deep inside, I knew when the moment came, I would not seize the advantage.

Anger rose, swift and uncontrollable. At the stranger beside me, simply for her existence. At myself, for my weakness in not pushing ahead, and for my self-preservation, so raw and shameful. I despised myself for it, even as it could not be denied. Ideals died amid the reality of battle, victory and honor and even Poland, once so golden and glorious, worthy of the greatest of sacrifices. In their place was an urge so primal it blinded all the rest. The will to survive, to clutch at life itself.

The firing subsided. The soldier turned, motioned with a wave. The woman and I looked at one another.

"Go," I said quickly, then added, quiet, "Godspeed."

"Thank you." She rose, left the gateway at a crouch. An instant's pause, then she flitted across, a sparrow taking wing. A shot rang out.

I approached the barricade, hunched low. I sensed the eyes of the soldiers on me, but they could do nothing but watch. My heart thudded, my legs shook. I swallowed, tasting dust and gun smoke. Fear. I tasted fear.

I wouldn't be fast enough. I had done it before, but this time, this time . . .

"Be brave, Hela."

Antonina's voice. An echo. When had she said it? I tried to recall, to catch hold of the memory.

It had been the morning of a recitation at school. We had been seven or thereabouts, and I'd been huddling in the corner of our bedroom in my freshly pressed dress and ribbon-tied plaits, my stomach churning, knowing what awaited me—a sea of eyes to make my face burn and my words stumble.

Antonina had knelt beside me, reached for my hand. *"Be brave, Hela. I'll be with you."*

I drew a slow breath, holding the image of my sister's face in my mind.

Then I ran, keeping low. Darting across the expanse, stumbling over broken cobblestones and tangled tramway cables and rubble. The street blurred, a haze of gray and brown. Shots spattered. I ducked and ran and kept running as bullets whined, finding purchase in the sandbags, striking the cobbles around me.

A glimpse of blue, a sprawled figure. Brown hair and a cratered skull, red and gray spilling onto the pavement.

Don't stop.

The *rat-tat-tat* of a machine gun. The slamming of my heart. The ragged inhales of my breaths. My feet pounded the ground, yet barely touched it.

In another time and place, in a sedate, human world, crossing the street would take a minute, perhaps two. How long it took me, I would never know.

A lifetime passed in that space.

But I reached the other side. Somehow.

Minutes later, I arrived at the building where the Radosław Group had their headquarters. A sentry stood in the entrance, holding a British Sten.

"I have a message." I pushed out the words, my tongue dry and swollen.

"Your pass?"

It was a common enough question. Since the battle began, all liaisons carried passes, permitting us to move freely through areas held by the AK.

But suddenly, I wanted to shout at him, to scream and swear. *Do you know what I've just done? Do you know what it took for me to come here and what it will take for me to return? Do you, standing here in your tidy uniform, holding a weapon you probably haven't fired once today, know even a scrap about what it's like out there, and how dare you—how dare you—ask me for my pass?*

My hands shook as I retrieved the typed and stamped slip. He checked my pass and returned it, then motioned me into the building.

In the corridor, I paused. Smoothed a hand down my front.

A tiny hole, like a cigarette burn, pocked the autumn-brown fabric near my chest. Frantic, I clawed at the smock, searching for the wound, waiting for my hand to come away slick.

My fingers brushed metal. I drew out the chain.

The medallion had been bent, the image of Christ twisted, compressed.

My fingers curled around the tarnished oval, squeezing hard.

For a long moment, I stood, trembling.

Then I went to deliver the message.

I had become a soldier.

Only in that moment did I realize I had stopped believing I would live to be anything else.

33

ANTONINA
AUGUST 14, 1944

The cottage sat back from the road, painted in the hazy brushstrokes of summer twilight. It had a thatched roof and blue shutters from which the paint had long begun to fleck and fade. Another building, likely the barn, stood a distance away. Between the two lay the yard, an expanse of hard-packed dirt and scrubby grass.

I followed the village elder up the path, Kasia in my arms. My skull throbbed and my back ached and I blinked hard to keep my eyes open.

We'd spent last night in an abandoned camp near Łowicz. Both a Polish aid organization and the townspeople had done what they could for us. Local women distributed bread and tea, a gesture of solidarity and sympathy for the refugees from Warsaw.

This morning, the process of finding lodging began. Those with relatives or friends in Łowicz would be placed with them. The rest would be dispersed to surrounding villages. Kasia and I had been sent along with a group of others to a village about twenty kilometers from Łowicz. The elder of the village had been tasked with housing us, our number dwindling as he escorted us through the village and the surrounding farmsteads. Though some accepted the displaced Varsovians without disagreement, arguments ensued as the locals, many of whom appeared near destitute themselves, protested at having to accommodate strangers. But they took them in the end. They had little choice.

As we approached the cottage, I wondered dully what sort of people my hosts would be. Whoever they were, their home couldn't be worse than the Durchgangslager. If the situation became unbearable, I could move on. I was free from the Germans, and whatever happened now did not matter so much. Survival, I had learned, is very simple. Success or failure. No in between.

A girl of about fourteen came out of the barn carrying a pail, her feet bare beneath the hem of her faded print dress. A younger boy darted out behind her. He drew up short at the sight of us and sidled closer to the girl. They stood in the doorway of the barn, eyeing our arrival with a mixture of shyness and curiosity.

The village elder knocked on the cottage door. A moment later, a woman opened it. The toll of hardship made years difficult to determine, but I placed her between forty and fifty, her frame sturdy, strands of gray threading her hair, her eyes set deeply in her weathered face.

"Praised be Jesus Christ." The elder gave the greeting long a custom in rural areas.

"Forever and ever, amen." The woman dried her hands on her apron. "Well, I expect you've come about the people from Warsaw."

"So I have, Pani."

"And who's to be put here?" She peered past his shoulder to where I stood.

The elder gave a nod in my direction.

I hesitated, suddenly conscious of how I must appear. My blouse and skirt dirty and marked with rusty stains, my head bandaged and my hair in matted strands, the child in my arms just as filthy and reeking of her soiled nappy.

"I'm Antonina Dąbrowska."

"Jaga Wadowska," the woman replied.

Kasia, who'd been fussy all day, began to squall. I shifted her wearily in my arms.

Pani Wadowska's brow furrowed. "This your child?"

"My daughter, Kasia." I doubted this woman would think favorably about giving shelter to an unmarried woman with a baby. In time, she would ask about my husband, and I would tell her my child's father had died, giving as few details as possible.

"I'd best be on my way." The elder nodded to Pani Wadowska and headed toward the road.

Pani Wadowska appraised me, a hand propped on her hip. "Children," she called across the yard. "Stop loitering and get on with your chores." She turned back to me. "You'd better come in. The child needs to be fed, and you look as if you haven't had a decent meal in a month."

"Thank you." I followed her into a low-ceilinged room furnished with a rough-hewn table and dresser. On one wall hung a faded tapestry; on the other, a simple crucifix. The rich scent of vegetables rose from the pot bubbling on the stove. My stomach gave a hollow gurgle.

"Sit yourself down. Supper won't be long." She stepped to the table, picked up a knife, and began slicing a loaf of dark bread.

I lowered myself into a chair. For days there had been only survival and death. Fighting for one, waiting for the other. Only now had I begun to awaken to the irrevocability of my uprooting.

"From Warsaw, are you?"

"Yes." I settled Kasia on my lap, trying to quiet her cries.

"Foolishness. Trusting the red plague to drive out the black one. Foolishness." She cut through the loaf, her knife making a sharp sound as it struck the wooden board. "No good will come of it." She raised her head, eyes weary in her hardened face. "Only more suffering than what has already been."

HELENA
AUGUST 16, 1944

"May I have your attention, please?"

I lowered my spoon. Bronek stood at the front of the room full of soldiers and nurses and liaisons eating plates of soup, cleaning weapons, performing the myriad small tasks we did at quarters. The brevity of the interludes the only certainty they held before we went out again, back to the barricades, back to the fighting.

Conversation dwindled. I swallowed, chaff from the soup sticking in my throat. Little else but the ache of hunger could have induced me to touch the stuff. Pluj-zupa. Spit-soup, prepared with barley that hadn't been husked, so dubbed because we had to spit out the sharp hulls as we ate, a practice I would find more disgusting if I had the energy to care. But food in the Old Town was too scarce to do otherwise than swallow whatever was offered and be grateful.

"I have an announcement."

At Bronek's words, I tensed. Until I saw their faces, for Jasia stood beside Bronek, her arm in a sling. She'd returned to us this morning after only four days in the hospital. In true Jasia fashion, she'd given the nurses the slip and made her way back to our quarters. "My right arm is still in working order and I can manage perfectly well," she'd said. "I'm not going to lie abed while you all go on without me."

She and Bronek had argued, as they often did, their spats as fiery as their romance. And as often happened, Jasia won, though Bronek could have used rank to his advantage and ordered Jasia to return to the hospital.

Now they both smiled, Bronek's arm at Jasia's waist.

"This beautiful lady and I are to be wed."

"This is news?" Jerzy called out and a few laughed.

"That's not what he means." Jasia kept smiling. "We're to be married now. Today."

Andrzej's brows lowered as he sat on a crate, cleaning his MP-40. "You're not serious."

"Never more so. We've already spoken with the company commander, and he's agreed to give us leave until tomorrow morning. In an hour, Father Paweł will bless our marriage. It won't take long. He's promised to do it quickly. We need only the simplest of solemnities to seal what is already in our hearts." Bronek's eyes softened as he and Jasia shared a glance. "We'll not wait another day, not while it's within our power."

My gaze went to Andrzej. How would he respond? A wedding at such a time, in a city under relentless bombardment, on what was nearly the front lines of an increasingly desperate battle.

"Well, then." Andrzej rose. "I think it only right I be the first to offer my congratulations." He clapped Bronek on the back, and the brothers embraced. "Congratulations." He turned to Jasia, clasped her hand. "Both of you, congratulations."

All at once, others surrounded the couple in a flurry of well-wishes and embraces and good-natured teasing.

"We were talking," Bronek was saying, "and I asked her, 'What are we waiting for? Stalin to accept our invitation? Why not do it now?' The old rules aren't worth a grosz anymore."

"That's the spirit," Jerzy said. "If there was ever a moment for carpe diem."

I hugged Jasia. "I'm so happy for you both."

She drew me aside. "You'll come, won't you? My mother and sisters won't be there, and you're as dear to me as a sister ever could be."

I smiled, a sudden catch in my throat. "Of course. Of course I'll come."

In the quarters shared by the women, liaisons and nurses fussed over the bride-to-be. I rummaged through my rucksack until I found my extra blouse.

"It's white, at least." I shook out the wrinkles. It wasn't really white, for the material had a pattern of pale blue checks, the blouse fashioned with a simple V-shaped collar. Not nearly fit attire for a bride, but none of us had anything better.

"As long as it isn't SS camouflage, I'll be a happy woman."

We burst out laughing, Jasia first, then the rest of us, giggling like schoolgirls at the sheer incongruity of these circumstances.

Another girl helped Jasia undo the sling and slip her injured arm through the sleeve, before fastening the buttons of the blouse. As we bustled about Jasia, I glanced at Malina who sat on a mattress, apart from the rest. I crossed the room and lowered myself beside her.

I hadn't found out what had been inside the notebook Sowa so urgently requested be placed in her hands. But one night in Wola, I came upon her holding the worn little book while tears trailed soundlessly down her cheeks.

Though she never spoke of her loss, in her gentle gaze dwelt fathomless sorrow.

One of the other liaisons swept Jasia's auburn waves into a loose chignon. "There. Lovely."

Suddenly, Malina rose and approached Jasia. "Here." Her voice was shy as she held out a small tube. Lipstick.

Not once had I seen her wear the cosmetic. She'd been saving it, perhaps gathering enough courage to use it, to be noticed. Though the quiet boy who poured his truest self onto the pages of a battered notebook had noticed her and loved her with the whole of his earnest heart.

"Thank you, Malina," Jasia said, her voice soft, as if she understood what this simple gesture had cost.

I held a compact mirror as Jasia carefully outlined the bow of her top lip before smoothing the color over her bottom lip and rubbing a bit on her cheeks. "Well?" She did a little turn, like a model for a fashion house, in my wrinkled blouse and her own navy skirt, her arm in its white sling, wisps of hair curling around her flushed cheeks.

Applause rippled among the women. "Beautiful."

And Jasia was. I'd never seen a bride more radiant.

"Irek won't have eyes for anyone else." One of the nurses gave a sigh, wistful at the romance of it all.

"Well, I should certainly hope not." Jasia grinned.

"This too." I picked up her armband from the pile of garments on the mattress, helped her fasten it around her uninjured arm, the white-and-red band standing out against the light blue checks.

Our uniform and the emblem of our freedom both.

"Thank you." Jasia's gaze encompassed the women around her. "All of you."

It took over half an hour to reach the church, navigating the labyrinth of cellars belowground and ducking behind barricades above. Only seven of us went—the bride and groom, Andrzej and me as witnesses, and a few friends. What a wedding procession, accompanied not by the strains of music but the muffled thunder of exploding bombs.

Jasia carried a bunch of petunias Bronek had plucked from "a very obliging window box." Before they left for the church, he'd slipped one in her hair near her ear, then kissed her there. The bloom had wilted by the time we arrived at the cathedral, its petals drooping, but she wore it still.

They stood, facing one another, before the priest who had been with our battalion since the outbreak of fighting, heard confession for soldiers before battle, offered comfort to the dying and administered last rites, and above all, presided over the mounds of freshly turned earth where our fallen lay. Now he carried out another office, his stole binding Bronek and Jasia's hands as they recited their vows.

"I, Bronisław, take you, Janina, to be my wife, and I promise to love and honor you—" In that moment, it mattered not that we stood in the bomb-blasted remains of a once-majestic cathedral, the marble floor littered with fragments of stained glass and debris. In that moment, Bronek held Jasia's gaze, and all else fell away, leaving only the radiance of their love. "—to be faithful to you and to not forsake you until we are parted by death. In fear of Almighty God, One in the Holy Trinity, and all the saints."

I glanced at Andrzej as Jasia repeated her vows. Our eyes met, his lips softening into an almost-smile. His fingers enfolded mine as we stood slightly behind the couple. I squeezed his hand, remembering our kiss.

The audacity of love. It rose from the ashes, defying circumstance that would snuff it out, only to burn all the brighter. It burned now, in Bronek and Jasia's eyes, as they pledged themselves to one another in the ruins of the cathedral. And as I looked up at Andrzej, it rose within my own chest, its flame steady and true.

The ceremony lasted no longer than ten minutes, for neither we nor Father Paweł could spare more time. In the crypts beneath the cathedral, a field hospital had been set up, and he must visit the wounded and dying there.

He made out the marriage certificate, using their real names, as they had during the ceremony, for Andrzej had the presence of mind to mention beforehand that doing otherwise could lead to their union not being recognized as legal later on.

At our quarters, a few of the others had organized a wedding feast—bread, tinned meat, and a bar of chocolate someone had saved from the German storehouse.

Jerzy held up a bottle of wine and presented it to Bronek with a flourish. "You'll need plenty of this to face the night ahead, my man."

"Liquid courage," Ryś said amid laughter.

Jasia grinned, blushing.

"Mind you don't insult your superior officer." But Bronek grinned too. He gripped Jerzy's hand. "Thank you."

"We have another gift for you," said one of the men from Bronek's platoon.

"A honeymoon suite at the Hotel Europejski," Jerzy broke in.

The young man from Bronek's platoon chuckled. "Not quite, I'm afraid. But there's a storage room on the first floor. We've cleared it out a bit and arranged a place for the two of you. You'll be quite alone."

Bronek and Jasia looked at one another. "Thank you." Jasia smiled.

Malina poured the wine into an assortment of glasses, and I helped her pass them around.

Ryś took out his harmonica and blew a few notes of "Sto lat."

Jerzy began to sing, raising his glass. "A hundred years, a hundred years, may they live!" We joined in, voices rising in hearty chorus. Bronek slipped an arm around Jasia and kissed her while we sang. "A hundred years, a hundred years, may they live! Once again, once again, may they live."

Bootfalls against floorboards.

The song died away, the harmonica notes squealing to a discordant conclusion as the company commander entered the room.

He took in the scene, features grim. "I'm afraid I must put an end to the festivities. Orders just arrived. Assemble your men. Briefing in ten minutes."

HELENA
AUGUST 18, 1944

The eighteenth day of the battle.

The eighteenth day.

Somebody had mentioned the date. When or why, I couldn't remember. Jerzy. Yes. He had a pocket calendar. He'd told me this was his mother's name day. Helena. Like me. Though, of course, Jerzy didn't say that. He didn't know it was my name day too. There would be no presents, no well-wishes. Because here, I was Emilia.

He didn't know where his mother was. He'd had no word from her since he left to join the battalion for W-Hour.

He had a mother named Helena and he didn't know if she was alive and I don't remember what I said because my mind had fixated on the date.

The eighteenth.

Less than three weeks since the outbreak of fighting.

How could it be possible? Time had passed without my marking it, without my even realizing it. Each day blurred into the next, becoming one long, relentless day. The sky passed from dawn to night but not to darkness, because the city never stopped burning now, the horizon aglow from the fires caused by incendiary bombs and rocket launchers. We called the rocket launchers "cows" because, as the shells propelled through the sky, they emitted a terrifying bellow like a beast in pain. Little could be done to extinguish the fires because the Germans had cut off the city's main water supply. Now we had to rely on the few wells that hadn't been buried under rubble or drill new ones. Water as precious as ammunition and food and hope and everything else we were running out of.

The battle for Warsaw had become its own eternity.

I went to the field hospital on Miodowa Street to visit some of the boys from our battalion—among them Ryś, who'd been wounded the day before. I still had a bar of chocolate from the German storehouse and had gone so I might cheer the boys with greetings from their comrades and bring back news of how they fared to the others. Jerzy had given me cigarettes for Ryś, his gaze earnest, anxious, as he pressed the packet into my hand. "Make sure the kid gets them," he'd said, and there had been none of his usual brash humor in the words.

Had I arrived twenty minutes earlier, I would have been inside when Stukas flew over the four-story edifice plainly marked with a large red cross, the planes diving with their terrible droning shriek, releasing their loads, bomb after bomb falling methodically, inexorably.

When I reached the hospital, it was all over. There were only flames and mangled walls. Twisted iron and the skeletons of staircases. The air murky with smoke. Figures coated in black grime and the dust of pulverized masonry, scarcely resembling human beings, clambered among the ruins. Somebody shouted and somebody else screamed and I couldn't tell from where either came. For a frozen instant, I stood, clutching the candy in its paper, the chocolate cracking under my grip, crushed to bits by my fingers.

I helped the doctors and nurses and civilians pull the living and the dead from the remains of the building. I kept looking for Ryś until I found his body, laid out alongside others, coated in dust and soot but startlingly whole, his copper hair falling boyishly over his forehead. I bent, placed the cigarettes on his chest, folded his fingers around the packet.

"Make sure the kid gets them."

Then I returned to our quarters on Franciszkańska Street and fetched the soup and brought it to our men who couldn't leave their positions. They'd nothing to eat that day, and we still had barley to make soup and so I carried the soup. It wasn't very pleasant, carrying a pail of soup under fire, but I had learned to do it. In the last eighteen days, I had learned to do a great many things I never thought could be done, least of all by me.

I didn't tell them about the hospital. It wasn't any different than what happened every day in the Old Town, and they would hear soon enough anyway.

Later I went back to our quarters. For a moment, I remained near the gateway, holding the empty pail, fully aware of the danger of standing there, out-of-doors, exposed. But I just stood, squinting into the bright blue of the sky, the heat sweltering against my skin.

Against the dazzle of the sun, a figure emerged.

I blinked.

A man, filthy, bloodied, walking slowly toward me.

He was carrying something in his arms.

My breath trapped in my chest. I wanted to press my eyes shut so

I wouldn't see it. Wanted to will my body or, at the very least, my soul to take flight from this place. But I couldn't move.

Bronek stared directly at me, but it was as if he saw right through me or didn't see me at all. He continued walking, each slow step.

Then he went to his knees, still cradling the limp form in his arms, holding it with such gentleness. As if it might shatter. As if it weren't broken already.

He bent over her, touching her matted hair with his broad, grime-streaked hand.

Jasia.

But it wasn't. Not her. Only what remained of her, her body little more than crushed remnants of human flesh. Her chest was a mass of dark blood and her right leg . . . it wasn't there anymore.

Do something.

The demand—desperate, driving—clawed at my chest.

But death came and snatched, and I could not hold it back.

I had never been able to hold it back.

Bronek's shoulders convulsed as he knelt on the debris-strewn paving stones, his sobs racking, noiseless.

I fell to my knees beside him. His camouflage smock was covered in blood. I couldn't tell if it was only hers or if he, too, had been wounded.

"Bronek," I said softly, but he made no move or sound save that nearly inaudible choking. That sound would never leave me, the weeping of a man whose heart had been torn from his chest. Nor the image of him kneeling on the ground, his helmeted head bowed, his arms sheltering Jasia's body, tenderly touching her cheek, running his fingers over her lips.

Loving her as truly as he ever had.

Hours later, when night had long since come to rest upon the battered city, I sat in a deserted corridor, its shadows surrounding me.

Bronek told Andrzej how it happened. They had been crossing the street, platoon leader and liaison, when an artillery shell exploded. By some miracle, or by some curse, Bronek had survived.

From elsewhere in the building came muted voices, perhaps commanders discussing tactics, debating where to concentrate men and weapons, how to hold areas that remained ours, how to take back what had been lost.

But though we might recapture an objective, succeed in driving the enemy from a building or street, every day we lost what could not be reclaimed. Though others might take up the weapons of the fallen, they could never replace the ones who would always remain the bravest and the best of us.

Memories rushed in. Jasia knocking on my door, asking if I had a room to rent, breezing into my shell of a life and infusing it with laughter and friendship and purpose. Jasia taking my measure with her keen gaze, demanding to know why when I asked to join the conspiracy.

"Because I want to fight."

"I wonder if you know what that means."

No, Jasia, I didn't know.

Jasia dancing with Bronek, smiling into his eyes. Jasia bolstering the others with her fearlessness, running under fire with orders. Jasia flashing back a retort at Jerzy's boasting—*"And if the ladies of Błysk but had the weapons of the lads, they'd drop twice as many Hitlerites, and don't you ever doubt it."*—grinning as she said it.

Jasia returning to the fight with her arm in a sling, indefatigable as ever. *"After all, you lot can't manage without me."*

You're right, Jasia. We can't.

Jasia standing in the ruins of the cathedral on her wedding day, shining with joy in a wrinkled blouse and a soldier's armband.

My breath shuddered.

Enough.

I pressed my eyes shut, bolting the door of my mind against the memories. I didn't want to feel anymore. Because I had lost and I had lost and I had so few left. Because it didn't matter any longer. Tomorrow, the next day, a week from now, my end would come. Every day, it came for more of us—soldiers, civilians. It didn't matter whether we wore an armband, we all died the same. In agony and helplessness and terror.

My turn would come. I only had to live until then.

Quiet footsteps. I raised my head. Father Paweł came down the corridor, the flame of his lamp pervading the darkness. The priest, whom we knew only by his pseudonym, had been there when Jasia and Bronek had spoken their vows. And he had been there tonight when Jasia had been laid to rest, uttering the same words he'd recited so often over the past eighteen days, he had surely lost count.

Both times he had been there and it had been only two days.

Two days.

I expected him to continue on his way, return to the hospital to sit beside men and women—but they were children, so many of them, no more than eighteen, twenty—who were dying alone, without mothers or sweethearts or even comrades, not one familiar face as they passed from this world to whatever lay beyond. That was where the priest should be. A comfort in a comfortless place.

Instead, Father Paweł lowered himself down, setting the lamp on the floor, stooping beside me in his cassock and surplice, which were as stained and filthy as the clothes we fighters wore. "You're from Błysk Battalion, are you not?"

"Yes." My voice was hoarse, as if I'd been crying, though I hadn't shed a single tear. Probably it came from constantly breathing smoke from the burning buildings and dust from the rubble. I could barely remember air that didn't taste of death.

"I thought so. You were there that day in church with . . ." He stopped, both of us knowing what he'd been about to say. I wondered why he stayed, but couldn't find the strength to speak. I'd come out here to be alone. So I wouldn't have to meet the eyes of the others, glimpse on their faces the rawness of grief, the numbing apathy of another loss upon all that had come before.

"Is there anything I might do for you, child?"

"For me?" I shook my head. "No. What should I need?"

"Perhaps there's someone you wish me to remember in my prayers?"

"Why? Do you think God is listening?" My words came sudden, bitter. I shouldn't have spoken so, not to this man. Though what did it matter? Whether I voiced the words or kept them to myself changed nothing.

But the priest said only, "He is always listening."

Of course that was what he would say. I used to believe that.

Once, long ago. I wasn't certain I still did. Not after all I had lived and lost.

"The mark of His presence is not in the absence of pain. For it is in the times of greatest suffering when I find I understand where faith truly lies. Not in life, because though there is goodness to be found in it, its depths of suffering and evil are so often incomprehensible. We must believe in something greater than life or else how would we find more than despair in its living? Or in its ending."

"There is no sense in anything anymore," I whispered, more to myself than to him.

He nodded. "So faith is all that is left to us, then."

Silence lingered. The glow of the lamp flickered across the wall, a mingling of light and shadow.

"I am afraid." The words were a confession. I could not say them to my comrades, the ones who needed my strength so they would not lose their own, but I spoke them now to this man, who had heard and harbored the secrets of innumerable troubled souls.

"You are afraid of death?"

I shook my head. "I know it will happen to me. It is everywhere. I—I suppose I am afraid, a little. That it will not happen quietly. But I have a sister." My voice was soft. "In Wola. Or, at least, she was when I saw her last. I don't know where she is now."

"When we love, it is only natural we fear. For the ones dearest to us, for ourselves, how we will endure their loss. But no matter what we are asked to bear on earth, our days are in the hands of God. So too is the hour when we pass into eternity and He receives us to Himself as a father would a child who has come home after a long and weary journey." He paused. "You are not forsaken in His sight. Even in this. You must pray to Him to help you believe it is so."

My throat swelled, aching fiercely. I swallowed, unable to speak.

He rose. "I will pray for you. And for your sister." For a moment, he stood, gazing down at me. "Dominus vobiscum."

The Lord be with you.

Then he walked away, the wavering flame of his lamp receding with his footfalls.

I leaned against the wall, my arms wrapped around my knees.

Wetness slipped down my cheek, a trickle of warmth against my skin. Alone in the darkness of the corridor, I wept. For Jasia and Ryś and the others. For my sister. For how I had failed to protect them, for how little I could do to protect anyone, for how small and frightened and powerless I was in the midst of the raging that had consumed us. For the hope I no longer had—in victory, in peace, in anything beyond this madness.

When I had no more tears, I lifted my face, still damp.

"So faith is all that is left to us, then."

"Please, God." My whisper came cracked. "Show me how to believe."

34

HELENA
AUGUST 23, 1944

The Old Town was dying. Crushed beneath the tons of bombs that fell one after the other every half hour from eight in the morning until seven at night. Blasted to rubble by artillery. Perishing in the flames of the burning houses. Strangulating in the airless cellars where thousands of civilians huddled, starved and despairing, hiding from the bombs and the light. They hated the Germans and spoke resentfully about the Russians, asking each other why the latter had not come, wondering if they would ever come, if we would not all be dead before then and if it would not, indeed, be better to be dead now.

Once the civilians had cheered us, given whatever we asked and given without being asked, looked to the soldiers of the Armia Krajowa with a pride such as there had not been since 1939. In the first flush of the battle, when everyone thought it couldn't last more than a few days, we had been golden in their eyes, a secret army rising from the shadows to drive out their foes. Now their gazes turned upon us with bitterness, the soldiers who had taken up this fight but had been unable to achieve victory. They looked at their city, razed to its very stones, and they looked at their dead, laid in hastily dug graves, strewing the streets, or buried beneath rubble. Husbands and mothers and children and friends. And they looked at us with apathy and accusation for what we had begun.

The Old Town was dying. Her lifeblood seeping out of her ravaged body, even as we fought to stanch the flow. Battle-beaten men and women continuing on after others had fallen.

But we had nothing but our hands.

Nothing but our hands, and they were not enough.

Since the fall of Wola, the Jan Boży Hospital and the adjacent church and monastery had been on the front line of the defense of the Old Town. Its buildings and grounds had been annihilated as AK troops grappled to hold their positions. After days of fighting, what we defended could not be called a hospital anymore, only gutted ruins, among which both sides battled for every meter of ground. Many of the patients and staff had been killed in the attacks on the hospital before they could be evacuated, and corpses lay unburied in the building's remains, their bloated bodies swarmed by hundreds of flies, the stench of rotting flesh sickening in the heat.

I'd scrambled and crawled and run under fire and somehow reached our positions, bringing food for the men who hadn't left their posts in over twenty-four hours. Gunfire pulsed as I crouched behind the wreckage of what had once been an interior wall. Near me lay a man who'd been shot in the jaw, fresh blood staining his dressing. He slumped against the wall, moaning, but I had nothing to give him.

Hunkered at a shattered window behind a barricade of mounded sacks, Jerzy cracked off a shot. At the next window, Andrzej fired a burst with his MP-40. Machine-gun fire drilled the air from German positions in the rubble beyond the hospital. From an upper floor came the answering rattle of our own machine gun.

"Wilk, grenade!" Andrzej shouted, voice hoarse.

Wilk crawled over, clutching a hand grenade. In a swift motion, he rose, hurled the grenade through the window. The next instant, an explosion reverberated. Distant yelling in German or maybe I only imagined it.

A whistling rush.

Someone shouted.

I threw myself over the wounded man.

A shuddering eruption. Bricks and flying plaster and smoke.

I raised my head, coughing on dust, sound a muffled echo.

A hole had been blasted in the wall not two meters away.

Through the haze, Jerzy picked himself up, checked his weapon, took up his position again. His grime-streaked features held stony resolve.

He hadn't been the same since we'd lost Jasia, since Ryś had been killed in the bombing of the field hospital. Ryś had revered his squad leader, copied his mannerisms, tried to be just as brash and funny and daring. Now Ryś was gone, and Jerzy had no one to look up to him anymore.

Thoughts came scattered, my mind strangely adrift.

Andrzej was shouting. I saw his lips moving, but my ears buzzed with an empty ringing.

One second Jerzy was at the window, taking aim with his rifle, the next, he jerked, fell backward. I crawled toward him, picking my way among the debris, keeping low. "Jerzy."

He lay motionless, eyes open. Blood spilled and spread under his head. Nearby lay his helmet, pierced by a bullet. I pressed my fingers to his neck. My breath shook.

No.

Did I say it aloud or did my heart only scream the word?

Jerzy. Tawny-haired, grinning, fearless Jerzy.

Deep in my chest, a raging built.

No more. I won't watch them take anymore.

There, among the detritus, lay Jerzy's Mauser.

I drew the rifle toward me. It was slick. With sweat, with the severing of life. I bent over Jerzy's body, fumbling with his ammunition pouch until it gave way. Clutching both pouch and rifle, I crawled to the window, the relentless beat of gunfire all around me. My fingers had a memory of their own, brought back to the hours of studying weapons until our minds had mapped every part, of shooting at targets. The howling in my brain did the rest.

I readied the bolt—a quick up, back, forward, down. Raised the rifle, its stock against my shoulder. Squinted down the sights. Out across the no-man's land of the hospital grounds, muzzle flashes surged amid the rubble.

I trained my sights on a gray-green helmet. Pressed the trigger. The rifle jerked. I drew the bolt up, rearward, forward, down, and again took aim. Fired.

The helmet wasn't there anymore. Whether its wearer had fallen, I didn't know.

My ears pounded with the *brrr-rrrr* of machine-gun fire, but I no longer felt fear. My mind emptied, my eyes became an extension of my rifle sights, my body a machine squeezing off shots. Pausing only long enough to reload, pressing a new clip into the magazine.

Another mortar blast shook the building. I ducked, but my fingers remained clenched around the Mauser.

I lifted my head, stared down the sights. The machine gunner.

Blinking against grit, I took aim. Drew a slow breath. Held it there, frozen.

I won't forget you, Jerzy.

Then I squeezed the trigger.

Abruptly, it stopped. The terrible battering fire.

Someone shouted. It wasn't a yell of pain, but I didn't pause to absorb what it was. I just kept firing.

"Hold your fire. They're withdrawing."

They were. Shadowy figures fled across the hospital grounds.

I aimed, fired. One of the figures stumbled, went down.

"Emilia." A strong hand gripped my shoulder. I jerked around, clutching the rifle. Andrzej crouched beside me, dusty features taut. "Enough." He took off his helmet, swiped the back of his hand across his forehead. "It's over." Then he fell silent, and I followed his gaze to Jerzy's prone form. For a long moment, he stared at the lifeless body, his jaw tight with held-in pain.

It wasn't over.

This ended only one way now.

HELENA
AUGUST 31, 1944

Dear Antonina,

Why am I doing this? Forming the words in my mind instead of on paper. But I haven't any paper, and even if I did, I don't know where you are, so how could I send a letter?

They gave me the Cross of Valor for taking out the machine

gunner. But it didn't matter. Because in the end, we lost the Jan Boży Hospital.

In the end, we lost the Old Town.

I kept Jerzy's rifle. When I wasn't running with messages or orders, I was defending our positions. I think Jerzy would have been proud. I know Jasia would.

I wish you could have known them, Tosia. I wish you could have known them as I did.

Two days after Jerzy fell, I carried the order for our platoon to withdraw from the ruins of the hospital. A few days later, Andrzej became the commander of Gryf Company. Our former commander was killed when Stukas bombed our quarters. Many died under the rubble. Fourteen from our company alone.

Death is all around me, my closest friends are gone, and somehow I am still alive. How, I do not know.

I suppose I should tell you what happened to me. I might leave it out so as not to worry you, but since you're never going to read this letter (because it isn't a letter at all), it won't matter if I tell you. And besides, I miss the days when there were no secrets between us.

The remaining soldiers of Gryf Company had been ordered to defend positions not far from our bombed-out quarters when the Germans mounted an attack. I took aim and then all I remember is a fiery swath of pain passing through my side and Andrzej yelling to Malina and, just before it went dark, thinking it had finally ended for me.

When I came to, I was in a field hospital. They told me I had been wounded in my left side, but the bullet had passed through cleanly. I don't know how long I lay in the hospital, but it couldn't have been more than a couple of days. Bronek was there too, badly wounded during the defense of the Jan Boży Hospital.

You remember Lidia Zawadzka from school, don't you? She's a nurse at the field hospital now, and she asked about you. I don't know. That's what I told her. I didn't mention Wola. I didn't want to see her face, the way they all look whenever anyone speaks of that district.

Today Lidia told me the news, quietly so the others wouldn't hear. The Armia Krajowa is abandoning the Old Town. The commander-in-chief and his staff have already left for the city centre. The remaining troops will soon follow by way of the sewers.

She said the Błysk Battalion was among those ordered to break through to the city centre, driving a corridor through enemy positions via which AK troops, as well as our wounded and the civilian population, could evacuate. The attack failed. She didn't know what happened to my comrades.

They're going to evacuate us, the wounded who are able to walk, to the city centre through the canals. When I asked what would happen to the others, she shook her head. The doctor did rounds to determine who was strong enough for the journey. They didn't tell the wounded what was happening; they didn't want to spread panic. I made myself get up and told the doctor I would go. When I asked about Bronek, the doctor said it wouldn't be possible, he was in no condition to be moved. I thought of Wola and what the Germans had done in the hospitals there. I thought of Jasia, who had given this man her love and would have given her life to save his, but in the end, war made the choice for both of them. I thought of Andrzej. And I thought of you, how birth isn't just a bond, because what can be forged can also be broken. It's part of you. Immutable. Irreplaceable.

And I stared straight into the doctor's eyes and told him I would not leave Bronek behind.

I'm not afraid anymore, Tosia. I'm not brave. I simply no longer have any fear for myself. Though I still fear for others, for Andrzej. He is giving the whole of himself to this fight. Not for Warsaw, or perhaps not only for Warsaw, but for the lives of us all. The men and women under his command. The inhabitants of the city we call our own. I see it in his face, the resolve to keep fighting for them, even as hope ebbs that our soldiers will ever be anything but alone in this battle.

I wish you could have known him too. I wish he and I could have had more than this fight, more than a kiss on a rooftop. Yes, Tosia. I kissed him. I didn't mean to do it, but I'm glad, so very glad, I did. I think I might have loved him if I had anything left of myself to give.

And for you, Tosia. I'm afraid for you and little Kasia.

We're going into the canals now. I don't know what will happen to us. I suppose it doesn't really matter now.

I still have Tata's medallion. I saw it in your eyes, the tears you kept back when you put it around my neck. I wanted to cry too. Maybe you already knew that.

I wish we could have cried together. I wish we could take back the time we lost. I wish . . .

Night deepened as I stood with the others. For over an hour we'd waited to enter the sewer and our turn had not yet come. The street seethed. Groups of soldiers pressed around us, many with bandages and slings, the white strips binding their wounds tinged violet in the falling darkness. Some could barely stand, could not have stood but for the support of a comrade. Shelling and gunfire, such familiar sounds now, battered the air. It was close. I didn't want to think about how close. I couldn't help but wonder if the enemy wouldn't simply target us from the air, wipe us all out with a well-aimed bomb or a couple of low-flying planes to strafe us as we awaited evacuation.

At the center of it all, the manhole on Krasiński Square. A barricade of sandbags encircled the entrance to the canal, protecting it from enemy fire. Near the entrance stood a man in a Polish officer's cap, shouting for people to keep back because of the shelling. He fired into the air with his Sten, whether at the Germans or to hold back the crowd, I wasn't entirely sure. His eyes had a strangely wild cast, as though he had gone a little mad.

Had I looked in a mirror, perhaps I would have found I, too, had gone a little mad.

Bronek slumped against me, his arm heavy over my shoulder, his pallor ashen. I'd nearly dragged him here with the aid of another boy from our battalion who had his right arm in a sling. My side throbbed, and I fought lightheadedness. Others entered the sewer ahead of us, crawling low, then vanishing into its void.

The *pock-pock* of gunfire and the din of shelling converged with the shouting of the man with the Sten and the distant panic of civilians. The military police had cordoned Długa Street, which led into the square, allowing through only those with AK passes. They must be under orders not to allow the situation at the entrance of the canal to dissolve into a free-for-all lest a surge of civilians obstruct the passage of the soldiers. I'd seen them, women with children, old people, emerging from the cellars, the crevices where they'd burrowed for nearly a month, to plead with the military police to allow them into the sewers, claiming some connection with this or that person of influence in the AK, only to be turned away, forced back if they did not go willingly. News must have spread that our troops were withdrawing from the Old Town, and few had not heard the stories of the fate of civilians once the enemy overtook a district.

Are we abandoning them to another Wola?

How could I leave? But even after the Old Town was lost, the fight for Warsaw would go on. I had to join my battalion or at least try. I had to take Bronek to the city centre, for he would not survive the journey alone.

Still, I could not think of the civilians without a sickening in my stomach.

Finally our turn came. I ran toward the manhole, bent low, Bronek's heft weighing me down.

The man ahead of me descended. I drew a shaky breath, crouching on my hands and knees, grit scraping my palms, staring into the dark hole in the cobblestones.

"Keep moving," someone shouted.

I lowered myself down. Better for me to be first, so Bronek could follow behind me. My foot found the first rung, dangled blindly before reaching the second. There was no ladder, just iron notches at intervals, a vertical descent into blackness. I groped for the next foothold. Pain flared in my side.

Dear God, help me.

My foot swung, met only air. Gasping, I clutched the rung, my fingers slipping on the clammy iron. My shoe found purchase on the next notch and I continued downward, step by step, the circle of red sky above growing faint and distant.

My feet touched the ground. I sank into muck, sewage soaking my boots. Darkness swallowed me. I gagged on the fetid air. My eyes watered.

Somewhere above came the drip-plink of water. I blinked, trying to adjust to the blackness. My chest tightened. I stayed near the entrance, staring up at the cone of feeble light outlining the opening.

The clink of footfalls against metal, the sound of scrabbling, then a pair of boots appeared. I waited in the clammy darkness as they descended.

"Bronek." The echo of the canal amplified my whisper. Over the past days, without realizing it, I'd stopped calling him by his pseudonym. What did all that matter now?

"I'm here."

"Take hold of my belt."

A pressure at my waist told me he had. I reached out until my hand met slimy brick. I took another step, keeping one hand on the curved wall, stretching out the other, groping my way forward. Bronek followed, holding on to my belt. I kept moving, sloshing in the rising water and sludge, the darkness of the tunnel suffocating.

Panic crept up my throat. Where were the others?

I bumped into something. Warm and living. I exhaled shakily, keeping close to the shadowy presence ahead of me. I wanted to cling to this stranger, another human to anchor me, but instead, I pressed my eyes shut against the blackness as we waited for our group to assemble, the silence belowground stark against the tumult of the streets.

"Listen up." A voice echoed from somewhere ahead. "No light, no talking. In a few hundred meters, we'll pass directly under enemy positions, and if you don't fancy the Krauts chucking in a grenade and blowing the lot of us to bits, you'll do this quietly."

My skin prickled. In the weeks the AK had used the subterranean passages to convey troops, messages, and weapons from one district to another, how many had met their end in such a way?

"We'll stop now and again, rest a few minutes, but we have to keep moving. Keep hold of the person ahead so no one gets separated. If you get lost down here, you'll be dead before you find your way out. If anyone can't make it on their own, the rest keep going. That's an order."

I swallowed hard. No one spoke. Water dripped.

"All right now, it's silence from here on."

We took the first steps. I clung to the coat of the man in front of me with one hand, feeling my way along the sticky wall with the other. I couldn't tell how many walked ahead, how many behind. The gurgle of water, the slosh of footfalls, and the occasional muffled cough all that could be heard in the stillness.

It took effort to keep my balance on the curved bottom of the sewer, the current of muck and water clutching at my legs as I pushed onward. The sewage soon came up to my thighs, my skirt sodden. I slipped, almost lost my grip on the man's coat. A few steps later, Bronek stumbled, nearly pulling me down with him.

I kept moving, one of a line snaking farther into the labyrinth of the canals. My forehead slammed against brick. I faltered, dazzled by the pain. I would have called out to Bronek to alert him, but the guide's warning about breaking silence returned to me.

I sensed the walls closing in, the space through which we passed narrowing. Before I had stooped, now I had to walk bent double, almost at a crouch, to keep from hitting my head. How the men managed, I could only guess. It quickly became exhausting to proceed this way, every step a battle against the current, but we did not stop.

Down the line, someone moaned. Another swore, the hiss of the curse echoing along the canal.

The mire in which we waded had a luminous film, blackness reflecting off blackness. My side pulsed, pain its own heartbeat. I drew shallow breaths through my mouth, but I could not escape the overwhelming stench. The stink of rotting and filth and excrement, and we had no choice but to breathe it in. Our need for air trapped us, the canal trapped us, and we could do nothing but keep walking, hunched forward, holding on to the body ahead of our own, putting one foot in front of the other, submerged in darkness.

The ground under my feet suddenly shifted, became soft. I bit back a cry as I stumbled.

I braced my hand against the wall to steady myself and kept going. The bottom of the sewer evened again.

I did not want to consider what I had trodden over.

Light trickled from above. We must have been passing under an open manhole. I held my breath as we glided past, a column of shadows. The Germans could be directly above us, listening for any sign of life from below. In the next moment, a grenade could fall, landing among us with a splash. Here, trapped below the surface of the city, there would be no escape.

The weak light illuminated the egg-shaped canal, the brick walls, the murky sewage. Something bumped against me. The bloated body of a cat floating in the mire. My breath shuddered.

Hours, or maybe only minutes later, we stopped to rest. The low ceiling made it impossible to stand upright, and my back ached. I shivered, soaked to my waist, dizzy from the throbbing in my side, from the stench. The rough wall of the sewer had cut my hand, and I thought vaguely about infection, but what could I do about it now? I drew Bronek against me, held him as if he were a child. He slumped in my arms, barely conscious.

In a few minutes, Bronek took hold of my belt, and I grasped the man's coat and we continued on.

Through the tunnel came a rushing echo, a cascade of water gushing from the ceiling. We passed under the stream, now drenched to the skin.

Suddenly, there was a slackening in the weight on my belt, then a heavy splash. I stopped, turned.

"Bronek," I called, forgetting the necessity of silence, my voice reverberating along the canal. I thrashed in the high water, groping in the blackness. "Bronek." Panic pitched my voice.

"Hush," somebody hissed. The line had halted its progress.

"He's here," came a voice.

I reached out until I found them. Supported by the man behind, Bronek coughed and gasped.

"I'll carry him, if I can." The white of the man's sling shone dimly in the inky dark.

"No." I swallowed, my throat dry. "I'll manage. Bronek, hold on to my belt. That's right."

Again, we plodded onward, Bronek's weight pulling me down, my side burning. I did not need to check to know my wound had reopened.

Time passed in darkness and stench, the groans of the wounded, the swash of dozens of pairs of feet slogging through mire.

The sewer narrowed again, a vise closing around us. I slipped on the bottom of the canal. Water rose around me, the current dragging me down. I went under, the rush of water in my ears.

I needed to pick myself up, keep moving. For Bronek. For Andrzej.

Be brave, Hela.

Antonina's firm voice, as I crouched in the corner of our bedroom, too frightened to go to school.

Be brave, Hela.

I wasn't. I had never been brave. Couldn't she see that?

She reached out her hand, palm up. Her eyes, so blue, on my face. Slowly, I placed my fingers in hers. Her hand clasped mine, and she drew me up with her, smiling.

See. That wasn't so hard.

I broke through the surface, coughing and sputtering. I found Bronek behind me, took a step. Then another, sewage plastering my hair to my neck, shivering in my sodden clothes, dragging a man when I could barely drag myself.

Father in heaven, be my strength, for I have none.

One step after another, one step after another, into the depths of the canal, into a blackness without beginning or end.

HELENA
SEPTEMBER 1, 1944

Strong hands grasped under my arms, pulling me to the surface.

I took a tottering step. Night had scarcely begun to give way to the first whispers of dawn, but I blinked as though against the brilliance of midday sun. Dark spots blinded my vision.

My legs gave out, and I sank to the ground. I turned my head as Bronek collapsed beside me, but I had no strength to move or speak.

Air. I gulped a breath. Fresh. Cool. So good. I inhaled and inhaled. I couldn't get enough, my lungs could never be full enough. My head spun like I'd swallowed a glass of vodka. I was drunk on air.

How long we had journeyed through the canals, I could only guess. Six hours, at least. Time had frozen in those subterranean corridors, that space void of light and air and life. Somewhere along the way, our guide had become lost. I wasn't sure how far we wandered before he realized his error and we had to return the way we came until we reached the branch in the tunnel where the mistake had been made. Once, passing under an open manhole, we heard voices speaking German. I had waited for the splash, for the concussive blast that would end us all, but it had not come.

I did not know how I had done it—would never know—but somehow, I had reached the other side, and Bronek with me.

There was victory in that. Or would have been, had I not been so desperately tired. Had our forces not been withdrawing, abandoning the Old Town and the thousands who remained there. Probably our commanders would call it straightening out the lines or some such nonsense, as the Germans had once done. But then as now, who could not fail to understand the truth?

Others emerged from the manhole, gasping for air, staggering, dropping to the ground, men strewn around the entrance to the canal like corpses. I turned my head slightly.

Buildings, their facades unscathed by bombs. The street clear of rubble, its cobbles unmarred by craters. In the shop across the street, they still had windowpanes.

I'd forgotten what that looked like, glass in a window. That something so fragile could be whole instead of in shatters.

How could it be possible? How could this be Warsaw? Or perhaps the question really was, how could the other place be the city I had known and loved all my life?

I lay unmoving on the cobblestones, my clothes sticking to my limbs, reeking of sewage, as the night fell away from the sky.

OCTOBER 3, 1944

SOLDIERS OF FIGHTING WARSAW!
THE HEROIC DEEDS OF POLISH SOLDIERS, WHICH
CONSTITUTE TWO MONTHS OF FIGHTING IN WARSAW, ARE
PROOFS, HOWEVER FULL OF HORROR, OF OUR DESIRE
FOR FREEDOM—OUR STRONGEST DESIRE. OUR BATTLE IN
THE CAPITAL, IN THE FACE OF DEATH AND DESTRUCTION,
STANDS IN THE FOREFRONT OF FAMOUS DEEDS OF POLISH
SOLDIERS DURING THIS WAR. THEY WILL BE A LASTING
MEMORIAL TO OUR SPIRIT AND LOVE OF FREEDOM.

BÓR, COMMANDER-IN-CHIEF, ARMIA KRAJOWA

35

HELENA
OCTOBER 4, 1944

Sixty-three days.

For sixty-three days, we fought. For sixty-three days, the bravest and the best of us fell on the altar of our city. On the last day, the sixty-third day, a delegation of the Armia Krajowa signed the act of surrender.

The rising that had burned so bright on the first day of August perished in the ashes of Warsaw.

The end of the battle found me in the city centre. I had not been there long. After the evacuation from the Old Town, I spent nearly two weeks in a field hospital, fighting the infection that had resulted from my journey through the sewers. As the middle of September neared, I was still weak, but I could no longer bear to be away from my comrades. Even in the hospital, word reached me of Soviet aircraft appearing in the skies above the city for the first time since the outbreak of the fighting, driving away the enemy Stukas that had been the terror of Warsaw for weeks. Once again, the low thunder of Red Army artillery could be heard from the east. The prospect of the Soviets coming to our aid infused a ray of hope into the lowering clouds of defeat, and I wanted to be with the others.

Casualties had been high in the battalion's attempt to break through to the city centre, but Andrzej and a group of others had—

in a maneuver so daring it had risen to something of a legend—managed to pass directly through enemy lines, their camouflage smocks and helmets disguising them as German troops. Others had evacuated through the sewers, and after a few days' rest, the battalion had been sent to Czerniaków, a riverside quarter of the city that had passed the first weeks of the battle in comparative peace. Bronek soon joined us there, not yet fully recovered but determined to return to the battalion.

As when we'd withdrawn from Wola to the Old Town, soon after the arrival of our battalion, the situation deteriorated as the Germans, having crushed the insurgency in the Old Town, concentrated their assault on the Czerniaków bridgehead. Rocket launchers and mortars soon did the grim work we had by now grown accustomed to, reducing to rubble the suburb with its wide avenues and well-spaced houses.

The days in Czerniaków passed in a nightmarish haze. The remaining soldiers of our battalion defended their positions in the ruined buildings, faces haunted, eyes glazed. Our comrades fell, the volunteers who replaced those lost in Wola and the Old Town fell, and we had become so exhausted, so numbed, we scarcely grieved. In fact, we hardly noticed. Once I curled up in a cellar and promptly fell asleep, waking hours later to find I had been lying on a corpse.

In the third week of September, the majority of the troops from the Radosław Group received the order to withdraw from Czerniaków through the sewers. A detachment of our battalion stayed behind as a rearguard to defend what remained of the bridgehead. Clutching at the fraying hope of a Soviet crossing, the remnant in Czerniaków battled fiercely to hold the sector, the fighting raging from building to building, upper floor to cellar. Many buildings fell into enemy hands, as did the soldiers who defended them and the civilians who remained.

Our battalion commander coordinated an evacuation of the wounded, our troops, and civilians across the Wisła. The night of the evacuation, which had been arranged with the Soviets by radio, we gathered at the riverbank and waited for the boats promised by the Soviets, but only a few small crafts arrived with promises of more. But we could no longer hold out in the inferno that had become Czerniaków. We'd run out of ammunition, men, and hope. Here, the battalion that had fought together since the start of the battle disintegrated. Some determined to rescue themselves by swimming across the river or crossing in makeshift rafts. Others remained with the wounded.

In a desperate attempt to break out of the district, our commander decided to lead a group through enemy lines to the city centre. If we had to fight our way out, so be it.

Hours later, we reached a building in the hands of the AK. Only five remained—the commander of the battalion and his liaison, Andrzej and me, and another soldier. Many had been killed. About the others, we didn't know. Bronek had been in the group that lost contact with the rest. Both the commander and Andrzej had been wounded.

We arrived in the city centre near the end of September. After that, not much was left. District after district had fallen, leaving only scraps of territory to which our army still clung. We had no electricity and little water. The shortage of ammunition had grown desperate. The city was starving. If we fought on, victory would not be achieved, but the destruction and death would continue. Day upon day, loss upon senseless loss.

On the first day of October, a hush fell over the ruins that had echoed with the crackle of gunfire and the deafening blast of explosions for nine weeks. The ceasefire negotiated with the Germans had taken effect, a two-day armistice from 5:00 a.m. to 7:00 p.m. to allow the civilian population to leave the city for the transit camps. Of course, shortly after 8:00 p.m., the bombardment resumed.

In our quarters in the city centre, we waited. All of us knew it was only a matter of time.

On the third of October, the news came. Representatives of the Armia Krajowa had met with the German command to negotiate the terms of surrender. The formal agreement had been signed the day before.

Our soldiers would leave the city as prisoners of war. They would be treated not as insurgents but as soldiers of the Polish Army, entitled to the rights of the Geneva Convention. This included members of auxiliary services—liaisons, nurses, and other noncombatants. There would be no reprisals against civilians. They would evacuate the city for the transit camps.

The entirety of the population would be expelled by order of the Germans. In a matter of days, it would all be over. We had fought for Warsaw, and now we would forsake her.

One of our officers assembled us to read out the surrender agreement. They issued the remaining provisions and our pay, five hundred złoty and ten American dollars apiece. I stared at the flimsy paper notes and choked back a rise of hysterical laughter. What use would they be to me now? What could I buy? Certainly not the loaf of wheat bread and chicken and fresh vegetables that I obsessively craved. Nor a hot bath and a cake of soap to cleanse the filth from my skin, for in the whole of Warsaw, only a few wells remained in which a little water could still be found, rationed by the glass. Nor could I purchase the return of my comrades, my freedom, or my city.

I crushed the banknotes in my palm, despising their touch.

We had two choices, the officer informed us. We could leave the city as soldiers of the Armia Krajowa or take off our armbands and join the civilians. Each must decide for themselves. Some, especially those with families, chose to return to the civilian population. During the fighting, we had been dealt with as bandits instead of soldiers, and it was difficult to believe our captors would now abide by the Geneva Convention. The fate of civilians, too, remained in question. For though they had been passing through the transit camps for weeks, who could say what would happen to those deported from there?

To march into captivity as soldiers and prisoners of war or to join the civilians and partake of their uncertain fate?

The choices of war are never kind. But in the end, I chose. As a prisoner of war, they would send me to a place where there would be no chance of searching for Antonina. Reason told me I had little possibility of finding her, of this whirlwind flinging us together instead of scattering us with no more care than dust, but that wasn't what mattered. Since taking the oath, I had given the whole of myself to fighting for Poland, but now that fight had been lost. I had tried to do my duty, but now I had another duty, one I had put aside, told myself there would be time for later, after freedom had been won. But there hadn't been time. For so many, there would never be.

I had become a soldier, but I had always been a sister.

And so, I chose.

I packed the few provisions I had been issued into the rucksack I'd carried since W-Hour. Footfalls and voices echoed throughout the building where we'd been quartered, everyone making preparations for the departure from the city. The soldiers had buried some of our best weapons, though according to the terms of surrender, they were to walk out carrying arms and hand them over to the Germans at a designated point. The Armia Krajowa would go into captivity with armbands on their sleeves and military decorations pinned to their coats. Those who had triumphed over us would not see us hang our heads in shame. We had fought as soldiers and would march as soldiers, disciplined and dignified. Even in our defeat, of that, we could be proud.

The tread of footsteps made me raise my head. Andrzej approached. A sling bound his left arm. He'd remained at the field hospital just long enough for the bullet to be removed before returning to us. The hospital had overflowed with wounded, the situation chaos itself, and we all wanted to be together at the last. Since then, I'd dressed the wound, which appeared to be healing.

"Here." He held out a small bundle. "I brought you this."

I unfolded the fabric, revealing a dress of wrinkled cotton, the pattern of small white flowers on a blue background faded to a dingy shade. With the dress was a pair of scuffed brown shoes. I glanced up. "Where did you find these?"

"Bought them from a civilian. You can't go"—he swallowed—"in those things."

For a long moment, he regarded me as I sat on an overturned crate, the dress and shoes in my lap. He must have queued for water, for he'd washed and shaved, his hair still damp, fresh comb tracks marking the dark strands. Soldiers who'd scarcely attended to personal hygiene during the final days of fighting now cleaned themselves and their garments as best they could, yet another way of maintaining their dignity as they prepared to march out under the gaze of the Germans.

His features tightened. "You'd best change." Then he turned abruptly and walked away.

In the privacy of a tiny lavatory, which had long ceased to function as such, I undressed. I unfastened the belt, then drew the camouflage smock over my head. One by one, I unlaced the boots I'd worn since Wola, each landing with a dull thud when they fell.

The trousers I'd taken from a dead German soldier in Czerniaków slid down my bony hips without my having to undo the buttons. I took off the men's shirt I wore beneath the smock, for the girlish blouse I began the fighting in had been ripped away in the moments after I'd been wounded.

For a moment, I stood, my bare skin prickling in the chill. The medallion lay against my chest, resting just below the hollow of my throat. Gingerly, my fingertips traced the sharp outline of my ribs, the taut ridge of the scar on my left side.

Then I put on the dress. The worn cotton hung on my whittled frame, the gathered waist baggy. I bent and laced the shoes, but not before retrieving my pay and tucking the banknotes under the right insole. The shoes pinched my toes, but I couldn't pass as a civilian wearing German boots. I slipped my arms into my cardigan, packed so long ago, in anticipation of W-Hour. The contents of my rucksack had remained comparatively dry during my journey through the canals, though the garment still carried an unwashed scent.

I faced the tiny mirror above the sink. Somehow it remained in place, despite the bombings, a crack running like a lightning bolt along the grimy glass. For the first time in weeks, I met my own reflection. Purplish bruises shadowed the skin under my eyes, my cheeks sunken, my gaze so hard and haunted I no longer knew it as my own.

I ran my fingers through the matted tangles of my hair, using my few pins to twist it into a knot at my nape. My gaze fell to the heap of garments on the floor, the brown-and-green camouflage lying amid the pile, my stained and tattered armband still affixed.

A flood of memories. Jasia stamping the bands by the light of a carbide lamp, a determined wrinkle in her brow. Ryś sliding one over his shirtsleeve, eyes alight, his boyish grin spreading wide.

"Dashing, isn't it?"

My eyes stung, white and red, a blur of heat. I blinked, hard.

Then I left the lavatory, the door shutting softly behind me.

I wandered through rooms and corridors crowded with men and a few women, packing, cleaning clothes or boots, smoking, eating rations, talking with comrades, or sleeping while they still could.

I asked a few if they'd seen Andrzej, but no one had. These weren't the boys from our company who looked to Andrzej as their revered commander, to me as a combination of older sister and fellow soldier. They were gone—dead or captured or simply missing—and all that remained were the faces of strangers.

I stepped outside, carrying my rucksack. A faded sky stretched above the shattered buildings, and a chill scoured the air. Autumn had come to Warsaw, but neither we nor the landscape had marked the passing of the seasons. In a few months, snow would drift from the sky to settle softly over the ruins, but who among us would remain to see it? There would be only a void where once a city had stood, only the wind to carry the echo of all who had gone.

Several paces from the entrance stood Andrzej, staring out across the remains of the street. At the crunch of my steps, he turned. He wore a civilian coat now, his camouflage smock discarded, for it was forbidden to wear any part of a German uniform when the soldiers became prisoners.

"You're going, then." His voice was weary, the words too blunt to be a question. There was none of the company commander in his stance.

He had told me to do this, thought I would be better off with the civilians. I did not know if he would prove to be right. I only knew what I must do.

I only knew I had to leave him.

"Shall I walk with you part of the way?"

I hesitated. He would be going soon with the other soldiers. And I needed to do this on my own.

"It isn't necessary. I'll be all right."

He nodded. Our gazes held, a wordless remembering of all we had shared and all we had lost, one comrade to another. Then he drew himself up, standing at attention. "The honor has been mine." How simply he said the words, yet they meant more to me than my Cross of Valor.

I raised my chin, eyes steady on his. "And mine."

He pulled me close with his uninjured arm, enfolding me with his strength. My rucksack fell to the ground, and I clung to him, breathing in the musk of his sweat, my cheek against the curve of his neck. Holding him and knowing I would gladly give all I ever possessed if only this could be our always.

He drew away, smoothing my hair, brushing my cheek with his thumb. Kissing my forehead, my lips. I kissed him back, rising up on tiptoe, framing his face with my hands. Trying desperately to catch hold of this moment and imprint it upon my memory, to draw it in for all the empty days that stretched ahead.

Why didn't we do as Bronek and Jasia did when we had the chance? Did we truly think we would ever have anything more than this moment? Why didn't I love you while we still had time?

"We'll come back to each other." His words came fierce. "Don't ever forget that."

My throat ached, so I could only nod.

"God be with you."

"And with you," I whispered.

Then I picked up my rucksack and turned, walking quickly away. This war had held too many goodbyes.

It wasn't until I stumbled that I raised my head. I stood in a surreal landscape, the charred skeletons of buildings piercing the sky, a barricade of paving stones and sandbags still standing, but no longer defended, the street a mass of rubble and craters. An autumn wind blew over the ruins, tugging at my hair, carrying the scent of ashes.

The devastation settled into my soul.

Sixty-three days of bitterness and bloodshed. Sixty-three days of suffering and death—so much death, so many lost while fighting in battle or huddling in cellars or walking down the street. Sixty-three days that had rendered these streets a graveyard.

Sixty-three days that had silenced a city.

We had been proud, so proud and eager to fight. We had tasted freedom in those early days, and those first victories had held such exultation. The fleeting glory of those moments would remain with all who had partaken of this struggle. We had known what it was to take up arms, to proclaim to those who had for so long oppressed us that the people of Poland had spirit and honor and the will to fight. We had withstood a mighty military force for two months, longer than our army had during Hitler's invasion, and our enemy had been forced to draw on vast resources to crush our resistance.

What had it all been for?

I could not answer that. Nor could I answer if I would still fight, if the choice lay before me again.

Perhaps what we had done held no more purpose than anything else in this mad war.

No. We had not given ourselves in vain. I had to believe that.

I made my way along the narrow path that wound through the rubble, following the aged, the young, the wounded, carrying bundles, suitcases, rucksacks, pushing little ones in prams. A river of humanity flowing out of the ruins. Silence hung over the procession as they took in the desolation, features weary, strained, grim. In the hush came the shuffle of footsteps. I merged into their ranks, became one of them.

I remembered Emilia Plater, whose name I had chosen, who had led her troops into battle more than a century ago, who had fought as desperately for her homeland then as we had now, and who had died, still a young woman, two months after the rising had ended without victory.

Until the end, she had stood with courage.

As I would stand now.

I walked onward, stumbling in my too-tight shoes, picking myself up, continuing on—a lone woman in a gray cardigan and worn dress—into the stretching wasteland of a fallen city.

HELENA
OCTOBER 7, 1944

The train hurtled onward, wheels clacking against tracks, light flashing through gaps in the wooden planks.

A freight car. Bare walls and hard floor. A high, barred window through which light and air passed in trickles. A bucket in the corner, communal toilet for more than sixty women pressed inside, crammed together, one body against another. Despite the chill, the air was close, heavy, choked with unwashed bodies and waste and despair.

The memory of childhood train journeys. Sitting on the cushioned bench, my feet in their shiny leather shoes not quite reaching the floor. Tata's strong, wool-clad shoulder brushing mine. Antonina wriggling on my other side as she stared rapt out the window at the passing scenery. "Tata, look!" she would call out at some new sight, and Tata would smile and remind her to lower her voice.

Hunched against the wall, one among a mass of strangers, I could still hear her childish voice, carrying across the years, merging with the clatter of the train. *"Tata, look!"*

Where are you, Tosia?

I'd spent three days at Durchgangslager 121. From the moment I entered the transit camp, I searched the endless crowd for Antonina, for friends or neighbors or anyone who might have news of her. Before I could continue my search, guards forced us into one of the halls for processing. When my turn came, I didn't know how to look, what to do. It happened so fast. One minute I was standing there, worrying I might somehow be detected as a member of the Armia Krajowa—they'd suspected one young man already, separated him from the rest—and then it was over and they herded me and a group of others into another building.

Hundreds, maybe even thousands, crowded the hall, and it didn't take long to realize our numbers were comprised mostly of the young and relatively fit. There were no women with small children among us. Barbed wire surrounded the buildings, each one isolated from the rest, guarded by Wehrmacht soldiers. The next day, I approached a guard and explained in perfect German how I'd been separated from my sister and her baby upon arrival—might he not send me to wherever they were? I held out a portion of my army pay, hoping to bribe him into conceding to my request. He'd taken the money, seemed ready to do as I asked, but then another guard approached and the one to whom I'd given the banknotes shouted at me to go back inside.

My third day in Durchgangslager 121 turned out to be my last. Early in the morning, they marched us to a column of freight wagons. Standing in the vast chaos of the yard, I searched, frantic, for a means of escape from this high-walled prison, from the cars that waited with gaping mouths to swallow us. But there was none, and I boarded the wagons with the rest.

What will become of us? The question filtered through the car. No one had an answer. People clung to some speculations and discarded others. One woman grimly predicted we'd end up in Auschwitz, that feared place into which countless Poles had vanished during the years of occupation. At that, one girl began to sob. Another told her to keep quiet—what good did tears do us now?

All of us knew the only certainty was the unknown.

Hours later, silence had descended over the car packed with girls and women. Some slept or tried to, others sat, features tight with fear or blank with shock, each alone in our collective suffering.

I searched my rucksack until my fingers met glossy wood. I drew the frame from the folds of my blanket, holding it in both hands as I sat, the rough wall chafing my back with the rocking of the car. The day we learned of the capitulation, I'd gone to Hoża Street, hoping Antonina might have somehow found her way to my flat, might be there with Kasia, waiting for me. The building wasn't there anymore. Well, it was, in the same way an animal is there after vultures have shredded its flesh and gnawed its bones and left them strewn. It had taken a direct hit.

For the second time in my life, I stood in the ruins of a place I called home.

In the murky dimness of the car, I brushed a thumb over the cool glass, touching the faces of my parents. Mama, in her gossamer veil

346

and gown, her hand through Tata's arm, a gentle smile on her lips. "You have her smile," Tata always said. And I did. Or had. Once. Tata, tall and youthful, his other hand covering Mama's. I traced his features, but the glass was cold, the black-and-white image lifeless even as it captured life.

I tried, Tata. I fought for Poland as you did. But we lost so much and it's over now and I don't know what will happen to me. I'm afraid and I wish you were here. No, Tata. I don't wish that. It would grieve you too much to see Warsaw now, how they left her a landscape of ashes. You're better where you are, far away from a world I never knew could hold such cruelty.

I don't know where Antonina is. I left her to fight as you left us, and now . . . I'm sorry, Tata. I'm so sorry.

I rested my cheek against the wall, drawing in sips of air through a crack in the boards. The frame lay in my lap, covered by my hand. My eyes slid shut as the train thundered down the tracks, the rhythm of its wheels converging with my voiceless prayers.

36

ANTONINA
APRIL 5, 1945

Once there was a city of bustling thoroughfares and serpentine streets, a city of baroque churches with soaring spires that brushed the clouds as if reaching toward heaven itself. A city of stately palaces where centuries-past kings had reigned. A city through which a river pulsed, a curving artery flowing through its heart, a river that had birthed the city and watched over her as she grew. A city of verdant parks where youths flirted with girls in summer frocks and children sailed boats on glistening ponds and coaxed their parents for a few groszy to buy ice cream from the man with a pushcart. A city of fashionable cafés and gilded concert halls and sparkling nightclubs, where music spilled and swelled, from Chopin's preludes to tangos and jazz. A city of elegant residences with iron balconies and small flats crowded with families. A city of life, bursting and unabashed.

Once there was a city . . .

Then came invasion and occupation. They left her battered, yet still she stood. Cracked but proud. Then her people rose and blood stained her streets and bombs fell upon her baroque churches and sparkling nightclubs, her palaces and tiny flats, rendering them ruins. Then she fell and the victors drove out her inhabitants, an exodus without a promised land.

But it did not finish there.

They who had crushed her would not be content with her destruction. Even her abandonment did not satisfy them.

No, she must be stripped, her rubble scavenged for anything of value, her treasures and the possessions of her citizens plundered.

In the end, they burned her. What bombs and artillery and tanks had not leveled, they gave over to fire. Dynamite and flamethrowers, a systematic annihilation. Then silence descended over the ashes, the silence of a vanished million.

Once there was a city . . .

I returned in February, but not to the city I remembered, not to my Warsaw. In its place I found a phantom landscape, charred and barren. Hollow windows stared sightlessly from blackened buildings. Fragments of walls stood amid a carpet of detritus. Streets had become canyons, mountains of rubble rising on either side of former thoroughfares. We became adept at clambering over the heaps, tripping and stumbling among the bricks and tangled tramway cables and shards of former lives. Rubble submerged even the resting places of the dead laid in hastily dug graves during the fighting, but it was the corpses that had never been buried, decomposing under collapsed buildings or in burned-out shells, that gave the winter air its stink of decay.

Block after block, kilometer after kilometer, the remains stretched, a desolate moonscape blanketed in snow.

A lonely few had remained in the city in the months after its destruction, living like castaways on a deserted island, hiding among the ruins, in constant danger of discovery by German patrols, barely surviving, emerging only after the Russians arrived on the seventeenth of January. Within days of the entrance of the Soviets—I would not call it liberation; another occupation, a lesser one, perhaps, but not freedom—the children of Warsaw began to return to her. After months of exile, they streamed into the city by the hundreds, then by the thousands. They came in search of their homes and businesses, their families and acquaintances, each asking the question, What remains to me?

Amid the ravages and the emptiness, few answers could be found.

Upon my arrival, I set about the urgent task of finding somewhere to live in a city that had been rendered mostly uninhabitable. Praga, on the east bank of the river, had seen the least destruction, and while nearly every structure in the Old Town had been razed, Żoliborz and Mokotów had suffered comparatively less damage. But as thousands returned to the city that winter, every semi-livable building assumed the value of a sought-after residence with several families crowding into a single flat.

Kasia and I spent the first weeks living on the ground floor of a ruined building, icy wind leaking through the tarpaulin that took the place of a wall. I had barely any money and nothing to sell, the family with whom I shared the dwelling no less destitute. But I had not endured more than five years of war without gaining a few lessons in resourcefulness, and so, using the little funds we possessed, the woman and I opened a stall selling hot soup. In this way, we survived the winter.

In the days after my return, I made my way to Wola to discover what remained of my flat. As I stood on the street, staring up at the fire-scarred walls, I began to shake, an uncontrollable racking that rose from deep within and spread outward, overtaking every part of me. I had shut out the memories, refusing to absorb, to relive, even to recollect that day. But I had not been free of them, had simply forced them back until I could do so no longer. Memories came in blinding flashes, images broken, yet startlingly vivid.

The heaps of corpses in the yard of the Ursus factory had been incinerated by order of the SS. Later the factory had been set ablaze. I could not return there, nor so much as pass by its gate. I doubted I ever could.

In streets and courtyards across the city, in the eviscerated buildings where soldiers had battled to the last, and beneath the rubble where none had yet searched, remnants spoke where voices had been silenced.

The children of Warsaw had come home to a graveyard.

Near the end of March, help arrived from an unexpected source, a chance encounter with one of my former associates, the woman I had known as Jolanta. I recognized her at once, her diminutive figure and brisk stride, her clear blue eyes. She'd dyed her hair, though, her blond strands now a reddish hue, likely for reasons of disguise rather than fashion.

"But you were in Pawiak."

"My colleagues arranged for my release. They"—she hesitated—"paid a great deal to do so. I was taken to be executed, but a Gestapo man led me away and I went free." She told of it in the same voice she'd once used when passing on information about a child—firm, controlled, but silent emotion passed across her face. The past months had held great difficulties for her.

When I told her where my child and I had been living, she gave me an address of friends in Mokotów and said I needed only to mention she had sent me and they would take me as a boarder.

"I've been searching for a place for weeks, but there are none to be had. I can't tell you how grateful I am, Jolanta."

"Irena now." She gave a faint smile. "We are all trying to remember who we used to be."

I told her of Róża and Łucja, how they had been with me in Wola. Though Irena had not placed them with me, someone else in our circle must know their fate, in case any of their family survived to search for them. I had done all I could to shelter them, but it hadn't been enough. How many Jews had spent years surviving the ghetto and the dangers of life under the surface of the city only to die as nameless civilians in the battle for Warsaw? The futility of it left me hollow. Irena's eyes held the same.

Just before we parted ways, I asked softly, "The children?"

"Many are safe. Of others, I do not know yet." She reached out and clasped my hand, her gaze steady on mine. "It was so little, what we did. But hope lies in every life. Hope and defiance." She pressed her lips together, both of us lost in the memories. Then she went on. "If you find yourself in need of work, come and see me. I'm at the health and welfare department at Bagatela 10. It's impossible to provide aid to everyone, but we do what we can. The task ahead is tremendous." She made a gesture encompassing the devastated street on which we stood—two boys scrounging in a hill of rubble, an old woman bending over a pot in front of the stump of a wall.

"I've no professional qualifications."

She tilted her head, giving me a look that dismissed my words as nonsense. "Marysia is there too."

I gave a little gasp. "Marysia? She's here, in Warsaw?" I had not been certain what had become of her, had feared . . .

"Working alongside me."

"Then I'll come within the week." I smiled. "Gladly."

"I'm afraid we can offer little in the way of remuneration at present, but we'll see to it you and your child don't go hungry."

"That's all I ask."

Irena gave a brisk nod. "Excellent."

The address in Mokotów turned out to be a burned-out building, but it had a roof and walls and a modicum of warmth, so it seemed a palace after spending weeks in a ruin with a tarpaulin for a wall. The family's eldest daughter agreed to mind Kasia during the day, so I began work at the health and welfare department.

In the face of a staggering magnitude of need, Irena and her colleagues possessed a remarkable ability for organization. The department set up welfare centers and distributed food brought from the surrounding countryside. Irena, whose concern was, as always, for children, arranged care for orphans living in the rubble. The department staff dwelt in conditions little better than those we sought to aid, returning at night to dingy rooms and cellars weary to our bones, often hungry, but somehow unflagging in purpose.

Perhaps my colleagues went about their duties out of a desire to ease the suffering of their fellow citizens, to do their part in the task of rebuilding. I wanted to help, of course I did. This was the city of my birth, and my heart broke at the sight of her ashes. But I went each day to the office for another reason.

In the hope that in an endless line of strangers, I might one day find my sister's face.

Thousands of AK soldiers had been sent to prisoner of war camps. Thousands more civilians had been deported to the Reich as forced laborers or—*please, no, dear God*—to concentration camps. Everyone I encountered seemed to be searching. For a child or husband or mother, missing, lost, unknown.

We searched and waited and would not stop searching and waiting until the ones we lost returned to us or until facts turned our hope cold and perhaps not even then.

But Helena would come home. The war would end—Germany had no choice but capitulation in the face of the inexorable advance of the Allies—and my sister would return to Warsaw.

Every day, I repeated this. Every day, I prayed for it to be so. Every day, despair or maybe reason whispered of other eventualities.

She'd died in the battle for the city. Even now, her body might be among the numberless buried under the rubble or in a crudely marked grave or one that hadn't been marked at all. She'd fallen in the fighting or been killed in an air raid—at least let her have gone that way, not driven in front of a tank with her hands in the air or captured and raped by the SS before they finally gave her the merciless mercy of a bullet or a rope around her neck—*No, I can't think it. Not Helena, not my sister.*

Dusk stained the sky as I made my way along Hoża Street. I needed to return to Mokotów and Kasia, but sometimes, when hope crumbled in my palm, I came here. To the flat we'd shared with Aunt Basia, where my sister and I last lived together.

The crunch of my footfalls mingled with the exhale of a thawing spring wind as I approached the ruins of the building. Navigating my way around the scree, I crossed to the wall. It rose against the falling twilight, lone and blackened.

I stilled.

The paper wasn't there anymore. Others were, but not mine, for I'd placed it there, below the shell of what had once been a window, wedged by a loose brick.

> For Helena Dąbrowska
> Antonina and Kasia are in Warsaw.

Below I had written my address.

Such notes appeared all across the city, bits of paper left on the walls of former residences to notify anyone who might be searching out the fate of their inhabitants.

> Ewa Lewandowska is looking for her sons, Bartosz and Jan.

353

Maria Bagińska is living on Targowa Street.

For Tomasz Kępiński. We have gone to Skarżysko. If you read this message, come to us there. We are waiting for you. —Your wife and daughters

Each scrap of paper a little world of fear and hope.

My breath shuddered. I went to my knees in the rubble. Tears ran down my face, and I let them fall, my body racked with gulping cries, too spent to fight. For so long I had fought, but I was alone, so terribly alone, and I couldn't go on anymore. I knew I must, for Kasia, but I had lost so many. They stretched just out of reach, a congregation of shadows. Tata. Aunt Basia. Marek.

Helena.

"She isn't gone," I whispered, but only the scuttle of the wind returned to me.

In the fading light, my gaze caught on a fragment of white. I reached out, tugged the paper free from under a broken brick. I smoothed my palm over the crumpled slip, the note stained and dirty, the penciled words faded.

For Helena Dąbrowska
Antonina and Kasia are in Warsaw.

I rose and secured the note, lodging it in place under the brick. It lay against the charred wall, a tiny white beacon in the shadows. *Bring her home, dear God. Somehow, please, bring her home.*

HELENA
JUNE 7, 1945

When I remembered that day, the day I returned to Warsaw, I would always think of the sky. It stretched above the city, a clear summer blue dotted with gently drifting clouds, as the train drew into the station.

How many times had I lived this moment in my memory? Hundreds? Thousands? On the journey, first to a transit camp in the

Reich and then to Berlin, I carried it with me. During the hours of grueling monotony in an armaments factory, I traced it in my mind, a dreamworld nothing could touch. Through the long nights, huddling with the other women as the building shook with the thunder of Allied bombs, I gave myself this day as a promise. In the aftermath, crossing war-ravaged Germany and Poland in freight cars, crowded passenger trains, and on foot, every rotation of the wheels and every step forward echoed the same refrain.

Home.

In all the months that had passed and the kilometers I had journeyed, I told myself it still meant something.

With a hiss of steam and a grinding of brakes, the train came to a stop. Passengers collected their belongings, rose from their seats, but I didn't move. I sat in the stuffy compartment, my hands clutched in my lap, my breathing uneven, as the bustle went on around me.

Only when the compartment had emptied did I rise and shoulder my rucksack. I alighted from the train and stepped onto the platform.

The Main Station had been obliterated, so trains arrived at the West Station. I paused, still in the midst of the coursing river of the throng, searching the faces of those on the platform and those who hurried by. Moments passed as I stood, waiting, as if from some pathetic belief that I needed only to set foot in the city to encounter the ones I sought.

Then I walked on, leaving the station behind.

And I was in Warsaw.

Whenever I dreamed of coming home, I always returned to the city of my memories, one unaltered by the battle for her freedom, untouched by bombs and artillery, unbroken by war. I had left her in ruins, yet still, I painted her as she had once been. Perhaps not as before occupation settled upon her, but still vibrant, somehow whole. Deep down, I'd known the truth, how futile and empty the fantasy I entertained, no better than a child with an imaginary playmate. But during the long months in Berlin, during the hunger and fear and despair, my dreams carried me away and I let myself drift. Not all the time, but for fleeting moments, sustaining me like bread.

Dreams. Hadn't I learned yet how foolish they were?

Now the bright spring sun laid bare reality.

Dust swirled, rising from the rubble in clouds, churned up by the footfalls of pedestrians and the wheels of carts and rickshaws. I covered my mouth, coughing, lungs still weak after the bronchitis I'd suffered during the winter. Carcasses of brick and stone lined the street, jagged walls etched against the sky as though a giant hand had swiped the building, collapsing half, leaving a stark and solitary remainder. Though the thoroughfare had been cleared, rubble lay in peaks and valleys that overflowed onto the sidewalk.

I had no destination. I simply wandered. Had I ever been so adrift, so alone as in those moments, lost in a city whose face had once been as familiar as a friend? I had returned to Warsaw, but she had become a stranger, a ravaged landscape in which I could scarcely find my way. Sometimes I passed a landmark—the café where we used to go with Tata for coffee and cream cakes, the bookshop where I'd once spent my carefully saved pocket money. Or a makeshift street sign told me where I stood and I remembered what had been before, but what was no longer. And if it yet remained, often it was altered almost beyond recognition.

Since the day I shed both uniform and armband in a pile on the lavatory floor, I had been Helena the civilian. There had been no place for Emilia the soldier during the months in Germany. Indeed, if anyone discovered her existence, I could have been sent somewhere far worse as punishment for concealing my participation in the Armia Krajowa. But she remained part of me still, Emilia intertwined with Helena, the two bound so neatly together it would be impossible to unravel one from the other. Emilia was not indomitable, for she could break too, but knowing her heart still beat as mine had given me strength.

I took in the ruins of Warsaw not only as Helena, the girl who had called this place home, but also as Emilia, the soldier who had fought for the life of this city and now beheld her lifelessness. I knew what the battle had cost. For these shattered streets, my comrades had fallen. For this city, they had sacrificed, and for the hope of her liberation, they had given their youth and their lives.

The war in Europe had ended. I'd spent its final months as an anonymous Polish laborer in the very city where Hitler took his own life as the Red Army surged into the capital. Germany's surrender followed within days.

But we had not gained freedom. Only loss and exile and devastation. To Poland had been given simply another occupation. Soviet ownership instead of German. The Russians had entered Warsaw only after the Germans had crushed our army's insurgence and rendered our city a wasteland.

I passed a group of men digging in a square. The rasp of their shovels came amid the clamor of traffic. The stench of rotting, like putrefying meat, only stronger, more cloying, nauseated the warm spring air. I had first encountered this scent during the siege of 1939 and again during the battle for the city when the odor of the dead overpowered the rubble in which we fought. One breath and I wanted to be sick.

The men drew something up, placed the bundle on a stretcher. Nearby a woman looked on, clutching a handkerchief to her nose. I paused beside her.

"Why are they digging here?"

She turned, glancing at me. "They're exhuming the dead buried last summer, so they might be identified," she said, voice muffled by the handkerchief. "Perhaps I will find him here," she went on softly, her gaze on the workers as they dug. "I want to bury him, you see. Just to know where he rests. Just to know . . ."

"I-I hope you find him." I nearly retched then, clamping a hand over my mouth for lack of a handkerchief. I turned away, the dull thud of earth following me as I hurried across the square.

If our commanders had not given the order, if we had not counted on Soviet aid in a matter of days, if we had not risen . . . then perhaps, we would now be spared this. Perhaps we would still have our city. Perhaps the ones lost would still be with us.

It wasn't regret. I did not regret what we had done—not the fight itself, nor the ideals that had birthed our struggle—only what had come of it in the end.

But it was grief. For the losses. For their senselessness.

On the site of a bombed-out building, men pulled at ropes attached to what remained of a wall. Movements rhythmic, they heaved at the lines, sweating from effort. I watched, strangely transfixed, as the standing wall swayed and crackled. Then, with a shout from one of the men and a mighty crash, the wall fell in a billow of dust.

Hasn't there been enough torn down?

"Indeed, Pani."

I turned. An old man in a frayed cap had stopped to watch the demolition. I stared at him, wondering why he had addressed me before realizing I'd involuntarily voiced my thought aloud.

"But we must clear away if we're to build again," he continued.

"Will we, do you think?" My words came quiet.

His aged features creased with a hint of a smile. "My dear, we are in Warsaw, after all."

I carried his words with me as I continued on.

Yes, we are in Warsaw.

For amid the ruins, there was life. On thoroughfares busy with carts and the lorries that served as rudimentary transportation in place of trams, stalls offered food and wares while hawkers peddled cigarettes and matches. A crude but neatly lettered sign near a burned-out build-ing announced that "Hot Dishes, Coffee, Tea, and Pastries" could be found through the courtyard on the ground floor. The clank of metal rang out as a man hammered a board into an empty window frame. Farther down the street, a group of men and women cleared rubble, tossing salvaged bricks into the back of a cart.

Varsovians reclaiming their ordinary.

It should bring hope, life emerging like green shoots pushing up, small and resilient, from a soil of ashes. But it did not reach my heart.

During the months in Germany, I had one purpose. To fight, to endure, to survive for the day when I would return here. But when I dreamed of coming home, it had not been to Warsaw.

Instinctively I reached for the battered silver oval where it lay beneath the bodice of my dress. My fingers curled around the me-dallion and clutched hard.

There, on the ruined street, my heart reached beyond the place where I stood, out into the silent chasm. Reached out and whispered words that felt so small, yet held a universe of hope.

I'm home, Tosia.

37

HELENA
JUNE 8, 1945

I had come home, but I no longer had a home.

For hours, I wandered the remains of the city. I went to the flat in Wola where Antonina had lived. Only smoke-blackened walls still stood. I searched for a message, for any sign of life, but found none. They papered buildings all over Warsaw, the notes. I read every one, the names, the addresses, the few lines, meaningless words with meaning to someone. How many would be written but never found?

I walked the streets of Wola, questioning those I encountered, repeating the same words over and over. "I'm looking for Antonina Dąbrowska."

A grim shake of the head, a glance of pity, a word or two. Their features hardened by mute suffering, few spoke of what had unfolded in this district. Not all had witnessed it, for many had fled Wola for the Old Town and the city centre in the early days of the fighting, while others living here had never resided in the district until their return to the city, but none remained untouched by what had happened in this place.

Every district had its own tragedy, but Wola was not tragedy. Wola was immeasurable.

Each time I turned away from yet another stranger who had no answers, the cracking in my chest deepened and spread.

I passed by the street where we'd captured the tanks, the cemeteries where we'd battled for every meter of ground, the school where we'd sung in the evenings, where Sowa recited poetry, and where I'd kissed Andrzej on the rooftop. The memories came in waves, mingled with the aftermath that spread before me.

The last time I saw Wola, I'd been with my platoon, retreating under heavy fire.

We did not bear the guilt for the crimes perpetrated here. Our soldiers had fought and died for this district. But as its desolation seeped into my bones, as my gaze fell upon traces of life—a broken teacup lying in a gateway, a scrap of blue cloth in a heap of rubble—I cursed the fight we had begun in all our shining idealism and fervor for freedom.

I left Wola with my heart hollowed.

In my wanderings, I encountered the new occupation. Huge posters had been plastered on whatever structures still possessed a wall to be defaced. They depicted a Russian soldier, the Soviet ideal of manhood, an Armia Krajowa soldier rendered as a hunchbacked dwarf cowering at his feet. The Polish soldier had been spit upon, the caption "The Spit-Covered Dwarf of Capitalism" unnecessarily reiterating the artist's intent. The Soviets would certainly not salute us for our heroism, and Poland's future in a Europe reordered by the Allies was a road paved in unknowns. Once again, our underground army must melt into the night.

I trudged down the street as rain spattered from a vacant sky. After I left Wola, I had gone to the building where Andrzej once lived, hoping I might find him there or, at least, to find a message from him. I didn't know where he'd spent the months as a prisoner of war or if he'd returned to the city, if he'd lived to return. I knew he and Bronek had a mother still living at the time the battle broke out, but I didn't know her name or address.

We had been Andrzej and Emilia, our true selves hidden in the shadows of resistance, and yet I knew the way his brows lowered when he was deep in thought and how one corner of his mouth tipped higher than the other when he smiled. I knew the way he led, steadfast and decisive, always the first to risk himself before another. I knew he had been afraid, not for himself but for the men and women under his command, yet had fought with courage, both for Poland and the ones beside him. I knew how he'd gone to Malina after Sowa's death and how she'd lifted her head at his quiet words as he sat beside her and the way he'd drawn his brother's head against his chest and clutched him as Bronek wept for Jasia. I knew how he wordlessly pushed a cup of coffee toward me on the evenings I'd stumbled into his flat after tramping across the city in the days of the conspiracy, how he insisted on giving me his bed on the nights I couldn't reach home before curfew and slept on the divan instead, lying on his back with one arm under his head and glancing over at me with a trace of a smile. I knew the way he'd tucked his blanket around me as I shivered in the darkness of a cellar in Czerniaków and how we'd stood together on a rooftop and he'd shown me what a kiss could be.

I knew all of this, but not his name. How many times had I thought that since leaving him, asking myself how I could care so deeply for this man, a stranger in so many fundamental ways? So much remained for me to know of him, for us to know of one another.

But the chance was gone now, so I supposed it did not matter.

I tripped over a broken cobblestone and went down hard. A rickshaw swerved, its driver shouting at me. I pushed to my feet and limped to a gateway, my knees and palms scraped and bleeding. In the entrance of a bomb-blasted building, I unshouldered my rucksack and sat, dabbing my stinging knees with the sleeve of my cardigan. Carts clattered and dark umbrellas bobbed along the street, concealing the figures sheltering beneath them, and still I sat, heedless of the rain landing in damp splotches on my hair and clothes.

What reason was there to move on? I had no home to which I could return, no one who would worry about my absence. For hours, I had walked, searching for a glimpse of familiar features, for someone to remember me.

But Warsaw had become a city of strangers.

I could search and keep searching and find no one. I squeezed my eyes shut, my breath shaking.

"You are not forsaken in His sight. Even in this. You must pray to Him to help you believe it is so."

I had never forgotten the priest who had given me those words. In the months in Germany, I had clung to them. One of the women at the armaments factory had a small Bible, and at night in our quarters, I read the words imprinted on the thin pages, the story of constancy and grace beyond compare.

He is with us. There could be no greater hope. No matter what this earth held, no matter how we were shaken and shattered, He alone endured.

Dear God, grant me the strength to believe it is so. Even in this.

I picked up my rucksack and made my way onward, my feet aching. I would return to the bombed-out building where I'd slept last night and eat the other half of the roll I'd purchased from a stall. I would need to find work or I would soon starve.

Nothing remained of my life before the battle that had engulfed the city. Engulfed and then laid waste to it. My flat, my work as a secretary, my place in the conspiracy and the camaraderie I had found there, my sister . . .

All gone.

How to live without a life? How to build with empty hands?

I continued walking along a street backdropped by skeletal buildings, the drab hues of the landscape blurred by the rain.

A voice called out. The sound caught inside me, distant, hazy.

A lorry rumbled up the street, passengers sitting on the wooden benches, a woman hurried past, a handbag over her arm.

"Emilia."

I stopped, turned. Droplets of rain struck my face and hair.

A man shouldered through the throng.

"Emilia."

My breath came out in a choked gasp.

Then I was running down the street, darting between rickshaws and umbrella-carrying pedestrians as I had once darted amid the hail of bullets and eruption of grenades. I had learned to run with the grim tenacity of a soldier.

Now my heart gave my feet wings.

We reached each other. He went still, a pace between us.

Time had worn away the edges of my memories, shadowed his

face even as I clutched at its recollection, but now he stood before me, near enough to touch.

Andrzej.

He wore a threadbare coat, the strands of his hair darkened by rain. His features had aged—by the battle for the city, by wherever he had been since—their contours sharper, his eyes deeply set. But he was here, he was whole. His lips parted, but he didn't speak, taking me in as though overcome by my reality.

Then my rucksack fell to the ground and I flung my arms around him. His came around me, warm and solid, lifting me off my feet. I pressed my eyes shut, clutching him, breathing in his scent.

"How I have dreamed of this," he whispered, voice hoarse. "How I have prayed to find you."

"I don't even know your name." Scarcely more than a breath, my words.

He drew back, lips easing with that familiar near-smile. "It's Stefan. Stefan Zieliński."

"Helena." My smile came soft. "Helena Dąbrowska."

He reached up and gently brushed a rain-damp strand of hair away from my face. "Helena."

Such a simple thing, my name on his lips. But with it, my heart came home.

He kissed me, there on the street, the taste of rain mingling with tears as we held each other in the midst of the crowd.

At last, I drew away. "And Bronek?"

He swallowed hard. "He didn't make it out."

A flash of memory—the group of soldiers, filthy, eyes glassy with fatigue, moving through the night, the rattle of enemy machine guns in the darkness, the yell of a man who'd been hit . . .

A tremor passed through my body, even as I willed the memories to retreat.

My chest ached at the pain in his gaze. Words didn't mend grief. Not such as this. Ease, perhaps, but never mend, for loss takes not only a life but also a part of those who remain. No heart can carry another's sorrow.

But love can stand with another through the breaking.

"We won't forget him," I said, my words soft but fierce.

He nodded, his features cracking.

They were with us still, the ones we had lost. They would always be with us, brave and bright-eyed, donning bands of white and red, striding to the fight on that sunny August day.

"Though dust, through them, the world reborn."

Sowa. Ryś. Jerzy. Bronek.

"Never forget the women," Jasia would say, a spark in her eyes. *"We were there too."*

I won't. I promise you, Jasia. I promise you all.

After a moment, he asked, "And your sister?"

"I haven't . . ." I swallowed. "I've only been back since yesterday."

"Where are you staying?"

I gave half a smile, remembering where I'd slept last night. "Nowhere yet."

"My mother and I are living on Warecka Street. It's a cellar, but at least it's out of the rain." He paused. "Will you come with me?"

I looked up at him, into the eyes of the man who knew Emilia but also Helena. The soldier I had been and the woman I had become. We would always know one another in a way perhaps few lovers ever could. For as we had been shaped by our experiences, so too they bound us as deeply as any two could ever be.

Emilia and Helena. I stood before him now as both. Loving him as both.

Then I bent and picked up my rucksack. Our gazes met, a silent question given and answered, then his broad hand closed around the strap, and he slung it over his shoulder. My fingers folded into his, and we started down the street as rain fell, droplets shed from the sky to wash the ruins around us.

HELENA
JUNE 11, 1945

Twilight swept the sky as I made my way along Hoża Street. I hadn't come here since the day we learned of the capitulation. Maybe because it hurt too much, returning to the last place I had called home, the last place Antonina and I had lived before so much that now seemed slight and meaningless pulled us apart.

I had returned to Warsaw with nothing. Now I had a roof under which to sleep each night, and with Andrzej—Stefan—I had a home. In the cramped cellar he and his mother shared with several others, the two of us talked for hours, whispering late into the night. We told one another of the months we'd been apart, me of my time at the armaments factory in Berlin, he of his captivity in prisoner of war camps throughout Germany. To speak at great length of those places, to return to them in memory, exposed wounds too raw to probe, but in what we kept silent as well as what we spoke, we understood one another. As the nights passed, we quietly talked of the future. In the middle of January, with Poland overrun by the Soviets, the Armia Krajowa had been formally disbanded.

But a group of prior AK officers and soldiers had begun to form a new organization—the birth of a second conspiracy. This time against the communist regime. Not long after his return to the city, Stefan had reunited with a comrade from our battalion, now the leader of a unit in the new organization, and upon learning of its existence, Stefan joined its ranks.

"Are we to spend our whole lives fighting one enemy or another?" I had whispered as we sat together on the folding bed, my head resting on his chest, darkness gathering beyond the cellar walls. "Isn't the war supposed to be over?"

"I'm not sure it ever can be." The words came quiet, his breath stirring the strands of hair near my ear. "Not for Poland. Not for us."

I raised my face to his. "I want a life, Stefan." My voice broke. "After everything we've come through, I just want to live."

He'd kissed me then, cupping my cheek, his lips tenderly exploring mine, and I kissed him back, trying to forget both the past and the future.

Now I stood, arms wrapped around myself, staring at the charred remnants of the building where I had once lived. Time unraveled, drawing me back to the day we came here to stay with Aunt Basia. Antonina had been bold and angry and dangerously in love with

Marek, and I had been frightened, desperately missing Tata, wanting only to flee from our reality.

We'd been so young then. Girls, really. War had shaped us into women. What would life have made of us had our course been set by another compass? Had the years left me stronger or had I simply been broken so many times I would never be anything but shards? I had pieced myself into a semblance of wholeness out of necessity, cracks and jagged edges unseen but irreparable.

I don't know how to be without us, Tosia. It's like a part of myself is gone and I'm just wandering through empty rooms, trying to find it. I wish I could come into our bedroom to find you'd left the armoire open and your clothes strewn everywhere while you were dressing to go out. I wish I could hear you practicing scales on the piano when I'm trying to read. I wish we could laugh again. I wish you were here and we could face all this together.

For long moments, I stood on the street, lost in recollection. The waning light touched the ruins, softening their scars. Since childhood, I had always found the gentleness in this hour, the hazy space before darkness held sway, when day converged with night.

Light and shadow. Shadow and light.

So much of life is lived in the meeting of the two.

I would never return to the girl I had once been, but perhaps, in time, I could find purpose, even peace, as the woman I had become. For in the moments when it seemed no heart could bear such emptiness, I had learned God is nearest in our shattered places.

I withdrew the note I had brought, the reason I'd come. I drew closer, the ragged wall towering above me, scraps of white standing out against smoke-stained bricks. I read the messages, one by one.

Ewa Lewandowska is looking for her sons, Bartosz and Jan.

Maria Bagińska is living on Targowa Street.

I reached out, my palm smoothing a stained and crinkled note against the rough bricks.

Then my breath stilled, my legs nearly gave way.
Two lines, penciled on a torn scrap, the words smudged.
But in them lay the sum of every hope a heart could hold.

ANTONINA
JUNE 11, 1945

Golden twilight. The scents of grass and soil. A child's laughter. The quiet miracle of the ordinary. Once I'd held such moments carelessly, accepting them like one who has never known hunger accepts a full plate of food. Now I gathered them close, for I knew how fleetingly they passed, how friable the commonplace could be. To find it now in this razed city became a miracle all its own.

The building where we lived had been a spacious villa with a garden. It had been burned out, but not bombed, and though it had no windows and furnishings, it had a roof and solid walls, and that made a real difference. It was remarkable—though less so after more than five years of war—how quickly we, like all Varsovians, grew accustomed to scraping out a life from the rubble.

The garden at the back of the villa must have once been a place where a family took tea in the afternoon or spent summer evenings, the children's laughter drifting across the lawn as they played, the others sitting on the terrace, the air heady with the scent of lilacs. No one tended the grounds now, the grass overgrown and stippled with weeds, the villa at its backdrop scarred by fire, boards nailed crudely into empty window frames.

But Kasia loved the garden. She took no notice of the ravages, perhaps because she was too young to remember buildings unmarred by bombs, or streets not lined with mounded rubble. Though perhaps it would have made little difference even if she had recalled the past. Children possess a special ability to chase joy, even in the midst of the improbable.

She toddled through the grass, stopping to pluck a weed. She held it up to me, her smile wide, utterly enchanted with her treasure.

"What did you find?" I smiled. "Oh, how pretty."

"Pwetty," Kasia repeated, twirling its stem in her tiny fist. I sat on a blanket nearby as she wandered across the lawn. When she strayed too far, I rose and swept her into my arms. "Not so fast, my little one." I kissed her cheeks, her curls, cradling her close.

She has your eyes, Marek. And when she smiles, there's a dimple in her right cheek, just where yours was. She's so curious, and yesterday she was banging her spoon on the table and it was like she understood what tempo was. Is that silly? No, you wouldn't think so. Your eyes would grow soft and you'd look proud and say, "She's bright, she'll make a fine musician."

When she's older, I'll tell her of you. I'll play your compositions—the ones published before the war, the ones that weren't lost—and she'll know what a brilliant man her father was. Someday I'll tell her how you gave your life fighting for your people. And though I cannot give her a better world in which to grow, she will be cherished. That I will always give. For both of us, my darling.

I lifted Kasia high and spun her around, her giggles spilling out, music on the summer evening. I laughed, my head tilted back, the grass soft under my bare feet.

"Tosia."

I stilled. Turned.

In the entrance to the garden stood a woman. She wore a gray cardigan over a faded dress, her honey-brown hair wisping around her cheeks, her eyes as blue as the Wisła in summer, blue as my own.

One look and all else fell away. My feet carried me across the grass, my mind scarcely conscious of their movements.

"Hela." My voice caught. "Hela."

She stared at me, eyes shining with tears. They trickled down her cheeks and my own spilled over. Then I was holding her and she was holding me, Kasia between us. We clung to each other, crying tears long held back. For the ones we had lost, for the time we had lost, for all that had come between us. For every day we had fought to keep hope for the other from fading and for disbelief and joy that this moment was real, that the other was here.

"You're home now," I whispered.

Our gazes held and there was only the two of us, Antonina and Helena, the sisters we had always been and would always be. For as the tide ebbs, but in the end returns, so too is the bond between sisters. Changing yet changeless. Indelible. Unbreakable.

"We're both home now," she said softly.

Kasia held up the weed still clutched in her fist. "Pwetty."

Helena and I looked at each other, our cheeks damp, and laughter escaped in a rush as cleansing as tears. "Hello, Kasia." Helena touched Kasia's dimpled arm. "Do you remember me? I'm your Auntie Hela."

Kasia held out the weed to Helena. "Pwetty."

"It is pretty." Helena took the wilted stem. "Thank you."

I shifted Kasia in my arms. "Come. Let's go inside."

Helena nodded, smiling, swiping her face with the back of her hand. Then she slipped her arm around my waist, and together we started toward the house.

Before us stretched a future as uncertain as the past had been. What the coming years would hold could be answered only by time. Darkness still hung over Poland. Perhaps it would not lift for a long while.

But Warsaw would endure. They had shattered her walls but not her spirit. For the spirit of a city is not inscribed in brick and stone but in the hearts of all who call her home. It is they who will gather up her fragments and restore the broken.

It is they who will give her life again.

I looked at my sister and my daughter, the two who would always be part of me, and a slow but certain unfolding began in my heart.

There is hope in us yet.

Historical Note

In exploring the multifaceted narrative of history, the stories I am most drawn to are those I call "the courage of the commonplace." Ordinary people who, when thrust into times that test the very substance of humanity, fight with quiet resilience to uphold and preserve that which should be most sacred to society—freedom, human dignity, and human life itself. Often their stories remain hidden, memories kept only by their witnesses. This novel is inspired by many such individuals who did not seek commemoration but whose legacies are truly worthy of remembrance.

The capitulation of Warsaw on September 28, 1939, and the subsequent arrival of German troops marked the start of five long years of oppression, brutality, and unrelenting terror. As Alexandra Richie writes in *Warsaw 1944*, "Nowhere in all Nazi-occupied Europe was the 'extensive machinery of repression' as great as it was in Poland."[1] More than five million Polish citizens perished during the Second World War, approximately three million Jews among them.

Though all Polish people suffered, the singling out of the Jewish population soon became apparent, first through restrictions, humiliations, and the plundering of their property, then by the establishment of a "Jewish district" in the autumn of 1940. Thirty

1. Alexandra Richie, *Warsaw 1944: Hitler, Himmler, and the Warsaw Uprising* (New York: Picador, 2013), 129.

percent of Warsaw's population was forced to exist in 2.4 percent of the city's living area. Between 1940 and mid-1942, 83,000 people died, mainly from disease and starvation. On July 22, 1942, what the Germans referred to as Grossaktion Warschau—Great Action Warsaw—began. Over the course of barely two months, the Germans and their auxiliaries carried out the deportation of 265,000 to 300,000 men, women, and children. The majority were sent to the Treblinka extermination camp.

Unlike occupied countries in Western Europe, where the authorities meted out lesser sentences—such as imprisonment in a concentration camp—providing aid or shelter to Jews in Poland was a crime punishable by death. Still, an estimated 70,000 to 90,000 Poles helped conceal Jews in the Warsaw area alone. Among them was Irena Sendler, a social worker for Warsaw's welfare department. Irena and a few colleagues received passes authorizing them to enter the ghetto. Initially they smuggled medicine, food, and typhus vaccines into the sealed district, but as the situation grew increasingly dire, they began arranging ways to bring children out. Children were smuggled through the law courts—which could be accessed from both the ghetto and the "Aryan" side—through cellars in buildings bordering the ghetto, in ambulances and trams, in crates and sacks, in work brigades leaving the ghetto, and through the sewers. Every small life slipped across the ghetto wall carried the greatest risk for the rescuers.

Irena recounted how fearful parents pressed her for assurances about their child's safety. "I spoke frankly; I said I couldn't even be certain I would safely leave the ghetto with a child that very day. Scenes from hell ensued. For instance, the father would agree to give us the child, but the mother would refuse. . . . Sometimes I would leave such a family with their child. The next day I would return to see what happened to the family, and frequently it would turn out that the entire family was already in [the] Umschlagplatz."[2]

Once the children had been brought outside the ghetto, Irena and

2. Anna Mieszkowska, *Irena Sendler: Mother of the Children of the Holocaust*, trans. Witold Zbirohowski-Koscia (Westport: Praeger, 2011), 74.

her colleagues arranged temporary shelter in one of the "emergency care units." In time, the children would be placed in orphanages, religious institutions, or foster families. In late 1942, Irena made contact with a newly founded organization—the Council for Aid to Jews, known by its cryptonym, Żegota. Irena became head of the section dedicated to providing aid to children. Żegota is not mentioned in the novel because it is unlikely someone in Antonina's position would be aware of its existence.

On October 20, 1943, Irena was arrested and taken to the Gestapo detention center on Szucha Avenue where she was subjected to brutal torture. Both her legs were broken. But Irena betrayed no one. Because she alone knew where all the children had been placed, her colleagues in Żegota set out to rescue her and succeeded in bribing a Gestapo officer for her release. Irena assumed a false identity and continued her work for Żegota until the outbreak of the Warsaw Uprising.

The story of Irena Sendler has become legendary, and as is often the case with such figures, certain details of her life and work remain obscured by a haze of myth as well as a lack of substantiated facts. Despite careful research, I was unable to discover exactly when Irena began using the alias Jolanta. Some evidence suggests she adopted this pseudonym for her clandestine activities before her initiation into Żegota. Thus that is how she introduces herself to Antonina.

Another ambiguity regards the number of children helped by Irena and her colleagues. Irena is generally credited with rescuing as many as 2,500 children from the Warsaw ghetto. According to testimony compiled by Irena and three of her closest associates in 1979, that figure encompasses the number of children aided by Żegota as a whole. Though the name of Irena Sendler has become renowned, she frequently reminded those who praised her that she had been but one member of a courageous fraternity. She later said, "I could not have achieved anything were it not for that group of women I trusted who were with me in the ghetto every day, and who transformed their homes into care centers for children. These were exceptionally brave and noble people. As for me, it was simple. I remembered what my father had taught me. When someone is drowning, you give him your hand. I simply tried to extend my hand to the Jewish people."[3]

Before the war, Poland was home to nearly one million Jewish children under the age of fourteen. Of those children who remained in Poland during the war, only an estimated five thousand survived, and most lost one or both parents. It is my hope that this novel pays tribute to the quiet valor of those who gave of themselves to protect the most vulnerable.

Following the mass deportations in the ghetto, a group of surviving Jews, the majority in their teens and early twenties, began to prepare for resistance. On April 19, 1943, what became known as the Warsaw Ghetto Uprising broke out. Approximately 750 Jewish combatants battled German forces in a revolt lasting twenty-eight days. Over 7,000 Jews—combatants and civilians—lost their lives. Thousands more were sent to Treblinka or other camps. On the other side of the wall, non-Jews looked on as the uprising unfolded. The festivities in Krasiński Square as the ghetto burned is an event mentioned in many accounts of the uprising. On May 16, 1943, the SS blew up the Great Synagogue in a symbolic declaration of victory. Of Warsaw's Jewish population, 98 percent perished during the Second World War.[4]

Another facet of history I touched on in the novel regards what has become known as the Katyn massacre. Following the invasion of Poland by Germany and the Soviet Union, the Soviets captured and imprisoned thousands of officers of the Polish Army. In March 1940, the order went out for the officers to be executed. Under strict secrecy, the NKVD—the Soviet secret police—carried out the killings at pits in the forest or in prison cellars. According to research by Polish historians, nearly half the officer corps of the Polish Army were murdered. In 1943, Germany announced the discovery of the mass graves to sway international opinion against the Soviets. The Soviets, in turn, declared the Germans had committed the crime.

3. *Irena Sendler: In the Name of Their Mothers*, directed by Mary Skinner, produced by PBS Distribution, 2011, DVD.

4. Gunnar S. Paulsson, *Secret City: The Hidden Jews of Warsaw, 1940-1945* (New Haven, CT: Yale University Press, 2013), 1.

Due to their political alliance with Stalin, neither the United States nor Britain challenged Soviet claims of German responsibility. In the following decades, Soviet disinformation masked the truth about Katyn, and only in 1990 did Russia formally acknowledge guilt.

The genesis of the Armia Krajowa—the Home Army—began long before the organization became known by that name. From the earliest days of occupation, the Polish people sought to establish organized resistance. By 1940, 140 underground groups had been formed in Warsaw alone. The history of the unification of the Polish resistance is long and labyrinthine, but on February 14, 1942, the organization officially became known as the Home Army. The Home Army wasn't merely a resistance group but the armed forces of the Polish Underground State, subordinate to the government-in-exile in London. By 1944, it had become one of the largest resistance movements in occupied Europe, with over 350,000 soldiers throughout Poland.

The Błysk Battalion was inspired by Zośka, one of the most famous battalions in the Home Army. The Zośka Battalion and its predecessor unit, "Jerzy," blew up railway bridges and German trains that supplied the eastern front, freed imprisoned comrades, and executed informers and members of the Gestapo and SS. The actions of the Zośka Battalion during the Warsaw Uprising included the capture of the Panther tanks, the liberation of the concentration camp in the ghetto ruins, the battles in the cemeteries, and the bitter fighting to hold the Jan Boży Hospital. During the Uprising, the battalion suffered a casualty rate of approximately 70 percent of its soldiers.

The Warsaw Uprising remains not only one of the most heroic chapters in Poland's history but also the most tragic. Even today historians remain divided about whether the failing of the Uprising was inevitable from the outset. "We wanted to be free and owe the freedom to ourselves," wrote the deputy prime minister of the Polish government.[5] His words encapsulated what many Varsovians felt.

5. Szymon Nowak, "The Most Beautiful Polish Battle," Institute of National Remembrance, July 30, 2021, https://ipn.gov.pl/en/digital-resources/articles/8492,The-most-beautiful-Polish-battle.html.

Not only would the Uprising be a battle against the hated occupiers but a fight for Poland's independence amid the threat of communist rule. 40,000 to 50,000 people fought in the Uprising, nearly 12,000 women among them.

In the first days of the battle for Warsaw, an atmosphere of freedom and euphoria prevailed as the Home Army captured large swaths of the city. However, they failed to gain control of key bridges, airports, and main military and police installations. Within days, the tide began to shift. In response to the Polish insurrection, Hitler and Himmler issued the order: "Every citizen of Warsaw is to be killed including men, women, and children. Warsaw has to be levelled to the ground in order to set a terrifying example to the rest of Europe."[6]

The Wola massacre is perhaps the greatest tragedy of the Uprising. It is also the "largest single battlefield massacre of the Second World War."[7] Before the Uprising, Wola was a working-class district of 85,000 inhabitants. Over the course of a week, an estimated 40,000 to 50,000 civilians were systematically and ruthlessly murdered by SS and police units, including the infamous Dirlewanger Brigade, made up of convicted criminals and prisoners of war.

The accounts of several survivors of the massacre, including a woman named Wanda Lurie, informed Antonina's experiences. The Ursus factory became one of the places designated for executions, and Wanda was taken there with her children, who were eleven, six, and three years of age. At the time, Wanda was in the last month of pregnancy. Wounded when the shooting began, she lay for three days in a heap of corpses—the bodies of her children among them. She managed to escape the factory but was soon recaptured and taken to St. Wojciech's Church. The killing of civilians in Wola was partially halted when the commander gave the order for women and children to be spared while the execution of men suspected of being insurgents continued. This wasn't done out of humanitarian motives but because of the impossibility of continuing mass slaughter while engaging in combat.

6. Richie, *Warsaw 1944*, 244.
7. Richie, *Warsaw 1944*, 255.

The toll of the Uprising is numerically staggering. An estimated 150,000 to 180,000 civilians and 18,000 Home Army soldiers perished during the sixty-three days of battle. After the surrender of the Home Army, the Germans expelled nearly the entire population of Warsaw. Of those processed through the transit camp at Pruszków, around 150,000 were deported to the Reich for forced labor, 60,000 to concentration camps, and hundreds of thousands more sent to other parts of Poland.

Following the suppression of the Uprising, Hitler reiterated the order that the city be razed to the ground, an act of revenge that had no military grounds whatsoever. The destruction of Warsaw amounted to over 80 percent of all buildings. The annihilation encompassed historic buildings, monuments, libraries, universities, churches, and countless homes—cultural and historical treasures lost to plunder or destroyed in the flames. The bustling capital of a million inhabitants had become a wasteland, a city erased.

On January 17, 1945, the Soviets entered Warsaw, but the postwar years proved Poland and its citizens had not regained independence. Following the agreements reached at the Yalta Conference, the eastern part of Poland was incorporated into the Soviet Union while the remainder became subordinate to a puppet communist government. Under the Stalinist regime, veterans of the Home Army were hunted and persecuted. Thousands were imprisoned or deported to gulags and labor camps. Many were executed. One former liaison from the Zośka Battalion had a one-year-old son at the time of her arrest; her imprisonment lasted more than five years. Meanwhile, resistance groups continued the struggle against another occupation. The repression of former insurgents eased with the "Thaw" of the mid-1950s, but only with the fall of communism in 1989 could the restoration of memory and identity begin.

From her ruins, Warsaw emerged reborn. The meticulous reconstruction of much of the Old Town took place in the decades after the war, centuries of architecture resurrected from rubble. Today Warsaw is once more a vibrant capital city of over a million inhabitants, but the scars of war remain embedded in her landscape. History is taught and preserved through museums while monuments commemorate the two uprisings that left a defining legacy. Every year at five o'clock on August 1, sirens resound across Warsaw and in towns and cities all over Poland. For sixty seconds, traffic stops and pedestrians still. Even as the sirens swell, a hush descends over the city that rose for freedom and rose again from its ashes. The white-and-red flag flutters, and Warsaw remembers.

Acknowledgments

Though the act of writing is often undertaken in solitude, the journey of bringing a story to the page is one walked in community. With every novel, I gain a deeper sense of this truth and remain profoundly grateful for those who travel this road with me.

To the spectacular team at Revell. What an honor and joy it is to partner with you all. Since the long-ago days when my teenage self filled bookshelves with Revell novels, I've been ceaselessly inspired by the excellence and dedication given to every title under your imprint. It humbles and amazes me to count mine among them. From editorial to design to marketing to sales, the ways in which you shape a novel and usher it into the hands of readers are too numerous to name, and this author is ever thankful for them all.

To Rachel McRae. The depth and nuance of your insight enriched this story in myriad ways. Our shared passion for Poland and its history made the process all the more special. I'm blessed to call you my editor and even more blessed to call you my friend.

To Robin Turici. Your editing instincts strengthened and shaped the words on these pages. What a privilege it is to learn from you.

To Rachel Kent, my wonderful agent. We've worked together for over ten years and on many books, and I am humbled by the ways you've invested in my stories.

I owe a debt of gratitude to Dr. John Radziłowski, historian and director of the Polish Institute of Culture and Research in Orchard Lake Village, Michigan. Thank you for allowing me to view the Home Army artifacts at the PICR. It still makes my breath catch to remember holding a helmet worn by a soldier during the Uprising and studying copies of the *Biuletyn Informacyjny*. The afternoon I spent at the PICR greatly enriched my research and remains one of the most memorable experiences of this project. Thank you also for your generosity in reading the portion of the novel related to the Uprising and providing valuable feedback. Of course, any errors are mine alone.

To my dad, who has always supported my creativity. With love, always.

To my mom. From concept to completion, you are so much a part of what makes every book possible. For reading everything from early drafts to polished pages, for giving of your wisdom to unravel the tangles of this story, for the unending ways—both seen and unseen, small and great—you support me on this journey and for the sacrifices you make to do so, and mostly for being the extraordinary woman you are, my gratitude is boundless.

To my sister, Sara. I'm sure you're the first person I told when this story was just a spark of an idea—you always are! You spent innumerable hours brainstorming, offered brilliant feedback on multiple drafts, and never failed to cheer me on through the days when writing was a fight to form words. At the heart of this novel is the enduring bond between sisters. What a gift it is to call you mine.

To my readers. Thank you for journeying with this story, for the notes and messages that bring encouragement to my heart (and often tears to my eyes), and for being part of the community of reading friends online and at events, both in-person and virtual. Part of the wonder of books is the ways they draw us together, and for that, I am abundantly grateful.

Above all, to my Savior. You are with us on the mountaintops and in the valleys and every moment in between. It is by Your grace that I write and for Your glory that I seek to live.

Amanda Barratt is the bestselling author of numerous historical novels and novellas, including *The White Rose Resists* (a 2021 Christy Award winner) and *Within These Walls of Sorrow*. She is passionate about illuminating oft-forgotten facets of history through a fictional narrative. Amanda lives in Michigan. Learn more at Amanda Barratt.net.

Connect with
AMANDA BARRATT

Sign up for her newsletter to receive bookish news, exclusive sneak peeks, and more!

🌐 AmandaBarratt.net | f AmandaBarrattAuthor

📷 AmandaBarrattAuthor | 🐦 AmandaMBarratt